TALKING

TO THE

SHARKS

TALKING
TO THE
SHARKS

A Daniel Jacquot Thriller

Martin O'Brien

– 9 –

They tear you apart... They leave no trace...

MOBUK
PRESS

Praise for the Jacquot Series

"Tall and tough, smart and sexy, Jacquot is a first-rate series hero."
– Kirkus Review (US)

"Well-drawn, and strongly flavoured. Rich, spicy, and served up with unmistakeable relish."
– The Literary Review

"Martin O'Brien creates a sexually charged atmosphere that is as chilling as it is engaging."
– The Sydney Morning Herald

"Well-written and compelling. Tight plotting, lyrical descriptions, and excellent characterisation mean Jacquot is here to stay."
– The Daily Mail

"French country life has never been so fraught with sinister atmosphere."
– The Rough Guide to Crime Fiction

"The Marseilles scene seems to be written by a native. O'Brien's ability to deliver a sense of place makes him worth watching."
– The Washington Post (US)

"Chief Inspector Daniel Jacquot of the Marseilles Police is fast becoming one of my favourite fictional cops."
– Henry Sutton
The Daily Mirror

"O'Brien's evocation of the hot, vibrant and seedy port in which everyone seems to be either a cop or a criminal, and sometimes both, is as masterly as Ian Rankin's depiction of Edinburgh."
– The Daily Mail

"Jacquot is an excellent character, no doubt set for a long and entertaining career, and the scenery of corruption in the South of France is very well painted indeed."
– The Birmingham Post

"A wonderfully inventive and involving detective series with vivid French locales creating the perfect backdrop. Jacquot is top of le cops."
– The Daily Express

Praise for the Jacquot Series

"A strikingly different detective, Jacquot walks off the page effortlessly."
– The Good Book Guide

"A French counterpart to Ian Rankin's Scottish Inspector Rebus, with a tough authentic voice, and deft plots."
– The Cleveland Plain Dealer (US)

"O'Brien, as always, makes effective use of his chosen setting – a sunny place for shady people."
– The Daily Mail

"Exotic and different, exceedingly well-written and entertaining."
– Huddersfield Daily Examiner

"Terrific!"
– Northampton Chronicle & Echo

"O'Brien is an elegant writer, and he's particularly strong on his scene-setting – you really will believe you're in Provence, admiring the scenery and partaking of some sumptuous meals."
– reviewingtheevidence.com

"A rich, colourful setting... O'Brien truly makes us feel, smell, hear, and see Marseilles. He writes skillfully, and the city setting simply reaches out and surrounds the reader. Definitely recommended."
– Mystery Scene

"Martin O'Brien's books featuring Chief Inspector Jacquot are fast becoming detective classics."
– Crime Squad

"Murder, mayhem, and the seedy side of Marseilles make for a truly mesmerising mix."
– The Northern Echo

"O'Brien does a good job in conveying the atmosphere of the place; above all, he manages to portray his characters without resorting to the stereotypes and caricatures that so often spoil Brit-written novels set in France."
– Marcel Berlins
The London Times

For Daniel,
Mathilde and Béatrice,
with thanks and love…

Prologue

At the dead of night, on a calm sea, a shark's dorsal fin breaking the surface sounds like a sharp, slicing whisper, followed by a gentle sucking as the whisper ends and the fish drops down into unseen depths. Sometimes the curved tip of a shark's tail will break the surface before it dives, but then the sound is altogether different – a flicking, excitable slash of water that, if there is moonlight or stars, might draw your eye to a scar of phosphorescence and, beneath it, the shadow of something menacing moving over a sandy seabed many metres below.

But on this night, at the end of July, on the edge of the Grand Lucayan Banks, there is no moon, there are no stars. Just a warm inky blackness, and the gentle lap of water on a drifting hull.

When the bleeding body is dropped overboard, just a few minutes pass before that first whisper can be heard, a single fin slicing through the water.

Followed by another, and then another.

It takes only a few minutes for the sharks to do their work. Tearing at the bloody bundle, shoving it this way and that as their greedy snouts push in for a bite. Scything tails slashing through the water for purchase and drive. Jaws snapping, black eyes rolling.

The arms, legs, and head are the first to go in this crunching, ripping frenzy. And when all that remains is a ragged torso the largest of the predators, a hulking bull shark, snatches what is left and drags it away, down into the depths.

__Old Friends__
Île des Frères, Martinique,
West Indies
October 2004

1

She was a beautiful woman. Everyone who saw her those first few days said the same.

Straight ash-blonde hair that curled at the shoulders. High, tanned cheekbones and clear blue eyes. Good legs, good figure. And good jewellery: a gold Omega Seamaster, a woven platinum Tiffany bracelet, and a sparkling diamond solitaire on her wedding finger, with matching diamond earrings. Worn with a comfortable familiarity, a sense of entitlement. Her voice was soft, and enquiring. French, but with the lightest American accent.

And everyone she met, she asked the same question.

"I'm looking for a man called Daniel Jacquot. Do you know where I might find him?"

She had taken an early morning American Airlines flight from Nassau, via Miami and San Juan, touching down at Martinique's Aimé Césaire airport a little over six hours later. One of ninety-four passengers on Flight 013. The name in her passport was Boni Stuyvesant, with a date of birth that tipped her higher into the thirties than anyone would credit.

"I'm looking for a man called Daniel Jacquot?" she asked the taxi driver who picked her up outside the airport Arrivals Hall. He said the name a couple of times, then shook his head.

She asked the same question of the concierge at her hotel on Parc Savane in the island's capital, Fort-de-France.

"Is he a guest, madame?"

When Madame Stuyvesant replied that he probably was not, the concierge widened his eyes, turned down his lips, and spread his hands. He was sorry, of course, but how could he possibly be expected to know someone who was not a guest at his hotel?

Up in her room, before she'd unpacked, Madame Stuyvesant began with the island phone book. Though she set no great store in this endeavour, it was as good a place to start as any. There were more than three hundred thousand islanders, and she was looking for just one man. There were eleven Jacquots in the directory, but only four with the same initial. Thirty minutes after sitting at the desk in her room, she put down the phone and sighed. She'd known it wouldn't be easy.

Nor did it get any easier. By the end of her first full day in Fort-de-France, she had visited the headquarters of the island's *Judiciaire*, the Mayor's office, the Tourist Board, three bars, two restaurants, and a bookshop and *Tabac* on rue du Créole. And at each of these places she received the same answer. A shrug, a frown, a shake of the head. Apologies…

On her third day on the island, Madame Stuyvesant hired a four-wheel-drive Nissan Pathfinder – not wasting the opportunity to ask the girl at the Hertz counter if she had ever rented a car to a man called Daniel Jacquot? And could the girl check her records to find out? Again, a shake of the head, a gentle apology… No such name, madame, *je regrette*.

For the first hour behind the Nissan's wheel, Boni Stuyvesant drove around the island's capital, both amused and intrigued by this cluttered clapboard French outpost in the middle of the Caribbean Sea. The same language, the same blue road signs, the same street names, and the same sombre memorials to islanders who had given their lives in two world wars on a continent far away. So familiar, but so distant, too. By mid-morning she had left the town behind her and was driving along the twisting coastal corniche to Case-Pilote and Bellefontaine where she stopped for lunch at a ramshackle wood hut on a bluff above the beach.

It was just the kind of place that Daniel Jacquot would love: locally-caught lobster grilled on a smoking *feu de bois* barbecue, split buttered tails served on thick china plates, eaten under a slatted *canisse* roof, at rough wooden tables whose legs sunk in the sand. Yes, she thought, this was the sort of place where she'd find him. But when she asked her waitress about Daniel Jacquot, and then the chef, and the barman, and two of the locals at a table near hers, the answer was the same. *Non, madame, je regrette…*

She went no further that afternoon, daunted by a narrowing road and the rising cloud-capped slopes of Mount Pelée. Instead she turned back to Fort-de-France, deciding over dinner on the hotel terrace that the following morning she would head out to the island's Atlantic coast.

Wherever he was, Madame Stuyvesant knew that she would find Daniel Jacquot on a beach somewhere, close to the shore, by the sea.

And she was right.

2

Two little girls, maybe four years old, played on Trinité beach with tin buckets and plastic spades. One was digging a hole, the other was using the shifted sand to build a castle. They played together happily, speaking to each other in a lilting island patois, while a large woman in frilled white skirts and colourful blouse, barefoot, her 'dreads' bundled up in a knotted headscarf watched from the shadows, cooled herself with a woven palm-leaf fan. Beyond the reef dark blue breakers showered up in silent white clouds of spray, but close to the shore the sea was a still, warm aquamarine.

Boni Stuyvesant had arrived on Île des Frères an hour earlier, following a tip-off from the harbour-master in Le Vauclin. Pocketing the fifty-euro note she'd given him and eyeing her Omega Seamaster, the old boy seemed to recall that there was a man called Daniel up around Le François, a short drive north along the Morne Courbaril highway.

At Le François, another fifty euros had secured the information that *un français* lived off-shore on Île des Frères. Since she'd missed the afternoon ferry, a further twenty euros secured her passage on a Boston whaler whose skipper was delivering supplies to a small guest house there. He could take her across, he told her, but he couldn't bring her back; he'd be unloading his cargo at the St-Christophe jetty and coming straight home. Just a twenty-minute turn-around.

Could she get a room at the guest house, Boni asked?

The man replied that she probably could; as far as he knew there'd been no more than a handful of guests the last month.

"Too 'ot dis time a' year, lady," he told her. "H-an' 'urricane season h-ain't real popular wid de tourists."

So, it was settled. He helped her aboard, and she sheltered from the sun in the small for'ard wheelhouse, wondering whether she'd be able to buy herself a toothbrush, toothpaste, and a change of clothes when she reached the island. But it was too late to do anything more than hope. Within minutes of coming aboard, the last crate of rattling beer bottles was handed down, and her skipper fired up the twin Johnson outboard engines. Cruising out of Le François' pocket-sized harbour and heading north-east, the skipper pointed out a small green smudge – Île des Frères – a twenty-minute ride off Martinique's Atlantic coast.

At Chez Chanson, a gingerbread balconied plantation house on a slope of sun-browned grass, decked with climbing shawls of hibiscus and shaded by leaning palms and blooming jacaranda, Boni Stuyvesant was shown to her room by the owner, a sun-wrinkled widow called La Veuve Chanson, and told that she could buy whatever she might need from the local store. When Boni asked if Madame happened to know a man called Daniel Jacquot, the woman's smile and nod made her heart beat a drum roll in her chest.

"Him wid de two gals? *Mais oui, certainment.* He on de odder side. Trinité." The old woman had glanced at her watch. "Be down on the beach by now, I'd guess. You wanna go, I get Samuel to drive you. Too far to walk anywheres in dis heat, ma'am, and de island bus h-ain't h-at h-all reliable."

And now she was here, on Trinité, leaving Samuel in the shade of a palm grove with the car doors open to catch the breeze. Stepping out onto the beach, she slipped off her sandals and felt a prickle of sweat through the stiff weave of her new cotton t-shirt.

And there, two hundred metres away, playing in the sand, were the two children, two little girls.

Boni didn't see the woman looking after them until she bent down to ask their names.

"You needs summat, missus?" the woman called out, and Boni took a step back, startled, shaded her eyes. The two little girls glanced up at her for a moment, and then went back to their play.

"I was looking for someone called Daniel Jacquot. I was told he lives here."

"Dat so, missus. And dat him dere, comin' h-up right behin' you."

3

Jacquot knew there was someone looking for him. Old Merluze at Le Vauclin's marina had phoned him before lunch, saying how he'd just made a fifty off him and would be happy to buy him a drink the next time Jacquot was down that way. And at a little after four, as he sawed through a length of planking for the deck outside the kitchen, the widow Chanson also made a call, telling him about her new guest.

"A fine-lookin' woman, she is, Daniel. Come in from Le François she done, h-and h-askin' after you. Told her she'd find you on de beach. Samuel's bringin' 'er over right this minute. Just mind you behaves yourself, y'hear? Remember your manners. Be nice."

The name 'Stuyvesant' meant nothing to Jacquot, and the Widow hadn't caught a Christian name. He wondered who the visitor might be, how she could know him, and why she should bother to make the trip across to the island and book in at the guest house just to pay a call? It had to be something important, he decided, but he couldn't for the life of him think what it might be. So he put down his saw, swallowed back the last of his beer, and rather than climb the low bluff that separated his house from Trinité's north shore, he swam round the point to wash off the sweat and sawdust. By the time he came ashore, he could see Samuel's yellow Peugeot parked in the shade, and the figure of a woman walking away from him towards the two girls.

He watched her reach them, bend down to speak to them, then start back when old Mama Loubertin called out from her perch. Jacquot chuckled. Mama Loubertin was as large as they come, wore the brightest clothes, yet she could disappear if she wanted to.

He was maybe ten metres away from them, when he saw Mama Loubertin point in his direction.

The visitor turned, and looked, and as she did so the two girls spotted him, the pair of them jumping to their feet when they saw who it was.

"Papa, Papa, Papa," they cried, and dodging past the woman they raced across the sand and hugged his legs, pleading with him to come play with them.

But his eyes were on his visitor.

More than ten years on, Jacquot recognised her immediately.

Never a moment's uncertainty.

Not Stuyvesant. The name was Milhaud. Boni Milhaud.

But he could see from the frown and the shadow of disappointment crossing her face that she didn't recognise him.

He reached down and picked up the two girls, one in each arm, cradled them against him.

He looked back at the woman, just a few steps away.

"It's been a while," he said at last.

4

Boni Stuyvesant felt a cold rush of disappointment when she turned and saw the man they called Daniel Jacquot. It wasn't him. Wasn't the man she'd been looking for; coming all this way, and now stranded on the island until she could get herself back to the mainland.

She should have known when Madame Chanson mentioned the two girls. The man's daughters. Jacquot didn't have any daughters, no children, none that she knew of. And nobody had mentioned children when she'd called the *Judiciaire* in Marseilles, and asked to speak to him. He'd retired, she'd been told. Four or five years before.

Did anyone know where she could find him, she'd asked? Did they have an address? A phone number?

The policeman she was speaking to explained that he hadn't known Chief Inspector Jacquot personally, but if she'd hold on he'd ask around. A few minutes later he came back with apologies. All anyone knew was that he had moved to the Caribbean, Martinique somewhere. That was the last they'd heard.

And now she was here. But the man she had come for wasn't this man. As tall as Jacquot, but slimmer, older, his hair a ragged, greyish-brown fall of sun-bleached tatters, his thick curling beard full around the cheeks and almost matted into the hair on his chest. He looked like a beach-bum, a Caribbean Crusoe. Dripping wet. Brown as a coconut.

But then, as he drew closer, she saw his eyes.

Jade green.

And heard his voice.

"It's been a while," he said.

And Boni Stuyvesant knew in that instant – the eyes, the voice – that she had found him. The man she'd been looking for.

And without meaning to, or wanting to, her shoulders slumped and she burst into tears.

5

"You've changed," said Boni. "I didn't recognise you."

"Island life," said Jacquot, walking with her along the Trinité shoreline. Their arms were linked and their steps in time, bare feet sinking in the sand, the water sluicing gently around their ankles. "It gets to you in the end."

The tears had stopped as swiftly as they had started. Jacquot had put the girls down and stepped forward, but in those first few moments Boni gathered herself. She put out a hand to stop him coming closer, wiped the tears away with the tips of her fingers, and had taken a deep steadying breath.

"How silly," she'd said. "How silly am I? *Vraiment*." She'd given a dismissive wave of her hand; easy and elegant.

Only then did she come to him and, holding his arms, she'd kissed his cheeks, three times, as though it were only days since they had last seen each other and not the best part of ten years.

Jacquot wasn't to be paid off so lightly. His arms went round her and he pulled her tight. Ten years on, she still felt the same. The warmth of her; the sinewy length.

"You look like a caveman."

"Like I said, island life. Razors don't feature too often."

"Clearly. And children, too?" she continued, kicking at the sea, swinging the sandals from her fingers. "I didn't know you had children. They're gorgeous."

"Béatrice and Mathilde. Béa and Matti," he said, glancing back the way they had come. The girls had returned to their sand castle, and Mama Loubertin remained sitting in the shade. "Béa's the soft one, Matti's the tough one. But when it comes to looks they take after their father."

Boni laughed. "Of course they do. And they're what? Three? Four?"

"Five in December. Christmas babies. An expensive time of year."

"And their mother?"

It was another three steps before Jacquot replied. "Their mother died," was all he said.

"I'm so sorry," said Boni.

Jacquot shrugged. "It was... a long time ago," he continued. "And she left me the girls. But what about you?" he asked. "Do you have kids?"

Boni smiled sadly, shook her head. "It never worked. Just a husband I love."

"That's good," he said. "Is he with you? On the island? Are the two of you on holiday?" Of course, Jacquot knew from Madame Chanson and the harbour master, Merluze, that Boni had come to the island alone, but he saw no reason to let her know that.

"No, he isn't. Which is why I am here. Looking for you."

"That sounds mysterious."

"It's a long story, Daniel."

"The best ones always are," he teased, squeezing her arm, lightening the mood.

And then, "Papa! Papa!" came a breathless voice from behind them; Béa catching them up. "Matti's being horrible… She's being mean to me. Tell her off, Papa."

Behind Béa, Jacquot could see Mama Loubertin lumbering over the beach towards them, one hand dragging Matti along with her, the other gripping her fan and a tangle of plastic spades and buckets.

He turned to Boni.

"Arsenic hour, I'm afraid. I'd ask you up to the house but I wouldn't recommend it. By the look of it there's going to be bloodshed."

"Of course, not a problem," said Boni. For a moment she looked surprised, and not a little put out, that their walk along the shore should be so suddenly and rudely interrupted. Someone not used to the demands of children, thought Jacquot.

"Why don't you give me a couple of hours to deal with the kids, and tidy myself up," he said, scooping up Béa, "and then come to the house for dinner, when the dust has settled? Say eight?"

Boni smiled, nodded. "Eight will be fine."

6

Jacquot stood in the shower and felt the salty tightness on his skin wash away. The girls had showered before him so most of the hot water was gone, just a lukewarm pattering rain in which to soap himself. Through the soft splatter of water he could hear the pair of them squabbling still, with Mama Loubertin telling them to mind their manners and eat up their supper or the Yam-Yam Man would come and get them. Not quite bloodshed, but close.

But Jacquot's mind was not on the girls. From the moment he'd waved her off in Samuel's car, all he could think of was Boni Milhaud, now Boni Stuyvesant, with her diamond ring, and diamond earrings, and a gold Seamaster hanging loose and elegant on her wrist. She had done all right for herself, thought Jacquot. She was what she had always wanted to be. Comfortable, and rich. But not, it appeared, altogether happy.

So what was the problem, he wondered? Why had she come all this way to find him, to seek him out after all this time? Because that's what she had done. She'd said so herself. And finding him wouldn't have been easy. It would have taken some effort. Only a few close friends back home in Marseilles knew where he was, and that was how he liked it. The past was gone. All he wanted was the present. The way he lived now. And whatever the future held in store. And the girls, of course.

So what did Boni want from him, he wondered? What was the 'long story' she wanted to tell him? It had to be about the husband, he decided, stepping out of the shower, towelling himself down, and wiping condensation from the mirror above the sink. Whatever the problem, it had something to do with the husband. And it was clear that Boni imagined he could help in some way. Which meant that whatever the problem was, it was a probably a serious one. Despite those initial tears – relief, he supposed, at having found him – she hadn't come all the way to Île des Frères looking for a shoulder to cry on. Not Boni.

Wrapping the towel around his waist, Jacquot rummaged through the bathroom cupboard, found a pair of nail scissors and, leaning into the mirror, he began to tidy up his beard. The whiskers were tough and knotted, even after what remained of the shampoo and conditioner, and as he snipped away at them he recalled the Boni he had known all those years ago in Marseilles. A flight attendant with Air France when they met, promoted to Chief Purser during their time together, working transatlantic routes out of Marseilles, to Boston, New York, Los Angeles and San Francisco. It was a life she loved, travelling the world, moving into his small apartment on place des Moulins in Marseilles' Le Panier district after she'd relocated from Paris. They'd been together the best part of two years – enough time for Jacquot to think himself in love with her – when, without a word, she had left him. Just gone. Disappeared. No note. Nothing. He'd come back to the apartment after two days away on *Judiciaire* business, and the place was empty, everything she owned, and even some things she didn't, packed up and taken away. Even the curtains.

He remembered, too, how hard he had taken her departure, how badly he had missed her those first few weeks. Such sadness. The weight of it. It wasn't the first time she'd gone off in a huff, but this time it was different. Because this time he'd known that she wouldn't be coming back, knew their time together was over. What he hadn't imagined was how long it would be before he saw her again.

Putting aside the scissors, Jacquot took up a razor and tidied the edges of his beard. A scrape here, a scrape there, stretching the skin, lifting the bristles from neck and cheeks and lips, hoping he didn't cut himself in this unfamiliar task.

And working the blade he remembered the last time he'd seen Boni.

In his bed, naked, asleep.

It was summer and the sheet was draped over her waist, her back long and tanned, her shoulder gently freckled, an arm flung up around her head. Her hair was a light brown back then, and he could see it now, falling over the side of her face, spread on the pillow. It was a Saturday morning, and he'd had to leave early, meeting with a colleague at a crime scene up country. He'd tiptoed around, not wanting to wake her, and then, when he was dressed and ready, he'd gone to the bed, knelt beside it, touched his lips to her shoulder. They'd argued the night before; something small, something petty, that had grown into something ugly. Something he'd said, something he wished then that he'd left unsaid. Something he wanted to say sorry for before he headed off. So he whispered his apology, wondering if she was feigning sleep, wondering whether she could hear him. But she didn't stir, just a soft easy breathing.

And that was the last time he saw her.

Until now.

Ten years later, here she was.

Looking for him.

7

"You have a lovely place," said Boni, casting her eyes around Jacquot's single-storey home overlooking Trinité beach. They were sitting on the terrace in a pair of low-slung cushioned plantation chairs, a glass-topped wicker table between them, halved coconut shells for ashtrays, tall tumblers of island punch for refreshment. Mama Loubertin had settled the girls in their beds, Jacquot had been called to tell them a story, kiss them goodnight and wish them sweet dreams, and now he and Boni were alone. Just some soft Brazilian jazz playing in the salon, the occasional clatter of dishes from the kitchen where Mama Loubertin was preparing their dinner. And close by, unseen in the darkness, the soft slap of waves and the hiss of sea sliding over sand.

"It's... charming," she continued. "So... homely."

Jacquot smiled. There was something in Boni's tone of voice, the way she'd paused, searching for the right words – *charming, homely* – looking around with politely interested eyes and a sharp little smile, that made him suspect his guest wasn't being altogether honest. It was clear that she was used now to a grander lifestyle and found her present surroundings just a little threadbare and make-do. The louvred panel walls open to the night's soft breeze, a high beamed roof of tightly-thatched palm, ceiling fans turning slowly, table lamps and overhead lights throwing pools of gold on the polished teak floors, the furnishings bare but serviceable – second-hand upholstered cane-weave armchairs and sofas, a long dining table with six chairs on one side and a church pew on the other, a mirror framed in driftwood, and low bookshelves made of wood planks and bricks. Charming, certainly, homely too, but clearly not what his guest was used to. He might not have known the kind of life Boni lived – in the Bahamas, she had told him on their beach walk – but he had a fair idea there was some considerable distance between their respective lifestyles.

Boni had arrived at the house an hour earlier, her hair still wet from a shower, in a colourful print dress that Jacquot recognised. He had seen it just a couple of days before, in the window of Madame Corale on rue St-Christophe. If Boni had had to buy a change of clothes, he reasoned, showing her out to the terrace, she must have come to the island in a hurry, on impulse. He had a feeling he wouldn't have to wait too long to find out why.

"Have you been here long?" she asked, putting down her drink.

"We came here after Claudine died, nearly five years now," Jacquot replied, reaching for his cigarettes, lighting one. "Claudine's daughter found it, persuaded me to come."

"Claudine was your wife?" asked Boni.

"Not exactly."

"You never married?"

"Not enough time," he replied.

"And her daughter?"

"Midou. From Claudine's first marriage. She's an oceanographer, works at the Vauclin Institute on the Morne Courbaril highway just south of Le François. You'd have passed it on your way here. Low and long and grey, like a university campus."

Jacquot leaned forward for his drink. Boni watched him pick up the glass, swirl its contents, take a sip. He was wearing a white t-shirt and black cotton trousers, bare brown feet in faded black espadrilles. He'd washed his hair, trimmed his beard, and when he'd come out to greet her, she'd smiled to herself as she kissed him, smelled shampoo not the sea. Tidied up, he was the same old Jacquot. How could she not have recognised him? But there was a sadness now in those green eyes that had not been there before, a sorrow she did not recognise. The loss of this Claudine, she decided, must have dealt him a deadly blow.

"It was a ruin," Jacquot continued. "An old boat shack. But I fell in love with it. Six months to turn it round and make a home. We stayed at Madame Chanson's during the work, and she and Mama Loubertin looked after the girls until I could move them in."

"Is there a school on the island?"

Jacquot smiled. He knew Boni. Practical Boni. It was just the kind of question she would ask.

"In St-Christophe, just along the promenade from Chez Chanson. A nursery, and primary school. When the girls are old enough, they'll go to the school in Le Vauclin. Either they'll stay with Midou, or come back home on the ferry. We'll have to see."

"So this really is home?"

"Home."

"Do you work? You have a job?"

"Don't need one. The rental from the house in Cavaillon, Claudine's insurance, my pension from the *Judiciaire*... it easily covers all we need."

"So what do you do all day?"

Jacquot shrugged. "I work on the house; there's still a pile to do. I fish, I swim, I spend time with my girls..."

"But don't you miss it? The good old days, back in Marseilles? Where was it? Rue de l'Evêché? The squad? All those scoundrels you worked with, and the scoundrels you chased?"

Jacquot sighed, leaned forward to tap ash into the coconut shell. "Sometimes good things come to an end. And you have to move on. It's what I did – what I had to do. And I'm... well, I'm starting to be happy again." He might as well have been talking of the moment Boni walked out on him all those years ago. And they both knew it.

Behind him a floorboard creaked, and a slim brown arm curled around his neck. A warm body pressed against him, then clambered over the arm of his chair and slid into his lap, curious green eyes settling on Boni.

"Papa, I can't sleep," said Béa.

8

By the time Jacquot returned from the girls' bedroom after settling Béa, Mama Loubertin had called Boni to the table.

"I done served your soups, and left de stew pot in de h-oven." She looked at Boni, and nodded, then turned back to Jacquot. "I be back in de mornin' like as usual, and it better h-all be clean, yo' hear me?"

Jacquot assured her that everything would be as she expected – he wouldn't dare do otherwise, he told her – and followed her to the porch steps, pausing a moment to watch her torch flick on and light a path through the palms.

"I thought she lived here," said Boni, when Jacquot came back to the table, settled himself, offered and poured the wine.

"Back near the road. Close enough to keep an eye on me." He picked up his spoon, dipped it into the iced Vichysoisse.

"Another Madame... Madame? What was her name? Your old concierge in Marseilles?"

"Foraque. Madame Foraque. A friend of my parents."

"She never liked me," said Boni, tasting the soup. And then, "Oh, *si délicieuse.*"

"She didn't like anyone."

"She liked you. It was just the girlfriends, I suppose."

"She was very protective."

"And Mama Loubertin?"

Jacquot shook his head. "Here it's different. Here they all want me married," he said. "Madame Chanson, Mama Loubertin, and all their friends. A single man with children and no wife upsets them. They'll all have heard about you by now, and they'll all want to know what's going on. It's worse in the season. Any single women staying at the guest house, Madame Chanson's on the phone, trying to get me round there for one thing or another."

"But there's no one... special?"

"No. Not yet. Who knows?" Jacquot pushed away from the table. "Here, let me take your bowl. Time for Mama Loubertin's celebrated *langoustes créoles.*"

Two hours later, memories dusted down, old stories rehashed, their plates washed and put away just as Mama Loubertin had instructed, Boni and Jacquot were back to the terrace. The warm tropic air was still and hot and heavy and smelled of the sea, and the night around them was silent save for the distant boom of surf breaking on the reef.

"Something to drink?"

"I should be getting back, or Madame Chanson might start phoning all her friends," said Boni, glancing at her watch.

"So that's a 'yes' then," said Jacquot, going back to the salon.

She heard him put on some more soft jazz, and the clink of glass. She turned and watched him. Leaner, slimmer, but such a terrible beard, even if he had thought to trim it between their meeting on the beach and her coming to dinner. But the ponytail had gone, which was maybe not so good; she had always loved that ponytail. Yet underneath all the whiskers it was still the same Jacquot. Older, maybe, sadder, too, but invested now with so much more bearing... more presence. Because of his children, and his loss, she supposed. A grown man now. And if he'd been attractive in Marseilles, she decided, he was even more attractive here.

"It's a local rum," said Jacquot, returning to the terrace, handing her a tumbler. Its coppery contents swirled around as she took it from him, and the air was suddenly filled with the scent of dark hot molasses. "I've tried all the brands," he continued, settling back in his chair, swinging a leg over the extended arm. "Dillon, Bally, Trois Rivières, Habitation St-Etienne... but this one comes out my favourite. St Clément. Single cask. Like the best cognacs, armagnacs, but just... different." He raised his glass to Boni, and she raised hers. "To Martinique, and its wonderful rum," he said. "And to old friends."

She watched him sip, savour, and then swallow his drink. No, he hadn't changed. She could still read him. He'd fall silent now, smile at her, look out into the darkness, and wait. She knew why. Deep down, the man was still a cop. He'd want to know why she was there, want to hear the story about her husband. Just second nature. And she was right. Resting his glass on his thigh, he smiled at her, then turned to the darkness beyond the terrace, no lights this side of the island, just an endless shifting blackness sprinkled with stars.

"So how did you meet?" he asked at last, when she didn't rise to the bait, just as she had known he would. "You and your husband. And you still haven't told me his name."

"Patric. Patric Stuyvesant. We met on a flight to Miami. He was up front, by himself. We got into conversation."

Just how Jacquot had met Boni all those years ago. On an Air France flight from Paris to Djibouti, stopping at Marseilles. Where the pair of them had disembarked. She'd reached the line of cabs before him, taking the Crew channel while he waited for his bag. She was dressed in flight attendant uniform – the light blue pencil skirt with its winking pleat behind the knees, the little jacket with three silver buttons and the silver wings on the lapel, the cap clipped over her regulation French pleat. All she'd removed was her name tag – Boni Milhaud. He even remembered her pick-up line as they shared a cab into town. "I don't go all the way on a Sunday, to Djibouti I mean." He'd known then how the evening would end. And he'd been right.

"And Monsieur Stuyvesant is French? American?" asked Jacquot, wondering when the two of them had met – before or after she'd cleared out the apartment in Le Panier?

"French. His parents lived in Lourmarin. Your neck of the woods."

"Wine business?" Jacquot asked, knowing the countryside thereabouts, its slopes ribbed with vines. "Or lavender?"

"Wine. Just a few hectares, but it's good. You'd like it. Château Clos des Roses. Local sales, nothing more. When his father died, his mother carried on for a while, but she passed away a couple of years ago."

"What happened to the house?"

"Patric kept it, rents out rooms during the season to pay for the upkeep. There's a *gardienne* and her husband who live in, take care of the place. She looks after the guests, and he works the vineyard."

"And what does Patric do now?"

Boni smiled. "He plays cards."

"A gambler?"

"A clever gambler."

Jacquot gave her a look. "Is there such a thing?"

"Yes. Patric. He runs his own casinos on the island. Nassau. Not like the big boys, not like Vegas, more like private clubs. Four of them actually. High-end, high-stakes private clubs."

"You knew that when you met him?"

"Not at first. I just thought he was this very successful, well-dressed businessman who could travel first class between Europe and America. Oh, and he was very good-looking, too."

"So when did you find out? About the gambling?"

"A little later, on that flight. We started talking. He asked if we'd be landing on time. I told him we would. He smiled, and said we wouldn't. I assured him that thanks to a strong tail wind we were already ahead of schedule. So he bet me we'd be late touching down. Seven minutes late, if I remember. And he pulled a twenty dollar bill from his wallet."

"Did you take the bet?"

Boni laughed. "Well, you know me. Hate to lose a cent if I don't have to. But I took it, of course. Seven minutes late? That exact? It was a no-brainer. The money was as good as mine."

"And?"

"We were held in a holding pattern over Miami. All the time we'd gained on the flight was lost. It was as if he'd arranged it. We touched down seven and a half minutes late."

"He take your money?"

"He told me I could buy him dinner."

"Which you did?"

"Stone crabs. At Joe's, on Collins." She said it with an easy familiarity, as though Jacquot would know the place, when in fact he'd never been to Miami.

"And you married him?"

"Eight months later. At his home on Lyford Cay."

A silence settled between them. Jacquot broke it. It was time for the story.

"So what's gone wrong?" he asked.

Boni sighed, twisted the ring on her finger. "He's missing, Daniel. Three months ago. End of July."

"Just like that? No warning?"

Boni shook her head, sipped her rum. "A friend of his, a partner in the business, called at the house, told me what had happened, and said that Patric was in trouble. He owed money. At first I wasn't too worried; the business was good and we had easily enough to cover any unforeseen shortfalls. A bad run at the tables, that kind of thing. It happens a lot. But then he told me how much was owed. And who Patric owed it to."

"How much?"

"Close to ten million dollars. Something like that. Apparently Patric had been skimming the take."

"And the who?"

"A local businessman. Ettore DiCorsa."

Jacquot shook his head. "I don't know the name." He reached for his cagarettes, lit one.

"No reason you should. Which is probably how he likes it." Boni sighed, took another sip of her rum, licked her lips. "What he doesn't like is having someone take his money."

"His money?"

"He was like a sleeping partner. He'd helped Patric out after some bad runs at the clubs in return for a small stake."

"Did you talk to Patric about it?"

"I never saw him to ask. He didn't come home, and he didn't call. I haven't seen or heard from him since he drove away from the house that last morning."

"Had he been acting strangely? You know, out of character?"

"He'd been quieter than normal. But that wasn't unusual, and I knew not to press. Sometimes it happens like that. The clubs, you know. Like I said, a bad run. You just have to wait for the upturn. Things usually got better. I knew that."

"You reported his disappearance to the police?"

"Of course. Two days later. Just another 'Missing Person'. No body, no suspicious circumstances."

"And now?"

"The police? Still a 'Missing Person'." Boni took another sip of her drink, leaned forward, put down her glass. When she looked up her eyes were sad. "Apparently he was having an affair. A girl on the island. She'd gone missing too, so the cops put two and two together."

"Girlfriend?"

Boni sighed. "Patric was a good-looking man. Very… personable. Good with people. Just so long as he was careful, so long as I didn't know about it, I didn't care. You know what they say: he played, but he stayed…"

"Did you know this one?"

She shook her head. "According to the police she worked at The Edgewater. A big club up there in Nassau. In guest relations…" She gave Jacquot a look, a wry smile.

"How did you find out about her?"

"Patric's partner told me. Apparently it had been going on for a few months, but he didn't think it was serious. At least, not serious enough for Patric to run off with her."

"Did you tell the police what the friend had told you? About the money? This DiCorsa character?"

Boni shook her head. "It didn't seem a good idea."

"And the business?"

"Still going strong. Patric's partner, John Ballard, the one who told me what had happened, stepped in, took it over."

"And you think Patric's done a runner? To get away from DiCorsa, settling down somewhere with his girlfriend? And the money."

"Either that, or he's talking to the sharks."

Jacquot frowned.

"A local expression, up in Nassau. As in dead," said Boni. "The girl, too, possibly."

"And you want me to find out what happened to him? Which of the two. Dead or alive."

"You're the only one who can."

Her wedding ring, the diamond studs in her ears, the bracelet of her watch glinted in the candlelight. And her eyes began to well. Her voice softened, pleading. "I just need to know, Daniel. One way or the other."

Jacquot sighed, spread his hands. Glass in one, cigarette in the other. He knew this would be hard, but it had to be done. So there was no mistake, no misunderstanding.

"Like I said, Boni, I'm retired. I don't do that anymore. I have a different life now. I have my home here, the girls." He leaned forward, stubbed out his cigarette. "That part of my life is over."

"But you're a *flic*. You always will be. I know you."

Jacquot shook his head. "Not any more."

9

"She's a nice lady," said Béa, dark curls tumbling over her tanned face, pudgy brown fingers scooping up the last slippery slices of her breakfast mango from the wood platter that served as a plate *chez* Jacquot. The two girls had broken so much china between them – as clumsy as their mother – that Jacquot had asked Samuel's father to fashion him a set of wood platters. "I liked her," Béa continued. "She had twinkly ears."

The diamond earrings, Jacquot supposed.

"Is she your girlfriend?" asked Matti, sitting back and watching her father sip his coffee.

Matti was always the more direct of the twins. Jacquot often wondered if she was the elder of the girls. He would never know, of course, but he liked to think so. If it were true, then those few minutes ahead of Béa had given her a kind of knowing confidence. Of the two girls, she had always been the leader, the instigator, and mischief-maker.

"A long time ago, she was," he said, putting down his mug.

"Before *Maman*?" asked Béa, looking at her sticky fingers. What to do with them? She licked them, finger by finger, then wiped them on her bare brown chest.

"Before *Maman*, yes."

"So…" began Matti, "has she come here to marry you? Is she going to live here? With us?"

Mama Loubertin lumbered in from the kitchen, picked up the girls' platters and made a job of holding them in one hand and wiping down the table with a cloth. She shot Jacquot a sideways look. She'd heard the question and was waiting for his answer, too.

"I don't think so," Jacquot replied. "She's just here for a holiday."

"Lotsa places to go take h-an 'oliday," said Mama Loubertin. And nodding in his direction, as though to underline her meaning, she waddled back to the kitchen.

"She didn't stay the night like some of the others," Matti continued.

There was a grunt from Mama Loubertin as she disappeared into the kitchen.

"Maybe she forgot to bring pyjamas," said Béa, frowning.

"And maybe it's time you two ragamuffins got yourselves ready for school," said Jacquot, pushing back from the table and clapping his hands. "Go on, the pair of you. *Allez-y. Vite, vite!*"

The school was a fifteen-minute drive from Trinité, and on the way there Jacquot had the two girls sing nursery rhymes when it became clear that, as far as they were concerned, the question of Boni's intentions – and Jacquot's, for that matter – were all they wanted to know about. And as they sang, he let his attention wander, back to the lover who'd left him all those years ago.

Her eyes – icy-blue and low-lidded, as though she were about to fall asleep at any moment; her mouth, lips always slightly apart, just a breath away from panting; her hair, twisted into a tight chignon or a pinned pleat for work, but loosened to fall around her shoulders when she climbed onto him, pinned him down; the catch in her voice, throaty, smoky, her whispered words just for him. Her hands, her fingers. Teasing, reaching, stroking. Her litany of soft pleading and harsh entreaty. He remembered, too, the clip-clip sound of her high heels on the tiled entrance hall of Madame Foraque's house on Moulins, the sharp points of her elbows when she set her hair, the way she hummed as she did it, and how she loved to take him shopping, lingerie shops her favourite destination, drawing him into the process, offering him the lacy cup of a bra to feel, the ruched strap on a suspender belt, or the silky bodice of a petticoat. Offerings filled with unspoken promise. Boni was... and probably still was... a consummate sensualist.

But Jacquot remembered, too, her deceit and her cruelty. The affairs he was sure she had – one he knew of, for certain – and the way she had left him. Without a word. Just gone. As though she didn't care what hurt she might inflict, what sadness he might suffer. Simply discarded. But all these years later, knowing what he knew, what he'd suffered, he was surprised to realise that he still felt a strong abiding affection for her, and for the time they had spent together. She was a real player, a great girl, and he felt an equally strong sympathy for her, for the situation in which she now found herself. Gambling could be a nasty business – that deadly mix of money and greed and chance – and the risks nastier still when you crossed the big boys. Which was what this DiCorsa sounded like. He hoped for Patric's sake, and for Boni's, that he'd taken the money and run, and not been caught. Talking to sharks was not Jacquot's idea of fun. But was it just an expression?

A figure of speech for a violent death? Did it mean a bullet in the head? Or a knife in the guts? Or a cord around your neck? Or were there really sharks? Were people actually thrown to the sharks? And were you dead before they dropped you into the water, he wondered? Or did they leave that to the sharks? The kind of people Jacquot had come across during his time in Marseilles would have left it to the sharks. Just for the sport of it. Whatever happened, there'd be little left for the authorities to work on.

"Papa just drove through a red light," said Matti, from the back seat.

Which brought Jacquot back with a start. They had reached the outskirts of St-Christophe and the thick stands of palm and banana that had lined the road from Trinité were now broken either side by brightly-coloured wood shacks with corrugated iron roofs and fenced gardens. Thank God there were no CCTV cameras on Île des Frères, he thought. And thank God there wasn't too much traffic; if the light had been red, there'd clearly been no other cars on the road or he wouldn't have got away so lightly. If indeed he had gone through a red light. It was just the kind of thing that Matti would say – true or not.

Taking a firmer grip on the wheel and sitting up straighter Jacquot concentrated on the road ahead, keeping an eye on the rear-view mirror for a flashing blue light. The last thing he wanted was a run-in with *Capitaine* Faubert, about the only person on Île des Frères with whom he had not become friends. Whatever the reason – Jacquot's reputation with the Marseilles *Judiciaire*, or having once played rugby with France's national squad – the island's chief of police had taken against him from the start.

A few minutes later, with no sign of Faubert to spoil his day, Jacquot parked outside the school, unstrapped the girls, and taking their hands he led them across the road, kissed them goodbye at the gates – Matti in a hurry to be gone, pulling at her sister's hand, while Béa reached up for a hug.

Back in the car, waving as the girls crossed the playground and disappeared into the darkness of the school's front door, Jacquot drove on to the end of the promenade, circled the roundabout, and came back the way he had come, taking the road on the left that led up to Madame Chanson's.

He had a date with Boni.

10

Boni Stuyvesant woke to soft golden sunlight shifting through the muslin nets around her bed. For a moment she had no idea where she was and then, through the open windows, she heard the slap of slippers on the terrace below her room, the laying of china, the rattle of cutlery, and the warm tropical scent of freshly-baked banana bread. Now she knew where she was. Madame Chanson's guest house, on Île des Frères.

Boni had arrived back at the plantation house at a little after midnight. Her evening with Jacquot had come to an end with a flash of headlights from the palm grove and a soft beep-beep from her driver, Samuel. Apparently it was a signal the two men used. If no one appeared after five minutes, Samuel would leave whoever it was with Jacquot. When Jacquot told Boni what it meant, that Samuel wanted to get home, she finished her rum and got to her feet.

"I didn't realise it was so late," she'd told him. "And I wouldn't want to add to your reputation," she'd teased, kissing his cheeks lightly, squeezing his hand a little harder, and leaving him on the terrace steps.

"I'll come by tomorrow morning. Show you around," he'd called out. "Nine-thirty? Thereabouts?"

Now Boni lifted her wrist, turned her watch. A little after nine. It had better be 'thereabouts', she thought to herself, and leaving the bed she hurried to the shower.

As the water splashed over her Boni closed her eyes and remembered Jacquot, the man she'd met on that flight from Paris. Remembered it as clearly as she did her dinner with him the night before. She'd been standing at the aircraft door, checking through the flight manifest while two of her colleagues welcomed the passengers aboard. He was one of the last down the jetway, one of the last to step inside, a little out of breath, a leather bag in one hand, his boarding card in the other. She remembered exactly the way he had looked. He was dressed in faded blue jeans, pointed cowboy boots, a white linen shirt and brown leather jacket. His hair was long and tied in a ponytail, his skin gently tanned. She could see him now. Big and broad and imposing. A man you didn't miss. A man who caught, and held, the eye. But what she remembered most of all was the voice, a roughly whispered '*je vous en prie*' when one of the flight attendants checked his card, pointed him to his seat. And his smiling eyes, of course, a shade of green she'd never seen before, webbed with laugh lines and set above a nose that was ever so slightly out of line. A sports injury, she later learned.

Soaping herself, she recalled that last flight out of Charles-de-Gaulle. Taking over from one of the girls for the safety procedure, catching his eye as she went through the drill, and keeping it on him as she tightened the straps on her lifejacket and tipped her lips to the jacket's whistle. And that was that, until Marseilles where she waited for a taxi until he came out of the Arrivals Hall. There was no shortage of cabs on the rank but she'd invited him to share hers. He'd accepted her offer with one of his crinkly smiles and three hours later, after he'd taken her somewhere he knew for a late supper, she'd invited him to the Mercure Hotel on Marseilles' Vieux Port, up on the fifth floor where the Air France crews put up. The Mercure. That's where it started. All those years ago.

What surprised her was how long their affair had lasted. She'd had no desire back then for any long-term relationship, moving contentedly from one brief affair to the next – pilots and passengers mostly. But there was something about him, something so beguiling: the easy, elegant charm of him; the strength and bulk of him; and his gentleness too. And such a natural easy lover; those large hands, light as a feather. The way, once, preparing their supper, he'd teased open the petals of a courgette flower, fingering his way in to clean out the dust and the insects. It had been enough for her to want him then and there, opening her up the same way. And that's what she'd made him do, right there on the kitchen table, among that golden pile of pollened blossoms. But most of all, what she noticed then, and remembered now, was his never seeming to know just how attractive he was. It was never a card he played, or would have known how to play.

After that first night together at the Mercure they met up whenever she landed in Marseilles, and a few months after that first encounter, without any pressure from him, she'd decided to let out her flat in Paris and relocate to Marseilles. Moving in to his apartment in Le Panier, under the watchful and disapproving glare of that old witch, Madame Foraque.

That had been the first real wrinkle in their affair. That wicked old woman. With her black beret and red frizzy hair, the greasy throat-thickening smell of her soups and stews on the stove in her *conciergerie*, and those stinking cheroots she favoured. And the way the old biddy looked at her – dismissive, cold, unfriendly. As though Jacquot were hers, and hers alone. Not to be shared.

And then, of all things, she'd fallen pregnant and everything finally came tumbling down. Not because she didn't want to settle down, didn't want to be a mother, be married – which, actually, she didn't, not right then, but was sure he did – but because she couldn't be certain the child was his. That was the other thing: he had been faithful, but she had not. It was just the way she was back then. Life for the living. The glamour of her job. Travelling around the world. Single and free. And then, three months into the pregnancy, she had lost the child, and something else died.

Stepping out of the shower, Boni towelled herself dry and, as she dressed, she wondered about the woman who had come after her, the woman Jacquot had found to take her place, to take his heart. What had she looked like, this Claudine? Tall, dark, short, blonde? Old or young? She had seen no photographs in the house on Trinité, nothing to remind him of her, and despite one or two probing questions he'd told her nothing. How had they met, where and when, Boni wondered? And what did she do? Was she another *flic*? A lawyer, a doctor? Knowing Jacquot, she'd have been special. That was the kind of man he was. And for just a moment, Boni felt an unexpected twist of jealousy, a whisper of regret for a time long past.

Coming down the stairs Boni opted for a table in the dining room, rather than the terrace, ordered a pot of coffee, the fruit plate, and some pastries, informing a hovering Madame Chanson that Monsieur Jacquot was an old friend she hadn't seen for years, and that he hadn't changed a jot. Which was when the two women turned to the opened windows as a battered Citroën 2CV came to a screeching halt at the porch steps. Its doors were red and the body blue, its green canvas roof was rolled back, and the window flaps were up. The sun caught on the windscreen, flashing like a dusty mirror, and it was only when Jacquot swung out of the driver's seat, that Boni realised who it was. Espadrilles, shorts, a pair of sunglasses he pulled off and latched into the collar of a white t-shirt. Silver bangles on his wrist. Island man. No worries.

She lifted her coffee cup, took a sip and stayed where she was, a yellow-breasted bananaquit hopping around her plate, pecking up crumbs.

Let him come to her, she thought.

Like the bird.

Let him come to her.

11

It seemed to Jacquot that everyone who worked at Chez Chanson was in attendance as he jogged up the steps onto its gingerbread porch. There was Madame Chanson coming out of the dining room, and Shérine, the waitress, and Nathalie, the upstairs maid, and Amélia, the cleaner and, leaning out of the kitchen window as though waiting for a passing breeze to cool her sweating jowly face, Chez Chanson's cook, Honorine. All of them with eyes on him as he crossed the terrace and came into the dining room. He was not surprised. This was how they were. This was what he'd expected. They would all want to know what was going on, and they would all want something to gossip about. And as he passed them, he nodded and smiled and wished each of them a cheery "*bonjour, bonjour, ça va?*", to which they responded with lilting bird-song replies and laughing eyes and twitching smiles. They were all here for the show, waiting expectantly, watching his every move. He decided not to disappoint them.

"And a good morning to you, *chérie*," said Jacquot, when he reached Boni's table. He put a hand on the back of her chair and leaned down to kiss her, smelling her favourite perfume and being swept back a hundred years. Down on the beach the previous day, and at dinner the night before, he hadn't noticed her scent. But he did now.

"*Coco.*"

"You remember."

"After you left, the flat in Le Panier smelled of it for months. It made life very difficult." He chuckled fondly at the memory, making light of her departure all those years before, not wanting her to know how much he'd missed her those first few weeks. But as the scent had faded, so, too, had his feelings for her. And more quickly than he'd imagined.

"You are a such a liar, Daniel," she said, pushing him away. Playfully. And then, lowering her voice, "You knew as well as I that we were going nowhere. It had been good, but we were two different people, wanting different things. It was time to call it quits."

Which, for Jacquot, had certainly not been the case. He hadn't known they were going nowhere, or that it was time to quit. Or maybe he wasn't prepared to accept it. As far as he was concerned it was just a rough patch they were going through; they'd get over it, he was certain. But they hadn't. And by the time Jacquot finally realised what was happening, it really was over. She'd gone. In another life she might have stayed, might have settled down, as he had wanted her to do. But it hadn't turned out like that. Which was how, in the end, he'd found Claudine. Fallen in love with Claudine. And now he was here, with their two girls. And life was starting to be good again. The past was the past.

Pulling out a chair, he sat down, made himself comfortable.

Shérine sauntered over. Tight white tunic buttoned down the front, swollen hips swinging, bare legs and mismatched flip-flops. "Café-Calva, Monsieur Daniel?"

He smiled up at her. "Not today, Shérine. Just a picnic box from Honorine. For two. Her best." He looked at his watch and then raised his voice a notch so Honorine would hear. "And ready by the time Madame Stuyvesant comes down from her room, s'il vous plaît. Which will be in five minutes." He turned to Boni. "Is that enough time?"

It wasn't. Five minutes was asking too much. But Jacquot wasn't too bothered. Island time was like that; he'd grown used to it. Thirty minutes later, at a little after ten-thirty, he started up the old Citroën, pushed it into gear and set off with Boni in the seat beside him, back the way he had come with the girls, but turning off along the coast road rather than driving across the island to Trinité.

"There are just the four roads on des Frères," said Jacquot, as the last clapboard houses fell behind them. "This one, the corniche, goes all the way round. Twenty-four minutes from start to finish. You would never even know you'd gone round in a circle. The other three roads cut through the interior. It's not a big place. A little over forty square kilometres, with a population around six thousand."

"And beautiful," said Boni, sliding her arm through the 2CV's window flap and looking out over aquamarine shallows to the dark blue sea beyond, and white rolling breakers.

"Oh yes, very beautiful."

"So where does the name come from? The Brothers' Island?"

"The two hills. One north, up ahead. The other behind us, the other side of St-Christophe. When you're sailing in from the ocean, the first thing you see are those two hills, like cowled monks facing each other. Two halves of an old volcano, and the reef that surrounds the island is what's left of the original crater."

"Is it safe?" asked Boni.

"No eruptions yet," said Jacquot. "I'm keeping my fingers crossed."

Thanks to the tinny rumpus of the Citroën's engine, the state of the road and consequent jouncing of the springs in their seats, there was little chance for further conversation as St-Christophe fell behind them and Jacquot increased his speed. Once the last houses were past them the coastal corniche took over, a steeply cambered tarmacadam road that cut a sandswept path through headland groves of palm, over rattling makeshift bridges built across dry stony streambeds, along stretches of deserted beach, and through small wood-shack settlements where barefoot kids watched them drive by. Sometimes a wave, often just curious eyes following their progress.

Nor was there much traffic to slow that progress, just a single horse and cart loaded with bananas, and two exhaust-belching lorries piled with sugar-cane that Jacquot passed easily and quickly. When they reached the blustery northern tip of the island where ocean waves rolled in through a gap in the reef and crashed onto the jagged rocky shoreline, Jacquot turned to the right and swooped down through a swathe of banana trees. After the sharp salty smell of the sea, and a vast expanse of blue, the air through the window and open top of the Citroën was filled now with a rich sweaty greenness, the view limited by the close jungle of vegetation either side of the road, long drooping leaves shading tight bundles of small green fruit bagged in blue protective plastic shrouds.

"The main crop after sugar," Jacquot said. "Sweetest bananas in the Caribbean…"

"I'll take your word for that. You should know how I hate bananas."

Before long the road began to climb. And as it climbed the air cooled, and Boni leaned back in her seat, tipped her head to feel it on her throat, watching the palm tops flash by above her.

Jacquot glanced across at her, the line of her neck and the open shirt, the crumpled shorts and long brown limbs, knees rubbing loosely together, swaying apart, as the road twisted and turned its way upwards. She was still, he thought to himself, one hell of a woman. And from nowhere he remembered the photos he'd taken of her back in Marseilles: at their favourite table outside Bar de la Marine on the Vieux Port; celebrating his birthday on the terrace at Mirador; at the

Jazz Festival in Juan-les-Pins (George Benson, no less, and their seats just three rows back from the stage); skiing in Val d'Isère; swimming out on the islands; diving the Calanques. Rolls and rolls of photos. She hadn't taken those when she left. And as he thought of them he remembered where they were. In a cardboard box in Le Panier, in the storeroom behind Madame Foraque's *conciergerie*. Packed away with the rest of his past. The old girl made him pay rent for it, of course, but it had proved a useful storage space when he moved in with Claudine. And knowing Madame Foraque, he knew they would still be there.

Ten minutes later they stopped for lunch at the highest point, the battlements of an old colonial fort used now as a paved belvedere where tourists came to take pictures and buy bags of peppered prawns from the Mamas who set up stalls here. But the tourist season had yet to begin, and they were alone, sitting on the belvedere wall, working their way through Honorine's hamper – radishes, spiced olives and slices of Créole salami, warm jerk chicken and a creamy potato salad, fruit, bread, and a Thermos of chilled white wine. Below them, they could see stretches of the road they'd taken from St-Christophe, the coastline's broken curve of green headlands and golden beaches reaching away to the south, and its necklace ring of reef – aquamarine shallows one side, cobalt depths beyond.

"Trinité is over there, on the other side," said Jacquot, pointing across fields of cane and maize and bananas with his chicken leg. "Just past the slope of the hill."

"Any crime to speak of?" asked Boni, distractedly, worming a finger through the tub of radishes, finding one she approved of, and biting into it.

Jacquot chuckled. "People get drunk sometimes… That's about it. Usually all they do is fall over and hurt themselves." He took a sip of wine, and reached for his cigarettes. "You know something? The people here refer to Martinique as the mainland? That's where all the bad stuff happens. Not here on des Frères."

Boni flicked away the green shoots of the radish and reached for another. "Do all your girls get the tour?" she asked.

Jacquot gave a start, caught off guard. Then he smiled. "Whatever made you think that?"

Boni gave him a look. Who was he kidding? "Pointing out all the sights on the way here? That ruined plantation house, the old sugar mill, those fishing boats called... called..."

"*Gommiers* and *Yoles*..."

"That's them, *Gommiers* and *Yoles*. And now Trinité. It sounds like you've done it a hundred times."

"Not quite that often, Boni."

"Well, I bet it works," she said, with a sigh. "Times like this, like last night... I can't think of a woman who wouldn't fall in love with you, Daniel. With your two lovely daughters, and that home of yours on the beach..." She looked at him, and smiled fondly. "You're a different man now. All... grown up."

"But all of it without Claudine," he said, quietly. "Without the woman I love. My daughters' mother."

Boni put out a hand, rested it on his knee. "Which is how it is for me right now," she said. "Without Patric."

There it was. What Jacquot had been waiting for since he'd picked her up at Chez Chanson. For Boni to start work on him again, trying to persuade him to take the job of finding her husband which she had begun so persuasively the night before. He knew she wouldn't let it rest, not Boni. But he knew it was a lost cause, that there was no way he'd accept the commission. Too old, too out of the loop. And a father now, with two children to care for. But he still had to tell her, still had to let her down. Again. And Boni, he knew, was not a person who had ever liked being let down. When she wanted something, she got it. He didn't suppose she had changed since their days in Marseilles.

"The thing is, I don't know what to do next," she continued, looking out to sea. "Or where to go, or who to ask for help. You were the only one I could think of. You were always so resourceful, so..." She took a deep breath, and shook her head. Then she suddenly brightened, as though she'd thought of something, and turned those ice-blue eyes onto him. "Of course, if it's money... why don't I pay you? I wouldn't expect you to do it for nothing. And a lot of money, I mean it. And if not for you, then for your daughters. To keep them safe. To give them a start."

"It's not money, Boni."

"A week. Give me a week, Daniel. Ten thousand a day. Up front. Seventy thousand. Call it a round hundred. I can have it in your bank by lunchtime tomorrow."

Jacquot reached for her hand, took it up, held her fingers, smoothing his thumb over her nails. From a distance they could have been lovers. But that time was long past.

"I told you, Boni, it's not a question of money. It's not a question of anything. I have all I want, right here. And the girls need me. I'm sorry, truly sorry I can't help you, but I have a different life now, responsibilities I never had before. And like I said last night I'm getting too old for what you have in mind. It would be like going back out on a rugby pitch. I wouldn't know where to start."

She slid her hand from his, and took up her glass. "Just come with me to Nassau, and bring the girls if you want," she said, swirling the wine, sipping it. "Think of it as a holiday. Stay a week, just talk to people, see if you can find something, anything. If you do, you're free to go and I'll get someone else to follow it up." And then, beseeching, sensing she might be getting through to him. "Say you will. For me?"

Jacquot smiled. Just as he'd suspected. The same old Boni. When she wanted something, she was relentless.

"No, Boni. I mean it. Those days are long gone," he said, starting to pack away the remains of their lunch. "Leave it to the police. Or hire yourself a really good private detective. Someone who knows his way round. Either one is better than me." He looked at his watch. "But right now, it's back on the tour bus. There's a lot more to see, and time's running short. The girls will be out of school at three."

12

That evening, with Mama Loubertin happily roped in to babysit Béa and Matti, Jacquot took Boni to dinner. Not at Chez Chanson, but at Gustave's, a Créole restaurant on the headland above the harbour. They sat on the terrace beneath a roof of split cane, a warm sea breeze rattling the palm fronds above them, the lights of St-Christophe twinkling below, and the sea a pitch black pool of darkness. Palm heart salads to begin, followed by grilled pompano in a *chien* sauce. On Jacquot's advice they ordered the local Bière Lorraine rather than wine. "Something cold to put out the fire. The *chien* can be a touch too spicy for some."

Three beers each had loosened their tongues.

"You took everything. Even the curtains," he said, pushing away the cleaned white bones of his pompano.

"I left you the grass. I could have taken that, too."

"That would have been a step too far. I'd have come looking for you, believe me."

As soon as he said it, Jacquot wished the words back. They had spent the evening reminiscing, talking again of their time together in Marseilles. But not once had they spoken of Patric, of Boni's offer to pay Jacquot to find him. Now the way was open for her, but she didn't follow through.

Instead, she told him she was heading home the following day, taking the morning ferry. She said she understood his reluctance to help; she was sorry for it, of course, but she understood. No hard feelings.

But Jacquot knew Boni, knew she wouldn't give up so easily. She had one more card to play, and he knew she'd play it. Knew what was coming. One more trick up her sleeve.

After dinner, arm in arm, they strolled back along rue St-Christophe, the sea and harbour on one side, a line of ramshackle roadside bars and restaurants on the other. There was a hot breeze whipping up sand on the pavement, and far away a jagged fork of lightning ripped silently through the night. Moments later the darkness groaned and shook with a distant thunder.

"There's rain coming," said Jacquot, raising his chin and sniffing the air.

"A hurricane?"

"Not us. Further south, maybe, down Tobago way. But there'll be a storm here for sure."

And as he said it the first drops smacked down around them. Just a few at first, as though the rain couldn't make up its mind. But then, the very next moment, it came down in a torrent, ghosting the promenade lights, making the pavement shine, and forcing them to run for shelter.

They waited under the awning of a bar, watching other late-night strollers run for cover, the rain beating a rattling tattoo on the sloping corrugated metal roof that sheltered them.

"Do you remember the rain in Marseilles?" she asked.

"Of course I do," he replied, recalling the storms that used to blow in from the sea at the end of every summer, or blast down the course of the Rhône. Stiff unyielding sheets of steel, cold and grey, that smacked onto your head with a numbing force, or hammered on the roof of your car.

"Will it last long?" asked Boni, clasping his arm, drawing close.

"This is just a taster. It'll stop any minute, but then it'll really rain. All night."

And that is what it did. One minute torrential rain, the next it had gone. Just a streams of water racing along the gutters, gurgling into the drains, and a thin steam rising from the road.

"Time to make a run for it," said Jacquot, and together they hurried along the promenade, turning up towards Chez Chanson, breathless now, the guest house driveway littered with jacaranda and hibiscus blossom stripped from the branches by the rain.

At the steps leading up to the porch, Boni did what Jacquot had been waiting for. She slid her arm from his, turned and drew him towards her, stepped in close, raised her mouth to his, started to brush her lips against his.

How it always started.

Then, coming closer still, she pressed her body against him, moved her lips to his ear and whispered, "What about it, Daniel? You want to come up? For old times' sake?"

And as she said it the rain returned with a vengeance, hurtling down from the black night sky, smacking onto their heads and shoulders, and soaking through their clothes.

13

At first, no one noticed the stain. It was small and dark, the size of a coin. On the ceiling of Madame Chanson's dining salon. It appeared as Shérine was laying tables for breakfast, at a little before seven in the morning. The rain had stopped two hours earlier and now the gardens and house steamed with a heavy clogging heat, barely stirred by the dining room's single fan.

When the first guest came down for breakfast   a medical supplies salesman from Fort-de-France – the stain in the ceiling had grown to the size of a side-plate. But still no one looked up, no one noticed it. Maybe it was a warp in the ceiling timbers, or a crack in the ancient plasterwork, or maybe the irresistible pull of vibrations from the fan, but one side of the stain soon began to drift towards the metal column from which the fan hung. No longer a circle, it resembled now the curved irregular shape of a yam, its leading point drawing closer and closer to the fan's ceiling bracket. And as it moved it began to change colour, not so much the rusty brown of leaking water, but a rich scarlet that showed up bright and sharp against the ceiling's creamy lime-wash coat. There seemed to be more of it, too, as though fed by some unseen source, and if any of the diners below had looked up, and looked closely, it is likely they would have seen it actually moving.

An hour after it first appeared, the tip of the stain reached the fan's ceiling bracket and trickled on to it, and over it, and down the brass column. A single scarlet stream, winding around the metal like ivy, drawn down by gravity and by the motion of the fan. At the bottom of the column, it gathered for a moment on the brass casing that concealed the fan's motor, then spilled out onto the first of the four blades. Slowly but surely, aided now by the blade's spinning centrifuge, the stream of scarlet increased its speed and quickly reached the paddled end of the blade, trembled there a moment before drops of it span off into the room

The first drop landed on an unlaid table by the door of the dining room, and went unnoticed, a spot of red on bare brown wood. The second drop hit a floorboard on the other side of the room and was similarly unnoticed. But the third and fourth drops found their targets, staining a white tablecloth with a single red dot, and smearing the salesman's newspaper. It landed on an inside page, just a few centimetres from his thumb, soaking slowly into the paper. He looked at it, frowned, and then tipped his head back, trying to see where it had come from.

It was exactly then that Madame Chanson came into the dining room, pausing at the door. As she had done in the parlour and in the hallway, she reached for the switch that controlled the speed of the ceiling fan and turned it to 'High'. The old fan took a moment or two to get up to speed, but when it did the little red drops started spinning off all four blades like water from a garden sprinkler, raining down on the room below. Dashes of red appeared on the muslin drapes at the windows, on plates and napkins and tablecloths, on the lime-wash walls, and on Madame Chanson's cheek and the lacy front of her white blouse. She touched the drop on her cheek, looked at her reddened fingertip, and then down at her blouse where a red stain was spreading through the cotton. Then she looked up, just as the salesman had, and saw the brown mark in the ceiling, saw the stream of scarlet trickling down the brass column of the fan, and saw the drops of red spinning off the tips of the fan's blades.

Shérine, the waitress, was the first to realise what the red drops were.

And the first to scream.

14

Jacquot was strapping Béa and Matti into their car seats for the drive into town when Mama Loubertin came waddling out onto the porch.

"Hey, dere's de phone waitin' h-on you," she called out, nodding back to the house.

"Can you take a message? We're late," he called back.

"It's the Widow Chanson. She done sound pretty urgent, you h-askin' I," replied Mama Loubertin, and lumbered back inside.

Leaving the doors open on the Citroën, and the girls strapped in their seats, Jacquot hurried up the steps and into the salon where Mama Loubertin was holding out the phone for him.

He took it, and looked back at the car to make sure the girls hadn't slipped their seatbelts, and made a run for the beach.

"It's Daniel," he said, "what's so import–?" He stopped talking, listened for a moment, frowned. "Hold on, hold on. Slowly, slowly now. Start from the beginning, s'il te plaît."

Less than a minute later, Jacquot had vaulted down the porch steps and was unstrapping Béa and Matti from their car seats.

"Change of plans, girls. No school today."

And as Mama Loubertin gathered them to her, Jacquot leapt into the driver's seat, fired up the engine and tore off down the driveway, slip-sliding through the mud from the night's rain, but finding a firmer surface when he reached the road.

As Jacquot drove, slowing the Citroën through palm-lined curves but pressing his foot hard down on the straights, he tried to make sense of what Madame Chanson had told him on the phone. "There been an h-accident, Daniel," she'd said, her voice shaking. "It's Madame Stuyvesant. I tink her gone dead."

The words had come at Jacquot like icy shrapnel. But only one made any real sense.

Dead.

It couldn't be, he thought, slowing for another bend in the road. Boni couldn't be dead. But that's what Madame Chanson had said, and she wouldn't have said something like that unless she was certain. After dismissing Madame Chanson's suggestion that it might have been an accident – what kind of accident could have killed Boni in the few hours they'd been apart? – Jacquot's immediate thought was suicide. She'd lost her husband – possibly dead, or at any rate holed up somewhere with a lover and a large amount of money – and when she'd come to Jacquot for help he'd misread the depth of her concern and desperation, and turned her down. Maybe after he'd left Chez Chanson the night before, after he'd declined her invitation to share her bed for old times' sake, she'd decided the game wasn't worth playing anymore.

That's how it sounded – a sudden, lonely desperation in the early hours that had made her take her own life. Even if she had booked passage on the morning ferry.

But try as he might, Jacquot couldn't believe it. Boni might indeed be dead, and his heart twisted at the thought, but he knew she wasn't the kind of woman who'd kill herself. Not when she'd seemed so intent on finding her husband.

So if it wasn't an accident, and it wasn't suicide...?

When Jacquot finally pulled through Madame Chanson's gateway and sped up the drive the first thing he saw was a blue Renault police car by the porch steps, and the white Peugeot with the red cross on the doors that belonged to Doctor Cornel. Pulling up beside them he was out of the car and up the steps before the old engine had stopped kicking.

Madame Chanson, her browned wrinkled skin a pale grey with shock, her hands clasped so as not to show the trembling, and her stained blouse exchanged for a white linen shift that came to her ankles, met him in the hallway. Behind her, in the parlour, her three other guests sat at a coffee table with Sergeant Balmet from the local St-Christophe *gendarmerie*. He had a notebook on his knee, a pen in his hand, and was asking questions. When Balmet saw Jacquot, he nodded and pointed upstairs. Which meant that his superior, *Capitaine* Faubert, was up in Boni's bedroom.

"I'm so sorry, Daniel," Madame Chanson was saying. "So sorry. H-it's such a..."

But Jacquot didn't stop. He took the warped stairs two at a time and when he reached the landing he headed for the open door at the end of the corridor. But Faubert wasn't there, just Doctor Cornel who'd recently taken over the island practice from old Doc Julien. The new man was sitting on the edge of a large four-poster bed draped with muslin, and had brought with him a weak but just discernible smell of antiseptic; the kind of clean, clinical smell one might encounter in a hospital corridor. He was packing up his medical bag. Beside him, Jacquot could see two bare feet, ankles delicately crossed.

"My condolences, Monsieur Jacquot," said Cornel, closing and latching the lid of his bag. "I understand from Madame Chanson that you knew the deceased; she was a friend?"

"A long time ago," said Jacquot, taking in the word 'deceased' yet even now somehow not believing it. But it was true. Boni Stuyvesant was definitely 'deceased'. He could see that the moment he stepped past the doctor and looked at the body. There was something punctured about it, something empty, drained. And it wasn't just the loss of blood. When you know someone alive, and then see them dead, it is often difficult to be absolutely certain it's the same person. Death crumples people, sometimes beyond recognition.

But Boni was an exception. Her body, punctured and drained though it was, was just as he remembered it. Long, and toned from exercise, but a little fuller in the hips than he remembered, and now a little less tanned. She was wearing white cotton pants but nothing else, her watch, her earrings, her bracelet laid neatly on the bedside table. It looked as though she had curled up on the bed to go to sleep. She was lying on her left-hand side, head resting on a couple of pillows, legs drawn up, her right hand tucked between her knees and her left arm straight out, over the edge of the bed. The arm was stiff, locked at the elbow, the lower half of the forearm red with blood, hardly any of which had soaked into the bedding, most of it coursing down from a deep gash on the inside of her arm, filling her cupped palm, to drip between her fingers to the floor. The blood had started to dry, but it still had a scarlet shine to it.

"She used a razor blade," said Cornel, getting up from the bed. The movement caused the mattress to rise and the body to stir as though Boni were about to wake. "As you can see it's a long deep cut following the line of the radial artery. Quite deliberate. She knew what she was doing. It wouldn't have taken long. The blade's on the bedside table."

Jacquot hadn't seen it at first, but now he did. A thin sliver of silver, a line of blood showing along its edge. If the blood had dried, Jacquot knew it would be difficult to lever the blade from the table's surface.

Kneeling beside the bed, keeping clear of the outstretched bloody arm, Jacquot reached out a hand and pushed back the fall of hair from Boni's face, tucked it behind her ear. The eyes were closed and the mouth slightly open, the skin pale enough to show freckles on her cheek and the bridge of her nose, freckles usually hidden by her tan. If not for the wound in her arm, and the spill of blood, she could have been sleeping. Curled up, snug, dreaming. A shaft of early morning sunlight slanting across her. Just the faintest trace of the perfume he remembered from the night before.

Ten years apart, just the last couple of days together, and now she was gone. This time he would never see her again, and Jacquot felt a great chilling sadness settle on him. He might not have loved her, not as he had loved Claudine, as he loved his daughters, but he and Boni had shared something special together, all those years before in Marseilles, and a wringing emptiness filled his heart. Such a terrible, terrible waste, he thought, and for a moment he felt a coil of anger fill the emptiness. On the drive into town, he hadn't been able to believe that Boni might kill herself, but now it was clear that she had. If only he'd accepted her invitation, he thought, if only he'd let his heart rule his head the night before, standing together out there in the rain – her body so close to his, her lips at his ear – then maybe, just maybe, she wouldn't be lying here now.

He moved his hand to her shoulder, the skin smooth as silk, not warm but not yet cold, then slid it down her right arm, over her raised hip, and onto her leg. As he had done so many times before with dead bodies, he pressed a finger gently against the muscle in her thigh. There was still some give beneath the soft golden down on her leg, but no white mark when the finger was withdrawn.

Cornel must have seen what he was doing.

"You were a cop once, weren't you? Someone said. Old habits, I suppose."

"That's right. Old habits."

"Well, I'd say she's been dead three, maybe four hours. Full *rigor* has not yet set in, but the neck and jaw have started to stiffen."

Jacquot got to his feet, and pulled out the chair from the dressing table. It was antique, delicate, and creaked as he sat on it. He took a couple of deep breaths and looked at the floor. There wasn't much blood. Whatever there had been had seeped away into the space between two floorboards.

"She was a beautiful woman," said Cornel, coming over to Jacquot and laying a hand on his shoulder. "Such a tragedy. I'm so sorry for your loss."

Jacquot nodded, and the doctor took a firmer grip on his bag and turned for the door.

"I'll be downstairs with Balmet if you need me," he said. "For now, I'll let you say your *adieu* in private."

15

Old habits, thought Jacquot, as he listened to Cornel make his way across the landing, the old floorboards creaking as he passed over them, pausing before he turned down the stairs. Creak, creak, creak. One step after another.

Old habits die hard.

Thirty years a cop in Marseilles, close on five years out of the game, and yet...

And yet.

Boni had been right. Once a cop, always a cop.

Because he knew, suddenly, sitting there at the desk in her room, that there was something wrong. Something not quite right. Something he couldn't quite put his finger on, but something definitely... wrong. Something at odds with what he was looking at. The bed. The body. It was instinct, just that, but an instinct that had served Jacquot well in the past. An instinct that he had learned to trust. And he trusted it now.

Something was wrong.

Something not quite right.

Getting up from the desk Jacquot went to the bathroom. The walls were timbered and painted a creamy white, and the floor tiled in red stone squares. An old cast iron tub on ball-and-claw feet, with a shower attachment and plastic shower curtain decorated with a repeating pattern of blue shells and scarlet starfish, stood along one wall, and in a metal rack on the side of the tub were a shampoo and conditioner. A mirrored vanity and single sink, a lavatory and bidet occupied the facing wall, and everything as it should be: a toothbrush in a glass, a tube of toothpaste, a hairbrush with a brand stamp from *Pharmacie* Fidèle in town, a pack of hair clips, lip balm, cleansing wipes, moisturiser, and a bottle of *Coco eau de toilette*. And everything new. No strands of hair in the brush, only a few of the wipes removed, the bottles of shampoo, conditioner, moisturiser almost full. It was clear that Boni had bought everything here on the island.

And there was the razor. A woman's razor. Pink and white plastic. Slim and elegantly curved. Four detachable heads, but only three in the dispenser. One missing. Jacquot found it in the waste-bin beneath the sink, along with a mess of crumpled packaging and used wipes. Or rather the razor head's shattered remains. Two thin blades, not three

like the others. The third on Boni's bedside table, covered in blood.
It would have taken some effort and determination, Jacquot decided,
to break open that moulded head and remove a blade. But, as far as
he could see, there was nothing to do it with. Once again, a niggling
doubt wormed its way into his head.

Back in the bedroom, Jacquot went to the wardrobe, an ancient
armoire with carved panelled doors that groaned and creaked as he
opened them. On one side was a rail, and on the other side three open
shelves and a single drawer. On the shelves were four neatly-folded
white t-shirts, two pairs of shorts, a cupped fold of white bras, an
opened pack of cotton pants similar to the pair she was wearing, and
hanging from the rail the coloured frock from Madame Corale that
Boni had worn when she came to the house that first night for supper.
He pulled open the drawer. Inside was the crumpled linen skirt she'd
been wearing at Gustave's the night before, a pair of shorts, a couple
of creased t-shirts, and a tangle of underwear. He closed the drawer,
and the armoire's doors, and stood back. On the floor beneath it, side
by side, were the cork-soled emerald green espadrilles she'd worn
with Madame Corale's frock, a pair of cream canvas espadrilles and
two pairs of flip-flops. He looked around. No case to carry anything.
As he had first thought, Boni had come to the island on impulse, with
no time to pack for her stay. Or maybe in a hurry, too.

He went back to the desk and opened its single drawer. A sewing
kit, a bible, some complimentary postcards of Chez Chanson, and a
few sheets of letter-headed stationery. He sat in the chair again – more
carefully this time – and leaned down to pull out Boni's shoulder bag
from under the desk. He put it on his lap and opened it up, looked
inside. It smelled of leather and perfume, a warm beckoning female
scent that he recognised. He brushed a hand through it, shifting the
contents. An opened pack of tissues, a Biro, a lipstick, mascara, some
chewing gum, a mess of old receipts, and a car key with a Hertz
fob on which was written a registration number and vehicle make.
There was also a wallet. Slim, crocodile skin, with a zip along the
edge. He dropped the bag to the floor, then slid the zip across and
opened the wallet. A driver's licence with a stern-looking photo of
Boni and a Nassau address behind a clear plastic window, a selection
of credit cards, a pocket filled with ten- and twenty-euro notes, and
a keycard for the Hôtel Ambassadeur in Fort-de-France, the room

number written on it in black marker pen. Using the Biro from the
bag and a postcard from the desk drawer, Jacquot copied down the
driving-licence address, reached for the Hertz car key, and removed
the hotel keycard from the wallet before zipping it up and dropping it
in the bag, pushing the bag back under the desk. Slipping the car key,
keycard and postcard in his pocket, Jacquot went to the bed and put
his hand on Boni's foot. Colder now. The doctor was right; she hadn't
been dead for long.

And then he frowned, shook his head.

Once again, that same nagging uncertainty. The feeling that
something wasn't right. Something at odds. But something shifting,
something he couldn't quite settle on. He looked at the body. The
drawn-up legs, the hand between the knees, the outstretched arm with
its bloody trails, the hair spread across the pillows.

Something... something... something...

When it finally came to him, it came slowly at first, a half-formed
thing, just a faded memory. Something from the past. From their
time together in Marseilles. In their bedroom under the eaves. And
the more he thought about it, the clearer the memory became, and he
knew he was right.

This was no suicide. Boni had not killed herself. No possibility.
Not a chance. Someone else had done that. And had staged the body to
make it look like a suicide. But whoever had killed Boni didn't know
her like he did. It made his blood beat a little faster. With a rising
anger, and the sudden satisfaction of knowing that he was right.

The razor.

The pillows.

The heart.

Down in the driveway Jacquot heard a car pull to a halt. He went
to the window and parted the drapes, tipped the blinds. An ambulance
from the island's hospital. A converted Renault Scénic. The driver and
his passenger, both in hospital whites, got out and went to the back of
the vehicle. One of them pulled out a gurney, the other reached in for
a body bag. In this heavy sultry heat, Jacquot knew that they would
want to seal the body and move it to the morgue as quickly as they
could.

Going back to the bed, he leaned down and kissed Boni's cool
shoulder, smoothed his hand over her hair.

"Don't worry," he whispered. "I will find who did this to you, and I will make them pay."

Then he stood up, took one long, final look at the body, his old friend and lover, and left the room.

16

Jacquot had reached the landing and was turning to go downstairs when the ambulance crew started up, carrying the gurney like a stretcher with the black body bag bundled up on it. He stood back to let them pass, pointing them to Boni's room. He watched them manoeuvre the stretcher through the door, and only when it closed behind them did he start down the stairs.

The house was unusually quiet. Whenever he called by, there was always noise and bustle, always someone about. Guests coming and going, or Shérine clearing tables with a clatter, or Nathalie, the upstairs maid, humming calypso as she went from room to room with her basket of soaps and linen, or Amélia, the cleaner, with her hoover, pan and brush, all three of them chattering away with Honorine, whenever Madame Chanson retired to her office behind the captain's table she used as a front desk. Now there was silence, just the singing whisper of insects, and the creak of the stairs beneath his feet.

When Jacquot reached the hallway he looked around. In the parlour, Sergeant Balmet had clearly finished with his questions and he and the guests had gone their separate ways. But the door to the dining room was closed, and behind it he could make out voices. He crossed the hall, opened the door, and looked in. They were all there: Sergeant Balmet and Madame Chanson watching Amélia and Nathalie holding a ladder for Shérine, who had climbed up to remove a fall of muslin curtain. As she reached for the clips that held it in place, wobbling dangerously as she did so, Jacquot could see long red lines staining the cloth, the same red as the dots and splashes on a pile of tablecloths taken from the tables and heaped on the floor. Looking up at Shérine he saw, too, the stain in the ceiling, directly beneath Boni's bed, and realised what the dots and splashes were. Her blood. Seeping between the floorboards, running along a beam maybe, soaking into the plasterwork beneath, and ending up on the paddles of the fan, now switched off but still dripping, a plastic bowl strategically placed on the floor below it.

Balmet was the first to spot Jacquot and, saying something to Madame Chanson, he came to the door, asked if he could have a few words, if Jacquot was up to it?

They went to the parlour, Balmet directing him to the coffee table where he'd been speaking to Madame Chanson's guests when Jacquot arrived. Through the room's French windows, Jacquot saw them now, the old couple, with a pot of coffee at the end of the porch, and down in the driveway Madame Chanson's other guest stowing an overnight case in the boot of a taxi. From beyond the trees, down the slope in St-Christophe, came the mournful hoot of the morning ferry.

"I'm so sorry 'bout your friend, Monsieur Jacquot. Just the mos' terrible ting."

Jacquot nodded, managed a swift smile.

"Tell me," began Balmet, sitting forward on his chair, assuming a business-like air. "I h-unnerstand from Madame Chanson dat you and your friend had dinner together last night?"

"That's right. Gustave's." It seemed a century ago, rather than just a few hours.

"And you done come back 'ere together?"

"Correct. About midnight. Just before the storm."

"And 'ow was her, Madame Stuyvesant?" asked Balmet, taking his notebook and pen from his shirt pocket. "Did her seem depressed? H-out of sorts, you know?"

Jacquot shook his head. "Not at all. It had been a nice evening."

Balmet nodded, took this in, then scribbled something in his notebook. He was young, late twenties, his hair like black sandpaper cut tight to his scalp and shaved high around the ears. He was a strong lad, with a wide spread of shoulders, bull chest, and bulging biceps that stretched the short sleeves of his blue uniform shirt. The voice matched the build, deep and sonorous, with a pleasing island lilt. His mother, Justine, worked at Madame Corale in town, and his father was a boat builder. In his short time on Île des Frères, Jacquot had come to know the family well, and had grown to like the young policeman.

"Do you normally question people so closely about suicide victims?" Jacquot now asked.

Balmet closed his notebook, pressing it shut like a prayer book between his hands. He looked uncomfortable. "Of course, we h-always like to 'ave some background."

Jacquot nodded. "She'd booked passage on this morning's ferry. Did you know that?"

Balmet flipped open his notebook, checked it, nodded. "Madame Chanson done mentioned it," he replied.

A silence settled between them.

"So where's the boss?" asked Jacquot. *Capitaine* Faubert had still to show up. A suicide at Madame Chanson's should have had him there in minutes, striding around the house, playing the big cheese. Jacquot was surprised he'd failed to put in an appearance, leaving the action to his subordinate.

"Comin' in by ferry," said Balmet, looking mournful. "He been over on the mainland dere the last coupla day. Out at the Lamentin 'ippodrome for the trottin' races. Loves the trotters, does the *Capitaine*."

"Not so good at picking the winners is what I heard."

"Good days and bad days, I guessin'. The way h-it go." Balmet couldn't disguise a smile.

"Does he know what's happened here?"

"I done call him, like I shoulda, let him know and h-all."

"So he'll be here soon."

Balmet shot Jacquot a resigned look. Could it be any different? A stage for his boss to strut on? The young policeman had clearly enjoyed taking charge of the case without his superior's interference, but he knew that his time was running out.

"Tell me about the guests," Jacquot asked. "The couple over there, the man in the taxi. Did they see or hear anything?"

"Nuttin', Monsieur Jacquot."

"Didn't they hear Madame Stuyvesant return, go to her room? All those creaking floorboards and squeaking doors?"

"The h-Oliels done gone bed early. Monsieur Tarrant, too, done same soon h-after. And dere was thunder, right? And rain on de roof, too."

"Do we know who they are?"

Balmet felt comfortable enough to answer without referring to his notebook, and slipped it back in his breast pocket, keeping hold of the pen, tapping it against his leg as he spoke. "Monsieur and Madame h-Oliel is regular 'ere. From Béziers. Dey comes every year and stays a month. Then dey home."

"And Tarrant?"

"A salesman, medical supplies. From Fort-de-France, he done said."

"Has he been to the island before?"

"He told me it his first visit. Callin' in at 'ospital and h-all."

"So what do you think?" asked Jacquot. "How do you read it?"

"Read it?"

"A woman has an evening out with an old friend, after booking a seat on the morning ferry," Jacquot continued, "and then kills herself. Strange, don't you think? I mean, suicide?"

Balmet was silent for a moment. With Faubert as his boss, he was clearly not used to being asked for his opinion. "Who can say what go on in someone's mind, Monsieur Jacquot? H-at night, in de early hours, and you'se on you own, strange tings 'appen, and strange thoughts clamber in, you know?"

"And you're happy with that, are you?"

Balmet shrugged, spread his hands, but the lips tightened and frown lines deepened across his forehead.

Jacquot saw the look, noted the young man's hesitancy, his uncertainty. It was a look Jacquot recognised. The same whisper of doubt he'd experienced just a few minutes earlier in Boni's bedroom. Something not quite right. But what was on Balmet's mind? What was puzzling him?

Jacquot leaned forward. "Faubert's not here. Go ahead. What do you really think? There's another reason you spoke to the guests, isn't there?"

Balmet couldn't help himself. His shoulders sagged and he let out a deep sigh, as though he'd been holding his breath the whole time. He looked around to make sure his boss hadn't crept up on them, then lowered his voice, just in case.

"Well, see, h-it's de razor, Monsieur Jacquot. Dat razor her done used. H-it just don' make no sense."

"How do you mean?"

"Well, see, dem blades is sealed tight in plastic 'eads. They'se difficult to take out. You'se need somethin' 'eavy, like an 'ammer, to break the 'ead open to get at dem blades, right? But dere was no 'ammer. Nuttin' dere in the room her coulda used. So how her do it then? How her get that blade outta dere? That's what I'm thinkin'."

"So you're saying someone killed her?"

Balmet jerked back, as though he hadn't dared take it that far, and was stunned by Jacquot's suggestion, even though there was really no other possibility.

"I don' know… I'se not sure. See, it just… It just, you know, I don't like dem questions when you can't find no answers on."

Jacquot gave a grim little smile. He knew exactly how Balmet felt.

"But if someone did kill her," Jacquot said, "it doesn't look like she put up much of a fight. There are no bruises on her, no signs of a struggle."

"No lump on de 'ead neither," said Balmet. "I checked. Nuttin' more than a broke fingernail was h-all I done see." And then, tipping his head to one side, "Was de lady a left-'ander, or a right-'ander?"

Jacquot had to think for a moment. "Left-handed. Why?"

"The 'and that shoulda made the cut?"

"I suppose…" said Jacquot, suddenly understanding what Balmet was saying, and realising what he'd failed to spot.

"So you gone look at de 'and between her knees? Them right 'and?"

Jacquot conceded that he had not.

"Well, dere weren't no blood h-on it. Nuttin'. Not a drop. I done look. But when you cuts a vein with a blade, like her done, even with a small strip a one, there be blood on dem fingers that 'olds de blade, for certain sure. Couldna not be no other way. And likely all 'cross the bed, too. So why her done gone make the cut with de right 'and an' not her left, and then not end up with no blood on it?" Balmet pursed his lips again, and started to shake his head. "De 'ole ting just ain't makin' no sense with me, Monsieur Jacquot."

Jacquot looked hard at the young man. He was smart, no question. Jacquot had the advantage of having known Boni, yet this young policeman was using his head. Putting two and two together and coming up with the wrong number. Or possibly the right number. But not altogether sure what to do with it, how to proceed, not sure if he was right or wrong. He was only a sergeant after all, and not used to making up his own mind, not with a boss like Faubert. Jacquot decided to give him a helping hand.

"Did you know that she didn't shave, Sergeant? She waxed. Legs, armpits, everything. Boni Stuyvesant was most particular when it came to her appearance. She waxed, she never shaved." He paused, seeing again the soft golden down on her bare legs. "There's something else, too."

Balmet leaned forward, all ears.

"She hated two pillows. Only ever used one. And do you know why?"

Balmet shook his head. Frowned. How could he possibly know?

"When Boni was seventeen or eighteen, she was in a road accident; her boyfriend's car back-ended by a drunk driver. She fractured a vertebra, and even after wearing a brace for months her neck was never quite the same again. Which meant she only ever used one pillow when she slept, because if she didn't she'd wake up with a migraine. Which would put her in a very bad mood. Yet here she is, upstairs, with two plump pillows supporting her head."

Balmet drew in a breath, his eyes widening.

"And that's not all. Now it might take some explaining to the authorities..." Jacquot continued, spreading his hands, "I mean, it's hardly the most convincing of evidence, but Boni never, ever, went to sleep on her left-hand side. On her heart side, she used to call it. She always preferred to sleep on her right-hand side. Without exception. 'My heart needs room,' she once told me."

Jacquot paused, smiled fondly at the distant memory, the pair of them in bed, spooning together when they went to sleep, usually with her cuddling into his back, her hand sliding around his waist to rest, tantalisingly, across his belly or the top of his thigh, the warm whisper of her breath on his back. Always like that. He looked at Balmet, and pointed to the ceiling. "Yet here she is, with her head on two pillows, lying on her left-hand side. If Boni was going to commit suicide, I'm certain she'd have arranged herself on the bed in her more natural and familiar position, just as she would have done if she were going to sleep."

"So you sayin' to me, certain sure, dat someone done kill her?" asked Balmet, quietly. "And set it up to look a suicide?"

"That's what I think," said Jacquot. "So you were right to be suspicious. Someone murdered Boni Stuyvesant."

"Murder? Did I hear someone say murder?" came a disbelieving voice from the parlour door.

17

Capitaine Jules Faubert may have arrived on the morning ferry after a few days partying at the Lamentin racetrack, but he had still found time to get himself in uniform. Which wasn't too much of a surprise. Jacquot could not recall a time when he'd seen Île des Frères' Chief of Police in anything other than his uniform. And always immaculate. His belt and bandolier as highly polished as his bald head. His shirt and shorts with knife-edge creases. Insignia and decorations gleaming, the short Malacca cane he carried as stiff and shiny as his black lace-ups.

Balmet leaped to his feet, saluted, and stayed standing.

Jacquot remained seated.

Faubert came into the parlour. "Ah, if it isn't Monsieur Jacquot. Helpin' us with our enquiries, I see. So good of you to take an interest. Your days in the Marseilles *Judiciaire* provin' hard to shake off, *n'est-ce pas?*" His voice had a gentle island lilt, but there was no mistaking its edge. He smiled, sympathetically, as though Jacquot were suffering from some unfortunate ailment which he really should try to keep to himself. "But I can assure you that everything is under control. I have just spoken to Doctor Cornel and he is in no doubt that the victim – a friend of yours, I believe? My condolences – took her own life." He turned from Jacquot to Balmet, tapping his sergeant in the chest with the point of his cane. "Suicide, Sergeant. Not murder. Unfortunate, of course, but there we are."

"Dere's jus' one or two tings, *Capitaine*, don't quite…"

Faubert held up a finger. "*Tsk, tsk, tsk.* This is Île des Frères, Sergeant. For all your wantin' it to be otherwise, this is not the mainland, and nor is it Miami. So please try to bear that in mind. The last time anyone was murdered here, the Emperor Napoleon was on the throne. Two hundred years, near enough. And not a single murder since. I think those facts speak for themselves, don't you?"

"Your sergeant is right, Faubert," said Jacquot. "There are things that don't quite fit. Madame Stuyvesant did not kill herself."

This was not what Faubert would want to hear, Jacquot knew. And not just because it was coming from him. The season was about to start, and rumours of murder would certainly put visitors off. Most were day-trippers, but there were always a few, like the Oliels, who booked into Chez Chanson or one of the island's other small *pensions* and stayed a week or more. And murder would likely mean a more senior officer than Faubert coming over from Martinique to run the investigation. Faubert wouldn't like that either. Having to share the limelight, or worse, play a supporting role. The local *Gendarmerie* and *Police National* were never easy bedfellows.

"In your opinion, *cher monsieur*. In your opinion. But that is not what Doctor Cornel tells me." Faubert walked to the French windows, tipped the cane to his forehead in a friendly salute at the Oliels, then turned back to Jacquot and Balmet. "A razor, a slit wrist. No sign of a struggle, I'm told. Not so much as a cushion out of place. But perhaps, given all your experience with the *Judiciaire*, you'd care to enlighten me? These 'things' that don't quite fit."

"I knew the victim."

Faubert nodded. "Which, as I said, the good doctor mentioned. And again my condolences." He said it in such a way that he clearly believed the shock of Boni's death had somehow unhinged Jacquot, had somehow reduced his powers of reasoning to a minimum.

Jacquot could see Balmet was just longing to say something, to come to his defence. So he spoke to spare the sergeant.

"For one thing, Madame Stuyvesant didn't shave. She wouldn't have a had a razor in her room."

Faubert frowned, gave this some thought. And then his face brightened. "Well, I'm not aware of many waxing facilities in St-Christophe."

Jacquot could see that Faubert was enjoying himself. He had it sorted. He wouldn't be persuaded. Certainly not by a retired Chief Inspector from the Marseilles *Judiciaire*. So Jacquot held back from mentioning how Boni liked to sleep on her heart-side, and only ever used one pillow. Like the shaving and the waxing, Faubert would make a meal of it. And love every moment of it. Instead Jacquot shrugged and got to his feet. He knew he'd need a lot more than personal observations   and his hard-earned instincts – to make Faubert take him seriously.

"So what will happen to the body?" he asked. And the next moment, is if on cue, the landing floorboards creaked and then the stairs, and the three of them turned to the parlour door as the medics stepped down into the hallway with the stretcher between them, the body bag strapped to it just a crumpled length of black plastic with no indication where head or feet might be.

"Madame Stuyvesant will stay here on the island until we've located and contacted the next-of-kin," said Faubert. "Which is what you, Sergeant, can do. Something to keep you occupied. As soon as we have details we'll set things in motion. So no need to worry yourself on that score, Monsieur Jacquot. In the meantime, Sergeant, you can bag up Madame's possessions and take them to headquarters."

And with a swish of his cane he pointed Balmet to the door, gave Jacquot a sharp dismissive nod, and followed his sergeant from the room.

18

Jacquot went shopping. Despite the heat he left his car at Chez Chanson, walked down the drive and headed into town, following the route he had taken with Boni the evening before. The violet jacaranda blossom and scarlet hibiscus that had been stripped from the branches during the previous night's storm lay like a bruised brown carpet of closed buds across the drive. They perfectly reflected Jacquot's mood. Sombre, downcast, his heart still wringing from the loss of someone dear to him, and the anger it brought. The last time he had experienced death at such close quarters, the last time he'd seen a body, it had been Claudine's, in a hospital corridor in Marseilles. Silent, still, and growing cold, just like Boni's. Never to return, never to be in his life again. And it had shattered him. Boni's death wouldn't change his life as Claudine's had done, but he still felt it, that leaden sense of loss. A loss he would get over, just as he'd survived their split all those years ago. But it was still a death, a suspicious death, and a death he intended to follow up. Someone had killed his old friend and he knew he wouldn't rest until he had found out who, and how, and why.

By now the sun was high and the heat relentless, shimmering off the pavement and road and turning St-Christophe's promenade into a greasy black band strung with sagging telegraph wires and thick power cables, the sun glare so bright that it was impossible to see any blue sky, the air as thick and still as treacle. It was, thought Jacquot, like taking a breath in a sauna, the damp heat scorching his throat. But there were still people around, going about their daily routines, most of them flitting desperately from shade to shade like moths after sunrise. Out in the bay, across the sea wall on his left, the departing ferry shivered in the heat haze, hardly seeming to move, but melting away as he watched.

The first shop Jacquot visited was Madame Corale, and he shifted his shoulders as he pushed open the door and felt the chill from the air conditioner sweep through his t-shirt and over his skin.

Sergeant Balmet's mother, Justine, greeted him with a big, toothy smile. She was like her son, broad and strong and tall, with her hair tightly ribbed in beaded rows.

"Yo, Monsieur Daniel. How's dem girls o' yours doin'?"

"Doing just fine, Justine. Always begging me to bring them

shopping."

"Well, dey's girls, ain't dey? It's what girls do best," she said, and a deep motherly chuckle rumbled up out of her. "So you's gettin' something for dem? We got some fine stuff jus' in."

"I came in about a dress you had in the window a few days back. A floral print?"

"Too late, she done gone an' sold."

Jacquot nodded. "I know that. I just wanted to know about the woman who bought it."

"All I hear," she replied, giving him an amused look, "is you done know dat lady just fine enough without me tellin' youse any ting."

The island grapevine. The old girls, thought Jacquot. The gossip mill. It hadn't taken long for word to spread, though it was equally clear that for all its well-oiled efficiency the grapevine hadn't yet supplied Justine with the news of Boni's death. Jacquot decided not to pass it on. Instead, he leaned up against the glass counter and asked if the dress was all she'd bought.

"Best day's sale for weeks," Justine told him. "Shorts, t-shirts, sandals… All de best stuff, too. You h-asks me, pity is she just stayin' a few days." There was a sense of reprimand in the observation, as though it was widely hoped, and expected, that Jacquot might make Boni change her mind. No chance of that now.

"Do you mind me asking how she paid?"

"Debit card, honey. Just as gold as her tan."

"You have the details?" he asked, wondering why he hadn't thought to check himself when he'd had the chance, up in Boni's bedroom, with her wallet in his hand. It wouldn't have happened back in the day.

Justine gave him another skewed look, and chuckled. "You lookin' to put something on her account, now?"

"Just the details, Justine. Nothing more than that."

Going to the till, she stooped down behind the counter and pulled out a ledger. It might have been the twenty-first century and credit card transactions a familiar enough means of purchase, but at Madame Corale they still liked to write it all down.

"She offered that Yankee Rapid. American Express. But I done told 'er we don't go tek 'em. So she paid it h-all wid Visa." Madame Balmet ran her finger across the line. "Behrens Bank. Nassau. Up dere in dem Bay-'amas."

Behrens Bank was not a name Jacquot recognised. But why should he? He decided it was probably the bank of choice for high net-worth clients who liked some anonymity along with the personal service. No teller windows there. Just air-conditioned panelled rooms, plump leather furniture, and whispered consultations. Boni would have liked that.

"Did she come straight in from Nassau, do you know?"

"Told me she'd been stayin' in Fort-de-France. Decided to come over on the spur – probably when she done heard you was about. Didn't have the chance to go pack a few things, she said."

"What did you make of her?"

"Well, she some fine-looking woman, ain't she though?" said Justine, closing the ledger and sliding it back under the counter.

Exactly the words that Madame Chanson had used when she'd called him just two days past to say there was a Madame Stuyvesant looking for him.

"Bright as a button, and a lovely smile on her," she continued. "And manners, too. She brought up good, and no mistakin'. Looked just a dream in that dress. Couldna sold it to a better lady." Justine gave him yet another crooked look, eyebrows dancing. "An' you likin' it, too, I'm bettin'."

"You're right," said Jacquot. "She did look good in it."

Justine nodded. "She surely did. And went just grand with that mighty fine ring on her finger." It wasn't a question, but it sounded like one. Justine's eyes latched firmly on his. So what was the story with the ring, she wanted to know; they'd all want to know Boni's status? Married? Divorced? Widowed? Justine wanted to get there first.

But Jacquot let it pass. Instead, he asked if there had been anyone else in the shop when Madame Stuyvesant visited.

"Not a soul save her," she replied, knowing she'd been sidelined. "The place to herself. And she done tek the full h-advantage, I'm tellin' you."

"Anyone hanging round outside? Waiting for her?"

"None so I could see." The frown returned, an eyebrow raised. Another question hovering, but one that Jacquot answered with a nod, and thanks, and a *"bonne journée,* Justine," as he pushed away

from the counter and headed for the door, shivering a little as it closed
behind him and he stepped back out into the midday heat.

His next stop was *Pharmacie* Fidèle a hundred or more metres
along rue St-Christophe, just a short walk but one that brought the
sweat into his hair, prickling over his scalp and through his beard.
The *pharmacie* was run by Madame Maudin who was winding down
its shutters when Jacquot tapped on the door. On the other side of the
glass, the *pharmacienne* gave Jacquot a disapproving look. Hands on
hips, lips tight and full, eyebrows lowering. She dropped her chin and
glared. It was her lunch hour and she wasn't the kind of woman who
liked her business hours played with. But Jacquot knew she'd open
for him; he had two daughters, after all, and one of them might be in
need of something.

"You done know the hours, Jacquot. You coulda made it earlier,"
she said by way of greeting, unlocking the door and standing back for
him.

Jacquot apologised and stepped inside, another blast of air-
conditioning chilling his skin.

"I just wanted to ask about a friend of mine who came in here
yesterday, maybe the day before."

"The fine-lookin' lady? Sure, she were here. Coupla day back.
I was just closin' but kept open for her. Jus' like you now. Bought
herself a ton of stuff, she done."

"A brush? Shampoo? Perfume?"

"And the rest. Creams an' tings, you know?"

"And a razor? A lady's razor?"

Madame Maudin frowned. "Don't remember no razor," she said.

Jacquot looked around, found the shelf of razors, saw the one in
Boni's room, and pointed it out. "One like this?"

Madame shook her head. "Only sold a one of dem dis week," she
said. "Yesterday, it was. And a man, would you believe? Told him we
had the men's kinda razors – Gillette and the like – but he said he was
gettin' it for his wife."

"A man?"

"A visitor. Not an islander."

"Did he say where he was staying?"

"Nope. Just wanted the razor. Paid cash and left."

"What did he look like?"

"'Bout your height, and build. But younger, you don't mind me sayin'. Maybe in his forties, but coulda been thirties even. Hard to say. Had himself a thin little moustache."

Which made Jacquot go cold.

The only moustache he'd seen in the last few days had belonged to the salesman at Madame Chanson's guest house.

The man Jacquot had seen with the Oliels and Balmet in Madame Chanson's front parlour.

The man stowing his overnight bag in the taxi.

The man who'd left on the morning ferry.

Jacquot glanced at his watch. Another ten minutes he'd be stepping ashore on Martinique. And gone.

19

Madame Chanson was in her office when Jacquot returned to the guest house. The door behind the captain's table was ajar and he could hear her talking on the phone – a one-sided conversation, no other voice to be heard. Apart from her sing-song murmuring, the rest of the house was silent. The dining room door was closed, the staff had gone off for their lunch break, and he suspected that the elderly Oliels had retired to their room to sleep through the heat of the day. He couldn't make out what Madame Chanson was saying but he had a good idea what the subject might be. He wondered what Madame Balmet and Madame Maudin would think when they heard the news that Boni was dead. There'd be condolences, of course, but a telling-off for sure, the next time he saw them.

He tapped on the open door and poked his head round. Madame Chanson waved him in, bangles jangling, pointed to a chair and brought her call to a close. She settled the phone in its cradle, without Jacquot being able to tell whom she'd been talking to, then sat back in her chair and looked at him sadly.

"Why it h-all just a terrible ting," she said. "Such a fine-lookin' lady."

Jacquot nodded, spread his hands.

"And you h-askin' me, you looks like you could do wid a drink. You an' me both."

Without waiting for an answer, Madame Chanson opened a drawer and drew out a bottle of pastis. Two glasses followed, with a bowl of ice and a jug of water from a mini-bar fridge behind her desk. Two healthy measures were splashed into the glasses, followed by a cube of ice for each and a smaller amount of water. The clear yellowish liquor turned cloudy as milk, and in an instant the air was filled with the smell of anise.

Jacquot took his glass, raised it to the ceiling – to Boni – and took a sip.

Madame Chanson, shaking her head, did the same. Then, licking her lips, she put down her glass and said, "You knows her a long time, she tellin' me."

"Back in Marseilles. Ten years ago. We were..." Jacquot paused, and Madame Chanson leaned forward. "We were very good friends."

But the Widow was not to be as easily sidelined as Justine. "And more, I'm guessin'? Don't get to look like you does right now, when it's just a friend gone passin' on."

Jacquot sighed. "You're right. More than friends. She was... special."

"Well, she were surely dat, and no mistakin'. So I'm very sorry for your loss, Monsieur Daniel. I truly am."

"I know you are, I know," he replied. "And she said how much she liked it here, how kind you all were."

"Why, dat's the job we do, Monsieur Daniel. Dat's why we's here. To make our guests feel welcome, part of the family."

Jacquot nodded, took another sip of his pastis.

"But what I can't go fathom," Madame Chanson continued, "is why a lady like she should want to go an' do such a ting. Such a fine-lookin' creature, she were, so young. And sad, too, I'm thinkin'?"

"I understand there were problems at home," said Jacquot, not wanting to give too much away. This was not a woman to confide in.

Madame Chanson nodded. "I knows dere were someting wrong, right from the minute she done step in de house. But she gone brighten up someting strong when she sets eyes on you, that's for certain sure. But seem like she carryin' too much for even you to lighten the load."

"I just didn't realise, I suppose. Just how bad it was."

A silence settled between them, as Madame Chanson considered this.

Which was the moment Jacquot had been waiting for, a way to proceed, to find out what he wanted to know without arousing the Widow's suspicions.

"I hope that your other guests haven't been too upset by all of this?" he began. "It can't be easy for them."

"Just sorry is all. For her, for you."

"Sergeant Balmet tells me the Oliels come every year."

"Always a month, this time a year."

"And Monsieur Tarrant? He seemed very familiar. I'm sure I've met him somewhere."

"A salesman. Medical supplies. From over on de mainland."

And I'm the President of the Republic, thought Jacquot.

"He's stayed here before?" he asked.

Madame Chanson took a long sip of her drink, the ice sliding down the glass and coming to a rest against her top lip. She put down the glass and shook her head. "First time, but said how him loved the place, said him lookin' forward to comin' on back sometime soon."

Jacquot thought it unlikely, but didn't say so.

"French? An islander?" he asked instead.

"American, but managed wid de French. Got de words, but not the h-accent."

"And when did he get in?"

"Came in on yesterday's ferry. Said him 'ad a meeting up de 'ospital, sortin' out some orders and such, and den him'd be 'eading back to de mainland. He done take the ferry dis mornin'."

Jacquot nodded.

"Do you have an address for him, a business card, a phone number?"

He knew it was unlikely, but worth checking all the same. A murderer was hardly likely to leave contact details. He wasn't disappointed or surprised when Madame Chanson shook her head.

"Just signed in, paid cash him did, and dat was dat. A quiet sort of gentleman, but very polite."

And very deadly, too, thought Jacquot.

20

A killer. A paid assassin. That's what Tarrant was. Someone sent to kill Boni. That's the conclusion Jacquot had come to by the time he left Madame Chanson's guest house and drove up the hill towards the island's hospital. But by now that killer would be back in Fort-de-France. And he'd be gone. Lost on the island somewhere, or straight to the airport and the first flight out. And all Jacquot had to go on was a thin moustache and more than likely a false name. And a moustache, he knew, could easily be shaved off.

He needed more. Much more.

And the hospital, where Tarrant was supposed to have come for a sales meeting, was the place to start.

Ten minutes later, a few hairpins short of the ridge above St-Christophe, Jacquot indicated left and drove along a palm-shaded lane to the island's hospital, a collection of long single-storey blocks with white lime-wash walls, red slate roofs, and covered walkways set in a wide green spread of tree-lined terraced lawns. With its parking area laid with gravel and ringed with white-painted stones, the hospital looked as tidy and regimented as an army barracks.

After parking the Citroën Jacquot headed for the main entrance, and at the reception desk he asked for Doctor Cornel.

"Him on his rounds right now," said the nurse on duty. "Won't be free another thirty minutes."

"Do you mind if I wait?"

"Sure ting. Dey're seats over dere, or benches out in de garden. Take your pick, you can. But me, I'd settle for de garden."

Jacquot made to go, then turned. "Tell me," he said. "Just out of interest. How do you source supplies for the hospital?"

The nurse shrugged. "Mostly dey done come in from the mainland, on de ferry. Regular orders and specials, both."

"Do you have salesmen calling by? You know, people from the big pharma companies?"

"Maybe once a blue moon. One, maybe two time last year. But like I say we's supplied by Martinique, so any salesman's go waste him some time come callin' here."

"Anyone in the last few days?"

The nurse shook her head. "None that I knows of."

Jacquot thanked her and went back out into the sunshine, spotting a bench in the shade of a jacaranda tree, its blossoms stripped from the branches and littering the lawn. He swept the seat clear of the fallen blooms and settled down, watching a hummingbird flit around what was left of the flowers. Such a delicate, but hardy little bird, he thought, with its blurring wings, shiny plumage and curved probing beak. He'd seen their nests around the house in Trinité, nests no bigger than an egg cup, made of downy feathers and spider web. Extraordinary creatures. But where did they go to survive a storm like the one last night, he wondered? Just a single raindrop would be enough to send them spinning.

Reaching for his cigarettes, Jacquot tapped one from the pack and lit it up. Looking back at the scatter of buildings, he remembered the last time he had been here. With Matti, with a splinter in her foot that she'd tried to dig out herself, only to have the wound become infected. The first he'd heard about it was Mama Loubertin telling him he better get the girl fixed up before they had to take the foot off. There'd been no sun that day when they arrived, just a thick mist that turned the line of trees around the hospital into grey ghostly walls. Now the gardens were bright and cheerful, fresh from the storm, insects buzzing, birds calling, a cool breeze up here in the hills. And yet, for Jacquot, the place was heavy with sadness. Matti might have survived the splinter, but somewhere close by lay Boni's stiff chilled body.

Jacquot didn't have long to wait. He was thinking about lighting a second cigarette when he saw the nurse step out of the entrance, look around, spot him, and wave him over.

Doctor Cornel, dressed in an open white lab coat with a stethoscope looped round his neck, was standing at the reception desk, finishing up his notes. When he looked up and saw Jacquot he offered his condolences once again, and asked how he could help.

"I'd like you to authorise a tox report on Madame Stuyvesant."

Cornel frowned. "Toxicology?"

"I have reason to believe that she did not commit suicide."

Cornel's frown deepened. "But that cannot be. You saw the body yourself. A deliberate cut to the…"

"She did not kill herself," Jacquot repeated. "But I need a toxicology report to prove it."

"I'm afraid I cannot authorise such a…"

"Of course, I'll be happy to pay for any costs involved."

"It's not just the cost, Monsieur Jacquot, it's..."

"Call it a favour, doctor. I'll owe you."

And without waiting for an answer Jacquot slipped a fifty-euro note into Cornel's breast pocket, shook his hand, and strode out of the reception area.

That evening, back at Trinité, Jacquot told Matti and Béa that his friend, Boni, had died. He could have said nothing, but he knew that sooner or later they would hear about it. And best that they should hear it first from him.

"How did she die?" asked Matti.

"She just... passed away," said Jacquot. "Sometimes it happens like that."

"Is she with the angels?" asked Béa, with a thoughtful expression on her face.

"Oh, I should think so, don't you?" he replied.

"Then she'll be with Maman, won't she? That will be nice."

"It will, won't it?" said Jacquot. He looked across the table at Matti, scooping out the last of the ice cream from her bowl. There was a furrow in her brow, and he knew there was something she wanted to say. Would it be about angels, Jacquot wondered? Or the likelihood of Boni actually bumping into Claudine when there were clearly so many angels in heaven? Or would she want to know exactly what had happened? What this 'passing away' actually entailed? He prepared himself as best he could.

"Papa," said Matti, at last. "Can I have some more ice cream?"

It was only later, after putting the girls to bed, sitting out on the terrace where he and Boni had shared rum and memories just two nights earlier, that Jacquot thought about fingerprints. On the razor and blade dispenser, and on the broken plastic head and razor packaging in Boni's bathroom waste bin. And fingerprints, too, in Monsieur Tarrant's room. A match between the two would give him all he needed.

He gave a grim little chuckle. How could he have forgotten the basics of a crime-scene investigation so thoroughly? Island time, he supposed. For five years there been no call for it.

He'd been right when he told Boni that he was out of the loop.

Not just out of it, but well and truly out of it.

21

Jacquot slept fitfully that night, dozing off, waking with a start, then dozing again. And in those moments of sleep, he dreamed. Vivid, unsettling dreams that forced him awake. Boni doing this... Boni doing that... A look, a gesture, a certain dress, a smile... They should have been comforting dreams, but they weren't. Boni was dead. That was the one thing he knew in every dream, and in the moment he woke up. Dead and gone. All she would ever be now was a dream, or a distant memory. Finally, at a little after four, when it seemed he was awake more than he was asleep, he got out of bed, peeling the sheet from his sweating body.

In the kitchen he brewed a pot of coffee, poured a measure of Calvados into a shot glass and, when the coffee had perked, he drank the liquor as he always did. A sniff of distant Normandy orchards to begin, a single sip followed by a swallow of coffee, then the rest of the Calva back in one, and another gulp of coffee. By the time he reached the beach he could feel the liquor and coffee getting to work.

And as he walked along the shore in the grey dawn light, all he could think of was Boni. Despite the pain of their parting all those years ago there had been so many good times, leaving him with so many fond memories. And she was still so young, so much to live for. Sad, and sorrowful too, as Madame Chanson had observed, but also determined. Determined to find her husband, to discover what had happened to him. With or without Jacquot's help. Coming to look for him on this same beach, and bursting into tears the moment she recognised him; joining him for dinner that first evening; going for their island drive the following day; then dinner at Gustave's, and that torrential downpour outside Madame Chanson's when, if he had accepted her invitation, her murder might just have been avoided.

Not that it would have stopped her killer, Jacquot decided. Sooner or later Tarrant would have found an opportunity to complete his assignment. Here on des Frères, or on Martinique, or back home in Nassau. What Jacquot couldn't settle on was why Boni should have been a target? Judging by what she had told him, he was in no doubt that the order to kill her had come from this DiCorsa character. The man her husband had crossed. The kind of man who had someone else do his dirty work. But why take it out on Boni? Did this DiCorsa think she knew something? Was it intended to put pressure on Patric and the girl, wherever they were? Or was it simply an act of revenge? Something to set an example? You take my money, you pay the price. Ten million dollars' worth.

But why bother to make it look like suicide? To avoid an investigation, obviously. But how had Tarrant managed it? No sign of a struggle. No bruising. Just a broken fingernail. Which was why Jacquot had asked Cornel for a toxicology report. If she'd been drugged, which Jacquot suspected, it would hopefully show up in tests. And if it did, and if he could find Tarrant's fingerprints anywhere in Boni's room, then he'd have something far more persuasive than two pillows, waxing, and lying on her heart side to support his suspicions. And when he presented those findings to Faubert, the good *Capitaine* would have no option but to change his report and mount an investigation.

Jacquot took a pack of cigarettes from his t-shirt pocket, tapped one out and lit it. The first of the day. His favourite. He drew deep then tipped back his head and whistled the smoke at the few stars that still remained. Far out at sea, the sky had already begun to lighten. A thin scarlet line marking out the far horizon. In another twenty minutes the stars would have gone, the first leading edge of the sun would rise out of the sea, and another day on Île des Frères would begin.

As he walked along the shore, he wondered how it would end.

22

Sergeant Balmet, with his peaked *képi* in one hand and his fingerprint bag in the other, was waiting for Jacquot in Chez Chanson's hallway. And standing beside him was Madame Chanson.

"I did what you done h-asked," she said, leading them upstairs. She was slow, one step at a time, both feet planted before she took the next, a wizened claw cuffed with jangling bracelets gripping the banister. Jacquot and Balmet followed behind, pausing when she paused. "I told Amélie not to touch nuttin', not to clean nor polish. Which suited her just fine, I'm tellin' you. H-all she'd done was change de linen – sheets, pillowcases, towels. Dat's all. And h-anyway, dere was other tings to keep her busy yesterday."

Tarrant's room was at the top of the stairs, on the right, at the side of the house. Madame Chanson unlocked the door with an old tasselled key that Jacquot knew was unlikely to provide any viable prints, pushed it open, and stood aside for them to enter. The room was smaller than Boni's but with the same antique furnishings: an armoire, a big brass bed, a delicate-looking desk and chair and, beyond the open bathroom door, an identical ball-and-claw tub. Unlike Boni's room with its view of the sea, Tarrant's room came with a balcony looking out over the gardens, just enough room within its wrought-iron railings for a striped deck chair and table.

The two men looked around.

"Start with the bed," said Jacquot, taking a pair of latex gloves from Balmet and snapping them on. "Should get something there."

"Along wid everyone else who done slep' there," replied Balmet.

"Excuse me, *s'il vous plaît*, but de brass on dat bed's done polished every change-over," said Madame Chanson indignantly. "Cleanest brass on de island. H-any fingerprint dere, it'll be Monsieur Tarrant for certain. But why you wantin' him prints anyhows?"

"Just a formality," said Jacquot, turning to Balmet. He gave him a look, and Balmet nodded.

"Procedure, Madame. For the record," the sergeant said, and put his bag on the bed, opened it up. Two jars of fine dusting powder – one powder dark for light surfaces, the other light for dark surfaces – and a line of finely bristled brushes. In one of the two pockets in the lid was a roll of clear cellophane and in the second pocket a pack of white backing boards and sticking tape.

"So, Madame," said Jacquot, "if you could just let me have the keys, you can leave us to it. Shouldn't take very long. Have you got any guests booked in?"

"Just the Oliels, an' none more till de end o' de week," she replied, handing him the keys. "So you can takes just so long as you likes." And with that, she turned and headed for the stairs.

It took no more than an hour for Jacquot and Balmet to dust for prints in Tarrant's room – the double bed with its fenced headboard of shining brass rails, the old-fashioned brass light switch inside the door, the black Bakelite controls for the fan, door handles, window latches, the pair of bedside lamps, the drawer handles on the bedside tables, and the handle on the armoire. In the bathroom Balmet dusted the lavatory flush, the wood seat, the mirrored cabinet above the sink and the taps for sink, bath and shower. And not a single print to be found.

"Him musta worn gloves, or wiped de place clean," said Balmet.

Very professional, thought Jacquot. A man who meant business. A man who didn't like to leave traces. "It tells us something, don't you think?" he said.

"I don't never woulda believed it," said Balmet, packing away his brushes and jars. "He stay in de room and don't leave not a single print?"

"Okay, we'll go to Madame Stuyvesant's room. Try there."

If Monsieur Tarrant's room had been clear of prints, Boni's was covered with them. Almost every surface Balmet dusted provided a full or partial print. Light switches, handles, latches… One of the most frequent impressions was a left index finger, easily identified by a line through the centre of the pad, an old scar. As soon as Jacquot saw it, he recognised it, remembered the blood and the tight little scream that went with it, when Boni cut herself on the opened lid of a tin of tomatoes in their kitchen. The wound had been long and deep and had taken three stitches to close. She was off work for a week, fully paid, so she and Jacquot had gone skiing.

When they'd finished with the bedroom Jacquot and Balmet went into the bathroom and dusted all the places they'd dusted in Monsieur Tarrant's. Another harvest of prints, but no sign of a scarred left index finger on the curved handle of the razor or on the blade dispenser.

Tarrant had probably put the razor and dispenser in Boni's hand to lift her prints, but he'd used the right hand to do it and not the left. Significant certainly, but not quite a game changer.

It was the waste bin under the sink, however, that Jacquot was interested in. Reaching into it he drew out the discarded packaging for the razor. He had no doubt that the blade that had opened Boni's arm would show only her prints, albeit the wrong hand, but he hoped that the packaging might reveal something more. Tarrant may have worn gloves on the night he killed Boni, but it was unlikely he'd worn gloves when he bought the razor at Madame Maudin's Pharmacy. And if he'd forgotten to wipe the packaging clean, they might just strike it lucky.

And they did. Three clear prints on the plastic see-through cover, but not one of them with a scar across the tip.

On the way downstairs Jacquot had another thought. Stopping at the office to return the two keys to Madame Chanson he asked if guests always used the same table in the dining room. She told him they didn't, they were free to sit wherever they wanted, in the dining room or out on the terrace. When he asked about Tarrant, Madame Chanson told Jacquot that he'd only had the one meal, breakfast the day before, and that he'd sat at a table just inside the door.

Telling Balmet to follow him Jacquot went to the dining room, found the table and using his foot he drew out the straight-backed wooden chair. For the next ten minutes Balmet dusted the chair's uprights and back panel, the most likely places that Tarrant would have chosen to pull out the chair from the table and push it back in. And at the end of that time he had lifted seventeen more prints.

If any of those prints matched the prints on the razor packaging in Boni's bathroom, it would be a fair assumption that Tarrant had been in her room. Jacquot knew that this kind of evidence wouldn't convict, but it would certainly bolster his case that Boni had not taken her own life. And that was all he wanted. The truth. He might know she hadn't killed herself, but if there was going to be any investigation then he had to provide evidence to persuade the authorities.

There was just one last job to be done before Jacquot and Balmet called it a day. For the purposes of print matching, Madame Chanson and her staff were fingerprinted in the parlour – Shérine, the waitress, Nathalie, the upstairs maid, Amélia, the cleaner, and the cook,

Honorine. When it was Nathalie's turn, Jacquot noticed that Balmet's hand shook when he reached for her fingers, pressing the tips into his black inkpad and pressing them onto the board. He was certain, too, that if a blush could have shown on Nathalie's cheeks it certainly would have.

23

The following morning, after dropping the girls off at school, Jacquot parked his car and took the ferry to the mainland. Twenty minutes later he arrived at Le François, the ferry's first stop, where Boni had hitched a ride across to the island just a few days earlier.

Le François was a small settlement, its green hillsides dotted with red-roofed houses, its tiny marina crowded with fishing boats and pleasure craft, and its jetty strung with drying nets and piled with lobster pots. Balancing on one of these pots, a lone pelican watched Jacquot step off the ferry's ramp and make his way along the jetty. As he passed, the pelican shook its wings, clacked its bill and dropped it disapprovingly to its chest. Where the jetty joined the road there was a fishing and chandlery supplies store with a small car park behind it, small enough for Jacquot to spot the Nissan Pathfinder that Boni had left there.

The car was brand new, just a few hundred kilometres on the clock, its showroom shine dulled with a thin layer of dust, its interior hot and airless after four days sitting in the sun, a confusing mix of warm leather and baked plastic. Sliding into the driver's seat Jacquot buzzed down all the windows to let in some air, then checked the back of the sun visor – nothing – and the door pocket – nothing – and leant across to open the glove compartment. Again, nothing, save a rental agreement and map. Firing up the three-litre engine, he backed the Nissan out of its bay, crossed the Morne Courbaril highway and took the N6 cross-country to Fort-de-France. Just a little over twenty kilometres, it was the shortest distance on Martinique between a wild and rolling Atlantic and the calmer Caribbean. And as he followed the road out of Le François into a landscape of swaying green sugar cane, he realised with a twist of sadness that the last person who had sat in this seat, the last person whose hands had held this wheel, was Boni.

As he drove Jacquot wondered whether Faubert had contacted the *gendarmerie* in Fort-de-France to have them check out where Boni might have stayed. Somehow he doubted it. In all likelihood the *Capitaine* was directing his energies in having Balmet trace her next-of-kin, presumably with the address on Boni's driving licence. And since Boni's next-of-kin was missing he didn't imagine that Faubert would get any real results any time soon.

When Jacquot reached the capital after an uneventful twenty-minute drive, he made straight for Boni's hotel, an old colonial mansion of coral stone blocks and wrought-iron filigree balconies overlooking Parc Savane in downtown Fort-de-France. It was, he realised, nearly a year since he'd last been in the city, and after the peace and tranquility of des Frères he felt almost overwhelmed by the sheer hurry and scurry of the place. The toot and blare of car horns, the crowded colourful pavements, the swirling *rond-points*, and the buzz of commerce. Leaving the Ambassadeur's doorman to deal with the Nissan, Jacquot passed through glass doors into the air-conditioned cool of the lobby, noting the bustle of the place, the comings and goings, businessmen and tourists, bags piled on trollies and pushed by bellhops in sky-blue tunics. It felt modern, but it was old, too. Caged lifts, large china urns filled with drooping palms, and a central chandelier whose crystal drops tinkled in the breeze from the entrance.

He didn't bother with Reception, just took the lift to the third floor and followed the numbers to Boni's room. In the unlikely event that the hotel had been informed of her 'suicide', and had let the room out to another guest, he'd soon find out when the keycard failed to work. But it did work. A red light near the handle turned green, the door lock clicked, and Jacquot pushed it open.

Like Chez Chanson, Boni's room was at the front of the building, with a view over the park to the city's port. It was clear at once that Housekeeping had been at work. The room was neat and tidy, the bed made, the windows slightly ajar to let in a breeze, and nothing out of place. On a stool by the wardrobe was a silver Samsonite case. He tipped the catches and swung it open. Empty. But the built-in wardrobe beside it – which he checked next, sliding open a door – was filled. Shelves loaded with neatly folded blouses, slacks, t-shirts, and shorts, dresses and frocks on wood hangers, with a mix of formal and holiday footwear on the lowest shelf. As he brushed his hand through the hanging clothes, Jacquot could smell her still.

He could smell her in the bathroom, too, the vanity ranged with her toiletries – expensive brand-name cosmetics, toothpaste, toothbrush… But no razor.

Back in the bedroom, Jacquot slid open the desk drawer as he had done in her room at Chez Chanson. Inside was a folder of hotel services and stationery, and an island telephone directory with a marker about half-way through. He opened it up at the marker, a boarding pass for the flight from Nassau to Martinique via Miami. The first column on the left-hand page began with the name Isola, P.J. and in the column beside it, half-way down, was the name Jacquot. Eleven Jacquots in all. Four of them with his initial. There was a cross beside each of them. He closed the book, looked at the phone and smiled. He could see her sitting here, going through the numbers. Somewhere to start.

Getting up from the desk, Jacquot went to the bed. Right-hand side first – the heart side. Opened the drawer on the bedside table. Empty. He went round to the other side and slid open the drawer. A French passport, a Ulysses Travel Guide to Martinique, an unopened foil pack of Ibuprofen, a pen with Edgewater Club engraved on it, and an American Airlines travel wallet with an open return ticket to Miami and Nassau. Premier Class. The clothes, the open return... She'd clearly planned on a long trip, giving herself time to find him. And he realised then that he'd never asked her how she'd found him, how she'd managed to track him down to Martinique. Sloppy, he thought, even for an ex-cop.

Slipping the ticket she would never use back into the folder, Jacquot closed the drawer, sat on the bed, and looked around. Once again, he wondered what he was doing there, why he had made the journey from his home on Trinité to Boni's hotel in Fort-de-France? Something to do, he guessed. Something to fill the time until the results came through on the tox sample and fingerprints, something to ease the nagging curiosity of a cop. But, most important, he admitted to himself, it was a way to keep up a closeness with Boni, to be a part of her world, if only for a brief time, after she had been taken away from him. Murdered.

He'd known all along that it was unlikely he would find anything of interest in her room, and he was right. There was nothing here that caught his eye, nothing that piqued his instinct as it had done in her bedroom at Chez Chanson. Nothing out of the ordinary. Just a visitor's hotel room. He lay back on the bed, head on the pillow where she would have rested her head, and looked at the ceiling, the ceiling she would have looked at, and from beyond the windows he heard the hum of traffic, and life on the street, just as she would have done. There was a certain comfort in it, that closeness, but a real sadness, too.

And he wondered then, lying there on her bed, why Monsieur Tarrant hadn't faked her suicide here at the Ambassadeur, rather than waiting to do it at Chez Chanson? What had made him delay? What was the difference between here, and Île des Frères? It would certainly have been easier at the Ambassadeur, and in a city like Fort-de-France far more anonymous, far more likely to be put down as a suicide. There had to be a good reason for the man holding back. Had Tarrant been told by this DiCorsa character to find out what Boni was doing in Martinique, where she was going, who she was meeting? It seemed a reasonable assumption. Which meant, of course, that Tarrant would know about Jacquot, would likely have seen the two of them together. But it was clear, too, that Jacquot was of no interest to them. With Boni dead, there was nothing more for them to do. The trail had gone cold.

With a sigh Jacquot got up from the bed and, with a final look around her room, he opened the door, stepped into the corridor and let it close softly behind him.

That final click. Green light near the door handle turning red.

Boni gone.

Just memories now.

24

Back in the lobby Jacquot stepped out of the caged lift and was walking towards the entrance when a thought struck him. He turned to the Reception desk, manned by two young women in matching blue blouses and blue plaid waistcoats. One of them was leaning over a map of the island with a couple of elderly guests explaining the route to the old capital, St-Pierre. Her companion was on the phone.

As Jacquot approached, the girl on the phone smiled at him, held up a finger and a moment later, with a final, *"Oui, oui. Ça marche. Je vous en prie"*, she put down the phone and gave him her full attention. She was young and pretty, the skin smooth and lightly tanned, her lips painted a soft scarlet, eyelids subtly lined in brown. Her ponytailed black hair shone and her eyes were a sparkling gold. A name tag on her waistcoat identified her as Cilla.

"Good morning, *m'sieur*. How can I help?"

"Tell me," he said. "Has Monsieur Tarrant checked out yet?" It seemed a reasonable assumption that if Tarrant had been following Boni, he might well have checked into the same hotel, just as he had done on Île des Frères. It was worth a punt.

Cilla turned to a computer concealed beneath the desk, worked the keyboard, and Jacquot watched her warm almond eyes follow the scrolling screen.

"Tarrant? Tarrant?" She looked back at him, started to shake her head. There was clearly no Tarrant on her records.

"A young man, younger than me," said Jacquot, repeating Madame Maudin's description at the *Pharmacie* on des Frères. "A little slimmer, maybe," he chuckled. "With a moustache?"

Cilla frowned, then her face broke into a smile. "Ah, *oui, bien sûr*. You mean Monsieur Torrance?"

"Of course, Torrance, that's right. I'm so sorry."

Her expression softened, saddened. "And I, too, *m'sieur*. I'm afraid you have missed him. He checked out this morning."

Jacquot gave a start. "This morning?"

So the man hadn't left on the first plane out. He'd stayed on. The nerve. That is, if Torrance was in fact Tarrant. But it seemed too close to allow for any other possibility. They had to be the same.

"He settled his bill after breakfast," Cilla continued. "An early flight, he said."

"Do you have a forwarding address?"

The receptionist checked the computer again. "Galveston. In Texas. That's all. Just a *poste restante.*"

"And how did he settle his bill?"

At this Cilla's helpful friendly expression faded, and she quietened, narrowed her eyes. She looked suspiciously at Jacquot.

Jacquot understood. Without a thought he said, "Chief Inspector Jacquot," and reached for his wallet, frowned, patted his pockets. "With the *Judiciaire.*" It was the first time in years that Jacquot had used these words. "I must have left my wallet in the car," he continued, and gave an apologetic shrug, relieved he'd dressed appropriately. His usual island attire would have got him nowhere, but the chinos, polo shirt and linen jacket he'd put on that morning looked respectable enough to put her at ease.

The tactic worked. Cilla went back to the computer, tapped away at the keyboard and checked the screen.

"Cash, Chief Inspector. Is he in trouble?" she asked.

"Just helping us with our enquiries," said Jacquot. "I had really hoped to speak to him again... Tell me, when did he check in?"

A glance at the screen. "Tuesday the 17th. So, a week ago, or thereabouts."

"And he was here the whole time?" asked Jacquot. If he'd been away three nights earlier, it would surely have to be the same man.

"I cannot say, *m'sieur*. Maybe Housekeeping would know if the room has been used the whole time. Would you like me to check?"

"That would be kind of you," he replied.

With a certain kind of look that Jacquot recognised, Cilla reached for the phone and dialled a single number. When she got through she asked if Room 46 had been occupied for the duration of the guest's stay. One floor above Boni, thought Jacquot.

Cilla put the phone against her breast. "Three nights ago, it seems the room was not used."

Jacquot nodded. It made sense. And then another thought struck him, and he said, "Will Housekeeping have turned his room round yet, or...?"

She glanced at her watch. "There were only a couple of guests leaving us today, so I would say for sure his room has been cleaned by now. But would you like me to check?"

"If it's not too much trouble?"

Cilla asked what he had asked, listened, nodded, and then put down the phone. "It was the first room they worked on," she said, with an apologetic, sympathetic smile.

"Never mind," said Jacquot. "It's not a problem..."

And then he frowned. Something he hadn't thought of. "Tell me, do you still have the keycard? For his room?"

"Of course," she replied. "But you'll need a new card if you want to see it. The old ones are wiped and recoded after a guest checks out, so they can be used again..."

"It's the old one I want. Do you happen to have it?"

Cilla bent down and reached under the counter, brought out a wooden box with an opening on the top. It looked like a child's moneybox.

"We put all the old cards in here," she said, levering off the lid. She spilled three keycards onto the counter. "I'm afraid I don't know which one belongs to Monsieur Torrance..."

"Would you mind if I take them all?" asked Jacquot. If Tarrant had written his room number on the card like Boni, he wouldn't have had to ask.

"You want them all?"

"If it's not a problem? And an envelope, too?"

An envelope was provided and Jacquot slid the keycards into it. Pocketing the envelope, he thanked her for her help and wished her a "*Bonne journée*".

"And you, too, Chief Inspector. And anything more you need, don't hesitate to call me."

The look that accompanied these words was as direct as the message was clear, and out on the hotel steps, waiting for Boni's Nissan to be brought round, Jacquot wondered if he'd read her wrong. Without thinking he turned and looked back through the glass doors. She was still watching him. She gave him a nod and a coy wave. No, he thought, he hadn't. And as the Nissan drew to a stop at the bottom of the steps, he felt an odd twist of discomfort. He was old enough to be her father. And then some.

"Gonna go rain, t'night, *m'sieur*," said the hotel valet, jumping out of the driver's seat and taking the tip Jacquot passed him. "So you takes care and keeps yo'self good an' dry."

Twenty minutes later, after losing his way on the drive out of town, Jacquot headed past the racetrack and airport at Le Lamentin and followed the road back to Le François.

If luck was on his side, he'd make the afternoon ferry.

25

The days that followed were slow and long and hot. In Marseilles, back when he really was a Chief Inspector working homicide with the *Judiciaire*, Jacquot had the rank and clout – the *piston* – to persuade all manner of people to do what he wanted. And as swiftly as possible, *s'il vous plaît*. From technicians in forensic labs and assistants in pathology departments, to bar men, taxi drivers, and police snitches. Here, on Île des Frères, it was a different matter. He wasn't a cop any more, and there was no pressure he could bring to bear on anyone. Instead he had to be patient. No point calling Balmet at the *gendarmerie* about fingerprints, or Cornel at the hospital about the toxicology report. They'd be in touch when they had something to tell him, and not before. And as he worked on the decking at the back of the house, or sat at the end of a nearby jetty with his fishing rod, or drove to and from St-Christophe to drop off and pick up his daughters from school, he wondered which would come first. The fingerprint analysis from Balmet's contact at the Laboratoire Médécine-Légale in Fort-de-France, including the keycards he'd passed on to Balmet after his trip to the Ambassadeur? Or from Doctor Cornel who, on receipt of his fifty-euro sweetener and an undertaking from Jacquot to pay for the report, had sent blood and tissue samples to the hospital labs on the mainland?

And as he sawed wood and hammered in nails, or watched the fish nibble at his bait, or listened to the chatter of his daughters, Jacquot thought about Boni. If matters hadn't taken a turn for the worse, if a certain Monsieur Tarrant, or Torrance, hadn't followed her to Chez Chanson and opened her forearm, she'd be back home in Nassau by now, having failed to persuade Jacquot to help her find her husband, and looking for someone else to do the job, leaving just a fond memory of her short stay on the island, an old friendship revisited.

But for all the sadness, there was anger too. That someone had killed her, so coldly and callously. And an aching frustration that the killer had so far managed to get away with it. Anger, frustration, and anxiety too: if the reports did not back up his theories, there would be little chance of persuading the authorities to take the matter any further.

Everything hinged on those two results. Fingerprints and

toxicology.

And the waiting was driving him mad. Now, whenever he heard the phone ring, he dropped his saw or his hammer and ran to pick it up, his hopes dashed time and time again.

And then, eight days after Monsieur Tarrant, or Torrance, caught the ferry for the mainland, the two calls he'd been waiting for came in quick succession. Followed soon after by a third.

The first call was from Balmet.

"Four of de seventeen prints we done took from de back of Monsieur Tarrant's chair gone match two of de three prints on de razor packaging in Madame Stuyvesant's waste bin," the sergeant said. "Dey also matches de prints on one of the Ambassadeur's keycards. A result, Monsieur Jacquot."

Jacquot felt his pulse quicken.

"And dere's more."

Jacquot's favourite words. "What more?"

"De print is on file. A murder in Tijuana four year ago. A shooting. Drug-related. De print was lifted from a retrieved shell casing, but back then there weren't no match on file. And de shooter was never apprehended."

The second call came twenty minutes later. From Doctor Cornel at the island hospital.

"Your tox report is back," the doctor began. His voice was uncertain, the tone perplexed, as though he couldn't really believe what he was saying. "It would appear that your money was well spent, Monsieur Jacquot."

Jacquot stiffened with excitement. "Tell me," was all he said.

"Well," Cornel began. "A couple of things. First, it appears that small trace elements of Pridoxamine have been found in the blood sample I sent for analysis."

"Pridoxamine?"

"That makes two of us," said Cornel, with a chuckle. "I had to look it up. Not a common drug," he continued. "Not at all. *En effet*, it's a narco-synthetic developed a few years ago by the US military and used extensively by their Intelligence units in Iraq. A psychoactive medication related to sodium thiopental, but far more effective thanks to the rapidity of its action."

"That's a truth drug, isn't it? Sodium Pentothal?"

"That's the brand name, and yes, it is used for that purpose. Altogether less messy than waterboarding. It's also the first of three drugs used in lethal injections in US prisons. Once it reaches the brain, it lowers one's resolve to resist. The same thing happens when it's used as a truth serum. The argument is that by decreasing a person's higher cortical brain function it becomes easier for them to tell the truth rather than lie. As I said, the only difference between Sodium Thiopental and this Pridoxamine is the speed with which it takes effect. Like the difference between… between a family hatchback and a Lamborghini."

"How would it have been administered?"

"Oh, intravenously, of course."

Jacquot frowned. How could Tarrant have given Boni an intravenous injection without her resisting? The broken fingernail?

"I know what you're thinking," said Cornel, with a gentle clearing of the throat. "Which brings us to the second thing. Something I didn't really take in at the time."

"Which is?"

"Madame Stuyvesant's lips."

"Her lips?"

"They were chafed, a little… rough. The kind of thing a patient might present if they were badly dehydrated, or happened to find themselves in a particularly dry environment, a desert, for instance. But this same chafing or roughness can also result from the direct application and inhalation of quick-acting anaesthetics like Halothane or Desflurane – say, a soaked cloth held over the mouth. At which point, of course, one could more easily administer the Sodium Thiopental."

Jacquot recalled the antiseptic smell in Boni's room, a sharp acetone scent like nail varnish remover that he had initially attributed to Cornel. "So what you're saying is that she could have been anaesthetised, and then given an injection of this truth drug?"

"That might easily be the case."

"Did you find any puncture site?"

"I didn't… I mean, I haven't looked…"

"So where does all this leave your finding of suicide?"

There was a silence at the end of the line, then a nervous cough. "I… Well, in the light of the toxicology report I would certainly have to reconsider that initial finding, and recommend that further tests be carried out. In this instance, a full autopsy would seem to be the best way forward."

The third call came an hour later. Jacquot was on the school run so he missed it. Instead, he saw the red light blinking on his answer machine when he returned home with the girls. It was Faubert at police headquarters. The call was as unexpected as the contents of his message, and it was clear when Jacquot heard it that Doctor Cornel had not yet informed Faubert of the toxicology findings.

"A courtesy call," Faubert began, his voice treacly and snide. "I thought you might like to know that Madame Stuyvesant's husband has arrived in Martinique and will be coming over this afternoon to organise the removal of his wife's body for burial in Nassau. He's arriving by helicopter, and will be landing at the hospital at around four-thirty. I assumed you would want to be there."

26

If Faubert hadn't known about the toxicology report when he called
Jacquot about Stuyvesant's visit, he certainly knew about it by the time
Jacquot arrived at the hospital. There were four of them waiting for
the Stuyvesant helicopter, gathered together on the upper lawn where
the air ambulances landed – Jacquot, Faubert, Balmet, and Doctor
Cornel – with the red roofs of the hospital blocks spread out below
them like a straggling line of railway carriages stranded in a jungle
clearing. Few words had been spoken as they climbed the steps in
single file to the landing pad – Faubert fuming, Cornel silent, Balmet
quietly pleased, and Jacquot unrepentant – but once there Faubert
began again, unwilling to let the matter of Jacquot's unofficial tox
report rest.

"You had no authority to–"

"As I said, it was a personal matter," Jacquot broke in. "A private
matter. My call, and paid for. It was clear that something was wrong.
I just needed to confirm my suspicions." He did not add that, had he
not asked for the tox report, and left everything to Faubert and Cornel,
then Boni's death would have remained a suicide. He knew he didn't
need to; both men were acutely aware of the fact. Which explained
Faubert's annoyance, and Cornel's quiet embarrassment.

Faubert's displeasure had been evident from the moment Jacquot
pulled up at the hospital, the island's police chief snapping his swagger
stick against his bare leg, his lips set in a thin grim line. This afternoon
he was wearing regulation shorts, long black socks and black lace-ups,
a white belt, and white bandolier across an immaculately pressed blue
uniform shirt. The climb up to the landing area had only increased
his irritation, small patches of sweat turning the armpits of his shirt a
darker blue.

"If you were unhappy with the doctor's findings, monsieur,"
Faubert continued, "you should have said something. You should
have come to me."

"I made it quite clear that I was unhappy with those findings,
but you would not be persuaded," Jacquot replied, deciding not to
mention the print matches that Balmet had secured. He'd do that later,
when the autopsy findings were in.

Faubert turned to Cornel. "And you, Doctor, should have had the courtesy to let me know what you were doing. That a toxicology report had been ordered."

"I tried to explain to Monsieur Jacquot that…"

"It's coming," said Balmet, interrupting an increasingly heated discussion. He tilted his head to one side, looked out to sea, then turned back to the slope of land behind them.

Now they could all hear it, a distant but growing thump-thump-thumping of rotor blades. And then, as the helicopter rose into sight above the ridge behind them and headed in their direction, the thump was replaced by a sudden rising clatter. Stepping back, their clothes whipped against them by the downdraft, the four men stooped their shoulders and lowered their heads as the helicopter came in to hover above them, sending up a stinging spray of grass cuttings and gritty dust, before settling onto the lawn.

As the engine whine softened, Jacquot looked up in time to see the passenger door open and a man climb out. He was dressed in a cream linen suit with a yellow tie and sky-blue shirt, and looked to be in his early fifties, tall, tanned, and slim with a full head of greying hair. Exactly the kind of successful businessman that Boni had described. Reaching back into the cabin he pulled out a small leather backpack, and, stooping low, he started towards them. By the time he reached them, the rotor blades had slowed and their weight had come into play, making them droop lazily as they turned.

So this was Boni's husband, thought Jacquot, sizing the man up. Right here, on Île des Frères. The man she had wanted him to find. The man who had walked off with ten million dollars of someone else's money. Had she been mistaken about his disappearance? Was there something she didn't know? Something she hadn't told him? This was going to be interesting.

Monsieur Stuyvesant went for the uniform first, swinging the bag over his left shoulder in order to shake Faubert's outstretched hand. Jacquot missed the first words of greeting, but after shaking Faubert's hand Stuyvesant turned to Cornel, shook his hand, and then turned finally to Jacquot with a questioning look on his face.

"And this is Daniel Jacquot, an old friend of your wife's," said Faubert by way of introduction. Jacquot took the hand that was offered, felt the dry strength of it, and looked into the man's stone-grey eyes.

"Monsieur Jacquot, it is good to meet you. I have heard a great
deal about you."

"And I of you," replied Jacquot. "I am sorry for your loss."

"And I for yours," said Stuyvesant, a thin smile to underline
the sentiment as well as the shared grammar, revealing a gap in his
front teeth wide enough to hold a cigarette. "So," he said, releasing
Jacquot's hand and turning to Cornel. "If you could show my team
where to go, Doctor." Behind him, two men in hospital whites were
unloading a stretcher from the back of the helicopter. By now, the
sound from its engines had faded to an oily murmur, low enough to
make out a gentle creak from the resting rotor blades.

But before Cornel could say anything, Faubert stepped forward,
took Stuyvesant's elbow and steered him to the steps leading down
to the hospital. Jacquot, Cornel, and Balmet followed, and as they
started down Jacquot heard Faubert begin with an apology. He had
tried to contact Stuyvesant before the flight out from Martinique,
Faubert explained, but he had not been able to locate him. Regrettably,
Jacquot heard him continue, there would now be a problem with the
transfer of Madame Stuyvesant's remains to Nassau.

Stuyvesant stopped and turned. "Problem?"

Jacquot and the others came to a halt behind them, two steps back,
looking down on the pair of them. Faubert did not look comfortable.

"It appears that your wife did not die of natural causes. Therefore,
Monsieur Stuy–"

"What do you mean, she didn't die of natural causes? She cut her
wrist, didn't she?" He looked back at Cornel for confirmation.

"*Capitaine* Faubert is correct," said Cornel. "It would appear that
the suicide, the cutting of the radial artery, was not self-inflicted."

Patric Stuyvesant frowned, tilted his head as though unsure he
had heard the words spoken, or had misunderstood them. "Not self-
inflicted? What, exactly, are you saying?"

Faubert fingered his bandolier and cleared his throat, but Jacquot
beat him to it.

"Your wife was murdered," he said. "By a man called Tarrant, or
Torrance. He followed your wife from Miami, possibly all the way
from Nassau, stayed in the same hotel in Fort-de-France, and followed
her out here to des Frères."

The colour drained from Stuyvesant's face. It was a reflex no one could have feigned. The news of her murder was as shocking to him as her suicide. Or maybe, thought Jacquot, it was the name. Tarrant, or Torrance. Did Stuyvesant know him? Or was it because a plan to disguise a murder as suicide had failed to convince the authorities? Had Stuyvesant been involved?

"And where is he now? This Tarrant?" asked Stuyvesant. "Has he been arrested?"

"He left Martinique a week ago," Jacquot replied. "An American Airlines flight to Miami."

"And no one stopped him?"

"We didn't know…" Faubert broke in, glaring up at Jacquot. "Your wife's death had been recorded as a suicide. Nothing suspicious."

"So how come it's suddenly murder?" he asked, looking back at Cornel.

"A toxicology report has indicated the presence of certain… chemicals," Cornel replied. "In her system. Your wife was drugged… before being killed. But everything had been set up to make it look like suicide."

Stuyvesant turned from Cornel to Faubert.

"Is this true?"

"I'm afraid–"

"So what happens now?"

"Well, arrangements have been made for your wife's body to be transferred by air ambulance to Fort-de-France for further tests. A full autopsy. I regret it will be some time before the body can be released to you for burial."

"Very well," said Stuyvesant. "If that's what has to happen, that's what has to happen."

27

"Boni told me you were either dead, or you'd run off with a girlfriend," said Jacquot. "And she wanted me to find you."

"As you can see, Daniel, I'm not dead," said Stuyvesant. "But you'll have to take my word that there is no girlfriend."

Jacquot and Stuyvesant were sitting on the terrace at Gustave's where ten days earlier he and Boni had dined on palm hearts and pompano, the night the rain came, Boni's last night alive. The two of them had come here from the hospital after Stuyvesant sent his helicopter back to Fort-de-France, saying he'd stay overnight on des Frères and return to Martinique the following day, in the air ambulance with Boni. Which had seemed reasonable enough except, unlike Boni, Stuyvesant had come prepared. With that leather backpack. But how, Jacquot wondered, had he known he'd be staying over? After all, he'd only flown in to pick up the body, sign any release papers, and leave; there had been no reason for him to stay. Yet there was that backpack. That's what had started Jacquot thinking. There was clearly something going on here. Some other agenda. Something else that Stuyvesant wanted.

Since Stuyvesant was unwilling to spend the night at Madame Chanson's plantation house, Jacquot had suggested one of the guest cabins at Gustave's. The accommodation wasn't as old-time grand as Chez Chanson, he told Stuyvesant, but the cabins were clean and serviceable, and he wouldn't have to go far to find a good meal. Jacquot had offered to drive him into town himself, and Stuyvesant had accepted.

"So why would she spin a story like that?" asked Jacquot, tipping back the last of his drink, and beckoning to the waiter for two more of Gustave's celebrated *ti-punches*.

Stuyvesant sighed, shook his head.

"Boni had been having some problems recently. Maybe you knew?"

Now it was Jacquot's turn to shake his head.

"No, I didn't know. Until a couple of weeks ago I hadn't seen her, or heard from her, for years. What sort of problems?"

"Money. More accurately, gambling."

"In your clubs?"

"Every now and again, of course. But mostly high-stake games in other private gaming rooms. In the last few months she lost a great deal of money."

"What's a great deal?"

"Hundreds of thousands of dollars."

"But not ten million?"

Stuyvesant frowned.

"The ten million she told me that you had taken from a man called Ettore DiCorsa. Before you disappeared with your girlfriend."

"Like I said, I'm not dead and I don't have a girlfriend. And last time I looked, I'm a little short of ten million." He gave Jacquot a grin, and played the tip of his tongue between his gap teeth. As well as showing the gap in his front teeth, Jacquot also noticed that the grin revealed a small angled scar on the side of his chin, like a misplaced, off-centre cleft.

The drinks arrived and both men removed the paper umbrellas.

"Your French is very good, Patric."

"It should be. I'm French, originally. Born in Paris and brought up in Biarritz. When I was seventeen my parents moved to Miami. I went with them."

Jacquot nodded. "So tell me," he said, settling himself into his chair and raising his glass to Stuyvesant. "How did you two meet? You and Boni?"

"Playing tennis. A game of doubles. She had a mean backhand."

Not with her neck, she didn't, thought Jacquot. She liked to watch the big tournaments on television, but she never played. Couldn't play. The real Patric Stuyvesant would have known that. Just as he'd have known that Boni never gambled because she hated to lose money, and that she and Patric had met on a flight to Miami and gone on to Joe's for a plate of stone crabs. But then the man sitting opposite him wasn't Patric Stuyvesant.

Because it wasn't just the overnight bag that had started Jacquot thinking. It was the fingernails, too, the first sure indication that Patric Stuyvesant was not the man he claimed to be. The nails were bitten to the quick and what was left of them deeply embedded in the tips of his fingers; it would have taken persistence and sharp teeth to find anything worth biting. And if it was the first thing that Jacquot had noticed, it would have been the first thing that Boni would have noticed, too.

Hands were very important to her. And nails, particularly. She simply couldn't bear bitten nails. "Can you imagine," she'd once whispered to Jacquot, after a waiter served them drinks, "having hands like that on your body?" And she'd shivered. Maybe the prospect of a wealthy husband made bitten fingernails a more palatable proposition, but somehow Jacquot doubted it. Other women, possibly. But not Boni.

And born in Paris? Growing up in Biarritz? According to Boni, Patric's parents had lived in Provence, a wine estate near Lourmarin.

Which was quite enough for Jacquot.

"So let's get down to business," he began, reaching for his cigarettes and lighting up. "Just who exactly are you? Because you're certainly not Patric Stuyvesant. If you were, you'd have known about Boni's neck, that she never played tennis; that she didn't like gambling because she hated to lose money; and that the two of you met on a flight to Miami. Oh, and Patric wasn't born in Biarritz."

Stuyvesant put down his drink. He smiled, nodded, and seemed not in the least discomfited that Jacquot had seen through him.

"You're right. I'm not her husband. My name is Ballard. John Ballard. Jean Boulard, originally."

The name rang a bell. "Patric's partner?"

"That's right. I'm the one who took over running the business when Patric went missing. And I'm the one who found out that he had taken something that didn't belong to him."

"The money?"

Ballard nodded. "That's right. A very large amount of money. The ten million you mentioned earlier, skilfully removed over a number of months. I had to report it."

"Report it?"

"To my boss. Ettore DiCorsa. The man the money belonged to. The man who put me in place to look after his investment. The man who hired Monsieur Tarrant to follow Mrs Stuyvesant and find out what she was up to."

"By drugging her and then killing her?"

The bluntness of the question seemed not to bother Ballard. "It turned out she had nothing to tell us. She didn't know what had happened to the money. So… she was of no further use." Ballard spread his hands, gave Jacquot a low, sideways look – as though they were in it together.

Jacquot went cold. He hadn't expected this, and for a moment he didn't know what to say or do. The man he was drinking with had just admitted that he had played a part in Boni's death. His initial impulse was to get to his feet, push away from the table, and hurl himself at the man, pummel his smug self-satisfied face, before calling Faubert to have him arrested. But he did none of these things. As swift as that initial impulse to attack, was the realisation that there was no way he could prove that Ballard had just confessed to his role in Boni's murder. And nothing he could do. At the very most he'd be able to prove that Ballard had lied about his relationship with Boni, that he had impersonated her husband. But so what? Some difficult questions to answer, sure. A slap on the wrist, maybe. But that was all. In Patric's absence, and as her husband's partner, it was understandable that he should come to identify and claim the body.

"Why didn't you kill her in the Bahamas? Or Martinique?" Despite the bile of anger churning in his guts Jacquot managed to keep his voice level. "Why wait till she came here?"

"We wanted to know what she was doing. Whether she was involved. Why she would want to come to Martinique. We wanted to know who she saw. Who she met. Who she spoke to. Monsieur Tarrant simply followed her and reported back."

A waiter stopped at their table and asked if he could get them another round. Ballard nodded, and the waiter disappeared.

Jacquot watched his companion, stunned by what was happening. They could have been two businessmen discussing a mutual project, rather than talking about the disappearance of Patric Stuyvesant with ten million dollars, and the subsequent murder of his wife.

"So you're still looking for Patric Stuyvesant?"

Ballard shook his head. "Not any more. We know where he is."

"You know?"

"Of course," said Ballard, sliding his tongue over his teeth. "I pushed him off the boat myself."

Jacquot remembered what Boni had told him, about talking to the sharks. "You killed him, too?"

"When it was clear he wasn't going to co-operate…"

"So now you have nothing."

"There is still the girlfriend. And, of course, we have you."

Jacquot frowned.

"You're a cop."

"I was a cop. Not any more."

"Once a cop, always a cop," said Ballard. "That's what Boni told Tarrant. A resourceful man, she said. If anyone could find her husband it was you. She said she'd come here to persuade you to help. Which is why I am here. To do the same. And she was right; you appear to be everything she said you were."

Jacquot bristled. "I told her I wasn't interested. Told her I wouldn't do it. And now I'm telling you."

"So if you told her 'no', if you told her you weren't interested in helping, how come she put a hundred thousand dollars into your account?"

"What are you talking about?"

Ballard gave Jacquot an indulgent look. "Please, Daniel. We are not stupid. You were prepared to help Boni. For money. And now it's time to earn that money, by helping us."

"I don't know anything about any money. She offered to pay me, sure, but I turned her down."

"Believe me, she paid you. The transfer went through more than a week ago. The day before she died. On the company account. Which is how I know about it. If you don't believe me, why don't you call your bank? Check your balance?"

"And if I say 'no'?"

Another indulgent look, and a soft, deadly chuckle. "Oh, Daniel, I can think of two very good reasons why you shouldn't say 'no'," said Ballard.

Jacquot went cold. He knew exactly what Ballard was talking about.

Matti and Béa.

"Ah," said Ballard, with a slow, spreading smile. "I see you understand."

New Friends
Nassau,
The Bahamas

28

The heat was immediate. Crisp and searing, with no breeze to stir it, to soften it. As Jacquot stepped down from the aircraft onto the shimmering black tarmac of Nassau's Lynden Pindling International Airport, he knew it was the air-conditioning on board the private jet that made the heat so immediately intolerable. The sun might have been past its peak, low enough now to cast shadows, but it still threw out a scalding, sweat-drying blast that prickled his skin and ironed out the creases in his linen trousers.

He glanced at his watch. Ten past three. Samuel would be picking up the girls from school, to deliver them back to Mama Loubertin at the house in Trinité, and Midou, Claudine's daughter, would be arriving this evening to keep an eye on everything. He had called her that morning, before joining Ballard for the flight to Nassau, and asked if she could take a few days off to look after her half-sisters. When she asked what he was up to, and why the short notice, he'd explained that he had some business to attend to in Nassau and shouldn't be away longer than a week. He hoped that that was all it would be, telling Midou he would keep in touch and let her know when he'd be coming back. In the meantime, he'd be grateful if she could keep the girls happy, and distracted.

Jacquot missed Béa and Matti more than he could ever have imagined, and remembered their tears when he told them he was leaving for a couple of days on business. Their shocked looks and disbelieving, desolate crying had torn his heart to pieces. It would be the first time he had ever been apart from them. And pushing away a nagging thought that he might never see them again, he swore to himself that he would return in one piece. No matter what he had to do.

It had been a swift but miserable journey. From Île des Frères to Fort-de-France in the air ambulance sent to pick up Boni for delivery to the medical examiner in Fort-de-France, and afterwards aboard a private jet to New Providence in the Bahamas. The flight had taken a little under three hours and for the first two hours Jacquot had been left alone, sitting in a plushly upholstered leather armchair by the rear bulkhead, looking through the tiny window at passing clouds and distant islands, green and brown pebbles set like stepping stones in a deep cobalt sea.

Soon after take-off from Aimé Césaire airport in Fort-de-France, a flight attendant in slacks and open-necked blouse had asked if he'd like a drink – which he did, ordering a pastis, just to see if they had it, which they did, brought to him with a tray of canapés. A late lunch followed, with a choice of grilled chicken, beef, or sea bass. He ordered the sea bass which was served with baby new potatoes, buttered carrots, and a half-bottle of Chablis. He ate alone, watching Ballard at the other end of the cabin work through a pile of paperwork, and being served beef and a bottle of water. It was only after their lunch plates had been cleared, and as the plane began its gradual descent towards the Bahamas, that Ballard picked up a file and his coffee and came to the back of the plane, slipping into the seat opposite Jacquot. Putting his coffee and the file on the table between them, he asked if Jacquot was enjoying the flight.

"I can think of other places I'd rather be," Jacquot replied.

"And you'll be in those other places just as soon as you like," said Ballard. "*Cherchez la femme. Cherchez l'argent.* Isn't that what you say? That's all you have to do. Find Patric's girlfriend, and find the money. Just tell us where she is, and you can leave the rest to us. You'll be free to go."

"And how do you propose I do that?"

Ballard pointed to the file he'd brought over. "Everything you'll need, everything we have, is in here."

Jacquot reached for the file, flipped it open. There was just a single sheet of paper with a photo attached. A head and shoulders shot of a pretty brunette in a light green open-necked polo shirt. It was the kind of photo you might find in any personnel department, informal yet somehow formal. Full face, wide smile, but with no real suggestion of character. Not quite a passport photo, but close. Except for one thing. A slightly raised eyebrow. There was, Jacquot decided, something challenging about it. An arch look. Something edgy and knowing. As for the typed information on the accompanying sheet of paper, there was no raised eyebrow there. Just the sort of basic information a personnel department might hold. Date of birth, address, telephone number, education, employment history.

"Her name is Sylvie Martin," said Ballard. "As you can see she was in charge of customer relations at The Edgewater Club. Twenty-four. Tall. Pretty. An islander. Mother a waitress and party girl at the Rex, out on the island."

"The island? Nassau?"

"Paradise Island. Linked to New Providence by a causeway. It's where the big casinos are. Rex is the biggest."

"And what exactly do you mean by 'party girl'?"

Ballard gave Jacquot a look. "When she wasn't serving drinks, she served the high-rollers."

"And got pregnant?"

"In one. Stayed on the circuit but it didn't last. Went solo, and somehow kept it all together, but died of an overdose around the time Sylvie left college."

"Father?"

"You're kidding, right?"

Jacquot sighed, closed the file. "So that's all you've got? All you can give me?"

Ballard threw Jacquot a companionable smile. "Shouldn't be too difficult for a man with your qualifications."

"If you couldn't find her, how am I supposed to do it?"

"I'm sure you'll think of something."

Jacquot sat back and from nowhere he started thinking about that arched eyebrow. "Is this the only photo you have of her?"

"You want more? I'll see what I can do."

"Did you know her?"

Ballard gave a shrug. "Around the club, I suppose. But I don't really notice staff. And she's young. Okay to play with, I guess, but I prefer my women a little more… seasoned."

Thirty minutes later, the Gulfstream IV had hit the runway at Lynden Pindling, braked and taxied to a stop outside a low building away from the main terminal. A black Lexus with its boot open was waiting for them. Beside it stood a driver, and a Customs official who checked their passports, wished them a happy stay, and walked back to the charter terminal. The pleasures of private jet travel, thought Jacquot, as he slid into the limo's back seat with Ballard. No check-in queues, no burdensome security or Immigration checks. Who said crime didn't pay?

"For the purposes of your… investigation, I've put it around that you are Boni's brother, come to tidy up her affairs before the

Stuyvesant property is sold. It seemed appropriate that you should stay there. It's a lovely house, right on the beach at Lyford Cay," said Ballard, as their driver slid the Lexus through a gate in the airport's perimeter fence and joined the road leading away from town.

"The house is being sold? What about Patric? He's listed as 'missing', not dead."

"The house is in the company's name," Ballard replied. "For tax purposes, you understand." He looked across at Jacquot and gave him another of his short little smiles. The gap teeth reminded Jacquot of Omar Sharif, but Ballard was missing the moustache and his features were far less benign. There was something icily cold and calculating about the man.

"We've also arranged temporary membership for you at The Edgewater Club where Boni and Patric were members," Ballard continued, "and where Sylvie Martin worked. It's just a short drive from the house. Boni and Patric have cars in the garage – take your pick – and the housekeeper, Beth, will show you where everything is." He looked at his watch. "You have a couple of hours to unpack and settle in, and then the car will be back to pick you up at seven. You're having dinner with Mr DiCorsa."

29

Ten minutes after leaving the airport, they turned off the coast road and drove through a pair of pink stone pillars set with spear-tip wrought-iron gates. The Stuyvesant house stood at the end of a short drive lined with dwarf palmettos and clusters of bougainvillea, its creamy stone façade overlooking a turning circle of crushed white coral that crunched beneath the tyres of the Lexus.

"Home sweet home," said Ballard, getting out of the car and jogging up the steps to the front door. It opened before he got there and the housekeeper, Beth, appeared. She reminded Jacquot of Mama Loubertin back on Île des Frères, not quite as tall but just as bulky, standing in the doorway in a tight white dress and trainers. Introductions were made, Jacquot's case was brought to the door by their driver and, with a reminder that he should be ready for the seven o'clock pick-up, Ballard took his leave, the Lexus crunching away over the coral and heading back down the drive.

"Pleasure to have you stay wid us, sah," said Beth, and stepped aside for Jacquot to enter.

If the outside of the house had been impressive, the interior was breathtaking. No wonder Boni had been so 'charmed' with his own home on Trinité, thought Jacquot, taking in a wide open-plan expanse of low cream leather furnishings, a wall of bookshelves, a coral stone hearth, a collection of vivid abstract seascapes, and a long wall of glass that ran the length of the room. Beyond it he could see a balustraded terrace set with rattan sun loungers, a slope of lawn and, through a bank of feathery casuarina and tamarisk, a wide stretch of azure sea.

"I done put you in the downstairs guest suite, sah. Just you follows me," said Beth, picking up his case and swaying it away from him when he tried to take it from her. Crossing the room she led him down a hallway on the right and opened a louvred door. The suite had the same wall of glass overlooking the garden and beach, and comprised a comfortably furnished sitting room, spacious bedroom, and well-equipped bathroom.

"You want for me to unpack for you, sah?" said Beth, hoisting his case onto an ottoman at the foot of the bed.

"No, that's fine, Beth. Thank you."

She nodded, then stood a moment by the bedroom door. "Just so's you know, sah, I's so sorry for your loss. Your sister was one fine lady. It's truly a tragedy what she gone and done, but the good Lord gonna make a place for her in heaven despite it, and that's for certain."

Jacquot smiled. "Thank you. And I think you're right."

"Is there anything I can get you, sah? A drink? Some supper?"

"I have a dinner appointment, so I'm fine. What I'd really like is a swim, and then maybe a drink?"

"Ain't no pool, but you got yo'self a big wide ocean for that, sah. Waiting for you right down there." She pointed to the sea. "Just follow the path through de trees and you'se dere in a second. As for drinks, I makes me a mean rum punch, you interested? Just come on through to the kitchen when you're set, and I'll have it mixed and ready for the drinkin'."

When she was gone, the door closing with a soft click, Jacquot unzipped his case and pulled out a pair of swim shorts, stripped off and pulled them on. With a towel from the bathroom draped over his shoulder, he went to the bedroom window and pulled it aside in a single easy sweep, stepped out onto the terrace and drew it closed behind him. It was still hot, but the sharpness of the heat had eased, tempered now by a light sea breeze that smelled of salt and dried sand. Barefoot he hot-stepped it over the terrace flagstones, crossed the lawn and passed through the stand of shoreline trees, drawn by the shifting sound of the sea slapping on sand. Following the path through a carpet of emerald green sea grape he came out onto the beach, the sand warm underfoot, the colour of bleached coral, soft as talcum powder, and not a soul to be seen.

The water was as warm as the sand and Jacquot dove in, pulling himself through it with long easy strokes, the water sluicing over his shoulders, through his hair, his beard. For the first time since leaving Île des Frères he felt clean and free and when he judged himself far enough out he turned, dropped his legs and doggy paddled lazily. Two hundred metres away the house rose above the windbreak line of casuarina, its coral stone blocks and glass walls turning the colour of butter in the lowering sun; the kind of house, Jacquot decided, that you'd pass in a boat and wonder with a spill of envy who lived there. He saw, too, that it occupied a point of land, its nearest neighbours at least a hundred metres distant either side, just red rooftops showing between a bordering line of palms. And as he floated there, Jacquot wondered how many times had Boni swum out like this, to look back at that house and think how far she had come? A beautiful home, a husband she loved, a life worth living. Except, now, for Boni, that life was over.

Back at the house, Jacquot showered, dressed in chinos, espadrilles, and a short-sleeved white cotton shirt, and set off for the kitchen where Beth presented him with a freshly-made punch.

"Good and heavy with the rum," he told her, feeling the fruity, warming strength of it in his chest.

"And nuthin' wrong wid that, is there? You seems the kind of man, you don't mind me sayin', looks like he takes his drinks on the strong side."

"I have a feeling you and I are going to get along just fine, Beth."

She gave him a strange smile, shook her head. It looked for a moment as though she were about to cry.

For a moment Jacquot wondered if he'd said something wrong.

"Are you okay?"

"Oh, me? Why, sure… It's just… It's just you sounds so like her. That accent. Mister Patric done almost lost his, but Mrs Boni she had it still, just like you. Gonna miss it round here, and that's for sure. And miss her, too." She pursed her fat lips tight, and nodded her head, looking down at the floor, putting a hand to the work surface as though to steady herself.

Without thinking about it, Jacquot set down his drink and went to her, put an arm around her shoulders, drew her to him. She didn't pull away, just dropped her head to his chest, and he could feel her body tremble against his.

"You and me, both," he said. "You and me, both."

30

Jacquot was lying back on a terrace lounger with a second of Beth's rum punches when she came out to tell him that his car had arrived. He had spent the last twenty minutes on the phone, talking to Matti and Béa at the house in Trinité, and when he cut the connection, after sending his love, wishing them sweet dreams, promising he would be home soon, and not wanting the call to end, he'd felt a great emptiness descend, followed by a grim and burning determination to see this whole sorry affair through as quickly and as safely as he could.

The drive was a short one, just a couple of miles before the same driver who'd picked him up at the airport indicated right and swung the Lexus off the road and down through a stand of shadowy tamarisk, coming to a stop on an open patch of ragged cracked concrete. It edges were overgrown with weeds and a rutted stone path led down to a small jetty. Tethered to the jetty was a motor cruiser in a sleek black and grey livery, its cabin lights glowing gold in the gathering darkness and its engine idling along with a low-throated rumble.

"I'll be waiting when you get back," the driver told Jacquot, and as he stepped from the car and closed his door the Lexus turned in a tight circle and went back the way it had come, a trail of dust rising behind it. Lighting up a cigarette, Jacquot walked down to the jetty at an easy pace, his footfalls scuffing the stony path but turning to a dull thump as he hit the wood-plank jetty.

As far as Jacquot could tell the cruiser was a good fifty feet in length – twice the length and probably twenty times the value of his own boat, *Constance*, currently berthed back home in Marseilles' Vieux Port. As Jacquot drew closer he could make out a flying dolphin badge on the side of the wheelhouse and recognised the image. A Mochi. Italian. Part of the Ferretti Group, and custom-built. Make that fifty times the value of *Constance*, he thought as he flicked his cigarette into the water, stepped off the jetty, and jumped down into the cockpit.

There were two men aboard, the skipper in blue shorts, scuffed deck shoes and cream jumper, and a larger man in black jeans, tight black t-shirt and black trainers. Without any word of welcome, the man in black cast off and the skipper in the wheelhouse pushed forward on the throttles, slowly at first, drawing away from the jetty, but then applying pressure until the bows rose and the speed increased, the dark roar of the engine, the sluicing splash of water and the battering of air making conversation unlikely. At a pinch Jacquot reckoned he could handle the skipper if he had to, but the man in black was altogether a different proposition. There was a solid, muscled thickness to him – legs, shoulders, and arms – but he moved with an athlete's easy tip-toe grace. As Jacquot settled himself on a leather couch in a corner of the stern cockpit he hoped it would never have to happen.

From where he sat it was difficult to say where they were headed. Out to sea, certainly, the lights of Nassau's shoreline starting to stretch out behind them but, as far as Jacquot could see, just darkness ahead. Ten minutes later, the skipper dropped the revs and the Mochi's bows sank back into the sea. Jacquot leaned out and looked ahead but could see nothing. Then, on the other side, a line of lights came into view. A row of lamps along another jetty, and beyond that the lights of a low single-storey house.

Coming in slowly, the skipper cut the power, the cruiser drifted into the jetty, and the man in black stepped up on the side, leaping effortlessly onto the jetty. A minute later the boat was secured and the man in black leaned down to help Jacquot out of the cockpit, gripping his hand and almost lifting him off his feet. Again, nothing was said, just a finger the size of a hammer handle pointing along the jetty.

Somewhere up ahead was Ettore DiCorsa, the man who had ordered the killings of Boni and Patric. Back in the day, Jacquot would have come here to question, or arrest, DiCorsa. Now, albeit against his will, he was coming for dinner.

31

As far as Jacquot could tell, the home of Ettore DiCorsa was built on a low cay with no beach to speak of, just a ledge of coral jutting out over the water, a stony mushroom, its stem eaten away by the slap and tug of the sea. The night air was warm, just the faintest stir of breeze, and the sky above him sprinkled with stars as he stepped off the jetty and started up a gentle incline, a twin line of cowled downlights marking out a path to the house.

The house was low and long, a row of coral stone arches set with picture windows. Between each window and placed below a shaft of downlighting was a tub of spikey aloe. As he drew closer, Jacquot could make out the interior: a vast sitting room occupying four of the arched windows, a dining area with two windows to the left of it, and a book-lined study behind another two windows on its right. Between the sitting room and study, at the end of a curve in the path, stood a massive front door that looked as if it had been carved from a single coral stone block. As Jacquot approached, the door swung silently open and an elongated square of light spilled out into the night. Stepping into this light was a slight and wiry Asian dressed in a white collarless cotton shirt and loose navy blue slacks that ended just above bare ankles and bare feet. Chinese? Vietnamese? Thai? Jacquot couldn't tell.

The man clasped his hands together in greeting, bowed, and straightened.

"Mistah DiCorsa in the kitchen," he said, in a quavering sing-song voice. "Please to follow me, sah."

With another bow, the man turned and led Jacquot across the sitting room, its walls hung with dark *settecento* oils of ruined temples and moonlit seascapes, alcoved display shelves set with ancient pottery, its floor of cream marble tiles laid with a frayed Persian rug and furnished with sofas and armchairs upholstered in flowery arabesques. The lighting was low, just the alcove lights and brass-shaded downlights above each painting, and everything that Jacquot could see looked both valuable and tasteful. An interior decorator, or was Ettore DiCorsa the man behind it, he wondered?

Turning to make sure that Jacquot was still with him, the houseboy passed through an archway into the dining room, his bare feet smacking light and quick on the tiles. The dining room was as softly lit as the drawing room, its walls covered with silk tapestry work – *chinoiserie* mandarins and courtesans and galloping warriors, lakes and trees, humped bridges and distant mountains. In the centre of the room and set on a deep scarlet rug was a twenty-foot mahogany table and sixteen chairs, its mirror-shine surface glowing in the light of a dozen temple candles lined down its centre.

When he reached the table the houseboy stopped and pointed to a black enamelled six-panel Coromandel screen at the far end of the room. Behind it Jacquot could see a pair of mahogany doors with a carved lacework grille in the centre of each.

"Just follow the music, sah. Mistah DiCorsa expecting you."

The music was opera, heard dimly at first in the hallway and sitting room but growing in volume as Jacquot crossed the dining room and pushed through the kitchen doors. The room was enormous, three walls set with cupboards and shelves and the latest kitchen equipment, the fourth wall a sheet of glass that, like the Stuyvesant house, rose from floor to ceiling. Beyond it underwater lights turned the dark sea into a shimmering pool of green.

And there, standing at an island in the middle of the room, was Ettore DiCorsa.

"*Bucatini alla carbonara*," he said, waving Jacquot over. "I am making my very favourite dish for our dinner. I trust, *signore*, that you like Italian food?" The voice was warm and welcoming, a deep, rich American burr but underscored with an unmistakeable Italian lilt.

Ettore DiCorsa was somewhere in his late sixties, possibly seventies, Jacquot guessed, dressed in long khaki shorts and a blue Hawaiian shirt patterned with what looked like pink hibiscus flowers. He was as tall as Jacquot but not as well-built, the legs thin and scrawny, the arms, too, his hair a rippled dyed black that swept back from a peak in the centre of his forehead. His eyes and eyebrows were as black as his hair, and his mouth a thin line of salved pink in a narrow brown face. His skin glistened, as though he'd just applied a handful of moisturiser, but the hand he held out for Jacquot to shake was dry and firm. "So? Do you? Do you like Italian food?"

It would have been a brave man, Jacquot decided, who would have said to Ettore DiCorsa that no, he did not like Italian food. Fortunately, Jacquot did.

"I like any food that is well-sourced, well-prepared, and cooked with passion," he said quietly, to cover the hatred welling up inside him.

"A man after my own heart," said DiCorsa, the pink lips splitting into a dentist's dream of a smile. Implants, thought Jacquot; had to be. "Pull up that stool, my friend, and I will show you how a real *carbonara* is made. How my mother used to make it. And here," he said, sliding a glass across the counter to Jacquot, and pointing to a bottle. "Help yourself. From my own vineyard."

Doing as he was told Jacquot hoisted himself up onto the stool and poured some wine, watching his host slide a blackened skillet onto a ring of blue flame and dig out a spoonful of white fat from a jar.

"*Strutto*," said DiCastro, dropping the fat into the skillet, working the handle until the lump of fat started to spit and melt and slide around. "Not olive oil, not butter... Just *strutto*. You know *strutto*? You have heard of it?"

Jacquot said that he had not.

"Pork fat, plain and simple," DiCorsa continued. "A dripping, if you like. I get it from a supplier in New York who brings it over from Italy. From near Rieti, in Lazio, where I was born."

From wherever the speakers were hidden the music came to a halt, and in the silence DiCorsa tipped his head, held up a finger. "And to go with the cooking of my favourite dish, one of my favourite arias. From Verdi's *Otello*. Act II. The great Italian baritone, Aldo Protti, playing Iago, singing '*Credo in un Dio crudel*'. I believe in a cruel God. I like to think of it as my signature tune." A deep devilish voice started up. "Listen to that. What a sound, eh? Just magical."

"I'm more a jazz and blues man myself. Music to dance to. I don't know much about opera."

"Jazz is good," said DiCorsa, unwrapping a fold of paper and removing a hunk of darkened wrinkled meat. He placed it on a scarred chopping board, reached for a knife, and began to slice and dice it, working the blade like a professional. "Blues, too, I suppose. And dancing has its place. Those rhythms that make your body want to move, of course I understand that. But opera... Oh, my friend, opera is king. Forget the body, opera goes straight to the heart, caresses it, squeezes it tight."

"Do you mind if I smoke?"

"If you must," said DiCorsa. "But it will kill you sooner or later. Like Puccini, eh? A prolific smoker. Died of throat cancer, he did. Cigars and cigarettes."

Jacquot pulled out his cigarettes, lit up. For the devilment now, as much as the pleasure.

"Not to mention, of course, the damage it does to your taste buds," DiCorsa continued. "Here, you can use this," he said, passing over a china bowl, before scooping up the diced meat with the side of his blade and dropping it into the skillet. The meat sizzled and danced in the spitting fat.

"There, you smell it? That is something special, eh? You know what it is, this meat?"

"If you're making a real carbonara, it won't be *pancetta*."

"Hah! You are right, my friend," said DiCorsa, shaking the pan. "So you do know your food. Not *pancetta*. Never *pancetta*. Just pussy pork, *pancetta*. It would be like asking one of these boy bands they have now to sing *La Traviata*. Not enough voice, you understand me? Not enough heart, not enough soul, or spirit. *Pancetta* – pah! Too thin, too fatty. So tell me, what do you suppose it is?"

"*Guanciale?*"

DiCorsa paused in the shuffling of his skillet, and gave a startled look. "Well, well. You have it in one. *Guanciale*. The cheek of the pig. Like the *strutto*, I get it direct from Italy."

"Your man in New York."

"*Sì, sì*," chuckled DiCorsa. "My man in New York. The best he can find, from a farmer in the Aniente Valley. And the Aniente is a very special place, I am telling you. I have heard it said that in the Aniente it is the ambition of every pig to have its cheeks turned by this man into *guanciale*. One week buried in a parcel of salt and thyme, and three weeks hung out to dry in the winds of the Appenini. What a way to go," he said, and chuckled again.

Moving the skillet from the heat, DiCorsa reached for a saucepan, filled it with water, tossed in a pinch of salt crystals and put it to boil on the same ring of flame. The movements were fluid, practiced, and Jacquot was in little doubt that this *carbonara* would indeed be spectacular. He only hoped he had the appetite to do it justice. For he could not forget that the man who was cooking his dinner was a ruthless killer. The man who had ordered the murders of Boni and her husband, and doubtless many others, too. And worse, more frightening still, the man who was holding his children to ransom.

"So now the *bucatini*," said DiCorsa, opening a cupboard and removing a long packet of pasta. "Is like macaroni, no? But long and straight, with the smaller hole. And always dried; never, never for this dish, fresh pasta. Nor garlic, nor onions, nor cream, nor peas, nor mushrooms, nor broccoli… No pointless… *decorazione*. For a proper *carbonara*, less is always more. You must remember, my friend, that this is, and always has been, a peasant dish. *Un piatto di contadino*, we would say. So it is simple. But simple does not mean easy."

When the water began to bubble, DiCorsa slid a sheaf of the *bucatini* stalks into the pan, pushing them gently into the water with the flat of his hand.

"And now the eggs," he said, reaching for a glass bowl, cracking two whole eggs into it followed by two additional yolks, letting the unwanted whites slide through his fingers into the sink.

"We mix like this, with the tip of the knife, and then…" DiCorsa looked around. "There, if you please, the pecorino." He pointed to a sealed plastic container, which Jacquot opened and pushed over to him. "Always pecorino, and not the horror they make now in Sardinia. Nor Parmigiano. It must be sheeps' milk, not cows' milk, you understand? And only the best pecorino… Only the best. From Monte Sibillini… Not Lazio, maybe, but close."

"Your man again?"

"*Si*, my man. What would I do without him, eh? Tell me that."

By now the *bucatini* was boiling furiously, but DiCorsa paid it no heed. Pulling a grater from a drawer he worked the lump of hardened sheep cheese into a fluffy mound then tipped it into the eggs. "The moment. The moment is nearly here…" said DiCorsa, moving the pan of pasta from the heat and replacing it with the skillet of cooled *guanciale*. He pulled out a strand of *bucatini*, bit into it and nodded. "*Perfetto*… if I say so myself. Not too much salt, you see? Never more than a tiny pinch for the cooking. The *guanciale* and the cheese do the rest."

Then, taking a spoon, he ladled some of the pasta water into the skillet with the *guanciale*, strained off the rest, and tipped the meat and its juices into the mound of steaming pasta. It was a masterful performance, and the kitchen was suddenly filled with a rich smoky scent that made Jacquot's cheeks pucker.

"So we let it cool a moment, off the heat, and finally..." said DiCorsa, reaching for the bowl of beaten eggs and cheese, "we pour the eggs slowly, slowly onto the pasta, mixing it in with a wooden spoon. Gently, gently, so the eggs don't cook, don't curdle. Just a cream, do you see? Like this. A golden cream." He dropped the spoon in the sink and stood back. "*Ecco. Bucatini alla carbonara.* Like you have never tasted it before; like my mama used to make it."

A serving dish was brought out from the warming oven, the pasta tipped onto it, and black pepper ground over it.

"So, now we eat, my friend, and then we talk business, eh?"

32

"*Infiltrazione*. This is what I do. This is my business, and I must protect it. If I don't..." DiCorsa shrugged, spread his hands.

Jacquot and DiCorsa were sitting at a table outside the kitchen's glass wall, on a glass-floored deck above an ocean floodlit from below. A deep green pool of light showed coral heads and ivory patches of sand, fleeting schools of fish and darker shapes that moved more slowly, on the prowl. The night was still and warm, the sea sucking and splashing lightly beneath them, and high above the lights of an aircraft blinked amongst the stars. From unseen speakers a soaring voice rose to meet it.

"Ah, *Tosca*," said DiCorsa. "Another of my favourite arias. The great Renata Tebaldi singing '*Vissi d'arte, vissi d'amoré*'."

"Infiltration?"

"Exactly. That is the name of the game."

"And the game is?"

"The moving of money. The cleaning of money. I am... a cleaner." DiCorsa sat back and chuckled. "Such a small title for such a grand and profitable endeavour."

"Money laundering."

Another shrug from DiCorsa. "I have many clients, my friend; clients with cash businesses, you understand? And many of them... no, most of them... they are not so legal, I am honest with you. Which means my clients have a problem. They have to make their income acceptable. And that is the job I do. The job I am good at. I clean it for them. So I place their money in decent, legal businesses in which I have built up an interest. Some cash when cash is needed, you know?"

"Companies like Patric's?"

"As an example, yes. He had a bad run a few years ago. Those little gaming clubs of his. He needed help. I gave it to him."

"At a price."

DiCorsa shrugged. "Price? What price? He survives a rough time. The business does not fail. And soon it prospers. Because now, in addition to his own legitimate earnings, he earns twenty cents for every dollar of mine he shifts through his business. He should be grateful, no?"

"And you place someone like Ballard in these businesses to see that things run your way."

"To protect my investment, of course. Like any good businessman…" And then, "Oh, oh, just listen. Listen," said DiCorsa, holding up both hands to halt the conversation. "There, do you hear it? Tebaldi at her best. A real *lirico-spinto* soprano, that voice cutting through the orchestra. So dramatic, so… powerful."

Jacquot gave DiCorsa a few more moments with his opera, and then said, "So Patric was a party to the laundering?"

"Of course he was. He must have known. And tried to make something of it." DiCorsa wagged a finger. "Which was not a good idea."

"So you had him killed. And his wife. My friend."

"But they wouldn't co-operate. They pretended they knew nothing about it, the money that had disappeared. They would not tell me what I wanted to know. So… I had to set an example. Regrettable, but necessary. As I said, I have to protect myself. If people think they can work one over on me, where would I be, eh? In trouble, is where I'd be. And my clients would not be happy."

Jacquot shook his head. In his years with the Marseilles *Judiciaire* he had met many killers. Men and women, young and old, sane and insane. Sometimes he had felt pity for them, sometimes revulsion, but in all that time he had never felt fear, nor the kind of seething hatred he felt now. With this man, Ettore DiCorsa. And he knew why. Matti and Béa.

"So, Mr Ballard tells me you're a cop. A Chief Inspector?"

"Retired," said Jacquot, biting back a rising bile of fear and hatred.

"In Martinique?"

"It was Marseilles. The *Judiciaire*. Homicide. A long time ago."

DiCorsa let out an unexpected bellow of a laugh. "Marseilles? Marseilles, did you say? Did you know that the great baritone, Victor Maurel, came from Marseilles? The first man to sing Verdi's Iago. At Teatro all Scala, in Milan. Ah, such fun, life, eh? So strange. You a cop, having dinner with me. Sitting at my table. Eating with me. Like old friends. Who would believe it? But there you are. As I say. Life." He reached for the wine, poured Jacquot a glass and then filled his own. "You like the *carbonara*? The wine?"

"I suspect it would be dangerous to say no."

For an instant DiCorsa's expression changed. A hooded darkness

replaced the bonhomie, as though Jacquot had crossed a line. But it
didn't last. This was a joke, of course, and the dentist's smile returned.

"As in all things you are free to say what you like, my friend, just
so long as you are prepared to pay the price."

Jacquot sighed, sat back, pushed away his empty plate. He knew
he had to hold himself back.

"I think that speaks for itself, don't you? And the wine is... well,
it really is very good. If I didn't know I would say a Barolo, or at a
pinch, maybe even a Nobile from Montepulciano."

"I like a man who likes his food, and who knows his wine."
DiCorsa reached for his glass, sipped at the wine. "Even if he is here
against his wishes, against his better instincts."

It was the first time that DiCorsa had brought up the reason for
Jacquot's presence in his home, and Jacquot knew that the mood was
about to change. He was right.

"I was not aware that I had a choice," he said, swirling the wine
in his glass.

DiCorsa smiled, a little sadly, sympathetically.

"Ah, of course, the *bambini*... Two girls, yes? Mr Ballard
mentioned them to me."

"Two little girls who are missing their father."

"But they have their mother, she will look after them while you
are away."

Jacquot sighed. "There is no mother. She died. I am all they have."

DiCorsa leaned back, looked hard at Jacquot as he considered this,
then smiled as though he had found a solution.

"So you must do your best to keep them safe, no? And to see them
again, you must provide. Like any good father. And what are their
names, these two little girls?" he asked, putting down his glass. And
then, holding up his hands, "No, no, don't tell me. I don't want to
know."

For a moment, just a moment, Jacquot felt a burning, visceral
urge to pick up his knife and plunge it through that flowery shirt
into DiCorsa's well-fed guts. He could hear Matti and Béa's sad but
excited voices on the phone, could feel the love and the warmth of
them. That's what made him want to kill DiCorsa. Finish him. Right
here. Right now. For making them suffer. For taking their father from
them. For this loathsome man's cold, heartless threat, putting them all

at such deadly risk. And he could do it. He knew he could do it. The hatred he felt for this man was starting to bubble over, as furiously as the pan of boiling *bucatini* back there in the kitchen. But he reined it back in, turned down the heat. He might kill the man, but if he did that he knew he would never get home, never see his children again. For now he must bide his time. Find a weakness. Find a way out. Or find the girl, Sylvie Martin. Deliver her to them. And the money. Then, surely, this man would let him go. Back to Matti and Béa.

"Ah," said DiCorsa, breaking into his thoughts. "Just listen to this. Just supreme. Uplifting. *Lo de' sospiri*. That contralto. Sublime."

For the next two or three minutes DiCorsa fell silent again, tipping back his head, mouthing the words of the aria, eyes closed, his right hand raised above the table, an invisible baton held delicately between thumb and forefinger. But finally the music died and DiCorsa sat up, pinned Jacquot with ice black eyes.

"So, as I said. We have some business to conclude. You are interested in what I do, so maybe you should see how we operate."

33

It was late, and Jacquot was tired. It had been a long day. But now was clearly not the time for bed nor for sleeping. Getting up from the table, Jacquot followed DiCorsa through the dining room and sitting room and out into the hallway. The houseboy was waiting by the open door, as though he knew that his boss was coming. He handed DiCorsa a cotton jumper, which the man flung carelessly over his shoulders.

"You have a sweater? On the boat?" he asked, turning to Jacquot and reaching out a hand to finger the sleeve of his shirt.

Jacquot said that he did not.

DiCorsa turned to the houseboy. "Duc, another sweater for the *signore. Pronto, pronto.* Quickly now." And then, taking Jacquot's arm in his, he led the way down to the jetty, walking quickly, smaller steps than Jacquot, but enough to set the pace. "It gets chill sometimes, out there," he continued, nodding to the sea, and letting go of Jacquot's arm he stepped down into the cockpit and made himself comfortable on one of the stern couches. Clambering down after him, Jacquot took a seat on the other couch, while the man in black set to with the mooring lines. As he stepped back on board, Duc, the houseboy, came hurrying up, bare feet smacking on the jetty's planking, trouser hems flapping. He was carrying the sweater that DiCorsa had asked for, and passed it down to Jacquot with a bow and clasped hands.

And then they were off, backing up a few metres before the skipper pushed down on the throttles and spun the wheel to port. In a tight wheeling arc that almost tipped Jacquot off the couch, the Mochi surged through the water and, following the curve of the cay rather than heading back to Nassau, the skipper set out into open sea, the lights from DiCorsa's home drifting away into the darkness behind them.

It wasn't long before the Mochi started hitting choppy water and spray lashed back. But such was the design of the boat, or the skill of DiCorsa's skipper, that not a single drop found its way into the stern cockpit. It wasn't long before Jacquot was pleased that he had a sweater, even if it was DiCorsa's. The night air was still warm, but the buffeting breeze had a rising bite to it now, out on the open sea. He looked back, over the foaming trail they'd left behind them, searching for the lights of DiCorsa's house, now impossible to make out against the distant line of coastal lights on New Providence.

They sped along at a steady rate for another twenty minutes, the line between sea and sky marked out by distant pinpricks of gold and yellow, separated by vast expanses of star-studded black. By Jacquot's reckoning they were heading north, cruising at about twenty knots, but there was no way of knowing for sure. It just felt like that. And then, after a while, the wind seemed to drop, the swell settled and the going became smoother. But rather than increase his speed in calmer water the skipper brought it down, the bows levelling off, the heavy roar of the engine dropping to a chortling grumble. The man in black who'd been perched beside the skipper now came out of the wheelhouse and swung himself up onto the bow. Through the wheelhouse windscreen Jacquot watched him lean over the for'ard rail and look down, pointing first with his left arm and then his right. And after following the man's directions the skipper cut the engine, and in the sudden silence came the frantic rattle of an anchor chain. Slowly but surely the Mochi swung round into the breeze and settled in the water.

It was clear that the man in black, the skipper and DiCorsa knew exactly where they were and what they were doing. A practised routine. But Jacquot did not, and he began to feel uneasy. They were so far away from anything, so isolated, that they seemed beyond any formality, any rules. You could do what you wanted out here, and there was no one to call on for help. If he hadn't had a job to do for DiCorsa, if the driver of the Lexus hadn't said he'd be there later to drive him back to the Stuyvesant house, Jacquot knew that his sense of unease would have been far more urgent.

Once the Mochi had settled, DiCorsa went to the wheelhouse and opened a cupboard, found a bottle and two glasses and brought them back to the couches.

"Something to keep off the chill," he said, pouring out a splash of brandy and handing the glass to Jacquot. He poured one for himself then sat back, the glass held in his lap, his arm spread over the back of the seat. "You see that glow over there?" he said, nodding astern. "That's Andros. And those tiny lights off to starboard are Abaco. And where we are, right here, is the very edge of the Grand Lucayan banks. What depth, Stephen?" he called out to the skipper.

"'Bout fifteen metres, boss," the skipper called back.

"Exactly what depth?"

This time Stephen checked the depth sounder on his console.

"Seventeen point three metres."

DiCorsa nodded. "That's what it is here, but just a bit aways the sea bed drops clean away. Maybe a thousand metres. Maybe more, who knows. But deep, whatever."

The man in black came back from the bows and swung down into the cockpit. He looked at DiCorsa, who nodded, waved his free hand as though to say, *get on with it.*

Dropping down on his knees, the man pulled up a pair of brass rings set into the teak decking and opened a hatch that Jacquot supposed provided access to the engine. Reaching down, he seemed to feel for something, and then, finding whatever he was looking for, he heaved back on his knees, the muscles in his shoulders hardening with the effort. And there, pulled out of the darkness of the hold like a rag doll, was a man, dressed in soiled boxer shorts and singlet, trussed like a joint of beef, hands bound behind his back, ankles tied, with a width of silvery duct tape slapped over his mouth. His hair was wispy and grey, his body slim, and his eyes wide and white with terror, wild eyes jerking between DiCorsa, Jacquot, and the man in black.

"Meet..." DiCorsa paused, frowned. "What's his name again, Brock?"

"Rodrigo Fuentes," said Brock, the man in black. They were the first words he had spoken. An American accent, but a voice pitched higher than his build suggested.

"That's right, Rodrigo. And Rodrigo, here, has been a bad boy, haven't you, Rodrigo?"

Rodrigo started to shake his head, mumbling something through the tape that covered his mouth.

DiCorsa turned to Jacquot. "You see, Rodrigo, here, is a runner. One of my boys. Head of a team that works the tracks at Calder and Hialeah over there on the mainland. Puts money with my bookies. Dirty in, clean out. A winner every time. Only Rodrigo, here, gets greedy. Starts skimming the take. A dollar here, a dollar there. Only it's much more than that, isn't it Rodrigo? Last six months he's taken close to twenty grand. Of my clients' money. And thinks I won't find out about it." DiCorsa shook his head. "A big, bad mistake."

What happened next, happened so swiftly that Jacquot seemed not to have time to move, to object, or do anything. With a simple nod from DiCorsa Brock dragged the bound man to the transom between them, and bent the top half of his body over the side. Holding him down with one hand, he drew a cut-throat razor from his trouser pocket, flicked it open, and with a swift passing stroke opened up the back of the man's neck. Nothing deep, nothing fatal, but enough to make the blood flow and stain the back of his singlet. With the next stroke he cut through the binding around the man's wrists, then caught him by the hips and sent him tumbling over the stern.

There was a splash, some gagging, and then a tearing sound as Rodrigo ripped the tape from his mouth. And he began to plead, the words spluttering in his throat as he spat out seawater, trying to keep himself afloat. As though he knew what was going to happen. Just as Jacquot knew what was going to happen. They were both about to learn at first hand what talking to the sharks was all about. So Jacquot would know the fate that awaited him if he ever got on the wrong side of the man, DiCorsa, who was even now tugging at his arm, pulling him from his seat.

"Come, come, my friend. This, you have to see."

There must have been a current running, nothing strong but enough to move Rodrigo astern, away from the Mochi. But it was too dark to see much, just the splash of water as Rodrigo tried to swim back to the boat, and his feeble, frightened cries.

"Switch on the lights, Stephen," said Di Corsa, turning to the skipper in the wheelhouse. "Let's have some lights for our guest. And music, *per favore*. Something Spanish for our friend, Rodrigo. He is Spanish, isn't he?"

The skipper nodded.

"Good. Good. He'll like this."

A moment later a line of lights set into the hull of the Mochi lit up the sea around them. And there was Rodrigo, slowly drifting away from them but still within the spill of underwater light, his squirming body a black mark against a sandy seabed maybe thirty feet below him.

And then came the music.

Low and hauntingly familiar.

Dum... di-dum-dum...

Dum... di-dum-dum...

And then a voice. Such a voice.

Piercing. Bold. A splinter of crystal. It made Jacquot shiver.

"Bizet's *Carmen*" whispered DiCorsa. "'*L'amour est un oiseau rebellé*'. Better known as '*Habanera*'. The National Opera of Paris. And Callas. *La Divina*. *L'ultima voce di soprano*. But we need it louder. Louder," he called out to the skipper.

The volume increased, and in that dark warm night the voice rang out over the sea. At any other time, even though he didn't much care for opera, Jacquot would have found the aria entrancing.

But not on this night.

Not here.

"There! There!" said DiCorsa, putting an arm around Jacquot's shoulders, and pointing his brandy glass at the water. "Do you see it? Do you see?"

At first Jacquot couldn't see anything, but then a long black shape darted out of the darkened water into the glimmering pool of blue-green light. As far as Jacquot could tell it was maybe ten metres below Rodrigo, cruising along the seabed, a couple of metres in length, circling now, scenting the blood that had spilled from the wound in Rodrigo's neck and laced the sea with its deadly lure. Round and around the shark went, rising higher and higher with each turn, drawing closer and closer, almost moving to the music, until, with a jerking sideswipe, the fish seemed to knock against the man's bound legs and shoot away.

Rodrigo felt the knock, tried to look down into the floodlit depths, and screamed. He knew what had brushed against him.

"There's more sharks round here than leaves on a tree," said DiCorsa, taking a sip of his brandy, and licking his pink lips. "And I like to think I've played some part in that. Of course, night is their favourite time. Feeding time, you understand." And then he pointed again, spilling some of the brandy over his fingers. "You see 'em? Now they're coming in. Hey, Rodrigo," he called out. "You got some friends come calling."

DiCorsa was right. Suddenly there were maybe a half-dozen slim grey shapes sliding over the seabed, long sinuous bodies curving and coiling around each other, rising slowly like the first shark, as they homed in on the spill of blood, just a thin pinkish stain seeping from the man's neck into the water.

And now Rodrigo could see them, too.

Paddling his bound legs like a mermaid shaking her tail, he looked down into the water, and started to scream. Long, gagging screams, seawater filling his mouth as he started to swim, arms lashing out at the water, trying hopelessly to put some distance between him and the monsters below, thrashing his way back to the Mochi.

Jacquot was numb. It was like watching a horror movie. Being in a horror movie. And nothing he could do. Perhaps if he closed his eyes and listened only to the music…

Beside him, he felt DiCorsa's arm tighten around his shoulders. "Look, look there. Here she comes," he whispered.

And without meaning to, without wanting to, Jacquot opened his eyes and looked down into the water. But the sharks, maybe a dozen now, were still some distance below Rodrigo, a carousel of sleek grey torpedoes circling round and round. What DiCorsa had seen was on the surface, maybe twenty feet beyond the struggling man and outside the spill of light, a high grey fin slicing through the water, a silvery wake sluicing from it, shimmering in the starlight like a phosphorescent trail as the shark headed in for the hapless, helpless Rodrigo.

In the moments before it struck, the fin dipped beneath the surface and a large black shape shot into the circle of light, hitting Rodrigo in the small of the back, sending him surging forwards, pushing him back to the boat, against the current, his flailing body propelled by the shark's hefty momentum and hungrily snapping jaws.

This time there was no scream from Rodrigo, just a mouth gaping in shock, lips drawn back over yellowing teeth, eyes wide with terror. And suddenly the pinkish stain in the water around him became a swirling scarlet cauldron, and from far below the other sharks rose up, striking the man one after another.

One crunching bite after another.

A snapping, thrashing melée that turned the sea into a bubbling, boiling jacuzzi of blood and limbs and guts.

And the music played on.

And Callas sang.

34

Jacquot was woken by a gentle knocking on his bedroom door. He turned, sat up, wiped his eyes with the side of his hand. For a moment he wasn't sure where he was, and then the door opened and Beth came in carrying a tray.

"I done let you sleep," she said, coming round the side of the bed, placing the tray beside him. A pot of coffee, fruit juice, pastries. "Long day yesterday. And you back late, I reckons. You want eggs, I can go cook 'em up for you?"

"That would be good," said Jacquot. "Give me ten minutes and I'll be there."

"Take your time. I'll start cookin' when I sees you." And with that, she left him to his coffee and juice and pastries.

Maybe it was the smell of freshly-perked coffee and pastries, but Jacquot realised he was very, very hungry. It didn't surprise him. His stomach was empty. The night before, after the horror of Rodrigo's savage dispatch, DiCorsa had bid him a curt goodnight, disappeared into his stateroom below deck, and the Mochi had sped back to Nassau. Halfway there, Jacquot had tipped his head over the side and thrown up every scrap and morsel of his *bucatini alla carbonara*, one thundering heave that had emptied the contents of his stomach into the Mochi's churning wake and coated his mouth with a stinging acid bile. When they reached Nassau, Brock hoisted him out of the cockpit and pointed the way to the concrete turning circle where a set of headlights blinked on. Ten minutes later he had stood under a shower and washed himself clean. Clean of salt and sweat and sick, but not clean of memories.

Jacquot was appalled by what he had seen. He had watched a man murdered – horribly. And he had seen the men who did it. Knew them. He was a witness to murder. And a police officer, too. Albeit retired. Sitting there in his bed, a few hours later, he could still hear the frantic splashing, the fearsome screams, and the familiar stirring soundtrack of *Carmen* blaring out over the ocean. Close enough to the spectacle to hear the grunting and snapping and tearing and crunching. For a moment he thought he was going to be sick again, but tipped back his coffee and took a couple of deep relieving breaths.

Ettore DiCorsa was a monster, he thought. A certifiable psychopath.

A charming host one minute, cooking him dinner, pouring him wine, chattering away about food and wine and opera, the next an excitable little boy tearing the wings off a fly. Only Rodrigo was no fly. Rodrigo Fuentes was a living breathing person, old enough to have a wife and children who would never see him again, would never know what had happened to him. Would never have a body to bury. Just as the authorities would never have a body to mount any kind of investigation. Just another missing person, like Patric Stuyvesant. Torn to pieces in a stretch of lonely ocean.

Rodrigo Fuentes... Jacquot would never forget the name.

And he would never hear Callas sing without hearing, too, that bloody, bubbling overture of screams and grunts and splashing.

He was thankful that Boni had not had to share the same fate. They had killed her, but she wouldn't have suffered. Not like her husband, not like Rodrigo, and not like however many others DiCorsa had dropped over the side of his boat into those shark-infested waters.

After he'd showered and dressed, Jacquot picked up the tray and took it to the kitchen. Beth was sitting at the table polishing silver photo frames. When she saw Jacquot she finished the frame she was working on, put down her cloth and got to her feet.

"You want them eggs? Scrambled? Fried? Boiled?" she asked.

Taking another deep breath – the thought of a fried egg! – Jacquot asked for scrambled, and sat at the table where Beth had been polishing. As she set about her preparations, he picked up one of the photos. A shot of Boni dressed in a light blue snow suit, goggles loose around her neck, leaning forward on ski poles, her hair caught in a matching blue headband. He put down the picture and picked up another This time Boni was in evening dress – a stunning emerald green, slashed in a deep V down the front, a small silver clutch in one hand, the other hand looped through the arm of a grey-haired man in white tuxedo.

Jacquot knew immediately that this was Patric. Exactly the kind of man that Boni would have been drawn to. Tall, slim, broad-shouldered, an easy smile crinkling his eyes and creasing his cheeks with two long lines, one hand sunk in his trouser pocket, the other raising a champagne flute to the photographer. The skin was lightly tanned and the greying hair long and gently curled, the kind of hair, Jacquot decided, that Patric would have spent a lot of time pushing back from his face. He sensed, too, that this was a man he'd have liked, a man he'd have got on with, a man whose company he'd have enjoyed. No wonder Boni had felt so lost without him. No wonder she had come to Îles des Frères asking for his help.

But how, he wondered now, had this same handsome, successful man been seduced away by the girl Ballard and DiCorsa wanted him to find, this Sylvie Martin whose photo was no more flattering nor suggestive than any other passport-style head-and-shoulders shot from a personnel file. She was young and she was pretty, certainly, and there was something in the loose span and easy tilt of her shoulders that suggested a slim and lissome body beneath. But how many other young women would Patric have met like that. Hundreds? Thousands? So what magic spell had this young woman cast to lure him away from Boni? What enticing secret had Patric found behind that single arched eyebrow? Whatever it was, it had worked.

"Now don't you done get no finger marks on them frames," said Beth, whisking up the eggs. "I just done finished polishin' 'em all." She leaned over and looked at the photo he was holding. "Good lookin' fella, ain't he? And a good man, too. They made a great couple."

"You work for them long?"

"I came wid de house, would youse believe? Like a piece o' furniture," she said. "Housekeeper for the Musgraves, who lived here before Mr Patric and Mrs B. Dey asked me to stay on, so I did. And glad of it," she added, tipping the eggs into a skillet. "Maybe stay on in the job for the next owners, iffen they wants me, that is?"

"What about Patric?"

Beth frowned, looked a little flustered. "Well, he been gone a long while now. Gotta guess he ain't comin' back no time soon. Wherever he is. And with Mrs B. dead and gone, ain't no way he gonna stay in this big ole place when he ever does come home. Too many memories, fo' sure."

"Boni told me there'd been problems." Jacquot left it vague.

"Problems?" said Beth, coming to the table, laying down a plate and a fork. Back at the range she turned off the heat, shuffled the eggs one last time, then came and served them.

"Between her and Patric," said Jacquot. He picked up the fork, scooped up some egg and felt its hot creamy goldness fill his mouth. Delicious. Beth certainly knew how to scramble eggs.

"Ain't my place to go spec'latin'," she said, reaching for her cloth and screwing the top on her can of polish. "But men is men, and on an island like this, there's lots of available attractions. And Mr Patric weren't no exception, I'm guessin'."

"Anyone in particular?"

"If dere was, he was cool and careful about it. Just like he shoulda been," said Beth, putting away the cloth and polish in a cupboard beneath the sink. "So what's your plans, sah, you don't mind me askin'? It bein' a Sunday and all. You needs me today?" It was clear that Beth had had enough of speculation; there were more pressing matters on her mind.

"I suppose I need to go through Boni's things. Start packing them up. Mr Ballard said you could show me round..."

"Ain't no need for any showin'. Just help yourself. Go wheres you please."

"And you?"

"Church down at Holy Spirit, then lunch wid my grandnieces. It bein' Sunday an' all. Iffen that's okay wid you? There's food in the fridge if you's hungry..."

"These eggs'll keep me going. And maybe I'll head over to The Edgewater for dinner. Mr Ballard said I could use Boni's car."

"They say it's a good spread at The Edgewater. Miss Boni done loved going there. Just a couple of miles up the road, up towards Old Fort. It's signed so you can't miss it. Cars in the garage. Keys in the box over there by the door. Help yourself. There's a remote, too. Opens the garage doors and front gate." Beth took his empty plate and stacked it in the dishwasher. "So, if you's okay, I'll be back in the morning?"

"I'll be fine, Beth. Thank you. Have fun."

35

The first thing Jacquot did, when Beth had gone, was call the girls. He dialled the number, listened for the connection, and heard the phone on Trinité start to ring. And ring, and ring. He saw the salon on Île des Frères, the bare wood floors and rugs, the louvred walls, the driftwood mirror, the phone on the table by the kitchen door – all so far away, yet suddenly all so close. In his mind's eye he saw the girls hearing it, hurrying to pick it up, squabbling to be the first to reach it. But his call went unanswered. He immediately worried. They should be there. Finishing their breakfast, getting ready for the beach. And then he remembered it was Sunday. Glanced at his watch. Mama Loubertin would have taken them to Sunday school, the pair of them in their Sunday best. Polished shoes and pretty dresses (which Matti hated, and Béa loved), hair combed and brushed, tied in swinging ponytails (Matti's preference) or braided pigtails (Béa's). He breathed again. He would try later.

But as he put down the receiver, Jacquot felt again not just the distance between them, the thousand or so miles that separated them, but the fact that this was the first time they had ever been apart. Truly apart. Even when he was building the house on Trinité, and they had been with Madame Chanson or Mama Loubertin, he had seen them every morning, every evening, changed their nappies, bathed them, fed them their bottles, sung to them in their cots. The softness, the smell of them, their tiny warm bodies pressing against his. But all that was a long way away now. Just as they were.

With a great effort of will, Jacquot put the girls out of mind and set about what he had to do. And what he had to do was find the girl, Sylvie Martin, and the money that Patric had taken. He might not know what he was looking for, and felt no real confidence that his efforts would be rewarded, but it was clear that Patric's home was as good a place as any to start the search, even if Ballard had probably turned the place over after Boni left for Martinique.

There may have been no body, no blood, no weapon, nothing remarkable here beyond the day-to-day lives of two people, but Jacquot did what he did in the old days, back in Marseilles, or in the Lubéron, whenever he visited a crime scene. He left the kitchen and went into the hallway, stopping a few steps from the front door, as though he'd just arrived, and stood still, listening to the house around him, taking it all in.

Kicking off his espadrilles he walked slowly through the ground floor rooms – the main salon with the ocean glittering beyond the glass wall, a study, a TV snug, a dining room, a cloakroom. Looking, but not touching. Not yet. Next, he climbed the marble stairs to the first-floor landing, running his hand along the banister just as Patric and Boni would have done a thousand times. When he reached the landing, he paused again. There were two doors to left and right. He went to the right-hand door first, tried the handle, opened it.

The room was large, more suite than bedroom. Sitting room, dressing room, bedroom, bathroom, with a sliding glass panel that opened onto a wood-decked terrace. A glorious view. A deep blue sea, scattered sails, a distant line of white cloud along the horizon. But nothing more than that. Just a guest suite, he was certain. Like a room in a display home. Something cold and soulless and empty about it. Waiting for guests, friends staying over. Nothing personal here. No toiletries in the bathroom beyond a selection of sealed shampoos and conditioners, unopened boxes of cotton buds and wrapped soaps. But no worn toothbrushes, no razors, no hairbrushes. He thought of the chaos back in the house at Trinité. A different world.

The second bedroom, across the landing, was different. He knew it the moment he opened the door. He could smell her immediately. Boni. Three weeks or more since she had been here, but her scent was everywhere. *Coco.* Soft and warm and seductive, as though somehow kept alive by the heat.

Like its companion across the landing Patric and Boni's suite shared the same layout: a sitting room, bedroom, dressing room and bathroom. But the bookshelves in the sitting room were filled, the coffee table was spread with magazines, and a collection of black-framed photos covered one wall. Colour, and black-and-white. Boni and Patric here, there, and everywhere: at the beach, on a sailboat, skiing, game-fishing, poolside at parties, just the two of them. Through an open Moorish archway was a super-king bed, its cover a blue native weave the colour of the sea shallows, banked with pillows, cushions, squares, and set against a panel of white coral stone. Passing behind the stone panel, Jacquot found the same bathroom he'd found in the other room, with a free-standing tub in the centre of the floor fed by gleaming copper pipes, a walk-in shower, a long marble vanity, dark marble tiles, and shuttered windows overlooking the driveway. But in this bathroom there were personal effects, personal toiletries; Boni's on one side of the vanity, Patric's on the other, all neatly placed, ranged according to size, towelling gowns on hooks behind the door, soaps and shampoos in the shower. Just as they'd left it. As though they'd be back any moment.

And as Jacquot wandered around the house, he saw them – Boni and Patric. Watched their lives unfold around him. The pair of them in the kitchen having breakfast, lounging in the salon, hosting a dinner in the dining room, drinks on the terrace, in bed, dressing for work, for the beach. Talking, laughing, reading, watching TV, making love. Everything about their lives in this house, until he could almost hear them, as well as see them. Patric down in the hallway calling up to Boni, in the bedroom; Boni and Beth discussing menus in the kitchen; loving whispers, and raised voices, too; the slam of a door, perhaps; music, a TV programme.

Finally, back where he'd started in the front hallway, Jacquot began his search in earnest. Starting in the kitchen and adjoining utility room he went through every drawer and cupboard, reaching up, bending down, peering into shelves of saucepans and skillets, china, cutlery, and glassware. In the cloakroom, he went through the pockets of every jacket and coat and windcheater that hung there. In the salon he tipped out the cushions in the armchairs and sofas, drew furniture away from walls to see if anything had been taped there out of sight, knowing that Beth would have done this a hundred times, cleaned anything away, just as she would have done in the kitchen, but still… He went to the bookcase, slid out books, half a dozen at a time, flipped them open, swiping his hand across each emptied shelf, looking for anything that either Boni or Patric might have hidden away for safekeeping. In the dining room he searched an oak buffet, shuffling his fingers, carefully, through cutlery drawers, squatting down to look into the backs of its cupboards, under the dining room table, the chairs, and in the TV snug worked his way through racks of videotapes, flipping open each case, and checking the emptied shelves. He still didn't know what he was looking for, didn't know what he expected to find, but he made sure his search was thorough. All the obvious places, and the less obvious.

Jacquot knew that Patric's study would take the longest to search so he left it, heading back upstairs to go through their bedroom: the magazines on the coffee table, the books on the shelves, tipping every one of the framed photos to see if anything had been taped to their backs; every drawer of Boni's dressing table, the dressing room – Patric's clothes on one side, hers on the other – dipping his hand into every drawer, every pocket; and in the bathroom opening the mirrored cupboards above the vanity – tooth picks, sleeping pills, analgesics, creams for bites and burns. Nothing out of the ordinary. Nothing significant. Nothing at all. And only Patric's razor.

Back downstairs again he went to Patric's study, reached through sliding doors off the salon. A dark panelled room with French windows looking out onto a small paved courtyard at the side of the house. Furnished with a weighty mahogany director's desk, Italian executive chair, a sofa and coffee table, and a glass-fronted cabinet with trophies for tennis and sailing. Behind the desk the wall was lined with bookshelves and photos: faded black-and-white photos of a young couple, arm in arm, leaning against an old Citroën DS; on the steps of a church in bridal gown and tails, waving off a hail of confetti; at a restaurant table, on horseback, on skis, and with a young child Patric? – swinging between them; colour photos of an older Patric in scuba gear on a wood deck with a thatched hut in the background; at a café table in Greece playing backgammon with a bearded local; in ski kit on a mountain slope; with Boni. These photos couldn't be tipped out like the others; they'd been screwed to the wall.

Jacquot started with the bookshelves, doing what he'd done in the salon, snug and bedroom. Not novels this time, but box files disguised with book spines: company accounts, tax records, business expenses, ownership documents, lease agreements. When he'd taken them all down, checked the contents, swept each shelf and put them back, he turned to the desk and sat in the black leather chair, swinging from side to side, taking it all in. Seeing what Patric would have seen on its scarlet hide-bound surface. An Apple iMac monitor and keyboard, a telephone, a bundle of sharpened pencils and roller pens in a china mug with "Boss" written on its side, a notepad with no notes or indentations, a leather-framed picture of Boni curled up on a sofa. Everything tidy, practically placed, polished. Put in order by Beth.

Leaning forward, Jacquot found the power switch on the iMac and pressed. An orchestral clash, and a moment later the screen blinked on.

A picture of a sailboat crashing through waves, sails full, spray flying. Race day. Other colourfully spinnaker-ed yachts behind. But not a single folder showing on the screen. He went to the hard disc icon, and clicked on it. Apart from the usual raft of applications, there was nothing there to find. No documents. No photos. Nothing personal. Patric's Apple had been wiped clean. Jacquot switched it off, pushed back his chair and looked down. Four drawers each side, small at the top for bits and pieces, the lowest deep enough for bulkier stuff. He went through each of them carefully, the top two on each side equipped with compartmental separators for all the usual things: pens, rubber bands, a stapler, ruler, and a boxed supply of business cards – Patric Stuyvesant, The Baize Inc., with an office address and phone numbers in Nassau. A tidy man, thought Jacquot. Everything just so. The larger drawers contained a Dictaphone (no tape), a Hewlett Packard printer and copier with no papers left by accident under the lid, reams of paper, personal stationery, but nothing out of the ordinary. In the two bottom drawers, he found a cigar humidor in one (empty), and a pile of correspondence in the other.

Letters, postcards.

He slipped off the rubber bands that held them, shuffled through them. The envelopes were addressed to Patric Stuyvesant, had French stamps, with the sender's address on the back flap. Patric's parents. M. *et* Mme. Stuyvesant, Clos des Roses, Lourmarin.

He slid out a couple of the letters, unfolded them. Handwritten, two distinct hands – Patric's mother and father. Maman and Papa. The father's letters were short and sweet – the vineyard, business, sport, local politics. The mother's were longer, breezier – news from home, family and friends, births, deaths, marriages, gossip, with motherly pleas to take care, to look after himself, to eat properly.

Putting aside the letters, he went through the postcards. Views of the Italian Riviera – San Remo, Amalfi; views of Berlin and Munich; London and Stockholm. It was clear that Patric's parents enjoyed their holidays; clear, too, that they missed their son. Wish you were here, in some form or other, had been written on every card. Holiday messages from M and P – Maman and Papa, Jacquot guessed. He put them back, closed the drawer. Everything as expected. But nothing to work on.

Sitting back in the chair, he looked at his watch. Nearly two hours searching the house, and he'd found nothing. Not a purse, or pocket-book, or wallet. No diaries, no chequebooks, not even a stack of mail to look through: no bank and credit card statements, no utilty bills, flyers, letters, invitations… Nothing personal. The place had been cleaned out. Nothing.

He leaned forward, reached for the phone, and called Trinité.

This time the girls were home.

36

That afternoon, after a smoked ham and mayo sandwich in the kitchen, Jacquot changed into swimming shorts, crossed the lawn, followed the path through the sea grape and casuarina, and stepped out onto the beach. The sand was hot and he hurried across it, tossing aside his towel and wading into the water, convincing himself that no shark would come this close to the shore, and that if it did he would see its dark shape or slicing fin in time to get back to the beach. The day before he had swum out some distance, but this afternoon he contented himself with waist-high water, splashing it over his shoulders, dunking himself down into its aquamarine shallows, playing his hands through its sparkling clarity. And as he did all this he wondered about Rodrigo Fuentes, something he hadn't thought about before. Just how long had the poor man been down in that space below the cockpit deck? Had he been there when the boat collected Jacquot from Nassau? Or had he been bundled aboard while he and DiCorsa shared their *bucatini alla carbonara*? However long it had been, it must have been hellish down there – the cramped quarters, the darkness, the heat and deafening roar of the engine, and the certain knowledge that the end was closing fast. But had Fuentes known the particular fate that awaited him? Had he known about the sharks? Jacquot hoped not.

Back on the beach he spread his towel, lit a cigarette and, forming the sand into a pillow, lay back, gazing up at the deep blue sky, enjoying the salty taste of the tobacco in his mouth, and the drying tightening heat of the sun on his body. Where next, he wondered, now that he had been through the house and found nothing? What should his next move be? Maybe dinner at The Edgewater Club would provide some leads? He hoped so. He finished the cigarette and buried it in the sand, closed his eyes, and listened to the shuffling rise and fall of the sea, felt a cool breeze slide over him. He opened his eyes. A cloud passing overhead. He closed his eyes again…

And then, suddenly, from nowhere, it came to him.

And he leaped to his feet, snatched up his towel and cigarettes, and hurried back to the house.

The letters.

The postcards.

37

He couldn't believe he'd been so stupid. So unobservant. How could he have missed it, he wondered, looking at the letters and postcards he'd spread out on Patric's desk? How could it not have registered? Talk about being out of the loop. Back in Marseilles and the Lubéron it would have been the first thing he noticed. But that was then, and this was now.

The addresses.

Four different addresses.

Patric Stuyvesant, Pirate Cay Dive Safaris, POBox 17, George Town, Great Exuma. The earliest letters that his parents had written to their son had this address on the flimsy blue airmails. Dating back to 1978 when Patric had first arrived in the Bahamas.

Patric Stuyvesant, Apt 16, The Idlings, Yamacraw Drive, Nassau East. According to the dated letters from his parents, Patric had lived here from 1985 to 1987.

Patric Stuyvesant, 16 Coral Close, Nassau. From 1987 to 1993.

And from 1993, the house on Lyford Cay, where Patric had lived with Boni after she had walked out on him in Marseilles. The only difference between these later letters and the earlier ones was the handwriting. The mother's only. Nothing from his father. Her last letter was dated 2002, a spidery hand, written from a hospice in Pertuis. An accompanying note from a senior nurse at the home – typewritten – informed Patric that his mother was frail, but managing, and that she was looking forward to seeing him. Jacquot wondered if he'd managed to get home before his mother died.

Whether he did, or did not, was of no concern to Jacquot. What interested him, what delighted him, was that he had suddenly found a trail to follow. Somewhere to start. A great deal more than he'd had when he went down to the beach for his swim. He reached for some paper, a pen, and wrote down the addresses. The only question was, had Ballard, or one of his men, found these letters, realised their significance, and followed up on them? There had certainly been no mention of it on the flight from Fort-de-France. If he had missed it, maybe Ballard had too?

Whether he had or not, Jacquot decided to keep it to himself, and not say anything.

38

Still buzzing with his discovery, Jacquot went to his room and showered. When he'd towelled dry he realised he didn't have anything to wear. Or rather, nothing that was likely to pass muster at The Edgewater. Two pairs of cream chinos and a pair of black jeans, all a little creased from the journey, a selection of t-shirts, two blue Levi shirts with pearl stud buttons, espadrilles and deck shoes. They were fine on Îles des Frères but they probably wouldn't work in Nassau's most prestigious private cub. There was only one alternative. He went upstairs to Boni and Patric's bedroom and went through Patric's wardrobe. He found everything he needed.

The next surprise was the garage, through the kitchen and utility room. It was the one room he'd forgotten to search – which made him shake his head – but he could see immediately that there was little there of any interest. Just bare breeze-block walls, a smooth concrete floor, some gardening equipment, a pair of wind-surf boards on a rack, two freezer chests (power off and empty), and two cars. A low-slung black Mercedes SLK roadster – Boni's for sure – and Patric's bulkier and more practical Ford Explorer 4x4. Both appeared to be brand new and were a far cry from his own dusty old Citroën on des Frères. Going back into the kitchen Jacquot found the keys and remote, and returned to the garage.

Bleeping the lock on the Ford Jacquot went through it carefully, as he should have done earlier. Door pockets, sun visors, glove compartment, running his fingers between the seats and seat backs, opening the hatchback and checking through it. Neat and tidy, like the man's study. All he came up with were a pair of Ray-Ban sunglasses, the car's manual and service log (the last garage inspection dated the end of March), a fold-up map of New Providence, a scatter of coins in the transmission pocket, and a tangle of rubber bands in the unused ashtray.

After searching the Ford, Jacquot turned to the Mercedes. Inside, just as he'd expected, was the scent of warm leather and *Coco*. And a mess of hand wipes, tissues, mints, an old lipstick, a hairbrush, emery board and breath freshener. He checked the rear bucket seats and the trunk but found nothing of interest, then stood between the two cars and wondered which one to take. He'd never driven either model, but he plumped for Boni's, the Mercedes, and dropped down into the driver's seat. With another bleep from the remote, the garage doors slid open and he reversed out into the drive, tyres screeching on the polished concrete and then crunching over the broken shells.

How Boni must have loved this car, he thought, turning out onto the road and heading back towards the airport, running the wheel through his hands, just as she would have done. A slinky, sexy machine and, when he touched the accelerator, a powerful one too, its three-litre engine growling like a lion, deep and throaty, the car surging forward.

He reached for the CD player, turned it on, pressed 'Play'.

And smiled.

Eric Clapton and B.B. King.

Good old Boni.

39

As Beth had said, The Edgewater Club wasn't difficult to find. Remembering to drive on the left, Jacquot passed the first sign about a mile from the house, and turned into its gated driveway another half-mile further on, its grand entrance pillared in cream coral stone and set with wrought iron gates. It was quite a spread. Towering royal palms and fan-shaped palmettos lined its drive, its tutored emerald lawns were edged with white picket fencing, and its spreading grounds dotted with riotous explosions of pink bougainvillea, white plumeria and scarlet hibiscus. Discreetly-placed arrow signs pointed out tennis courts, guest cottages, swimming pool, and marina, and, up ahead, set on a rise above a long curve of private beach, stood a grand old plantation house painted a soft sunset pink with white corner stones, window frames, shutters and gingerbread verandah. Quite a spread indeed.

When he pulled up at the entrance a valet in crisp whites leaped forward, opened the door and gave Jacquot a numbered ticket. By the time he reached the first scarlet-runnered step leading up to the verandah the Mercedes had been driven away, and when he walked into the main hall, open to sea and driveway, he was glad he'd rifled through Patric's wardrobe rather than rely on his own creased chinos and a Levi shirt. Strolling through the hall were tanned tennis players with rackets swinging, polo-shirted yachties in deck shoes and necklaced sunglasses, even the more elderly and less sporty all elegantly turned out – the men craggy and important and wealthy, the women lean, attractive and perfectly coiffed.

"Good afternoon, sir," said a man at the reception desk, not so much a desk as a beautifully ornate Directoire console that made Madame Chanson's captain's table look shabby and rough. Jacquot had not approached this desk, had indeed been walking some twenty feet away from it, but the man behind it had clearly spotted him and not recognised him. He was as well dressed as the club members, in pressed shorts, long white socks and a cream polo shirt emblazoned with the same entwined 'E' and 'C' as the valet.

Jacquot changed direction and headed over to the desk.

The man smiled. "Are you a guest, sir? Can I find someone for you?" The message was clear: If you're not a member, you go no further than this point. Until you are claimed, you stay right here.

"My name is Daniel–" He was about to say 'Jacquot', but caught himself. "...Daniel Milhaud. I understand a temporary membership has been arranged for me by John Ballard."

"Of course, Mr Milhaud. Welcome to The Edgewater. Mr Ballard is not here at present, but please make yourself at home. Anything you need, just call one of our boys."

"I was thinking a drink might be useful."

"Our rum punches are the pride of the island, sir. And you have the choice of the Churchill Bar over there," he said, pointing across the hall at a darkly panelled room, "or the Roosevelt down by the pool, or if you'd prefer a stroll, the marina's Horatio Bar is always popular at this time of day."

"Maybe I'll start in the Churchill, and work my way through," said Jacquot with a smile.

"And why not, sir? A capital idea. And as I said, if there's anything you need..."

With a nod and a smile of thanks Jacquot crossed the hall and stepped into the panelled confines of the Churchill Bar. Outside the sky might have been blue and the sun still high, but here in air-conditioned gloom there was no sense of the day outside, no window to let it in. And everywhere photos of the great English statesman – not the familiar, formal portraits with bowler hat and V sign, but colour and black-and-white photos taken of Churchill in more relaxed mode, and clearly at The Edgewater: in an open-necked white shirt by a tennis net; at a poolside table with a fat cigar; in a linen jacket and spotted bow tie with assorted friends on the club's front steps; in a panama hat sitting at an easel with paintbrush in hand. And as Jacquot perched on a stool his eye was drawn to a withered brown stub of an Aroma de Cuba cigar in a glass case behind the bar.

"Good evenin', sah. And what can I get for you?" asked an elderly bar steward, appearing from nowhere.

"I'm told the rum punches are good."

"The best, sir. Large or small?"

"Let me start with the small, and see how I get on."

"A wise precaution, sah," the steward replied, and turned away to set about his mixing.

Jacquot looked around; he was not alone. Three men were closeted at a corner table, and two more sauntered in, to sit a few stools along from Jacquot. Both nodded in his direction, and he returned the silent greeting.

"One small punch, sah," said the steward, putting down the tumbler and a bowl of smoked cashews. "Shall I put it on a tab?"

"Milhaud," said Jacquot. And then, "No, make it Ballard."

"Of course, sah."

The punch was delicious, but very strong. He'd been right to start with the small. As he went to put down the glass he noticed the coaster. Something was written on it. He turned it so he could read it: "*When you're going through hell, keep going...*" Beneath the quotation, was the name Winston Churchill. He found his cigarettes, tapped one out, and lit it. The steward, who'd finished serving the two new arrivals, returned with a silver ashtray.

Jacquot thanked him, and then asked, just a general enquiry, whether Mademoiselle Martin was in the club?

The steward frowned.

"She's a member of staff. The last time I was here, she gave me the address of a tailor in Marseilles, where I live, and I just wanted to thank her for the recommendation."

The steward nodded. "I remember her now, but I'm sorry to say she doesn't work here now. She left a few months ago. Some time in the summer."

"Do you happen to know where she went?"

The steward gave it some thought and then shook his head sadly, not simply because he didn't know, Jacquot suspected, but because he wasn't able to be of help to a member – albeit a temporary member – of the club.

"Is there anyone who could let her know I was here, to thank her from me?"

"You could try the club secretary, sah. He's not here right now, but he'll be in tomorrow."

"Thanks," said Jacquot. "I'll be sure to ask for him. In the meantime…" He held up his glass.

"Another small? Right away, sah."

By the time Jacquot's order had been served (with another coaster and the words, "*I am an optimist. It does not seem much use being anything else...*"), the Churchill Bar had started to fill. The three men at the corner table had been joined by their wives, the two men who'd followed him in had become part of a larger group, and there were now three stewards behind the bar mixing drinks for the members. As far as Jacquot could see he was the only one drinking alone.

It didn't last long.

40

Jacquot felt a hand fall across his shoulder.

"Daniel, how nice to see you."

It was Ballard. He was dressed in tennis whites. His bare arms and legs smooth and tanned. He caught the eye of the steward. "The usual, Joe," he called out. "And another for my friend." There was no stool free so he leant in against the bar, and turned to look at Jacquot. "So, how was your dinner?" he asked. A smile hovered across his lips, and the gap in his teeth seemed to wink.

"I'm sure there's no need to tell you," said Jacquot. "The food was good, the company less so. As for the entertainment..." He shook his head. No words.

Ballard shrugged. "Mr DiCorsa knows how to show his guests a good time. So, how is everything going?"

"Slowly," said Jacquot. "I'm finding my feet."

"Take my advice, my friend, find them quickly."

Their drinks arrived. Ballard reached for his, a whiskey and water. Jacquot left his on the bar.

"So," Jacquot began, keeping his voice low. "Why don't we start with the money Patric took. What are we talking about? Cash, bearer bonds, portable assets?"

"Cash. At least, to begin with. From the four clubs, during counting or safe-keeping, or during transfer to the bank. After that..." Ballard shrugged. "I'd say redirected to another account, and then moved on. Possibly somewhere offshore, somewhere that doesn't ask too many questions, somewhere the money can be easily accessed. That's how I would do it."

"What kind of money are we talking about? The takings, I mean. Not the money skimmed."

"All four clubs are profitable, of course. But ours is a business based on chance, the fall of a card, the spin of a wheel. I mean, we're not retailers or wholesalers here, selling a product and marking up. Most times, of course, the house wins – on a good week a million plus for all four clubs – but sometimes we can take a hit. One of the clubs has a bad run. It's the name of the game."

"So helping yourself to ten million is going to take some time?"

"Not when there's money to clean," said Ballard. "Then the take is larger. More cash to skim. I assume that Mr DiCorsa explained the procedure?"

"Yes, he did," said Jacquot. "So who does the counting?"

"Accounts and security boys. End of business at each of the clubs. Often double-counted, too, by Patric or me, just to make sure."

"How long does the money stay on the premises?"

"Couple of days, maybe."

"And how does the money reach the bank?"

"By car. Driver and armed guard. But nothing to attract attention. No security vans, just a company vehicle. Twice a week. Money in the trunk."

"Four deliveries, from the four clubs, or just the one?"

"Just the one. Starting from Baize Central and doing the rounds."

"How long does it take?"

"Depending on traffic, on the selected route, maybe two hours start to finish."

"Selected route?"

"A different route every time. Different times of day, too."

Jacquot thought about this. As far as he could see, the only place to make the skim was at one or other of the clubs, before the money was moved. Anywhere else would mean other people involved.

"So tell me about Patric's car," Jacquot continued, changing tack. "Boni told me the last time she saw Patric was when he drove off that last morning."

Ballard sighed, "So she says."

Jacquot ignored the inference. "So if he drove off and she didn't see him again, how come his car's back in the garage?"

"Because I drove it there," Ballard replied. He took a sip of his whiskey, licked his teeth.

"And when was that?"

"Two days later. When I realised the accounts were short and he'd gone missing."

"He left the car at the office?"

"No, here. At The Edgewater."

"Picking up Sylvie Martin?"

"That's our guess. The club has staff accommodation. She checked out the same day Patric went missing."

"But he left his car here?"

Ballard nodded, took up his glass.

"So he took a taxi?"

"Martin had a car. A Honda. It wasn't in the employee's car park."

"What about Patric's passport? I couldn't find one at the house."

"He took it with him."

"But didn't use it?"

Ballard shook his head. "The first thing we did. No record of either Patric or the girl leaving the island. Checked Immigration, and airlines, and we have contacts at both. Reliable contacts. This is the Bahamas, remember?"

Why was he not surprised to hear that Ballard, and DiCorsa, had contacts like that? They probably 'owned' the island. Instead, he said, "There are always boats, small charter aircraft."

Ballard shrugged. "Which they didn't use."

"You know that for sure?"

"Like I said, we checked. The airport, marinas."

"Planes, maybe, but there'll be a lot of boats. Yachts, speedboats, cruisers. What is it? Two hundred miles to the American mainland? Even less to one of the other islands. It wouldn't have taken long, and Patric surely had friends with boats? A boat of his own?"

Ballard shook his head. "Take my word for it, she's on the island somewhere, we're sure of it, even if the money isn't."

"It's a small place to go missing. And stay missing."

"Which is fortunate for you. But not so fortunate for Patric."

"So where and when did you find him?"

Ballard grunted dismissively, as though he would have made a far better job at disappearing. "Maybe a week later. End of July. Down around Yamacraw on the lower east side."

"Yamacraw?" asked Jacquot, wondering, with an icy shiver, if they'd traced Patric there through the letters in his desk drawer.

"Not his usual beat, that's for sure. But he'd been taking out money from various ATMs down there on one of his debit cards. Brock and a couple of his colleagues started watching the outlets, and one night there he was. Simple as that."

Jacquot breathed a sigh of relief. "And the girl?"

"No sign of her. And no sign since." Ballard took a drink and looked hard at Jacquot. "I'm glad to see you're taking this seriously, Daniel. Seems last night's after-supper show served to focus your attention."

Jacquot let the comment pass, but felt again that worm of loathing twist inside him. What he wouldn't give... Instead, he picked up his drink, and swallowed it down. "I want to visit one of the clubs," he said, "Take a look around. Later tonight would be good."

"Which one?"

"The closest."

Ballard nodded, took a card from his wallet and laid it on the bar. Baize Two, a phone number and address. "I'll let them know you're coming." He smiled. "Anything else?"

"I'll also need two sets of business cards. Both in my assumed name. One should be 'Private Investigator', and the other 'Lawyer'. With Boni's address and home telephone as the contact point."

Ballard nodded, put down his drink. "I can do that. You'll have them by lunchtime tomorrow. So, you have plans?" He pulled out the coaster beneath his glass, read the words. Jacquot could read them, too: "*Without victory, there is no survival...*"

"You want me to tell you?"

"Not if you don't want to. Just make sure you keep me posted. Every day. Think of it as... parole conditions." Ballard smiled.

"There's another thing," said Jacquot. "I want a list of everyone you've spoken to about locating Sylvie Martin. If I'm going where you've gone, I need to know."

"That can also be done. You'll have the list with the business cards. Anything else?"

"I don't want anyone following me. Brock, or whoever..."

"There is no one following you. Because there's no need to have you followed."

Jacquot frowned.

Ballard called over the steward, and asked that everything be put on his tab. "Are you staying for dinner, Daniel? It's very good at The Edgewater."

"I don't have much of an appetite," he replied. "But why is there no need to have me followed?"

Ballard gave him a look. "You still don't seem to understand, do you? This is not a game we're playing." He tipped back the last of his drink, and squeezed Jacquot's arm. "Good talking to you, Daniel. Oh, by the way, our friend, Mr Tarrant, said how pretty your daughters looked when they went to Sunday school this morning. I thought you'd like to know."

Jacquot's blood turned cold, and another icy shiver raced across his shoulders.

Tarrant was back on des Frères? It couldn't be.

"If anything…"

"If anything, what?" Ballard gave Jacquot a questioning look, laced with the thinnest gap-toothed smile. "As I have made perfectly clear to you, and as Mr DiCorsa made clear to you last night, this is a serious business. All you have to do is find the girl, and find the money. And quickly. Keeping an eye on your children while you are away is simply… Well, why don't you think of it as a courtesy on our part. And an encouragement, too, of course."

And with a friendly pat on Jacquot's shoulder, Ballard turned and left the bar.

41

Back in Boni's Mercedes, Jacquot drove through The Edgewater
gates and turned left, following the signs for Nassau Centre, and the
directions for Baize Two given to him by the valet who'd brought
him his car. A twenty-minute drive, the valet had told him, staying
on the coast road and taking the second right after the Paradise Island
causeway. He found the turning with little difficulty, drove three
blocks down from the wharf as instructed, and made another right
into High Strand Lane, a narrow road lined on either side with candy-
coloured townhouses. Greens and pinks and yellows, with equally
colourful shutters. As far as Jacquot could see this was a residential
street, with no bars, or shops, or restaurants, just a dozen plots either
side of the street with cars in driveways and TV aerials on the red-tiled
roofs. Unsurprisingly there was no sign for Baize Two, just the name
in slanting white paint on a green door. He passed it, but could find no
parking slot. He drove on, round the block, and came back in time to
see a white Buick pull out from the opposite kerb, leaving him all the
space he needed.

Crossing the road, Jacquot walked up the front steps of the house
and was reaching for the bell when the door was opened by an islander
just a few kilos lighter and a few centimetres shorter than Ballard's
man, Brock. He wore a black suit, white shirt, and black string tie,
and when he heard the name Milhaud he nodded his head and waved
Jacquot in, closing the door behind him.

"My name is Milo," he said, "Mr Ballard said to expect you, sir. If
you'll follow me."

Milo led Jacquot into the first room on the right of the entrance
hallway. It was a bar, but not like the bar he had just left at The
Edgewater. All the bottles and glasses and paraphernalia for mixing
drinks were ranged across the top of a grand piano occupying a
corner of the room between the front and side windows, both of them
shuttered, so that there was no view of the street or grounds outside.
And no way of looking in. Telling Jacquot to help himself to a drink,
and that the manager would be down in a moment, Milo left the room.

With three of Joe's small punches inside him, Jacquot poured
himself a glass of Badoit and tapped out a cigarette. There was no one
else in the room, so he had the choice of a pair of fatly cushioned sofas

either side of a coral stone hearth filled with stiff-stemmed gladioli, or any of a half-dozen equally comfortable armchairs. Instead, he walked around the room with his cigarette and glass of water, looking at the prints on the walls – a series of eighteenth-century horse-racing scenes – until a woman's voice broke the silence.

"Good evening, Mr Milhaud. It's a pleasure to have you here."

Jacquot turned. The woman standing in the doorway was an islander, with short tufted black hair and full red lips, her eyes slanted, dark, and delicately shaded in a light blue. She wore a business-like charcoal grey pantsuit, a widely collared white silk blouse and sharply pointed heels that peeped out from below the hems of her trousers. "My name is Louise Higgins. I'm the manager here at Baize Two. Mr Ballard called to say you might be dropping by. I understand you wanted to take a look around?" Her voice was soft and smoky with a lilting Bahamian burr

"I'd like that very much," said Jacquot, stepping forward and reaching out his hand. Hers was slim and bony, dry as paper, with long lacquered nails and heavily-lined pink palms. She looked like a high-ranking company executive, rather than the manager of a private gaming club.

"You're investigating Mr Patric's disappearance, I believe?"

"That's right. Trying to make sense of it all."

"You're French, aren't you? Mr Patric was French."

"From Marseilles, originally."

"Never been there," she said. "But I hear it's some city." She pointed to a pair of armchairs and the two of them sat down. "And now there's this dreadful news about his wife. Suicide. Such a tragedy. Poor Mrs Stuyvesant. Such a lovely lady."

"I never met her."

"Well, you missed something, I can tell you. A real classy lady. Just the sweetest, the kindest... And so elegant. So... beautiful."

Jacquot smiled, remembered the air stewardess he'd first seen on that long-ago flight.

"So, what can I tell you? How can I help?" Louise asked, adjusting the crease in her trousers and crossing her legs.

"Why don't we start with the last time you saw Patric."

"Back end of July. He'd been playing poker with some high rollers from Miami. Left here about four in the morning."

"He played?"

"Oh, yes. He was a superb gamesman. And poker was his game."

"How did he do that night?"

"Very well. As usual. Got out at the top end."

"Any chance that someone at the table didn't like his winning?"

Louise shook her head. "Three of the players were members, two of them guests. All known to the House."

"But they lost a lot of money."

"Nothing that would worry them. And having Patric at the table would have made up for it."

"People enjoyed playing with him? Losing to him?"

"Like I said, he's one of the great players. Right up there. You win a hand against Patric and it's something to talk about, believe me. But not many do."

"So what kind of man was he?"

"A been-around-the-block sort of guy. But debonair, charming, like the block he'd been going round was in a good part of town, if you know what I mean. Good with people, too. Real friendly. And a gambler, of course. A natural. For Patric everything was a throw of the dice, a turn of the card, one little raindrop reaching the windowsill before the other."

"So what do you think has happened to him? Nearly four months, and not a sign of him."

"You ask me, he keeping his head down a while. Something's got to him. Someone . . He just waiting till it's safe to come back out into the sunshine." Louise sighed, shook her head. "Sometimes it's like that in this business. I just keep hoping he'll come in through that door one night like he's never been away."

"He's gone missing before?"

"Now and then. A week sometimes, maybe more. Playing off the island maybe, tournaments, that kind of thing."

"So you don't think anything bad has happened to him? Something not nice…?"

"I don't know. I just don't know. But I surely hope not."

"Tell me, how long have you worked at Baize?"

"From the beginning. Back when Mr Patric started up. I was a croupier at Baize Central, his first place over on the east side. Guess you could say I worked my way up."

"So Baize didn't start here?"

Louise shook her head. "We started up in an old bond warehouse round Winton way. Rough area, rough times. But Patric knew what he wanted. Soon as he had the funds, he ante'ed up."

"It looks like a slick operation. Very classy."

"That's what Patric wanted. No slots, no razzle, nothing Vegas. Just gambling as a gentleman's sport, and the surroundings to back it up."

"And by the look of it, it's worked."

"Yes, indeed. It's worked." She looked around the room, and smiled proudly. "He done really well. Four clubs around the island. Baize Central, this one here, and two others."

"So what kind of money are we talking about? I mean, how does Baize work? Bets, the takings, that kind of thing?"

Louise straightened, stiffened a little. Ballard had already provided him with the figures, but Jacquot saw no reason not to double-check. She might not like it, but he knew she'd be expected to co-operate.

"You know anything about gambling houses?"

"Spin of the wheel, red and black, that's about it. And aces can be high or low." He wasn't being entirely truthful.

"Our kind of gambler," said Louise, with a smile. "Well, I'll try to keep it simple. Baize membership is a thousand Bahamian a year. That's par with the US dollar in case you didn't know. And we got maybe a thousand members here on the islands, and from the States. Bring a guest and it's two hundred each one every time. And members are responsible for their guests' losses if they can't cover. Drinks are free, of course, because we like our players liquored up when they hit the tables."

"What's the most popular game?"

"Depends on the punter. Some like cards, some like dice, others work the wheel. Blackjack, baccarat, craps, roulette... The usual. Some leave it to Lady Luck, others think they can beat the system."

"Can they?"

"Sometimes, sure. But let's just say the House has the edge."

"What about poker? How does that pay?"

"Poker, bridge, backgammon, the House takes a rake..."

"'Rake'?"

"Games where the House don't have its edge, when it's just player versus player, we take a cut on bets laid. A small percentage. Poker it's up to the final pot. Backgammon it's on the winner's take, bridge the same."

"And how high do the pots go?"

"You name it. Usually high. The higher the better. With poker it's about twenty big games a week in our clubs, average pot around twenty thousand."

Jacquot nodded, and in the brief silence that followed he felt a familiar sensation. Slowly, but surely, it was all coming back. Old habits, he thought. Five years out of the game, maybe, but thirty years with the *Judiciaire* were starting to stir, to make themselves felt. And just as he'd done so many times before in the interview rooms on Marseilles' rue de l'Évêché, he suddenly changed lanes.

"What about using clubs like this for money-laundering?"

Louise's eyes widened. "It happens, so I'm told. But not here. Not at a Baize club. Patric wouldn't have tolerated that."

"You're sure?"

"I'm sure."

"And what's the House take when it does happen?"

"Varies, I guess. But around twenty per cent on whatever goes through is what I heard. To the House."

Jacquot paused, considered this. "And what happens to the takings? Legitimate takings. I mean here, at Baize?"

"Safes as big as Fort Knox in the basement of each of our clubs," Louise replied, a little more comfortable now, back on familiar ground. "Counting done in-house. Takings banked twice a week with the Central Bank of the Bahamas. All above board. We don't make the big roll. Not like Vegas or Reno or Atlantic City. But it's still a good roll."

Jacquot nodded again, taking it in. It was time for another change of direction.

"So tell me, did you know that Patric was having an affair?"

Louise laughed. Jacquot hadn't expected that.

"Unh-unh. No way," she said.

"You sound very certain?"

"That's 'cos I am. Real certain. He might have played some before Mrs Stuyvesant happened along; I mean, he was some good-looking guy. But once she was on the scene it was all change. Mr Patric and

Mrs Stuyvesant, they were tight. I mean… tight. And not just 'cos she kept any kind of leash on him. He finish here of an evening and it was straight home. He loved her, and that's for damn sure, you can take it from me."

She gave him a look, a stubborn defiant look that made him feel sorry for her. If only she knew.

"So you want the tour?" she asked, getting to her feet. "Take a look-see?"

42

It was just a little past nine, but the house on High Strand Lane was starting to fill. The front door opening and closing. Members and guests. The genial murmurings of welcome, the soft hush of money, the tightness of expectation. That quiet thrill of chance, and the prospect of a good run. Leaving the house richer than when you arrived. Or not.

Louise and Jacquot started their tour on the ground floor, Louise walking ahead of him, Jacquot loitering, looking, taking it all in. The house was much larger on the inside than it appeared on the outside. The same width, two rooms either side of the hallway, but the property opened up after that, stretching down through a maze of open-plan rooms connected by archways, each carpeted in thick blue tartan and furnished with whatever gaming tables the rooms were given over to: a long oval roulette table, a high-sided craps table, bacarrat and blackjack tables with leather-seated high chairs, each table manned by croupiers – men and women both – in black trousers and red waistcoats, each of them discretely supervised by black-tied pit bosses who looked like they knew as much about the games as they did how to contain any unwanted trouble should it arise. Already a crowd was gathering in each room, most of the members and their guests men, with a few good-looking women amongst them. No one wore formal evening wear, but the clothes were elegant, expensive, and Jacquot noticed some fine-looking jewellery. He also noticed a range of close-circuit cameras above the action. One in each corner of the room, one above each table. In the last room on the ground floor, under a glass roof, four square tables with four leather chairs drawn up to them were set out in a neat diamond shape. One of the tables was occupied, an elderly gentleman in open neck shirt and cravat dishing out cards for a round of bridge, pads and pencils beside each player.

"And the poker?" asked Jacquot.

"Upstairs," said Louise. "Follow me."

Going back into the hallway, she turned up a flight of stairs, its wide mahogany steps set with a tartan runner down the centre, held in place with old-fashioned brass stair rods, an ascending line of greyhound prints matching each step. The stairs creaked as they climbed, and led up to a circular landing with three panelled doors. One door was closed, but the other two were open.

"There's a game going on, so you'll have to be content with one of the empty rooms, if that's alright? Poker players don't much like an audience."

The room she showed him was dark and low-ceilinged, but unlike the rooms below there were no windows. It was carpeted in the same tartan weave, two of its walls were set with bookshelves, and two panelled in light walnut, a long buffet table along one of them equipped with a well-stocked bar and tall flower-filled vases, with a pair of leather-back chairs drawn up either side of it. In the centre of the room was a wide circular table maybe six feet in diameter and covered in a tight green baize. Set around it were six more of the leather-back chairs, with space for at least another four if they were needed. Above the table, like all the rooms below, hung a plantation-style ceiling fan. More for looks than usefulness, Jacquot decided, noting a narrow grille at the base of each wall and the low hum of air-conditioning. Not that the paddle fan or air-conditioning or vases of flowers on the buffet did much to cover the slightly stale scent of sweat, cigars, and cigarette smoke.

"The tables are re-covered every month, can you believe that?" said Louise, her fingers trailing over the baize. "Worn away by elbows mostly, or stained with spilt drinks, or burned from cigarettes or cigars. Four hundred bucks a time."

"I notice you have security cameras in each of the rooms..."

"And you'd like to see where we keep an eye on things?"

"Why not?" said Jacquot, with a smile.

Without saying anything she led Jacquot out onto the landing and pushed on a panel between the two open doors. It opened with a tiny squeak and revealed a steep narrow staircase. There were no prints on the wall, just a line of sleeved wires and padded ducts leading upwards. At the top of the stairs, the house's loft had been transformed into a control room. A long desk against three of the walls, and a man at each desk, watching a pair of monitors, each monitior split into four frames. Black-and-white pictures taken from the corners of each room below, and from directly above all the gaming tables.

"We can catch most things up here, but the card counters are the hardest to spot. Most times we leave that to the pit bosses. Hey, move over, Clyde, give a girl some space, why don't you?"

Clyde, dressed in chinos and sports shirt, did as he was told and

Louise drew up a chair.

"Something you might like to see," she said to Jacquot, reaching for a drawer, pulling a CD from a row of discs, and sliding it into a player on the desktop. "Something I've kept. Just can't seem to wipe it."

Jacquot put a hand on the back of her chair and leaned forward. The screen flickered and jumped into life. A single frame, from above. Five men and a woman at one of the poker tables below. Drinks set down, chairs drawn in, ashtrays within reach. Louise flicked a switch on the control panel that Clyde had surrendered and the monitor screen split into four. She selected one of them and the monitor flicked back to a single frame. Two of the men, sitting side by side. One was bald, in his fifties, sweating and overweight. He held a cigar in one hand and scooped up the two cards dealt to him, fanned them out an inch from his nose. The other man left his where they were on the table, just turned up their corners and leaned back to check his hand.

Jacquot knew what Louise was doing. He remembered the photos from the house on Lyford Cay. It was Patric. And the date in the lower left-hand corner was 7/22/04; time, 03.32. Just a few days before his disappearance.

Jacquot studied the man. The picture was not the greatest quality but it wasn't difficult to spot the easy elegance, a confident looseness in the way he sat at the table, leaning forward to push forward his ante chips, sitting back to watch the other players.

"Can you zoom in on the hands?" asked Jacquot.

"Sure thing," Louise replied, and the camera closed in on his head, a curl of light, greying hair, a long thin nose, a gentle smile as he said something, teeth white and even.

"There's no soundtrack, I'm afraid," said Louise. But it didn't matter.

Another tiny twist of the control and Louise centred the camera on Patric's hands, one resting on the baize beside his cards, the other working at a column of chips. Long tapering fingers, finely turned nails an even creamy colour against his dark tan. Boni would have loved those fingernails.

The game that followed was over in a little less than eleven minutes. Three of the six players had thrown in their cards after two rounds of betting, leaving just Patric, a man in a leather waistcoat and sunglasses, and a woman with piled blonde hair and a plunging cleavage.

"Who's the woman?" asked Jacquot. She was young, attractive.

"Mrs Drumgoole. A big name on the island. Old school. Family came in with the settlers. Loves poker and plays a mean game. The boobs help, too. Difficult to concentrate when you're looking at a rack like that. And she knows it."

"And the man beside her, in the waistcoat?"

"Avery Phillips, out of Reno. A pro. Plays the tournaments and makes a comfortable living. Very comfortable."

One by one the three remaining players pushed another stack of chips into the centre of the table.

"What are the chips?"

"Fives. Five hundred a piece."

Jacquot whistled. Louise had been right about Baize's high rollers. At a conservative estimate the pot must have been close to a hundred thousand dollars.

"Eighty-five thousand, in case you were wondering," said Louise. "But it goes higher. Just wait and see."

A few minutes later, Mr Phillips flicked his cards into the centre of the table and slumped back in his chair. Now it was just Mrs Drumgoole and Patric. The betting continued. The chips in the centre of the table grew in number.

And then Patric took one last look at his cards, laid them down and pushed his remaining stack of chips over the baize and into the pot. He sat back, put his hands behind his head, and smiled.

Mrs Drumgoole didn't move. Just watched him, watched the smile. And then, with a shake of her head, she tossed her cards onto the table. A good hand. A pair of jacks, and two threes.

Patric nodded, as though he'd known exactly what he was up against. Then reached out his arms and brought the pot towards him.

"You ever see a happier looking guy?"

"What did he have?"

Louise shook her head, chuckled.

"Knowing Patric, nothing."

43

"So you got everything you need?" asked Louise, coming down the stairs behind Jacquot and closing the control room door with a soft click.

"I'd like to see where the money goes. The counting room?"

"Basement level," she replied. "Just follow me."

In the short time they'd been in the control room, the house had filled and a murmur of voices reached up to them as they came down the stairs, sprinkled with groans of dismay and exultant cries of delight.

"Craps players," said Louise, over her shoulder. "They always make the most noise. You know where the name comes from, by the way? Craps?"

Jacquot admitted that he did not.

"And you a Frenchie? Just goes to show," she said. "Comes from your word '*crapaud*'. Toad? Frog?"

"Toad."

"If you say so."

"Any reason?"

"The way they used to play, still do sometimes, when they don't have a table. Squatting down to throw the dice against a kerb or wall or skirting board. Street craps, basically. Still see it certain places over the east side."

They reached the front hallway and she led him into the second of the rooms either side of the front door. Like the bar where they had met, the room was shuttered and warm, but the light was much lower, just two green-shaded frilled lamps hanging just a metre or so above a pair of antique backgammon tables. Not boards, but actual tables with raised borders, lacquered black surfaces inlaid with faded red and white points. Each of the tables was set with a tray of yellow and blue checkers, a pair of leather cups, black and white dice, and an ivory doubling cube. Two chairs faced each other across the board, with a third drawn up along one side.

"Three chairs?" asked Jacquot, as they passed the tables.

"Like I said, any game that's player versus player, the House always has a watcher. Someone to keep score, look out for any foul play, and tally up the betting and House take."

At the far end of the room, Louise took a keycard from her pocket, swiped it through a lock and pushed open a door. "And here's where it all ends up," she said, leading the way down into the basement.

If the lights were low in the rooms above, here they were eye-squintingly bright, three lines of halogen downlighters that reflected off the polished concrete floor and four chrome counting machines. Each of the machines was set on a square metal table, and at the end of the room was the door to a steel vault.

"From midnight on we got three men down here – two counters and a watcher. We work a rota between the clubs, so the counters and watchers never know who they're working with."

"How does the money get here?"

"See over there?" Louise said, pointing to what looked like the up-and-down sliding doors of a dumb waiter. "Connects with the Cashier's till in the first gaming room. Chips for cash. Cash for chips. A simple in and out. Every hour, the cashier sends down takings over and above the agreed House float. Weekdays that'll be about ten thousand dollars. Weekends maybe double. If there's a big payout, the money needed is sent right back up."

"And those machines do the counting?"

"Yes, indeed. Cost a thousand bucks apiece, and we got maybe twenty of them spread around the clubs. Each one counts and sorts fifteen hundred notes a minute, with UV and Magnetic detection for anything counterfeit."

"And after the counting?"

"Into the safe. A Commodore double vault. Nightly take in first vault, then moved to second vault for the next night. Every third day to the bank."

"Combination?"

"One for each vault. House manager has the combination for the first vault. Only Patric and Mr Ballard have the both."

"Which of them checks most often?"

"Varies, I guess. Here it's usually Mr Ballard, but the other clubs could be Patric."

"Anyone ever help themselves? A few notes into a pocket?"

"No pockets on the counters or watchers, so not an easy one to swing."

"Does it ever happen?"

She gave him a look. "Not on my watch, it don't."

44

Jacquot came awake quickly, with questions hurtling through his head. It had always been like this at the beginning of an investigation, and it was no different now. Questions, questions, questions.

Questions like, why would Patric steal ten million dollars when he had everything a man could want? A successful business. A beautiful wife. A good and satisfying life. Ten million? It didn't make sense. Of course, with ten million he could always start again somewhere else if he really wanted to change his life. Ten million went a long way, and he could always gamble, play the tables if he needed more. But with someone like DiCorsa after him, he'd always be a marked man.

And why take a lover like this Sylvie Martin and run away with her when he was married to a woman like Boni, a woman whom, by all accounts, he loved? And when there were so many other women to choose from? Mrs Drumgoole might have been married, but she was a beauty. And the girls he had seen at Baize the night before – the croupiers, a couple of the waitresses – were no slouches in the looks department. As Beth had said, there was no shortage of good-looking women on the island. *Available attractions* she'd called them. So why Sylvie Martin? But Jacquot knew that a single photograph from a personnel department file barely scratched the surface. Just a mug shot, a likeness, nothing more. It was only when you met a woman in the flesh, face to face, looked into her eyes, held her hand in yours, that you properly understood what attraction was all about.

Questions, questions, questions. But as yet no answers.

Except for one certainty. After his tour of Baize Two the previous evening he knew how easy it would have been for Patric to remove whatever money he wanted. With the combination to both vaults he could have taken what he liked – a little bit here, a little bit there. Over weeks, over months he could have amassed a very large amount. But it wouldn't have been more than months. Sooner or later, someone would have noticed the shortfall. And they had. Or rather, Ballard had. And Ballard seemed the kind of man who would pay attention to the nitty-gritty mechanics of business and accounting practices whereas, it seemed to Jacquot, Patric was more free-spirited, more at home at the poker table, or out on a yacht, or skiing, or diving. A figurehead for the brand.

The business cards that Jacquot had requested arrived while he was having breakfast on the terrace, mulling over what he'd seen and learned with Louise. He opened the two boxes and checked the contents. Stiff white card, his name and contact details in an embossed black copperplate. One with "Attorney-at-Law" beneath his name, the other with "Private Investigations". He took a half-dozen from each box and slipped them into the inside pockets of Patric's linen jacket. Left for lawyer, right for private eye.

There was also a folded sheet of paper with a dozen names and addresses. All of them were island addresses. Half of the names had '(EC)' after them. People employed at The Edgewater. The others were teachers and school friends '(BSHS – Bay Street High School)'. But there was nothing, he was pleased to see, for Yamacraw Drive, or Coral Close, or Pirate Cay.

The last thing Jacquot pulled from the package was an envelope containing eight colour photos. He tipped them out on the table and arranged them in a line, portrait and landscape, all of them group photos from The Edgewater Club. And in every single photo – with a straggle of life-jacketed children at the marina, at a Pirate Night cocktail party, standing in line to greet some visiting dignitary, sharpening a carving knife over a Thanksgiving turkey, decorating a Christmas tree in The Edgewater lobby – Sylvie Martin stood out from the crowd. Whether she was dressed in her Edgewater uniform of shorts and polo shirt, in a blue sequinned cocktail dress, or as a moustachio'ed bucanneer at the Pirate Night party, she simply filled the space around her, commanded attention. Her wide, easy smile, her sparkling, mischievous brown eyes, her lustrous fall of hair, the sense of fun and energy and youthful brio that radiated off her, none of these had been apparent in the photo that Ballard had given him on the flight from Martinique.

But there was one photo in particular that Jacquot went back to, lingered over. It was the marina shot, with Sylvie standing beside the line of kids. She was barefoot, in a bright yellow one-piece swimsuit, with a striped scarlet sarong knotted at the waist, a breeze catching her hair, both hands reaching up to hold and control it for the photo. Not quite side on to the camera, her figure was shown to wondrous effect: a slim waist, wide athletic shoulders, and full cleavage, and that troublesome breeze catching not just her hair but the edge of her sarong, too, billowing the hem to show the swimsuit beneath, cut dramatically high on the hip, her legs long and brown, a knee coyly bent. She looked stunning, so young and fresh, so effortlessly alluring and playful.

These were the pictures that Jacquot had needed to see. And suddenly he understood.

Sylvie Martin might not have been Boni, might not have had her class or elegance. But she had youth and vibrancy on her side, and an irresistible allure. Now the raised eyebrow in that first photo made sense. Because Sylvie Martin knew what she had, and that eyebrow just defied you to come and try to take it.

A challenge, a dare. Were you man enough?

And the gambler, Patric, had fallen for it.

"You here for lunch, Mr Daniel?" asked Beth, as he passed through the kitchen on the way to the garage, taking the key fob for Patric's car this time.

"Out all day, thanks, Beth."

"Well, I'll leave you something for supper, case you's hungry when you gets back."

"A jug of your rum punch wouldn't go amiss."

"Already done an' coolin' for you. Jus' give him a shake, add some ice, and you be flyin' first class."

45

Jacquot unlocked the Explorer, climbed into the driver's seat and, reaching across to the glove compartment, pulled out the map of the island. He opened it up, laid it on the passenger seat, and then reversed out of the garage.

For the first few miles, Jacquot followed the coast road in a westerly direction, away from the house and The Edgewater Club, with the sea on his right hand side, flashes of creamy sand and azure ocean winking through the trees. And every couple of minutes he glanced in his rear-view mirror to see if he was being followed. Ballard might have said they weren't going to bother tailing him, that there wasn't any reason. But when did anyone believe a killer? Not to mention money-laundering and whatever other criminal activities the man indulged in.

At the end of Western Road Jacquot swung right and followed the sign to Clifton Point along a dusty track where the Explorer came into its own, ironing out the bumps and ruts without causing Jacquot too much discomfort. There was quite a lot of dust thrown up behind him, which reduced his visibility, but when he hit the tarmac into Adelaide township he could see that there was no one behind him. He supposed they could have put some kind of trace in the car so they could follow his movements, but somehow he doubted it.

Turning away from the coast, Jacquot now followed South Ocean Road inland around the Albany golf course, and finally hit Carmichael Road, a seven-mile straight that led into the southern fringes of downtown Nassau, its humpback course marked out by telegraph poles, pastel-shaded wood frame houses, dusty yards, and stray dogs trotting beside the kerbs. Halfway along, the sky suddenly darkened and a brief shower of rain raced across the road, splattering against his side window and smearing the creamy dust on his windscreen. And as it swept down through the trees, spattering over the road, and sending the dogs running for shelter, Jacquot wondered if this was the northern edge of the same storm that had hit Île des Frères that last night with Boni, recalling her words, her whispered invitation, as the rain slashed down around them, soaking through their clothes in just seconds. And as he remembered the storm, the pair of them standing outside Madame Chanson's guest house, there was a bleep from the

Explorer's instrument panel and a red light. He needed petrol. And, he realised with a start, he needed money, too. The only cash he had was a wad of euros. At the next service station he pulled into the forecourt and filled the tank, watching the rain haul away to the north and a blue sky slide up over the palms. In the shop he paid with a credit card and asked where he could find the nearest bank or ATM. Back in the Explorer he followed the directions he'd been given for Flamingo Gardens, found a bank, and after checking his balance – Boni really had credited his account with a hundred thousand dollars – he withdrew a stack of Bahamian dollars.

Back in the car, he checked the map for Yamacraw Drive in East Nassau where Patric had lived when he first came to New Providence. He found it easily enough, then looked up Coral Close where Patric had moved in 1987. The two addresses were about four miles apart, separated by a crowded grid of streets that made up central Nassau. Not really knowing what he might find, Jacquot decided to start where Patric had started, on Yamacraw Drive.

Set back from a dusty strip of highway, The Idlings looked like an old American motel that had seen better days. The lime green wash was fading, stained grey with patches of mildew, and the paint on the storm shutters had peeled and blistered. When he pulled into the front lot, it didn't take long to see that the Ford Explorer was a great deal more valuable than any other car parked there, no less than two rusting, wheel-less vehicles propped up on breeze blocks within a hundred metres of the motel's entrance. Patric had certainly come a long way in a very short time. Which was why, probably, he'd ended up in DiCorsa's pocket, stretching himself too far, too quickly; taking too many risks that hadn't paid off. So not the consummate gambler he was made out to be, thought Jacquot.

Locking the Explorer, and relieved that he hadn't been driving Boni's Mercedes, Jacquot walked across the forecourt and through an arch into an interior courtyard that accommodated an empty swimming pool, a few dusty palms, and a line of stacked sun loungers. Surrounding the pool were the guest rooms, eight a side, four on the ground floor and four off the first-floor walkways. Just inside the archway, a painted arrow and the word *Office* pointed to the right. He followed the directions, found the office door, knocked and pushed it open. A small room with a tiled floor, more peeling paint and a warm damp smell which a beating ceiling fan did little to shift. The only furniture in the room was a square metal desk, a wooden office chair, and set along one wall a sagging leather sofa. Stretched out on the sofa and reading a folded newspaper was a man in yellow shorts and blue t-shirt, fifty or so, with long greasy hair and grey stubble. He looked like a car mechanic on his break.

"You lookin' for a room, we got some spare," the man said, without looking up from his paper. It was an easy lilting island voice.

"I'm not looking for a room."

"Then you come to the wrong place, pal."

"I'm looking for a man called Patric Stuyvesant."

When Jacquot said the name, the man put down his paper and swung his feet to the floor. He wore plimsolls on bare bony feet.

"Stuyvesant?"

Jacquot nodded. "He used to live here. Apartment 16."

"Nope. Room 22. Ain't no apartments here nowadays. Stayed a coupla times back in the summer, week or so apart, then beat it. Never seen him since. Owes me money, too, laundry and such like."

"Summer?" asked Jacquot, lightly, in an attempt to cover his surprise. He'd been hoping for some background to work with, but hadn't expected anything like this, that Stuyvesant, by the sound of it, had stayed here following his disappearance. But he guessed it made sense. An old haunt, somewhere he knew that would be suitably anonymous and discreet. It was certainly a good place to lie low. No one would have come looking for him here.

"End of July sometime? Got it in the book, in a drawer there," the man said, nodding to the desk. "And you are?"

Jacquot reached for his right inside jacket pocket and brought out his 'Private Investigations' card, handed it over. The man looked at it, then looked back at Jacquot.

"You got a funny voice, mister. Where you's from?"

"Marseilles. France."

"You come a long way for that Mr Stuyvesant. He in trouble?"

"That's what I'd like to find out. Was he here on his own?"

A sly look slid over the man's features. He rubbed a hand across his stubbled chin. "Mighta been. Might not 'a been."

Jacquot reached for his wallet. Slid out a ten-dollar note.

The man grunted.

Jacquot added two more.

"Fifty gets you all you need."

Another two tens followed, and Jacquot handed the notes over.

The man folded them and slipped them away into a back pocket. "And?"

"With a girl the first time, on his own second time round."

"A girl?"

"Oh, yeah. And then some. The real package, I'm tellin' ya. I mean, real pretty. Legs you wouldn't believe, and everything where it should be."

"You ever see her before?"

The manager shook his head. "None like that round these parts. More your north-shore variety. Well-dressed, looked good, like I said. Well-kept. Tell the truth, couldn't work out what they's was doin' down here. Seemed like they could afford a whole lot better, you know what I'm sayin'? And didn't go out much, neither. Guessed they musta been in some kind of trouble. Guess I was right."

"Did they have a car?"

The man nodded. "One of those Jap things."

"They have much luggage when they checked in?"

The man frowned. "Now you're askin', can't say as I remember."

"He leave anything after the second visit? You said laundry?"

"Yup, shirts and stuff. Kept 'em a while case he came back, but must 'a throwed 'em out when he didn't show."

Jacquot gave him a look. It seemed unlikely that he would have thrown away any of Patric's shirts. Probably sold them, or kept them for himself.

"I heard he lived here a few years back. Apartment 16."

"Mebbe. Can't say. Only been here a coupla year mesself."

"What about the girl? What happened to her?"

"Just seen her those first coupla days after checkin' in. Never set eyes on her since. Like this Stuyvesant. Here one minute, gone the next."

Jacquot looked round the office. There was nothing more for him here. With a nod to the manager, and fifty dollars poorer but well spent, he left the office and went back to his car.

46

Checking his map again, Jacquot decided to take the coast road rather than face the narrow grid of streets and likely snarl of city traffic that made up downtown Nassau. It was the longer route but it didn't take long to realise that he'd made the right decision. Up past East End Point, onto Eastern Avenue and along a road with the ocean on one side, brightly-coloured houses on the other, and only the lightest of traffic. He switched off the air-conditioning and buzzed down the window, a blast of warm air battering the arm he latched over the door frame, filling the car with the fresh briny scent of the sea. And as he drove he saw that developers were hard at work, beach-front lots boarded with postered wood-ply fencing, and newly completed beach-front apartment blocks rising above the tree tops. Rising higher than any of them was the pink plaster façade and giant archway of the Atlantis Hotel on Paradise Island now coming into view up ahead. Wild horses, thought Jacquot, shaking his head. It would take a herd of wild horses to drag him there for a holiday.

Twenty minutes later, Jacquot turned off West Bay Street, having pretty nearly circumnavigated the island, and started looking for Coral Close. He found it five blocks back from the highway, the houses far better-kept than Yamacraw, sitting in their own small plots, their gardens tidier and more colourful. And not a wheel-less rusting hulk to be seen. Definitely a step up in the world for Patric, thought Jacquot, as he spotted the house he was looking for and parked in the shade of a blooming jacaranda.

Number sixteen was a two-floor house painted peppermint green, with a stone porch, a red tile roof and glaring scarlet shutters on the five windows facing the street. Sitting on a swing rocker on the porch was an old lady in a blue housecoat. Her hair was grey, loose, and lightly dishevelled, her winged white-framed sunglasses the kind a Hollywood starlet might have worn in the sixties, and the cigarette clamped between bony claw-like fingers had been smoked down to a dead browning stub. A wood-slat picnic table was drawn up beside the rocker, and what looked like a glass of iced-tea – but could as easily have been a tall whiskey and water – had been placed within reach. The housecoat was loose on her skinny frame and her chest was brown and wrinkled. She reminded Jacquot of Madame Chanson, but a more disreputable Madame Chanson. She raised her head when she heard the gate open and she watched as Jacquot started up the path before calling out to him in a raspy, liquor-soaked Irish brogue.

"You come about the a-partment, it's done gone."

Jacquot came up the steps, wished her a good morning, and said that he hadn't come about the apartment.

"Well, if you've come to sell me something, sonny, then you can just skedaddle back where you came from. This old girl ain't for buyin' nuthin', less it's for drinkin' or smokin'.'."

"I haven't come to sell you anything, madame. I've come to ask you some questions."

"You the police?" she asked, reaching for her drink and taking a swallow. She kept the glass in her lap.

Jacquot went for his right-hand pocket and brought out one of his business cards. The one for 'Private Investigations'. He checked it, just in case, before he stepped forward and handed it over.

"You expect me to read that," she said, glancing at it before dropping it on the rocker beside her. "Print's damn smaller than an ant. And you don't see too many of them at my age neither."

"I'm a private investigator, madame," he said, settling against the porch rail.

"Don't see many of them neither." She tipped the sunglasses down her nose, and peered up at him. "Big fella, ain't you? Guess you'd have to be in your line of work. Good-lookin' too, save the beard and that nose on you. Someone break it, did they, for stickin' it where it shouldn't be goin'?"

"A long time ago. Playing rugby."

"Your own fault, then, either ways. So what is it you've come investigatin' for, way out here on Coral Close? Don't have no murders nor nuthin' hereabouts. Respectable neighbourhood is the Corals."

"I'm looking for a man called Patric Stuyvesant. I believe he lived here a few years back."

Jacquot could see that the name registered immediately. According to his parents' letters Patric had moved out ten years earlier, but it was clear his old landlady still remembered him. She gave him a beady look, sharp grey eyes narrowing, then pushed the sunglasses back into place. "You from the south? Alabama way? Louisiana? Or them Frenchie islands?"

"Martinique."

She nodded. "And what's your name again, Mister…Mister…?"

"Milhaud. Daniel Milhaud."

The old girl nodded. "That's French alright. Even your name's Smith I bet you'd make it sound French. Me, I'm Mrs Swanson, so that's what you can call me. So what you lookin' for Patric for, you don't mind me askin'? He in trouble again? Always in trouble, that one. One thing or another."

"He's gone missing. I'm trying to find him. I had this address. I thought I better check it out."

"You got a light for a lady?" she asked, lifting her hand with the cigarette. "Damn thing keeps goin' out."

Jacquot reached into his pocket for a lighter. He stepped forward, flicked the wheel and lit what was left of her cigarette. It didn't take more than a moment to know that she wasn't smoking tobacco. And it was strong, too. The smell of it ripe and pungent. He wondered how much he'd get out of her, if anything at all. But then maybe he could work it to his advantage. There was no time to waste.

It was as if she knew what he was thinking. "Not what it used to be," she said, waving the joint, letting out a wheezing plume of smoke from deep down in her bony chest. "Nowadays you take a toke and you're out all day. You better ask your questions quick, junior, or I'll nod off again."

"I wanted to know about Patric Stuyvesant."

"Best tenant I ever had, French, like you. Same kinda voice, the pair of you."

"You remember him?"

"Ain't one to forget. Always droppin' in after he left. Stays in touch, you know? Every birthday, Christmas. Sometimes just passin' by – for a chat, see how I am."

"When was the last time you saw him?"

Mrs Swanson took her time over that one, as though she was trying to recall, or work out the best answer. "Christmas, thereabouts. Brought me a bottle and a baggie. Like he always does."

"That's a long time. Not since then?"

She gave it some more thought, then shook her head.

"How did he seem?"

"No different. More money, bigger car, but just the same. Naughty boy, too. Always a naughty boy, that one."

"Naughty?"

"Girls and cards. What else?"

"He had a lot of girlfriends?"

"Different one every week. But that's why we're young, ain't it? The practicing years, gettin' our eyes in. Pity is, it don't last." She chuckled, lost her breath, and coughed fruitily. "Damn stuff, it's gettin' tougher to keep down..." She looked at what was left of the joint and flicked it over the porch rail into the garden. "Gonna stop one of these days... me and the smokin' both."

"The apartment's on the top floor? Where he lived?"

She seemed pleased by the change in direction, away from the tricky stuff, where she had to think. "That's right. Got its own staircase round the side. You come and go as you please. So long as you're quiet and don't make a ruckus I'm happy." It sounded like a well-used pitch.

"You put ads in the paper?"

"No need. People hear the place is free, come and ask..."

"So personal introductions?"

"That's the best way. I'm picky who I shares my home with."

"Patric ever send you someone?"

Mrs Swanson raised her glass, swallowed the last of her drink, then put her foot to the table and started to swing her rocker. She looked as though she hadn't heard the question.

"How long did she stay? The girl Patric brought here." It seemed to Jacquot a reasonable assumption. He'd taken Sylvie to The Idlings, why not here? Moving around; safe places no one knew about.

The old lady took her foot from the table, and the swinger slowed. "I ain't that stoned, Mister whatever-your-name-is."

But Jacquot knew she was.

"How long?"

"Not long. Coupla days, maybe. Hardly heard a squeak." She sucked in her breath as though realising she'd said more than she'd intended.

"What was she like?"

"Like I said, quiet as a mouse."

"Pretty?"

"Oh, they was all pretty."

"Was her name Sylvie?"

"Might have been."

"I need to know where she is," said Jacquot, quietly.

"She in trouble?"

"She could be, if the wrong people find her."

"Are you one of them wrong people?"

Jacquot shook his head.

Mrs Swanson grunted. "Strange thing is, I believe you."

"So where did she go, after she left?"

"Off the island, is all Patric said. Somewhere off the island. Somewhere safe." The old lady rested her head against the back of the swinger, looked away, past Jacquot, over her garden.

For a moment he thought she'd fallen asleep.

But then, with a long deep sigh, she said, "Tell me, Mr Private Investigator, is my boy, Patric, ever coming back?"

"I don't think so, Mrs Swanson."

She tightened her lips, nodded. "That's what I guessed. Always the good ones first."

47

It was late afternoon when Jacquot turned into The Edgewater Club. At reception he asked for the Club Secretary and a few moments later a pink-faced Englishman appeared, shook his hand, and introduced himself as Dickie Forbes-Temple. With the lightest touch to Jacquot's elbow, Forbes-Temple steered him to a nest of wicker chairs on the verandah. A waiter appeared and asked if he could get them anything. Forbes-Temple looked at Jacquot with raised bushy eyebrows. Jacquot shook his head, and the man was sent on his way with a word of thanks, and congratulations on his being awarded 'Employee of the Week'. Forbes-Temple's voice was starched and clipped, his body lean, stiff, straight-backed, but his manner was warm and kindly. A military man, Jacquot decided, or something in government. Late sixties. Retired, put out to grass, but landing on his feet. Churchill would have approved his appointment as Club Secretary. The Edgewater would be in safe hands.

"I was so sorry to hear of your loss, Mr Milhaud," Forbes-Temple began, as they settled themselves. "Your sister was a lovely lady. The Club has lost a dear friend and a valued member. In that order, I might add. Friend first and foremost, don't you know? And her husband, too," he added, shaking his head. "Still missing, I believe. Just a dreadful business."

A warm breeze stirred the leaves of a potted palm behind their table and from somewhere in the grounds came the distant drone of a lawnmower. Forbes-Temple passed a hand over his thin, combed-back grey hair.

"As you may know, Mr..." but Jacquot got no further.

"Oh, do call me Dickie. Everyone does."

"Of course, so, Dickie, as you may have heard from Mr Ballard I am here to put my sister's affairs in order. And also to do what I can to locate my brother-in-law. There are certain matters that will need his..." He pretended to cast around for the right word.

It was enough. Forbes-Temple was already nodding. "Quite. Quite. Yes, I understand. A difficult position, Mr Milhaud..."

"Daniel, please."

"Of course, of course. Daniel." And then he frowned. "But how can I be of assistance? I have no idea..."

Jacquot leaned forward, as though to speak privately. Forbes-Temple did the same, drawing closer, tilting his head to the right. A military man, for sure, Jacquot decided. No hearing aid that he could see, but the right ear was clearly not as reliable as the left when words were softly spoken. Too much gunfire did that to a military man.

"I understand that Patric... That there was a... That he had taken up with someone at the Club," Jacquot began. "One of your staff. A Miss Martin? It seems to me that if I can find her, or find out what I can about her, then possibly I might be able to find Patric."

"Most regrettable," said Forbes-Temple, with a shake of the head and tightly pursed lips. "It happens, of course, such... indiscretions, but still. We do all we can to discourage that sort of behaviour. The first rule of service, of course. Simply not acceptable. If I had known about it... A private word with Mr Stuyvesant, a stern warning in terms of membership, what? As for Miss Martin, ah, well, reprimanded at the very least, probably dismissed, I'm afraid to say." He sat back, spread his hands.

"So what can you tell me about her? What was she like?"

"Oh, a first-class girl. Absolutely first class, don't you know? Started here right after college. Bright, enthusiastic, nothing she wouldn't do..." Forbes-Temple coloured a little, realising what he had said, but carried on regardless, covering himself. "After the initial training programme, I believe she started at the crèche, looking after the members' children – sailing classes, tennis, that sort of thing. Later we brought her into the Club. Organising events – Christmas, New Year, our annual regatta – and then Guest Relations. The perfect job for her. A natural. She was so good with people... had the touch, if you know what I mean? Not the least bit star-struck or intimidated by some of our more... how shall I put it...? Our more high-profile members. Always at pains to make people feel at home, that nothing was too much trouble. And of course the members adored her." Again Forbes-Temple faltered.

Jacquot nodded. "She lived here at the Club, I understand?"

"That's right, yes. We have quarters for our unmarried executive staff down by the marina, if they choose to stay here. A dozen or so small apartments. Nothing grand, of course, but perfectly acceptable. Some do, but others have homes of their own; wives, children..."

"And before she moved in to your staff quarters?"

"As I said to Mr Ballard, after her mother's death and during her internship here she lived in the family home, a rental somewhere."

"She was able to afford it? The rent?" asked Jacquot, not surprised to hear that Ballard had already spoken to Forbes-Temple.

Forbes-Temple raised his hands. "She was a hard worker. Maybe she took a part-time job when she wasn't here. A bar somewhere, a coffee shop... something like that? Or maybe her mother had savings, though I wouldn't be too sure about that."

"And what do you know of her parents? Where she came from? Her family?"

Forbes-Temple sighed. "Ah, yes. Well, Miss Martin hadn't had the easiest time before she joined us. Her mother was... not the most reliable of parents, if you know what I mean? I believe she worked out on Paradise Island, at the casinos. Got in with a bad crowd, got mixed up in drugs, that sort of thing, and died of an overdose. Which made Miss Martin's success here all the more admirable."

"And her father?"

Another sigh. "I'm afraid I don't know anything about that. You probably won't know this, but it often happens like that with some of the islanders. Here one day, gone the next. It's in their nature, as I'm sure you'll appreciate. Regrettable, of course, but there we are."

"So The Edgewater wasn't just a job, it was..."

"Family. Exactly. Everything she'd missed out on. Which made the... this... this misalliance with Mr Stuyvesant all the more regrettable. She had come so far, was doing so well, and then to let it all slip away. And he is... well, a married man, and so much older than her."

"Apart from Patric, were you aware of any boyfriends? I mean, she was a very pretty girl."

Forbes-Temple shook his head. "None that I know of. Certainly no one on the staff, though I'd hazard a guess there would have been advances of that sort."

"Do you have any idea where she may have gone? Do you suppose she and Patric...?"

"I can only assume they are together, somewhere. Here on the island, maybe, or one of the out-islands. Maybe even the mainland. Who knows? But despite everything, despite what happened, I do... Well, I do wish her well. She was a lovely girl. Really lovely."

And that is where it ended. A group of people came up the steps, and one of their number came over, asked if he could have a word with Forbes-Temple. Jacquot could see that the man was relieved at the interruption. A tricky conversation brought to a convenient halt.

"Just one more thing," said Jacquot, as Forbes-Temple made to leave.

He turned, raised his bushy eyebrows again. "Of course, Daniel, anything at all." He looked suddenly uncomfortable, clearly wondering what Jacquot had in mind to ask, and in front of another member.

"Is there a phone I could use?"

48

Although Ballard had assured Jacquot that he wasn't being followed, there had been no such assurance that his phone calls would not be intercepted. For this reason Jacquot had decided that the Stuyvesants' home phone should only be used for calls to the house on Trinité. If he wanted to make or receive any other calls, it would be better to use a public phone.

The Edgewater phone was in an old-fashioned mahogany booth in a hallway behind the reception desk. One of four such booths, each with folding glass doors, and a comfortable chair. A notepad and pen with The Edgewater crest lay beside the phone, the island directory was housed in an embossed leather folder, and a vase of night-flowering jasmine scented the air.

"Just dial nine for an outside line," Forbes-Temple told Jacquot, and left him to it.

Closing the door he sat down, lifted the receiver and put a call through to the *gendarmerie* on Île des Frères where, Jacquot hoped, Sergeant Balmet would answer and not Faubert. Much to his relief, it was Balmet.

After a round of surprised greetings, Jacquot got down to business.

"There is a possibility," Jacquot began, "that our old friend from Chez Chanson may be back on the island, or possibly on Martinique… Yes, that's right… No, no, don't do anything yet, just keep your eyes open, and whenever you can, just drop by the house… No, no. Nothing official, and no uniform. Just a friend passing by… Exactly… And I'll be calling Midou later tonight so she'll be expecting you…" Before he ended the call he gave Balmet The Edgewater's telephone number, and told him to leave any messages for Daniel Milhaud.

The second call Jacquot made was to an old friend in Marseilles. After a another round of equally surprised greetings, he told his friend what he wanted and said he'd call back the same time the following day.

"Make it a little earlier," the friend told him. "I was just dropping off."

The third and final call was local. A brief enquiry, and a booking confirmed.

And that was that.

Looking forward to one of Beth's rum punches and an early night, Jacquot tipped the valet for bringing round Patric's Explorer and returned to the house on Lyford Cay.

49

At a little after ten o'clock the following morning, Jacquot clambered
onto the starboard float of a single-engined de Havilland Beaver
moored at the end of a jetty on Arawak Point. Behind him a mechanic
in oil-stained blue bib overalls loosened the mooring rope, pulled it
clear, and the Beaver moved lazily away from the pilings. Following
the man's instructions, Jacquot caught hold of a wing strut and hauled
himself up through the hatch. The interior was dark and cramped,
thick with a hot airless mix of oil and fish and stale vegetables. There
were six canvas-covered seats, but no other passengers. The pilot, a
man called Marlon, beckoned him up to the cockpit.

"Come up front, Mr Milhaud. You're the only freight I'm carrying,
and I could do with the company."

Jacquot did as instructed and, keeping low, he worked his way
along the aisle, squeezed into the cockpit, and slithered down into
the co-pilot's seat. Marlon pushed a can of Kalik beer between his
thighs and reached out to shake his hand, then took the money Jacquot
handed over, counted it and tucked it away in the door pocket. He wore
a green safari shirt with short, cuffed sleeves, a pair of grimy cream
shorts, woollen socks and laceless Timberland boots. There was a
dark, wiry stubble on his cheeks, his black hair was thick and tousled,
and his brown eyes webbed with red veins and couched in wrinkles.
He looked like the kind of man you'd want on your side in a bar-room
brawl, thought Jacquot, noting the faded tattoo of an anchor, an eagle,
and trident – the insignia of US special forces – only dimly visible on
the dark skin of his upper arm. Jacquot had liked the growly sound
of the man's voice when he'd booked the flight the previous evening,
and now that they'd met he liked him even more. Jacquot had found
him in The Edgewater's leather-bound phone directory under 'Charter
Island Air'. Four hundred dollars, cash, Marlon had told him, from
Nassau to the Exuma Cays and back. Jacquot had agreed terms, and
now he was here.

"You ever fly in one of these?" asked Marlon, leaning forward
and firing up the ignition. Through the windshield the single engine
coughed and spluttered and a thick black smoke belched back at them.
The three-bladed prop stuttered and fluttered and, with a final half-
hearted jerk, spun into silvery motion.

"First time," shouted Jacquot over the roar. "Looks like fun."

"Oh yeah, man, bundles of fun. So buckle up, put on the headset, and let's get going."

Pulling away from the jetty, Marlon steered out into the bay and increased the revs. The de Havilland picked up speed, a flock of pelicans scattered to port, and the floats started a slow staccato drumbeat over the water. Leaning forward over the pilot's yoke and peering through the windshield, Marlon found a passage of clear water and pushed the throttles forward. Twenty seconds later, the plane rose into the air and swung north, tipping round the western edge of Paradise Island and following its northern coastline. If Ballard had anyone following him, they'd lose him now.

"Like I said on the phone, you're looking at a hundred and thirty miles or thereabouts which means just a little over an hour's flight time each way." Through the headset Marlon's voice sounded distant and tinny. "Should get you to Pirate Cay round lunchtime. You need a beer to keep you fresh, there's a pack of Kaliks under your seat where the life vest usually resides. Having it patched at the moment so got myself some room for the more important things in life."

Strangely, the thought of no life jacket didn't bother Jacquot. He'd always teased Boni about the way commercial aircrews advised their passengers that in the unlikely event of coming down at sea they could use a life jacket. As far as Jacquot was concerned, if you came down at sea the chances of having an opportunity to strap on a life jacket and get out of the plane were slim to non-existent. At least this plane had floats if they had to come down in a hurry.

"So how long have you been flying out here?" asked Jacquot, as the east end of New Providence slid beneath their starboard wing and the ocean began. Somewhere down there was Yamacraw Drive and Coral Close.

"Few years now. Got laid off, bought myself some wings with the pay-out, and here I am."

"You're military, right?"

"How d'ya guess?" said Marlon, flexing his bicep so the tattoo moved. "Beach balls on noses."

Jacquot was puzzled.

Marlon saw the frown, and laughed. "You know... Beach balls on noses. Like in the circus." He took his hands off the controls and slapped them together like a pair of flippers. "Woooof! Woooof! Woooof! Seals? SEALS?"

"I get it. I get it," said Jacquot, chuckling. "You see any action?

"Panama, Kuwait, Mogadishu."

"What made you leave?"

"Disillusionment. Everything right, for the wrong reasons. Or everything wrong, for the right reasons. Down to what you're smokin' at the time, I guess. Whichever, the usual bullshit. Too much Company work, you know what I'm sayin'?"

"CIA?"

"Like it says on the tail. Charter Island Airways. You?"

"French police. Retired."

"Least you got that far. Me, I opened my mouth. Honourable discharge. Took the money and ran. My own boss now. Free and clear. Nothing like it."

"American?"

"American dad, island mother."

By now the Beaver had reached its cruising altitude and levelled off. Marlon finished his beer, slid open the window and tossed out the empty can. Far below the sea was just a dull silvery cloth with no other colour to show. And then, without warning, the silver gave way to a clear dazzling turquoise as the sun slipped out from behind a bank of cloud, flashing across the windshield and winking off the prop

With a gentle forward movement to the yoke, Marlon tipped the plane into a shallow dive and pointed ahead.

"That there's the start of the Exumas. Beacon Cay. And they carry on another hundred some miles, down to Williams Town and South Exuma. An island for every day of the year, so they say. Guess I'll have to take their word on that 'cause life's too short to go count 'em for myself. You ever been down these parts?"

"First time," said Jacquot, watching the distant stepping stone pattern of cays and sand bars and islands draw near and pass beneath them. "It's beautiful, in a kind of… fragile way. So much sea, so little land."

"Nature of the game, my friend," said Marlon. "You see here this side? All the light blue, the shallows? That's the Grand Bahama Bank. And over there, the other side of the islands, the real dark blue? Well, that there's the big deep of Exuma Valley. Thousands of feet down, it is. Like there's no end to it."

As though he was sitting at home watching TV, Marlon took his hands off the joystick and patted his pockets, pulled out a pack of cigarettes and lit up. "Hey, you mind reaching under the seat for another beer? Just time for a quick one before we reach Pirate Cay."

"Only if I can join you."

"Hell yes, man, hate drinking alone."

By the time they'd finished their beers, the de Havilland had dropped to a few hundred feet, the sea racing beneath them, the islands passing by on their left like a stately procession of green and white flatbed trucks.

"There she is," said Marlon, nodding to a low scrubby patch of land on the port side, and after they'd all but passed it by he brought the de Havilland round in a steep turn into the wind. A minute later they came down with a jarring thump-thump-thump as the floats smacked the water, and spray washed up over the windshield. Reducing their speed, Marlon steered for a wood jetty running out from a pink sand beach and line of weeping tamarisk. Three yachts and two sleek motor cruisers were moored in the cove, and a hundred yards to the right was a small marina with a half-dozen thatched roof dwellings set back from the quay.

"Place you're looking for is over the far side of the cove," said Marlon, pulling off his headset, killing the engine, and clambering out of his seat. "Pirate Cay Dive Safaris. Just keep walking till you run out of beach. You can't miss it. When you're done you'll find me in the marina bar. But right now, you want to help with the mooring?"

50

A warm offshore breeze was rippling the sea, scurrying across its surface, as Jacquot set off along the jetty. After the traffic-clogged streets of Nassau, Pirate Cay had a fresh salty scent to it. At the end of the jetty, he took off his shoes, rolled up his chinos, and walked down to the shoreline, the water sluicing and sucking round his ankles, the seashell pink sand squeezing between his toes.

Somewhere safe, Mrs Swanson had said. Patric had taken Sylvie Martin somewhere safe. Just the place, thought Jacquot, slipping on his sunglasses and casting about. A long strip of pink sand, a thin border of sea grape and tamarisk, and a scatter of timber frame buildings set around the quay.

He found the Dive Centre where Marlon had said he would, a hundred metres past the marina office, chandlery and beachside bar, a thatched wood cabin built out over the water from the rocky side of the cove. On the hillside behind it stood another four cabins, each built of thatch with palm weave walls, each connected by stepped duckboard walkways and each one with a hammock strung up under the eaves. There was an easy, laid-back feel to the place and from somewhere came a throbbing Reggae beat, loud enough to tap your foot to but not loud enough to cover the pile-driving chug of an air-compressor hidden away somewhere behind the main shack.

Jacquot recognised the place immediately, almost unchanged from the photo in Patric's study back on Lyford Cay: the same dark interior, the same lines of drying wet suits, weight belts and buoyancy vests, open shelves of masks and fins and snorkels, and a tall American fridge covered in various Dive Club decals. The same wood sign, too, hanging above the open doorway. 'Pirate Cay Dive Safaris'. So this is where Patric had come, thought Jacquot, back in the eighties. His first home in the Bahamas after the lush vined slopes of Lourmarin. Not a bad place for a young man to start out in a new world.

Stepping off the beach, Jacquot climbed a set of worn wood planks with a rope handrail and came out onto a duckboard walkway leading to the main shack. A long wooden dive boat was moored up alongside it, and a group of divers were suiting up in the shade of a canvas awning. A dive master in faded black neoprene was checking buoyancy vests and belt clasps, his face, hands, and feet as brown as a coconut husk, his hair a blonde salt-stiff thatch. As he moved from diver to diver he went through the drill: "Twenty metres max, stay with your buddy, and watch for the current when we get to the Point." When he spotted Jacquot he said, "Too late for this one, mister, but if you check with the boss we can probably set you up for an afternoon dive."

Jacquot thanked him and watched the party clamber down into the boat, taking their seats either side of the inboard engine housing. Pushing the bow away from the jetty, the dive master jumped down onto the for'ard decking and the skipper, an islander in cut off jeans and t-shirt, banked the craft away from the pilings and headed out into open water.

"You don't look to me like you've come for a dive," said a voice from the shack.

Jacquot peered into the shadowy interior. An enormous belly was the first thing he saw, round and brown and matted with grey hair, then thin legs spread out, knees wide apart, and a pair of flowery shorts. Their owner was sitting in a deckchair beside a wood plank table set on trestles. On the wall behind him was a framed cinema poster for "The Big Blue", and a sign that read: *"Plan your dive... Dive your plan"*. He wore a baseball cap that had lost all colour in the sun, bleached to a thin pink, and an equally faded and frayed strip of scarf knotted around his neck.

"And you don't look like you could take me for one," said Jacquot, stepping into the gloom and reaching out a hand.

The man took it and squeezed it hard. *"Touché,"* he said. "I like a fella who speaks what he sees. Dangerous habit, though." Keeping a grip on Jacquot's hand, he hauled himself out of the chair and stretched his back, hands on hips, belly swelling out in front of him. "So if you're not here for diving, what can I do for you, Mister...?"

"Milhaud. Daniel Milhaud."

"Jack Cooper, like the beer. Talking of which..." He waddled across to the door, leaned out, opened the fridge and found himself a can. "You want one?"

Jacquot said that he would. Jack reached in and brought out another, came back and handed it to him.

"Canadian?"

"French."

"You come in with Marlon?"

Jacquot said that he had.

"You stayin' on the island?"

"Nassau. I'm looking for an old friend. Patric Stuyvesant."

"Patric?" Jack pulled the tab on his beer, put the opening to his mouth and tipped back his head. "You come about twenty years too late, my friend," he said with a soft belch. He lowered his chin to his chest and let out another one. He waddled back to his chair and settled himself down.

"Twenty years? You've got a good memory." Jacquot cracked his own can, and sipped at the frothing ice cold beer

Jack Cooper took a deep breath. "People like Patric, you don't forget in a hurry. So what do you want him for? 'Cos you're a cop, aren't you? I know a cop when I see one. Pull up a chair, make yourself comfortable, and tell me what that bad-ass son-of-a-bitch has been up to now."

"Sounds like you like him," said Jacquot, pulling out a chair from the table. Its planked surface was rough and ring-marked, littered with a stack of diving consent forms under lead belt-weights, and a pile of *Dive* magazines. Beside them was a conch shell with flyers for '*Pirate Cay Dive Safaris*' stuffed into its pink mouth, and a well-thumbed guide to Caribbean fish. Above it, a single hurricane lamp hung from a rafter hook.

"Like him? Love the bastard. Best damn dive master I ever had, and about the luckiest guy with a deck of cards you ever set eyes on. Helped me build this place, back in the day. Most of it round a poker table. Reckon I wouldn't be here without him."

Somewhere outside, behind the shack, the air compressor shut down with a final clanking rattle, and just the Reggae beat remained, up in one of the cabins.

"He's gone missing," said Jacquot. "Three months."

"And the cops are checking back twenty years?"

"I'm retired. A private investigator now." Jacquot reached into his right-hand pocket, pulled out a card and handed it over. Jack took it, turned it to the light to read, then laid it on the table.

"So who's put you up to all this? Who's your client?"

"Patric's wife."

"Boni?"

"You know her?"

"Went to the wedding. Wouldna missed it. He got all the aces with that one, and that's for damn sure. She's a beaut, alright."

It was clear that Jack had heard nothing of Boni's 'suicide' on Île des Frères. Out here on Pirate Cay, it seemed like the rest of the world and its teeming business was a very long way away. Island time, thought Jacquot. Sunrise, sundown… A beer, a dive, another beer. It was easy to get into the rhythm, and forget. He'd done it himself.

"They ever come down here, Patric and Boni?"

"Came down couple years back. Big smart yacht. Oyster. Bit of sailing, bit of diving."

"So it's not twenty years since you've seen him?"

"Didn't say it was."

"So when did you see him last?"

"Didn't say I had." Cooper took another swig of his beer, and fixed his eyes on Jacquot. "Was it Boni told you about me?"

Jacquot nodded. "She thinks there's another woman involved."

"That's the trouble with married life," said Cooper, with a shake of his head. "One or the other's always sniffing. I mean, suspicious, or just plain sniffing, you get my drift?"

"Is she right?"

"Reckon that's their business, don't you? They're grown up, right?"

"She just wants to know."

"She says," said Cooper, with a chuckle that sounded like it came from bitter experience.

"She also said you'd be the first he'd go to, if he was ever in trouble." It was a lie, but it sounded reasonable.

"So it's trouble he's in now?"

"That's how it looks."

"Who with?"

"Bad people."

Another swig, another low belch, more like a hiccup. "Had to happen sooner or later."

"How so?"

"You ever meet Patric?"

Jacquot said that he had not.

"Well, I'll tell you; he trod a thin line, did Patric. And a gambler down to his bootstraps. Put the two together, and that thin line gets thinner, till one day it ain't there at all. Guess that's what must have happened to them. Time to get out of town…"

"Them?"

Cooper paused, frowned.

One too many beers, thought Jacquot. Just an elementary slip, but a slip all the same. Cooper was trying to get a handle on the conversation, trying to get his story straight, and he'd tripped up. Just like Mrs Swanson. The more you volunteered, the harder it was to stay in line.

Jacquot put him out of his misery. "When were they here?"

Cooper fixed another look on Jacquot, sizing him up. A good guy, or one of the bad ones? That's what he was thinking. A breeze came into the hut, stirred the consent forms on the table and set the hurricane lamp squeaking on its hook.

"July? Can't recall exactly when. Came in with Marlon, the pair of them…"

"They flew here with Marlon?"

"The same. Patric stayed just a few hours, the girl longer. He went back to Nassau, phoned the next morning and told her he was sending Marlon back with instructions. Seems they were going to meet up in Miami, and go on together."

"Go on? She say where?"

"Hey, man, I'm a dive master, not a travel agent."

"How did Patric seem?"

"Oh, cool. Always cool that one."

"Not rattled?"

Cooper spread his hands. "You never could tell with Patric."

"And the girl?"

"Happy to do whatever Patric told her. Didn't like it when he said he was heading back to town without her, but she sucked it up."

"She didn't know he was leaving her here?"

"Didn't seem like it."

"Did you spend any time with her?"

"She stayed in her cabin mostly. Went for a few swims. A dive. Maybe we had a beer. But that's it. She kept to herself."

"What did you think of her?"

Cooper ran a finger under his scarf. "One word. Hot. I mean,

Boni's right up there, but this girl wasn't far behind. And young, too. Guess that's what made up the difference."

51

Marlon was sitting on the terrace at the marina bar when Jacquot came to find him. He'd taken off his socks and boots and opened up all the buttons on his shirt. His chest was broad and solid, his breathing easy, eyes closed, hands clasped in front of him. Jacquot went in to the bar, asked for a menu, ordered two grilled snappers, a mixed salad, and a bottle of house white. The wine was American, from the Napa Valley, and for a house wine cost more than Jacquot could believe. The bottle was opened, buried in an ice bucket, and Jacquot took it out to the terrace with a couple of glasses.

"You probably thought I was sleeping?" said Marlon, opening his eyes and pushing himself up in his chair. "But I wasn't. Just a good way to get a client to buy the lunch and refreshment. Place like this, it's a tab you don't want to get left with."

"How come it's so expensive?" said Jacquot, drawing up a chair and looking around. It was like any beach shack operation he'd ever seen. Palm thatch terrace, wood decking, a low thumping Reggae beat from unseen speakers, and pretty tanned girls in sarongs waiting on tables. The sarongs reminded Jacquot of Sylvie, but none of the girls here came close.

"The people who come here can afford it, don't you worry. When you're looking to sail or dive, there's nowhere like Pirate Cay. So it costs. Anyway, how was my old friend, Jack? He give you any trouble?"

"Nothing I couldn't handle," Jacquot replied, pouring the wine.

"He may be fat, out of shape, but make no mistake, man, he knows how to look after himself. I've seen him put a lot of men down. A New Zealander back in the day, so he knows how to fight like he knows how to drink. Course, he lost the accent a while back. Everything but the cussing."

Jacquot sipped the wine. Ice cold, and dry as onion skins.

Marlon reached over, pulled the bottle from the bucket and looked at the label. "Like I said, I'm glad you're getting the tab. You order anything to eat?"

The snapper arrived a few minutes later. The marina bar might have looked like a shack but the food and service were first class. The snapper was stiff and lightly charred at tail and fins, served on a bed of watercress, the skin scored and silvery, eyes white. As for the girl who served them, she was in her early twenties, long limbed, tanned, no make-up that Jacquot could see. Just young and healthy and wholesome.

"You're new, aren't you?" said Marlon, giving her a big smile.

"First week," she replied, laying down the cutlery. "The name's Aimée."

"What happened to Issy?"

Aimée shrugged. "She took off on a boat. Calum needed someone so I got lucky, I guess. Now, if there's anything else you gentlemen need, you just let me know, okay?" And with a dazzling smile she left them to their lunch.

"Now you know why I just love coming to Pirate Cay," said Marlon, and picking up his knife and fork he peeled back the skin on the snapper, slid the fillet off the bone, and scooped up a forkful of the glistening pearly flesh.

"Where does everyone live?" asked Jacquot, starting with his salad. Crisp lettuce and the sweetest tomatoes, doused in a soft mustardy vinaigrette. "There doesn't look like there's a lot of rooms around."

"A few," replied Marlon, nodding back to the slope behind the marina. "But most of the people who visit stay on their boats, and those who work here live in town, a little settlement the other side of the island. A twenty-minute walk is all. If that. Pirate Cay ain't much more than what you see."

Jacquot started in on his snapper. "So Jack mentioned you know my friend, Patric? Patric Stuyvesant?"

"Stuyvesant?"

"Tall, grey hair. Around fifty," prompted Jacquot.

Marlon took another slice of fish, reached for his wine. He frowned trying to place the name. "Yeah, yeah. I know him. Good-lookin' guy. Flew him down here a few months back. Him and his girlfriend."

"Girlfriend?"

"That's sure as hell how it looked. A real honey, man. A little young for him, but hey... lucky guy. So how is he? Bearing up?"

"He's missing, and his wife is worried."

"Ah. I see. So you're not so retired, Mr Policeman?"

"Just checking things out for a friend."

Marlon peeled away the spine of the snapper like a waffle of a buttered hot plate and set the bones aside. "Don't know the wife, but my guess is she's right to be worried. A girl like that on your arm, you'd kinda want to go AWOL. No offence, you understand."

"Jack said Mr Stuyvesant left her here?"

"That's right. I took him back to Nassau, and then came down a coupla days later to pick her up. He wanted me to fly her to Miami, the Watson Island Seaplane Base."

"Did you and Mr Stuyvesant talk on the flight back to Nassau?"

"Had other passengers down here and back, so no chance to chat."

"When you came back for the girl, did Mr Stuyvesant give you anything for her?"

"Yeah, he did. A letter, a flight ticket, and a briefcase."

"Did he tell you what was in the briefcase?"

Marlon shook his head. "All I know is I had to give her the stuff, and fly her on to Miami. And I'm tellin' you, man, it was real tight on fuel, that flight. Nassau to here, and back to Miami. Swear I came in on fumes."

"Do you know where the ticket was for?"

"Didn't look, didn't ask."

"Did she sit in the co-pilot's seat on the flight to Miami?"

"Sure did."

"She say anything?"

"Just chat, you know? Company. Let her fly the old bird for a bit. We had a laugh."

"How did she seem?"

"Pleased to be off the island. Ready and waiting when I got here. Excited, I guess."

"And Mr Stuyvesant?"

"I was supposed to take him to Miami a couple days later, but he never showed. Last I heard of him."

Jacquot sat back, fell silent, looked out over the beach.

So what was the plan, he wondered? What had Patric set up? And when he didn't show up in Miami, what did Sylvie Martin do? Where did she go with that flight ticket? And did she know about the money? Did she know the trouble Patric was in? If she didn't, she must have guessed that something was wrong. All that to-ing and fro-ing. Hiding out at The Idlings and Coral Close, and here on Pirate Cay. And what had Patric sent her in the briefcase? Instructions? Addresses? A stack of bearer bonds?

"You file flight plans?" asked Jacquot.

"Should do, but often don't. Not too keen on people knowing where I am, where I'm going, and when I'm coming back. Which makes it my look-out if I come down."

"And this trip?"

Marlon pushed the plate away, shook his head, then slid a pin from his shirt collar and started in on his teeth.

"I think I forgot," he said.

"That's probably good."

"Oh yeah, how's that?"

"Because when we get back to Nassau, there's a possibilty you're going to get a visit from a man called Brock. About twenty kilos bigger than you. He'll want to know where you took me."

"I hope he asks nicely."

"I'd be surprised."

"I'm guessing you don't want him to know about Pirate Cay?"

"Your guess is correct."

"So where should I tell him?"

"You tell me."

Marlon sucked on his pin, gave it some thought. "What about Harbour Island? Over to the east."

"And why would I want you to take me there?"

"Well, there's no airstrip to speak of, so no scheduled flights, which makes my kind of operation a saleable item. Also, there's a great little restaurant there called the Lazy Palm. Everyone raves about it. You just told me you were meeting someone there for lunch. I didn't pry. Just did what you paid me for. Hung around and brought you back. How does that sound?"

Jacquot gave it some thought, and nodded. "Sounds perfect."

52

When they landed back at Arawak Point later that afternoon, Jacquot thanked Marlon for his help and asked him to call The Edgewater if he got a visit from anyone. "Just leave a message for Milhaud," he said.

"No problem, man. Nice doing business with you." The two men shook hands. "Any time you need anything, the CIA is at your disposal."

Back in Patric's Explorer, a furnace when he opened it up, Jacquot buzzed down the windows, turned the air-con high, and headed off for The Edgewater.

There was one message waiting for him. From Balmet.

In the booth behind reception he picked up the phone, dialled for an outside line and followed it with Balmet's number. It was picked up on the third ring.

"I been to h-all the places 'ere on de island," the sergeant said, "and done rung round de 'otels on Martinique, but they don't got nothing on no Torrance nor Tarrant. Nothing in neither name."

Jacquot wasn't sure whether he should be worried or relieved at this news. But there was no time to think about it. There was something else Balmet had to tell him.

"Which gone puzzled me after what you done said about 'im being here, and h-all," Balmet continued. "And after what I done found out dis afternoon. Fact is, 'e couldn'ta been 'ere."

"And why is that?"

"Because five day ago 'is body was found in a dumpster truck in Galveston. Shot four time. Dey got de guy who done it. Some local hood. A drug bust gone wrong, them sayin'."

Jacquot frowned. It didn't make sense. Ballard had been quite clear that Tarrant was back on the island. That he had been there on Sunday and seen Béa and Matti in their Sunday best. But if Tarrant had been shot in Galveston he couldn't have been there. Did Ballard know his man was dead, or was he just trying to put the screws on Jacquot? Making sure he kept in line? But how would he have known about Sunday School? If it wasn't Tarrant reporting in, then someone else must have been watching the house, and tipped him off? Who else had Ballard sent to the island? Another of his heavies? Or maybe it wasn't just the Bahamas where he and DiCorsa had contacts.

"Well, someone's got to be watching the house," Jacquot said. "So keep an eye out, will you?"

"Okay, Monsieur Jacquot. Youse can count on h-it."

"And have you been out to Trinité? How are the girls and Midou?"

"Been out a coupla time and everyting just fine."

"Great. Thank you. If you find out anything more, you know where to get me. I'll be checking in every day."

The next call Jacquot made was to the number in Marseilles. This time the phone rang a lot longer but eventually it was picked up. The voice was as gruff and businesslike as it always was.

"Peluze."

"Claude, it's Daniel."

"So last time you call, I'm in bed. And now I'm having my supper."

"Then you better be quick, or it'll go cold."

"And quick is what you'll get. So keep your ears open. I won't be repeating it. First, DiCorsa. Ettore DiCorsa. Not a thing on file. Not so much as a parking ticket. Checked with a contact in Rome and nothing there either. Nor Interpol. Clean as a whistle. Like he doesn't exist. The next one's different. Your man Ballard. Originally Boulard. Jean Christian Boulard. Forty-seven. Like you said, born in Paris where he earned his stripes – gang-related mostly – before moving to Biarritz with his parents where petty crime went big time. Everything from assault to racketeering, but intimidation was his thing. A fixer for the big boys, but not an enforcer. He left the messy stuff to other people, which is how nothing stuck. Couldn't find anyone prepared to identify or incriminate him. Picked up a dozen times, but never spent a night inside. A nasty piece of work apparently. Current whereabouts unknown. Or maybe you can tell me...?"

"He's here in Nassau. Works for DiCorsa."

"Well, whatever he's up to now, he's a bad one. My advice is steer clear."

"You mean, because I'm not a cop any more?"

"What I hear, Boulard isn't the sort who'd worry too much if you were a cop or not. What I mean is, he'd know someone who wouldn't mind if you were a cop. Remember that *mec*, LaFresne? The one from Toulon with the floppy hair and the smile? We brought him in one time, just before the Waterman case? Babyface, they called him. Anything but. Shot a couple of off-duty cops in a crowded bar but no-

one saw a thing. Couldn't get anyone to finger him. So that's the kind
of man you're dealing with, old friend. Just watch yourself and tread
careful. Anything else you need, make sure you call before dinner
time and bed time."

53

The girls were screaming. Matti, always the stronger swimmer, had nearly reached the boat, but Béa was floundering. And the sharks were closing in on her, a half-dozen fins slicing through the water. She'd never make it, she'd never get to the boat in time...

Jacquot woke in a sweat, heart racing. When he realised where he was, and the screaming and splashing faded, the relief was instant. By the time he pushed open the kitchen door, hair slick from the shower, he'd put the dream out of mind. It could never happen. That's all it had been. A nightmare.

"Ain't the world just an horrible cruel place," said Beth, as the door swung closed behind him. She was sitting at the kitchen table, elbows either side of the morning paper. "Here one minute, gone the next." She pushed the paper aside and went to the cooker. "There's fruit and cereal, or I got some ham and eggs iffen you feelin' hungry?"

"Ham and eggs would do fine," said Jacquot, taking her seat at the table and drawing the newspaper towards him. It took him a moment to see the story that Beth had been reading. At first it made no sense, and then his blood ran cold.

A single six-line paragraph below a two-word headline – *'Accidental Death'* – and a blurred black-and-white photo. The winged, white-framed sunglasses were unmistakeable.

> *"Long-time landlady, Martha Swanson, 78, was found dead yesterday by tenant, Tyler Wisden. 'She must have fallen down the stairs from my apartment,' said bank-teller Wisden. Swanson, a colorful and much-loved local character, had lived in Coral Close for more than forty years."*

Accidental Death? Somehow Jacquot didn't think so. Martha Swanson might have liked a drink, and liked a smoke, and she could easily have had a dizzy moment and tripped at the top of those stairs – she was nearing eighty after all – but he didn't think so. He remembered, too, what she had said to him, sitting on the porch as she smoked what may well have been her last joint: *Don't have no murders nor nuthin' hereabouts. Respectable neighbourhood is the Corals.*

And then, a little lower down the page in the Late Press section, another story caught Jacquot's eye, and his blood ran cold again. If there appeared to be no suspicious circumstances in the '*Accidental Death*' of Martha Swanson, the same could not be said for the victim named in another six-line paragraph under the headline '*Yamacraw Killing.*'

> "*The mutilated body of long-time Idlings Motel manager, Nelson Gittings, was found late last night on Yamacraw Drive. Gittings, 54, had been tied to a chair and savagely beaten. Police believe the killing may be drug related, and a murder enquiry is under way.*"

A plate of ham and eggs appeared at Jacquot's shoulder. Beth caught his eye and shook her head grimly.

"Ain't nuthin' but death and despair," she said, reaching down with her free hand to push away the paper before settling the plate in front of him. "Wonder sometimes why we bother to buy them noose-peppers. Plain ruin the day, they do. By the way, Mr Daniel, Mr Ballard done called to invite you to lunch. At The Edgewater. Round midday. I said I'd pass on the message."

54

Two people who'd known Patric, and whom he, Jacquot, had tracked down in the course of his investigation, had died in the last twenty-four hours. He'd have been a pretty lousy cop if he'd put two and two together and failed to come up with a satisfactory answer. Whatever had happened to Martha Swanson and Nelson Gittings had happened because he had visited them, because they might have known something about Patric's movements… And Ballard had wanted to know what it was. And all because he, Jacquot, had been followed. Ballard may have assured him that he would be working alone, but it was clear now that the man was lying. No surprise there, thought Jacquot. What was a little lie compared to multiple murder. It hardly registered.

And as of this morning, there was something about Beth, too, that made the hairs rise on the back of his neck. The way she'd been reading that paper when he came down for breakfast, the way she'd caught his eye as she served the ham and eggs, shaking her head with a beady, almost knowing '*tsk-tsk-tsk*' as though she'd left the paper there deliberately. Teasing him. Are we, or aren't we, watching you? He couldn't be sure, but he didn't quite know what to make of her anymore. Had she really worked at the house for so long, before Boni and Patric arrived, or had she been placed there by Ballard to report back to him? Had she been watching what he got up to, where he went and whom he met? Or had she been forced to do it. A threat made? Something held against her? He remembered the first time they'd met, her quiet tears in the kitchen, how he'd hugged her tight and felt her trembling. For all his doubting her now, he was certain those tears for Boni had been real. But whether he was right or wrong, he was glad he'd taken the precaution of leaving nothing around for her to find, and that he'd decided to limit his calls from the house to the girls on Trinité. As Jacquot turned into The Edgewater, he wondered whether Ballard's influence reached as far as Forbes-Temple and the Club's switchboard. He hoped it didn't, but if it did he'd probably find out about it sooner or later.

If Jacquot needed any further confirmation that he had been followed it came as he passed the reception desk at The Edgewater. One of the front-desk assistants intercepted him with a sealed envelope with the Club crest on it. Another phone message. At least all member messages came in sealed envelopes, thought Jacquot, though that didn't necessarily mean much when it came to Ballard. He opened it, slid out the note. Three letters. CIA. With a shrewd idea what Marlon's call was about, Jacquot went to the line of phone booths. The one he'd used before was occupied, so he took the next one along. The same leather-bound directory, the same pad and pen, but this time a single strelitzia stem rose spikily from its glass vase.

"It's me," said Jacquot.

"You said twenty kilos, man. More like thirty."

"So you got a visit?"

"You musta been watchin'. 'Bout an hour after you left."

Now Jacquot knew for certain he was being followed. "And?"

"Just like you said. He wanted to know where I'd taken you."

"And you told him?"

"Not immediately. I mean client confidentiality and all. And who was he anyway? What business was it of his?"

"And?"

"He just smiled, drew a chrome-plated cut-throat razor out of his pocket and pressed the blade against my nose. Right there on the jetty. Like he didn't care."

"He doesn't."

"So I said I'd taken you to Harbour Island, some lunch at the Lazy Palm…"

"That's all you told him?"

"That's all I knew, remember?"

"And it was enough?"

"I still got my nose if that's what you mean."

"I'm sorry you had to go through it."

"You have dangerous friends, man. If I'd known, I'd have charged you double."

"I'll be happy to make it up to you."

"Any time, just say the word. You know where to find me."

55

After a contemplative small punch in the Churchill bar (*"A man does what he must..."* on the coaster), Jacquot strolled out onto the club's lunch terrace and said to the Maitre'd that a table had been reserved in the name of Ballard. Apart from his daily calls to Ballard, there had been no contact between them since their flight from Martinique and their drinks together on Sunday. At least, no contact that he'd been aware of. Jacquot was not looking forward to the encounter.

"Right this way, sah. Get you settled, no trouble. Mr Ballard ain't arrived just yet. Can I get you a drink while you waitin'?"

"Menu and wine list will do just fine," said Jacquot, taking the chair that was drawn back for him. He reached for his cigarettes, lit up, and looked across the tutored lawns to the marina. A line of single-sail training boats were being towed out into the bay by a jet-ski, each of the sailboats manned by a boy or girl in matching red life-jackets. A young woman manned the jet-ski, standing on the footrests and looking back to see that her charges were doing what they were supposed to be doing. It could have been Sylvie Martin.

By the time Ballard arrived, a bottle of Pouilly Fumé had been opened, tasted, and then buried in a bucket of ice.

"Sorry to keep you waiting, Daniel. Some high rollers in town, and they need to be coddled."

Jacquot knew he wasn't sorry at all. Ballard was not the kind of man who did 'sorry'. But he let it pass with a shrug, as though the tardiness was of no concern.

"So, how is everything going?" said Ballard, casting an eye over the lunch card.

"You told me no one would follow me," Jacquot replied, getting right to the point. He kept his voice low and level. "I believed you."

"Ah, well, there we are. A lesson learned, my friend."

"And two people dead."

Ballard shrugged.

A waiter arrived at their table.

"Omelette, green salad," said Ballard, and handed him the card. No eye contact, no 'please', no 'thank you'. The man did not exist. Jacquot wondered if Ballard ever left a tip. He doubted it.

"And for me, The Edgewater crab cakes, please." If the company was unpalatable, at least he'd make sure that the food and wine would satisfy. This was his first meal at The Edgewater and everything told him – the attentive service, the china and cutlery, the starched napery, and the gleam of the wine glasses – that he was in for a treat.

Before leaving with their orders, the waiter reached for the wine bottle.

"That's fine, we'll do it ourselves, thank you," said Jacquot, beating him to the bucket and lifting the dripping bottle from the shifting ice. He offered the wine to Ballard, who shook his head. "Water will do just fine," he said.

Tant pis, thought Jacquot, and poured himself a second glass. He sipped it – cool and crisp with just a blink of smokiness – and tried to remember when he'd last had lunch with someone who didn't drink. If it had ever happened, it had been a very long time ago. Lunch, in Jacquot's book, was possibly the best meal of the day. Certainly, now that he was getting older, dinner was ceasing to satisfy. Only lunch held all the cards for him. But not this lunch, or rather not this lunch companion.

"So how did you find her, that landlady? And the motel manager?" asked Ballard, reaching for the water carafe.

"A cop never reveals his source."

"Oh, I can think of ways to make him," said Ballard, with a sly grin, pouring himself a glass of water. "And Harbour Island? How was your lunch?"

"Interesting," said Jacquot, stubbing out his cigarette. He was pleased to see the last of the smoke drift lazily in Ballard's direction.

"Any leads? And just so we're clear, Jacquot, it would be helpful if I didn't have to drag everything out of you."

"Okay, how about this? Sylvie Martin left the Bahamas around the same time that you found Patric."

Ballard shook his head. "Not possible. We checked. I told you that."

"Then whoever checked for you didn't do their job. Or you didn't pay them enough."

"Or we didn't have their children... dangling." Ballard shot him a thin, dangerous smile.

Jacquot leaned across the table, caught hold of Ballard's wrist as he reached for his glass. "If I haven't made it clear enough, *conard*,

I'll tell you one more time. If you so much as touch my children, I will come after you and make you suffer like you have never suffered before. And then I will make you suffer some more."

Another soft, malicious smile. "If you're a cop, don't you have to read me my rights first?"

"I just read them to you."

When their lunch arrived, just moments later, the two men ate in silence. Ballard sliced through his omelette like a man sawing a log, and speared his salad like someone dipping his pen into an inkpot, nervous jab-like motions most of which missed their target at the first attempt. When he succeeded, he lifted the dripping leaves to his mouth and pushed them in with fork and finger, his scarred chin glistening in the sun.

As for Jacquot's crab cakes… Well, they didn't disappoint. Served on a bed of sweet spinach, each of the three muffin-sized croquettes gave way to his fork with a steaming surrender that spilled the shredded meat onto his plate. If he'd expected a generous hand with the breadcrumbs, or any over-cooked dryness, he was mistaken. Just the oozing richness of the crab, beautifully mixed, with a delicate follow-through heat from paprika and sweet chili. For a moment Jacquot thought about ordering mayonnaise, but decided against it. The cakes didn't need any cream, didn't need anything, just the dry smoky kiss of the Pouilly-Fumé to make them memorable.

Across the table, Ballard took the last of the omelette, wiped the napkin across his mouth before he'd finished eating, then dropped it onto his plate.

"So where did she go, Miss Martin?"

"Miami."

"Your friend at the Lazy Palm told you this?"

"Not exactly."

Jacquot could see that Ballard was getting cross. It gave him a small shiver of pleasure.

"And she's still there? In Miami?"

"That's my guess."

"Do you know where?"

"There are a couple of possibilities I need to check out. Which is why I'm going to Miami. This afternoon." Jacquot scooped up the last of his crab cakes, then put down his fork and reached for his glass. He took a sip, licked his lips, and drew the bottle from the bucket. Ballard watched with an icy disapproval as he poured himself another glass. "And this time I really don't want anyone following me."

Ballard spread his hands. "I'm not sure that's a good idea."

"Then my investigation stops right here. And I get the next flight home."

Ballard's eyes widened, and then he chuckled, as though he couldn't believe what he'd just heard. "Aren't you forgetting something?"

"I don't think so. I've told you what I will do if anything happens to my children."

Ballard started to shake his head, a thin teasing smile stretching his lips. "I'm not sure you're in a position to…"

Jacquot slammed the table with the palm of his hand so hard and so fast that the cutlery rattled on their plates and their glasses wobbled. Conversations at nearly tables stopped, and faces turned in their direction.

Ballard suddenly looked uncomfortable. He nodded, tried to squeeze out a conciliatory smile. "If that's what you want…"

"It's what I want," said Jacquot, leaning across the table. "And while I'm about it, you can tell Beth her services are no longer required."

Ballard looked startled, and then even more unsettled. "The housekeeper?"

"There's no other Beth I know."

Jacquot watched Ballard's reaction. Had he been right about Beth? Had she been planted? When he saw Ballard shrug, spread his hands, like a man accepting the inevitable, he knew he'd been right.

Their waiter approached, leaned down to clear their table.

"Can I get you gentlemen anything else?" he asked. "Some dessert? Some coffee?"

"Just the bill, for my friend," said Jacquot.

The waiter looked relieved. He loaded their plates on his arm, nodded and left.

"How long will you be away?" asked Ballard, eyes narrowed.

"Three or four days."

"In Miami?"

"To start with."

"And when do you intend to leave?"

"I told you. This afternoon."

Ballard sat back in his chair, as though to consider Jacquot's plan of action.

"You'll go tomorrow," he said at last. "Tonight, there's a party at Baize Central. Lots of action."

"Your high rollers?"

"Exactly." Ballard pushed back his chair, and got to his feet. "I'll send the driver to pick you up. Ten o'clock. Dress smart."

And with that he turned on his heel and left the terrace.

56

Too many 'coaster' quotes in the Churchill bar. That's what had done
it. That's what had finally made Jacquot snap. Having to do what
Ballard told him, being complicit in his and DiCorsa's criminality,
had finally made Jacquot see red. Made him bang his fist down on
the table. Made him turn on Ballard and hurl the man's threat to his
children back in his face, and follow it with a threat of his own. Like
for like. And as he went down the front steps of The Edgewater and
waited for his car to be brought round, he could feel himself trembling.
Trembling with rage, and with fear, too. Playing with his daughters'
safety like that. What had he been thinking? What had he done?

For more than thirty years he had been a cop, a good cop, yet
now he found himself on the other side of the law, helping these men
in their efforts to retrieve ill-gotten gains, knowing innocent people
had died in the commission of that aim. And all because Ballard
and DiCorsa had threatened his children, putting him in a position
where any false move might prove fatal to his daughters. But they
were dead anyway, as was he, no matter what happened. Whether
Sylvie Martin and the money were found, or not. In Ballard's and
DiCorsa's world there were never any loose ends. It was the way
they worked, how they survived. Cold and cruel and utterly ruthless.
Patric, Boni, Martha Swanson, Nelson Gittings, all of them had died
because they had crossed Ballard and his boss. And Rodrigo Fuentes,
too. Some poor racecourse runner who'd maybe, or maybe not, tried
to skim what didn't belong to him. Twenty thousand, wasn't it? Just
twenty thousand dollars, and the man was thrown to the sharks. And
how many others had suffered that same fate? What was it DiCorsa
had said when the sharks first put in an appearance and honed in on
Fuentes. *There's more sharks round here than leaves on a tree. And I
like to think I've played some part in that.*

Which was why, finally, Jacquot had behaved the way he had. The
only thing that he could do now, his only hope, was to fight back.
And fight back hard. And be smart, play smart. It was all a game.
Like poker, nothing more nor less. Everything hanging on the cards
in your hand, the cards in your opponents' hands. A good hand, or
a good bluff. And as Jacquot swung up into the Explorer's driver's
seat and accelerated away from the club, he remembered Patric in the

video clip at Baize Two, sitting at that round table, facing the woman with the plunging neckline, and winning; and probably, as Louise had suggested, winning against all the odds. If Patric could do it, then so could he.

After leaving The Edgewater Jacquot drove into town, parked in a side-street behind Government House and found a phone kiosk. Using his credit card he made three calls, the first to Balmet at the *gendarmerie* on Îles des Frères who assured him that everything was okay. He had taken it upon himself, he told Jacquot, to bring in friends to watch the house round the clock, and to follow Midou and the girls whenever they drove into town. There had been no sighting of anyone suspicious anywhere near the house, he had a check on all incoming visitors to the island, a watching brief on all the island's various accommodations and, with his father's help, was even keeping an eye on any vessel coming into island waters. Jacquot could tell that Balmet was confident he'd done everything to ensure the girls' safety, and was grateful for it. But then Balmet didn't know the opposition. He'd done all he could, all anyone could. Jacquot only hoped it would be enough.

"You comin' back soon, Monsieur Jacquot?"

"A few more days," Jacquot had told him. "Early next week at the latest."

The second call he made was to the house on Trinité, and it was Midou, Claudine's daughter, who picked up the phone.

"She better be pretty," was the first thing Midou said when she heard Jacquot's voice. It was just what her mother would have said, in that same challenging, teasing tone. They might not have looked alike, but whenever Jacquot heard Midou's voice on the phone it was like talking to Claudine. And the two women shared the same kind of bantering tone.

"The prettiest I could find," he replied. "But she's hard work."

"You'll be used to that, then," said Midou. "You were with Mama long enough, you must have learned something." And then her voice dropped a note. "But it's not a girl, is it Jacquot? And it's not business, either. It's something else. Something not so nice."

"I'm afraid you're right. Not so nice."

"I guessed. The place is crawling here. I can't sneeze without blowing someone over, or have someone pop out from behind a tree and offer me a tissue. Are we in danger?"

Jacquot sighed. "You could be. That's why Sergeant Balmet and his boys are there, keeping an eye on things."

"Does it have something to do with that friend of yours? The one who committed suicide?"

"Yes, it does. And she didn't commit suicide."

There was a pause on the end of the line. And then, "I had a feeling, you know? Balmet was real touchy about it, didn't want to say the wrong thing."

"He's a good guy, he'll see you right."

"What about going back to Martinique? Taking the girls with me? No one would find me there, no one would know where to look."

It was something Jacquot had considered, but he knew that with Ballard and DiCorsa there was nowhere really safe, nowhere Midou and the kids could go without being found. Better they stayed where they were, on their own turf, with Balmet and his boys to look out for them.

"I'd be happier if you stayed where you are. If you need to move, I'll let you know, but for now..."

"And you? Are you safe? Are you going to be okay?"

"For now. For now. But I've got my guardian angel looking out for me. You know the one?"

"I know the one," said Midou, with a tremor in her voice. "So you're in good hands."

"Are the girls about?"

"You've only been away a few days and already you've forgotten?" Another Claudine jibe. "They're at school, Jacquot, like every other day, but with a half-dozen yardies hanging around the school gates to look out for them."

"Give them a hug from me and tell them I'll be back soon."

"I'll do that. No problem."

"And take care, you."

"I'll do that, too. Miss you, Papa."

It wasn't till he'd hung up, that he realised what Midou said. That last word. He couldn't decide if it made it easier, or harder, to do what he knew he had to do.

The third call was to his new friend, Marlon, at Arawak Point, and by far the longest call he made.

As he walked back to Patric's car he realised that for the first time in a long time he was frightened. Really frightened. For himself, and for those closest to him.

There was so much at stake, so much to lose.

And Jacquot knew all about loss.

57

There was no sign of Beth when Jacquot returned to the house on Lyford Cay. Just two hours since his lunch with Ballard, and the place was deserted, the rooms silent, the air dead and heavy. The kitchen, where Beth had served him ham and eggs that morning, was spotless, and soulless. He opened the fridge. Empty. No milk, no butter, no cooling jug of punch. Nothing. As though the unit had been cleaned out. He checked the cupboards. Again, nothing. No coffee, no sugar, no dry goods of any description. Beth had clearly made good her departure, taken everything with her, and done it in the last couple of hours. As he went from cupboard to cupboard, Jacquot wondered if Ballard had told her to do it – to take everything. It wouldn't surprise him. But good riddance to the pair of them, he thought, and going to his room he stripped off his clothes, pulled on his shorts and headed out to the beach.

The swim soothed him. The clear warm water, sluicing through his hair and beard, the sun sparkling over its surface, the clean, sharp, salty taste of it. And as he swam he thought of his daughters, swimming with them at Trinité. He'd taken them to the ocean within days of arriving on Île des Frères, a squirming little body in each arm, sitting himself down on the shoreline with the pair of them in his lap, letting the curling, bubbling wavelets wash up between his legs and over their tiny feet and pudgy legs. They'd screamed like banshees, waved their little arms as though to shoo the sea away, but he'd kept at it until they could sit unsupported and kick the incoming water with their legs, laughing and gurgling instead of screeching, squeezing handfuls of sand in dimpled fingers. When they were old enough, when they knew how to keep themselves afloat, he took them out further, flipping them onto his back and swimming around, whichever one was upfront – usually Matti – gripping his hair like the reins of a horse. He could feel that weight now, the pair of them on his back, their little legs clenched against his ribs, heels digging in, their screams of delight when he ducked down and the water threatened to unseat them. And he missed it, longed for it.

When Jacquot returned to the beach, wading ashore, he felt fresh and clean, flipping his hair back from his eyes and rubbing his hand through his beard. He hadn't brought a towel but he was dry by the time he reached the house, sliding open the door to his room and stepping under a cool shower to wash away the salty tightness of the sea. And then, lying naked on his bed, he closed his eyes and slept.

He woke to darkness in his room, and in the garden beyond, and for a moment imagined himself at home, in his own bed, waiting for the girls to scamper in, burrowing under the sheet for their morning cuddle. And for a moment he waited for that comforting familiar sound of bare feet pattering on a wood floor, until he realised it wouldn't come, he wasn't there. He peered at his watch, his cheap diver's Swatch, saw the time, made sense of it, and realised with a suddenly sinking heart that it was time to get up, and get ready, and face whatever new slide Ballard had in store for him.

Thirty minutes later, he looked himself over in the bathroom mirror. Patric's white tuxedo, a pair of double-stripe black trousers, a crisply tailored white shirt and black bow tie. Even the black patent pumps he'd found in Patric's dressing room fitted easily. Jacquot adjusted the tie, just visible beneath his trimmed beard, worked the collar of the shirt, just a centimetre or so too tight, and saw the green eyes wince and tanned skin tauten. He took a breath, and was whistling it out when the front door bell rang. He glanced at his watch. Just a few minutes before ten. He tucked the watch under his cuff, worked his neck again, and then left the bathroom.

It was time to play with the high-rollers.

58

It took about twenty minutes to reach Baize Central, the first club that Patric had opened, a long brick warehouse three blocks back from a marine engineering works and dry-dock, and a mile or so past the island's ferry terminal. Once they'd left the main strip the traffic thinned and the streetlights stood further apart. There was no sign of life here, and few lit windows. The same man who'd driven him that first day on the island – picking him up at the airport, and then driving him to DiCorsa's boat and back home again – pulled into a fenced forecourt and parked beside a low red Ferrari and a pair of silver Porsches.

"Just ring the bell," he said, the motor running. "Someone'll come fetch you."

Jacquot opened his door, climbed out and, straightening his jacket and tie, walked across the parking lot to a pair of high wood doors set with a small Judas gate. A single light bulb in a wired metal frame was set above the doors and illuminated a brass plaque engraved with the name *Baize Central*. There was no bell that he could see, but when he was no more than a few feet away, the Judas gate swung open. Behind it stood a man who'd have been a fair match for Brock, dressed in a tight-fitting evening jacket and blue velvet bow tie that had clearly been clipped into place, moving to one side and opening the gate wider, as though the clothes Jacquot wore were enough to gain him entrance.

Bending his head Jacquot stepped through the door into a brick-walled, thickly-carpeted reception area that was decorated, like Baize Two, with sporting prints. Below two fine oil paintings of famous Triple Crown thoroughbred winners was a long low reception desk manned by an island girl in a slim cream suit and orchid buttonhole. Her hair was lacquered and her smile was sweetly fixed.

"Good evening, sir," she said. "And welcome to Baize Central. If you'd care to sign in," she said, sliding a large leather-bound ledger across the counter, and opening it for his signature. It was a clean page, no other names visible.

Jacquot signed, pushed the ledger back, and the receptionist checked his name.

"Mr Milhaud, a pleasure to have you with us this evening. Mr

Ballard isn't here yet, but he asked me to give you this." She leaned below the counter and brought out a small package.

Jacquot took it, opened it, and found a long plastic box. He flipped the lid and saw that it was filled with a stack of gaming chips. He tipped them out – a mix of fifty and hundred-dollar chips – slipped them into his jacket pocket, and returned the empty box to the receptionist. She took it, smiled, and pointed him towards a set of baize-covered doors studded around the edge with shining brass tacks. "Just go on through," she said, "and have yourself a very good evening."

Jacquot thanked her, smiled, and did what he was told.

So this is where it all began, he thought, as he stepped through the studded baize doors into the gaming hall of Baize Central. On a thick red carpet, under green shaded lamps, stood roulette, baccarat and blackjack tables, two craps tubs, and on a raised platform along one wall a number of green baize-covered poker tables. And spread around the room club members and their guests placed their bets, or checked their cards, or threw their dice, or simply watched the action as girls in black tights, high heels, and blue satin swimsuits wove between them with trays of drinks. There was a low hum of conversation, the rattle of roulette balls hitting the wheel, and occasional shouts of delight. Above the shaded lights was a long blue cloud of cigar and cigarette smoke, and playing in the background a soft classical soundtrack.

As far as Jacquot could estimate the room was at least fifty metres long and half that wide, an old bonded warehouse with a high raftered ceiling and ballast brick walls. There were no windows that he could see, and at the end of the room a scarlet-runnered staircase rose up to another level, its mezzanine balustrade hung with concealing black drapes. A braided scarlet rope on two brass posts had been set up at the foot of this staircase, and was guarded by another formidably-sized Brock relative.

Jingling the chips in his pocket, Jacquot slid in between two punters at the first roulette table he came to. He was not a gambling man – or rather, not a man who gambled on a regular basis – but he knew more than he'd let on to Louisa at Baize Two. He dipped into his pocket and brought out three chips – two fifties and a hundred. He placed the fifties on 30 and 26 and the hundred on '*Impair*'. The varnished wheel spun, the ivory ball was flicked against the spin, and the croupier in silver satin waistcoat sounded the well-worn phrase "*Rien ne va plus*" as the ball tripped and gave a rattling indecisive hop, skip and a jump before settling into the red pocket marked 13. The odds had been stacked against him on the numbers, but his hundred-dollar stake on '*Impair*' had increased dramatically. He stayed for three more spins and was watching the wheel slow on the final turn when an arm slid through his and a voice whispered in his ear.

"666 – the nature of the beast."

Jacquot turned as the ball dropped in the pocket next to his number and his chips were raked away. The arm belonged to one of the most beautiful women he had ever seen. Long black hair falling over bare shoulders that supported the thinnest straps on a sleek red satin dress that seemed to be made from the same amount of cloth one might use for a cushion cover. And nothing else. Her skin was a dark golden brown, her eyes black as a moonless night, and her lips as red as her dress. And as he turned to her, the arm slid away from his and long fingers curled onto the lapel of his jacket. She was close enough to kiss and they both knew it.

"666?" asked Jacquot.

"Didn't you know? You add all the numbers together, it's 666. The beast. The devil."

Jacquot smiled. "But it's an American wheel. One to thirty-seven. 703."

She frowned, then tossed her hair, smiled a sly, complicit smile. "Close enough, Mr…?"

"Ah," came another, familiar, voice, and Jacquot looked up to see Ballard coming towards him. He was immaculately dressed. His shirt crisp, lapels a satin shine, the evening jacket trimly-waisted, beautifully tailored. "Daniel, Daniel, so pleased you could make it," he said, as though lunchtime's harsh words had never been spoken. He glanced at the girl, nodded, smiled, and Jacquot felt her fingers tighten on his jacket. "I see you're having fun. Any luck on the wheel?"

"Some," said Jacquot. "My friend here was telling me how to beat the odds."

Ballard gave the girl a beaming smile, as though she'd done him a personal favour. "Good, that's good. At Baize we like to provide our guests with all the help we can. A House rule." And then, switching seamlessly into English, with only the slightest French accent, he turned to the girl and said, "But if you'd excuse us, young lady, my friend and I have some business to attend to."

The girl tipped her head, and drew away, melted into the crowd. She clearly knew who Ballard was, and knew to do as she was told.

"So sorry to interrupt when you're making friends," said Ballard, switching back to French, with a sharp little smile and raised eyebrow, "but there's something I'd like you to see. Something that might interest you."

"And that is?"

Ballard nodded across the room. "You see the man over there? At the *Caisse*? The tall one with the goatee, carrying a case?"

Jacquot looked where he was instructed and saw the man Ballard had described. He carried a ribbed aluminium case which he passed through an opening in the barred grille, receiving a small rack of chips in exchange. It was a swift and practiced transaction. With a nod of thanks to the girl behind the grille, Goatee turned, looked around the room, and headed for the nearest craps tub.

"Inside that case there's near enough five hundred thousand dollars belonging to Ettore DiCorsa's clients. Sometimes it's more – anything up to a million – and sometimes less. But always a considerable amount. Two or three times a week, at one or more of our clubs. Of course, high-stakes' evenings like this one are the perfect time to do it, when large amounts of cash will be changing hands. So why don't I show you how that half-a-million dollars gets cleaned and accounted for?"

59

Leaving the roulette table, Ballard led Jacquot to the stairs where the Brock lookalike unhooked the braided barrier rope and stood aside for them. At the top of the stairs Ballard drew back the black drapes and gestured Jacquot through onto the mezzanine level. The same brick walls, a spread of blackened timbers supporting the roof, the same plush red carpet, and three round baize-covered tables each set with nine leather chairs, eight of the chairs with a name card in front of it and a stack of chips – round ones like those that Jacquot had been given, but piles of rectangular pearly plaques, too.

At one of these tables three croupiers in red satin waistcoats and three pit bosses in black tie stood together, whispering amongst themselves, waiting. None of them was drinking, none smoking. That was happening at the bar where Ballard's high-rollers were gathered – a large group of them talking and laughing amongst themselves. They all seemed to know each other but despite the hum of bonhomie and exuberance Jacquot detected a frisson of caution, a coldness to the gathering, a sense that these people were here for a great deal more than friendly small-talk.

All were dressed formally, though it was clear that Ballard's high-rollers had a different take on formality. Here were frilled shirts in flamboyant colours, lizard waistcoats and shiny silk jackets, string ties with topaz clasps, velvet trousers, leather trousers, high heels, trainers, and cowboy boots. And jewellery to match: chunky gold watches, jangling bracelets, and rings as thick and as threatening as knuckle-dusters. As far as Jacquot could determine the women in the group were either players themselves, or companions – the former older, harder, with tight smiles and sharp searching eyes, the latter younger, like the 666 girl Jacquot had met earlier by the roulette table. Were these younger ones like Sylvie's mother, Jacquot wondered? Good time girls working the casinos, working the clients, laid on by Ballard to keep his high-rollers happy? It seemed highly likely that they were. All part of the service.

As Jacquot took in his surroundings, and sized up the company, Ballard pushed ahead through the crowd, making for the bar, shaking hands on the way, introducing Jacquot as Patric's brother-in-law. The men and the women he was introduced to looked at him hard, as though he were another hand at the table, more competition, sizing him up.

"So where you hidin' Patric?" one of them asked Jacquot, while Ballard waved to the barman for drinks. The man wore a long string tie secured with a set of spreading silver bullhorns. His cheeks were as red as the croupiers' waistcoats, and his hair a greasy flick of black strands.

Jacquot smiled, shrugged. "Out of town, I heard, probably playing a table somewhere. You know Patric." And as he said it, he wished that it were true, that Patric really was playing a table somewhere, that he had avoided those last desperate thrashing moments, alone in a dark sea. But he hadn't, and Jacquot felt again a deep hatred for the man just a few feet away, ordering drinks, the man who – by his own admission – had pushed Patric off the boat, the man who was holding Matti and Béa to ransom. That his influence could reach as far as Trinité made Jacquot's blood run cold.

"I know Patric, okay," said Mr String Tie. "Came all the way from Houston to play him, get my money back from our last game. Seems like I'm gonna be disappointed."

"Takin' it from his House is just as good," said the woman standing beside him. She was the one in the lizard waistcoat and looked at Jacquot as though he were something served up for her dinner. Her hands were old and gnarled but the skin on her cheeks and forehead shone.

"Maybe so, maybe so, but I don't get to see that big smile of his crumple when I lay down the aces."

"You ever see his smile crumple," said another man, short and wiry as a jockey, with deep vertical lines creasing his cheeks. "Best poker face I ever seen."

Ballard came back with their drinks, passed Jacquot a tumbler of whiskey that rattled with ice, and turned to the players. "Patric sends his apologies, of course. Sorry not to be here with you folks, so he can take all that money you've brought along."

Before they could respond, a buzzer sounded and one of the pit bosses, now prowling the outer edges of the group, called out, "Ladies and gentleman, if you'd like to take your seats. Dealing in five. Take your seats, please. Take your seats. Five minutes…"

It didn't take long for the group to disperse, as though they'd been waiting for the moment and were impatient to begin, and Jacquot watched from the bar as the players found their places and settled at their tables. Lighting cigarettes, cigars, taking a drink, setting their glasses on the green baize, reaching for ashtrays. Jackets shrugged off, slung on chair backs. Cuffs unbuttoned, sleeves rolled up. The group had panned out just as Jacquot had suspected, the older women taking their seats with the men, the prettier, younger girls holding back at the bar. And as the players settled, the lights around the room dimmed save for the tasselled lamps above each table, their baize tops illuminated like three green pools in the darkness, wisps of cigarette and cigar smoke rising into the light. In short order, the pit bosses handed sealed packs of cards to the croupiers, the packs were opened, Jokers removed, and the cards expertly shuffled. Moments later, simultaneously, on each of the three tables, as though the croupiers had been choreographed to the second, with a flick of the wrist the first cards of the evening flipped across the baize.

"Ten thousand dollars a chair, twenty-four chairs," said Ballard, coming up beside Jacquot. "No wonder the House always wins."

"Who are they? Where do you find them?" asked Jacquot.

"Professionals, World Series players… They can be anyone so long as they pay for their place. And deposit a further hundred thousand play money with the House. That's the chips you can see, which they're free to add to whenever they wish, or need to. Which we hope they will. As well as the chair price, the House takes a further two per cent of all winnings from each player. You end up below your minimum hundred thou stake, you walk away free and clear – if a lot poorer. But when you're up, you pay the House when the sessions end. That's two per cent of a minimum two point four million dollar pot. And that's before the first card's dealt."

Jacquot whistled softly. "Win win."

"That's right. Win win. Big time, which is how that million or half-million downstairs just gets lost in the pile."

By now the three croupiers had dealt each of the players their first two cards, and at each of the three tables antes were being placed, chips pushed out into the pot. More cards followed, three per player, slickly spun over the baize. Carefully gathered.

"And it's just straight poker, like this?" asked Jacquot.

"Draw, Stud, Five-card, Seven-card, Texas Hold 'em. You name it.

Everything but Strip."

"How long do the sessions last?"

"Depends on the players. All night? All day? Who knows? Longest we had was two days, three nights. With breaks, of course."

"I don't think I'm going to last that long," said Jacquot, glancing at his watch. "It's time I went home. I have a busy day tomorrow."

"You have, indeed. But, ah, there's been a change of plan. I'm afraid you're going to have to book your Miami flight for the afternoon."

"Why?" asked Jacquot, suddenly alert.

Ballard smiled. "Because, my friend, at ten-thirty tomorrow morning you have a funeral to attend."

60

She'd be on her back, thought Jacquot. She wouldn't like that. If he had had any part to play in the arrangements for Boni's funeral, he would have asked that she be put on her side, the right side, with a single pillow, hands between her knees. But then he hadn't known about the funeral until the previous evening at Baize Central when Ballard had told him that Boni had been brought back to the island after her autopsy in Martinique.

When he'd asked about the autopsy's findings, Ballard had told him that thanks to the small traces of Pridoxamine a verdict of unlawful killing had been returned, and that an order had been given for the local *Judiciaire* to mount an investigation; to find, charge, and prosecute those held to be responsible. Ballard had smiled, spread his hands. Whatever happened with regard to that investigation, it was clear that neither he nor Ettore DiCorsa would lose any sleep over it. *Tant pis.*

Now, ten hours later, Jacquot, the dearly-departed's brother, sat alone in the front pew in a catholic church off Lyford Cay Road. The church was old and small, dating back to colonial times, with a wooden spire and timbered porch, its coral stone blocks painted a blinding white against the palms and sky and distant sea. Inside, the walls were more colourfully decorated with rainbow murals and scenes of island life that looked as if schoolchildren had painted them. It was cool in the church and smelled of candles and incense, wood polish and fat waxy blooms. Boni's casket had been placed on a draped trestle at the altar rail and decorated with a bouquet of spikey scarlet strelitzia. About forty mourners had gathered for the private ceremony. Apart from Ballard in the pew opposite, with Forbes-Temple from The Edgewater beside him, and a smartly-dressed woman in the row behind them whom he recognised from Louisa's video as Mrs Drumgoole, Jacquot knew none of the mourners. It was enough to receive their sad consoling smiles and sympathetic nods whenever he looked around.

For now, though, as the service proceeded as funeral services always do, with hymns and prayers and blessings for Boni Stuyvesant, Jacquot couldn't help but recall the last time he'd been to a funeral. In France, five years earlier. A service that had broken his heart. There had been a dusting of snow on the ground back then, at Abbé de Laune in Salon, where Claudine's body had been laid to rest. At the service in the brick-vaulted Laune chapel he had stood in the front pew with Midou beside him, each of them with one of the girls in their arms. Béa, whimpering, unsettled, being rocked and shushed by Midou; Matti, eyes wide and round, watching, listening, hardly stirring, as though she didn't want to miss a thing.

And as he sat there in that church on Lyford Cay Road Jacquot remembered yet another funeral he'd been to just a year before Claudine's. At Saint Vincent de Paul, in Marseilles. The funeral of Isabelle Cassier, a Chief Inspector with the city's *Judiciaire*. Three funerals in six years, three women, all of them special, all at one time or another an important part of his life. Two of them murdered, the one closest to his heart taken in childbirth.

Isabelle's casket, and Claudine's, had both been mahogany, but Boni's was white, as gleaming white as the church's coral stone walls, the red petals of the strelitzia spilling like blood over its lid. And beneath that lid, Boni. So close, but now so far away. And though he didn't feel the numbing heartbreak and utter loss that he had felt with Claudine, he was still filled with sadness – and anger – that such an old friend was gone, no longer a part of his life. Just a memory now. But taken so cruelly, so unjustly.

He wondered what she'd look like. Had they made her up? Would they have covered the autopsy's savage scarring? That raised, roughly stitched 'Y' of a scarlet incision, running from her shoulders to her sternum and down to her abdomen. And what clothes would she be wearing, he wondered? Probably nothing more than a hospital gown from Martinique. And what of the jewellery? The watch and the ring, the bracelet and earrings? Where had those ended up? A light-fingered hospital orderly in Martinique? Or Ballard, taking possession of Boni's personal belongings – as her husband; everything from Île des Frères and Martinique bundled up and sent back to Nassau along with the body?

A sudden pause in the proceedings, followed by a shuffling of feet, brought Jacquot back to the church on Lyford Cay Road. Ballard and Forbes-Temple and four other men were gathering around the casket which, with a practiced ease, they hoisted up on to their shoulders. Heads tilted, arms clasped, and cheeks pressed against the sides of the coffin, they started down the aisle in a matching slow step. As soon as they'd passed him, Jacquot left his pew, too, and followed them out of the church, keeping his eyes on the narrowed end of the white coffin where Boni's feet would be. Would they be bare? Or had someone put shoes on her? He tried to think of anything that might keep his mind off the fact that the man carrying her casket was the man who had ordered her death, and murdered her husband. He wanted, once again, to leap on Ballard, do him damage, denounce him at the very least. But he knew he couldn't. Not yet.

Outside the sun beat down, a bright, squinting light, just lacy pools of shadow beneath the palms. A hearse was waiting, its rear hatch door open. As Jacquot and his fellow mourners gathered around the porch, the coffin was lowered by the pallbearers and then rolled into the hearse's glass-sided interior. The hatch door was softly closed, and, with just the barest crunch of coral stone gravel beneath its tyres, the hearse drew away, off to the island's crematorium.

Where would the ashes go, thought Jacquot, with no family left to claim them?

Where would Boni want them to be spread?

Jacquot knew a place.

"Mr Milhaud, our condolences, sir," said the first mourner, an elderly gentleman whom Jacquot had seen at the club, taking and shaking his hand, followed in a line by the rest of the congregation, young and old, men and women, in their dark linen suits and sombre weeds, with their whispered and sorrowful sympathies, until only Jacquot, Ballard, and Mrs Drumgoole remained. She was taller than Jacquot had expected, and slimmer than she'd appeared in the video clip at Baize Two. He wondered how old she was. Early to mid forties, he guessed, dressed in a close-fitting charcoal grey suit, its collared mandarin jacket buttoned to the throat, the hem of its skirt clinging tightly to her knees, the calves of her bare legs tightened and sculpted by the high heels of her pointed black shoes. Her blonde hair was drawn up under a veiled black straw cap, its narrow brim throwing a dappled shadow over her face, her skin lightly tanned, smooth and flawless. If she was wearing make-up it was hard to detect beyond a lightly applied brush of pale red lipstick. There was no jewellery that Jacquot could see, but the high collar, long sleeves, and her black leather gloves could have hidden it. In that beating, pulsing heat, in the shadowy closeness of the porch, she smelled of the shower, fresh and citrus-y, with just the lightest note of tuberose and coconut. It was a wealthy, independent, confident scent. Not too much, not too little. But there all the same.

"Can I offer you gentlemen some lunch?" asked Mrs Drumgoole, after Ballard had made the introductions. "Sounds awful, I know, but funerals just always make me real hungry." Her voice was firm and southern, a no-nonsense sort of voice, and though the invitation had been extended to both of them she kept her eyes fixed on Jacquot. It was clear that Ballard was not included. Jacquot saw a thin flare of irritation tighten his lips, and felt pleasure in it. He doubted this was the first time that Ballard had been so delicately sidelined.

"How kind," Ballard said, with a smile he must have mined from somewhere deep, deep down, "but I do have some business in town to attend to. And Daniel, I know, has a flight to catch." This time the smile was more genuine, the satisfaction of the last word.

"You're surely not leaving us so soon, are you? Why, I understand you've only just arrived on the island." Mrs Drumgoole's grey eyes sparkled with mischief, the tiniest crease of laugh lines settling around them.

"A short trip," replied Jacquot. "I hope to be back in a few days."

"And, pray, what time is this flight of yours?" she asked, in a tone of voice that suggested flight times could easily be juggled whereas business in town might not be so readily re-scheduled. It was another snub to Ballard, though subtly and lightly delivered. To soften the blow she reached out a gloved hand and laid it on Ballard's arm, though she kept her eyes firmly on Jacquot.

"At five. To Miami."

"And are you packed? Ready to go?"

"All packed. Ready to go."

"Well, my dear man, that gives us just an ocean of time for a little bitty bite to eat, wouldn't you say? If you're hungry, that is?"

Jacquot spread his hands in submission.

"So, there we are. It's agreed," she declared, as though there could have been any other outcome. Opening her black clutch she pulled out a pair of sunglasses, raised her veil, and slid them on. "Do you have a car?" she asked.

"Just down the lane," he replied, nodding towards Patric's Explorer.

"Well, since you won't know the way, why don't we have my driver take the lead and you can follow? Or better still, why don't we have him take your car, and I'll drive you. Why, we could even pick up your case on the way and then lunch can be as long as we like." As she spoke, a long black Bentley drew up at the lych gate. "Clarkson always gets very bossy about the car," she continued. "Won't hardly ever let me drive. But this time I'm going to insist." She looped her arm through Jacquot's and nodded to Ballard. "Mr Ballard, so nice to see you again, and I am so sorry you can't join us. But do let me know the minute you hear from Patric, won't you? Last time we met, he cleaned me out, and this girl's looking for some payback."

61

"What a loathsome, horrible worm of a man," said Mrs Drumgoole, as she turned the Bentley into traffic on West Bay Road, tugging off her gloves finger by finger with her teeth and tossing them onto the back seat. A chunky gold bracelet and gold Cartier watch now made an appearance, along with a large diamond ring. Her hands were long and slim and elegant with plainly lacquered nails. Handling the car with an easy confidence, she now unpinned her black straw hat, tossed it into the back with the gloves, and loosened her bun. As the hair tumbled across her shoulders and she raked it out with her fingers, her scent slid across the seats, and Jacquot felt the warm fragrant closeness of her. "He makes my skin just crawl," she continued, shuddering to give the comment some emphasis. "I mean, the way he looks at you, you know? All sly and hungry, and sideways, like he knows something you don't, or wants something you're not in a month of Sundays ever going to give him. And those teeth, my Lord. That gap. Looks like the coin slot in a kiddie's moneybox. So... lascivious. The way he licks it, too." She gave another shiver. "But now, of course, having said all that, you're going to tell me he's your greatest, oldest, dearest friend. Please say he's not. He couldn't be, surely?"

"Rest assured, madame, that is not, and will never be, the case," said Jacquot with a smile.

"Well, I'm deeply comforted to hear it," she said. "And it's Elaine, please. I love being called 'madame' in that accent of yours, but why don't you try Elaine for size?"

"Elaine," he said, drawing out the name in response to her gentle flirting. She was, he decided, a quite delightful companion, and not just because she loathed Ballard. She made him feel as though he'd known her forever, and certainly made him feel that he'd like to know her better.

"Aha, I was right." She glanced across at him and smiled, coyly. "Just as I suspected. Even better than 'madame'."

Ten minutes later, with his suitcase tucked away in the Bentley's boot and the Stuyvesant house locked up, they joined West Bay Road once more and headed towards town.

"You know something?" said Elaine. "You don't look anything like her. Boni, I mean. The same voice, maybe, but that's just the accent. But everything else? No likeness whatsoever."

"Sometimes it happens like that."

"Maybe. Just strange is all. And quite an age gap for a brother and sister?"

Jacquot was impressed. And suddenly alert. It was the first time anyone had made any mention of the age difference. "Our parents blamed her on a *balon* too many of an aged bas-Armagnac. At their twentieth anniversary dinner." He wondered where that had come from. Such a smooth, plausible lie.

"Fact is," Elaine continued, "you look more like Patric. Same kind of build, same kind of knowing look. Same kind of confidence, too, you don't mind my saying."

"You've known him a long time?"

"Way back. Soon after he started his first club. As for Boni, it took a bit of time, but we got there in the end. I think at first she considered me an old flame of her husband's and therefore someone to keep at arms' length. None of that 'keep your friends close, and your enemies closer'. Don't blame her, I suppose. But it didn't last long. A couple of girly lunches and we were just tight as mating mayflies."

"And were you? An old flame?"

Elaine chuckled. "There you go. Just the kind of thing that Patric would ask. You really could be brothers."

"And?"

Elaine Drumgoole looked ahead, as though she hadn't heard the repeated question, or if she had she didn't altogether approve of the prying. Her chin was raised, her eyes looking down the bridge of her nose to the road ahead. There was something stiff-backed and patrician about her, and for a moment Jacquot wondered if she might not be looking for a spot to pull in, to leave him and his suitcase on the side of the road. But she didn't. She just shook her head.

"I tried. Just after my husband died. I was sad and lonely, and Patric used to call by. Bring me little gifts. Some funny little trinket he'd seen in a market someplace, or some fruit, you know? Like I was sick, and he was visiting a bedside. Which wasn't that far off the truth. But that was as far as I got him. The bedside. And when Boni happened along, why the only time I played with Patric after that was over the green baize."

"I hear he's good. A good player." Through the Bentley's shaded windows, Jacquot watched the turning for The Edgewater Club pass them by.

Elaine frowned. "You don't know him? Haven't you two ever met? Your sister married to him and all?"

Jacquot realised with a start that he'd let his guard down, would need to cover. He was Boni's brother after all. More lies were called for. More explanations. Elaine, he realised, was as sharp and canny as she was beautiful. Not someone he should underestimate. Which rather pleased him.

"I missed the wedding," he replied. "I was in hospital. Broken leg."

Elaine nodded, but the frown still hovered. "But never any other time?"

"We always seem to miss each other. Different countries, I suppose. I'm in France, he's here. Speak to him on the phone now and again; we're always planning to meet up… It's just never happened."

Which seemed finally to satisfy Elaine, playing the Bentley's steering wheel through her hands.

"Well, your loss, is all I can say. Your sister hooked herself a good one and that's for sure and certain. A real gem. And when it comes to cards – or any game, for that matter – he is…. Well, I've known some fine players in my time, believe me, but he's in a different league. And I've never beaten him, you know that? Not once. Not a single game. Poker, backgammon… deck or dice don't signify. Which makes me mad, I'm telling you. Sometimes, when I throw down my cards and look at him across the table I just know I had the better hand, would have beaten him. But with Patric, you never can be quite certain. Not certain enough. Nerves of steel, and a poker face to beat all-comers. No tell, no give-away. Just that slow smile of his. A smile you can't ever read." She turned to Jacquot, lowered her chin and gave him a sharp enquiring look over the top of her sunglasses. "So tell me about you, Daniel Milhaud. What's your story?"

"A lawyer, in Marseilles. I specialise in shipping. Maritime law." Another lie, smoothly delivered; he was getting good at this.

"Guess that's as good a place as any to do it," she said. "You married? Family?"

"Not married. But… I suppose you could say I'm a widower."

"You and me both. Two of a kind. Kids?"

"Two daughters. You?"

"Two step-sons. Layabouts the pair of them. Think they know it all, and just hate the fact that I'm the one who writes the cheques."

"What do they do?"

"One's a film-maker in LA, the other's in the music business, New York." She shot him a look. "Couldn't take a photo, or put on a record between them. Thought they'd lucked out when I married their father."

"And he was?"

"Harry Drumgoole. A painter. Canvases, not buildings. Kind of successful locally, but nothing great. What I mean is, he won't get to see the inside of Sotheby's anytime soon. But a kind and lovely man all the same. I miss him."

"So... where...?" Jacquot paused, spread his hand around the Bentley's plush interior. The polished burr walnut dash, the cream leather seats, the thick carpet beneath their feet.

"...Where does the money come from?" She laughed. "Just like Patric. Just the thing he'd ask. Fact is, it's the family business. Behrens Bank."

It took Jacquot a moment to register the name. Île des Frères. Justine Balmet behind the counter at Madame Corale. Boni had bought that floral print dress with a Behrens Bank debit card. But he didn't tell Elaine that.

"Not a name I know," he said instead.

"No reason you should, unless your maritime law business is paying you big bucks. Very big bucks. Minimum holding for prospective clients at Behrens Bank is a million clear. Which means no ties on it. To be kept on deposit. Current accounts need another million to set up and run. Go below it and you get your money back, minus commissions and handling fees, of course, with a recommendation to contact another house."

"You don't look like any bank manager I've ever met," said Jacquot.

She gave him a brief look. "Let me guess. Crédit Agricole?"

Jacquot nodded. "So where did the bank come from?"

"Great-grand-daddy. Settled on the island with his ill-gotten gains, met himself a pretty little Austrian girl called Trudi Behrens and married her. Her family had a trading store and chandlery up on Sayle Point, Behrens Trading, which he built up into Behrens Retail Stores, Behrens Associates, and finally the Behrens Trust Bank. Been in the family since back in the 1800s. When I married Harry, his boys just thought they'd died and gone straight to heaven. Just waiting for me to do the same. Go to heaven, I mean. Only trouble is their daddy beat me to it."

By now the Bentley had passed the wharves and warehouses of top-end Nassau town and was heading along East Bay Road. Jacquot wondered how far they were going. It wasn't more than a few minutes more before he found out. Just past Montagu Bay, a long high coral stone wall draped in cloaks of morning glory and topped by a thick grove of palm started its run along their left-hand side, cutting off any view of the ocean. Jacquot had passed the same wall as he drove from Yamacraw Hill to Martha Swanson's house and had wondered what hid behind it.

He was about to find out.

62

With a casual flick of her little finger, Elaine Drumgoole hit the
indicator stick and turned off the coastal highway onto a single-track
side-road. Up ahead a set of high wood gates swung open and the
Bentley passed through into what was clearly a private estate. A line
of palmetto either side of the drive; stands of jacaranda and tamarisk;
a pair of peacocks trailing their tail plumage like a bride's train over
lawns as trim and tutored as The Edgewater's – but not an arrowed sign
in sight. To the right, through a latticed fence of frangipani Jacquot
spotted a thatched pool house and diving board, and on his left the
wired sides of a tennis court. And the house, when they finally reached
it, was only a tad smaller than The Edgewater, a two-floor colonial-
style property painted a soft canary yellow, with white shutters on a
dozen windows, and a wrap-around gingerbread verandah. Built on a
rise of land above a broad swathe of private beach, the ocean glittered
beyond it.

After only a few days on New Providence Jacquot had learned
that property prices far exceeded anything on Martinique or Île des
Frères. On Lyford Cay where Patric had set up home a prospective
buyer would be hard pressed to find even the smallest plot for under
five million dollars, and over on Paradise Island starting prices for the
Ocean Club domain were maybe double that. Which made it almost
impossible to dream up the kind of figure that might approach the
asking price for these sumptuously tended headland acres. As Elaine
pulled up by the front steps and killed the engine, Jacquot decided it
had to be one of the most beautiful houses he had ever seen.

"The old family home," said Elaine, as she led him up the steps to
the verandah and across the burnished mahogany boards of its entrance
hall. "My great-grand-daddy built it way back. Made his fortune
on the Mississippi steamboats. Not owning them, you understand.
Playing on them. That's him there," she said, pointing to a painting
above a coral stone hearth filled with flowering cacti. A stout man with
whiskers, waistcoat and cigar, an arm resting on a green baize table, a
tumbler of whiskey and a spread of cards at his elbow. "Up and down
the grand old Mississippi. Natchez and Mobile to New Orleans, and
back again. Hardly ever set foot on dry land lessen it was to visit the
whorehouses, so I'm told. Either a great and lucky player or a clever

cheat, but a gambler down to his itty-bitty toenails. Guess it runs in the family," she said, leading Jacquot through sleekly furnished salons to the back of the house, and out onto another gingerbread-trim verandah overlooking a slope of cropped lawn, a drooping line of wispy casuarina, and a sparkling ocean. A table for two had been laid for lunch, and a pair of maids in grey tunics and white pinafores were waiting for them, drew back chairs for them to sit. Before she took her seat, Elaine unbuttoned her jacket, slipped it off and handed it to one of the maids. The blouse beneath was a dark blue silk, with a tightly-pleated bodice and a double strand of grey-blue pearls in its open neckline.

"You knew I'd say 'yes' to lunch?" asked Jacquot, as they settled at the table.

"Let's just say I was hoping you would," Elaine replied, snapping open a napkin and laying it on her lap. "There are things I need to know, and I think you're the man to tell me."

"If I can be of any help…" replied Jacquot, noting the new and sudden business-like tone.

"Well, why don't we start with my investment in Baize?"

"Your investment?"

"I have a ten per cent stake in the clubs."

"I didn't know that."

"No reason you should. It was a few years back. Patric needed some backing to start the second club and asked if Behrens would lend him some money. I told him I had no sway with the board, but that Behrens would view a start-up gaming enterprise with some considerable suspicion. Instead, I offered to back him myself. I could afford that small stake, and it seemed to me a reasonable investment back then. But how safe is it now, with Patric and Boni gone? What's that little toe-rag, Ballard, got in mind?"

Before Jacquot could answer, the maids returned. One of them carried two bottles of Kalik Light on a silver salver, and her companion an iced silver tureen. The bottle caps were levered off with a steamy hiss and set in front of them, and from the tureen a chowder vichyssoise was ladled into their bowls. It was thick and creamy and smelled of the ocean.

When the maids retired Elaine picked up her Kalik, and tipped it to Jacquot. The necks of their bottles chinked together. "To new friends," she said and took a sip straight from the bottle. Then she picked up her spoon, dipped it into her bowl and tasted the soup. "Homemade," she said. "I think you'll like it. But anyway, I interrupted. About Ballard?"

"All I know is he's taken over the day-to-day management of the clubs in Patric's absence. Pretty much what he was doing anyway." He, too, took up his spoon, and started in on the soup. "You're right. It's delicious." And it was. Light as air but packed with deep-sea flavour.

"So what will happen to Patric's stake?" asked Elaine.

Jacquot shrugged. "Nothing. As far as I know he's still the majority shareholder. So he still owns Baize."

"Leaving Ballard in control."

"Is that so bad? He seems to be doing a good job of it. Bringing in the high-rollers and making them feel special."

"He's low-life. I don't like him. Don't trust him."

"Well, it looks like you might be stuck with him."

"You mean, because Patric's dead?"

Jacquot was startled, hadn't expected that.

"Come on, Daniel. Let's stop pussy-footing around here. He's been gone three months now and no sign of him, no word. You ask me, he got himself into trouble and paid the price." She tipped her bowl and slid her spoon through the last of her soup. "We have a saying hereabouts..."

"Don't tell me. Talking to the sharks."

Elaine smiled. "That's exactly right. No body, and never a body. Nothing left to find. One day it's Patric running things, and the next minute Mr Gap-Teeth turns up." She put down her spoon and reached for her napkin. "Is he gay, by the way? There's just something about him..."

Jacquot frowned. It was the first time he'd thought about it. He'd certainly seen no woman with Ballard, nor heard about any. But then he remembered what Ballard had said to him on the flight from Martinique: *I prefer my women a little more... seasoned.* It struck him now as an odd thing to say. And a strangely non-committal observation. Maybe Elaine was right. Maybe he was gay.

The maids reappeared, the soup bowls and tureen were whisked away, and a moment later two waxed takeaway cartons with the words *Earl's Smoke Shack* slanting across the lid in a flamboyant red copperplate were placed in front of them. Jacquot looked at his carton and frowned.

Elaine saw the frown, and smiled. "You've heard of talking to the sharks, but you haven't heard of Earl's Smoke Shack?"

He shook his head.

"Open it up," said Elaine. "You won't be disappointed. The best damn ribs you ever ate. Cook throws a fit every time I send out for them, which is why I asked him to knock up a chowder – just to keep him happy, you understand – and the maids are always trying to set 'em up nice and dainty on plates. But me? I like to know where my food comes from, and I like to know it's the best I can get. Like the beer. So the cartons stay. And let me tell you, it doesn't get any better than old Earl's. Go on now, dig in, why don't you?"

The moment Jacquot prised open the carton's waxed lid, the hot scent of ribs rose up and filled his head. Sweet, smoky, sticky. Four fat ribs lying in a tangle of bleached bone and charred meat.

"Use your napkin," said Elaine, reaching in with her own. "The bone'll be hot still."

Following her example, Jacquot bunched his napkin around a curve of white bone and lifted a rib from the pack. It steamed in front of him and a line of black sauce ran to the end, threatening to spill back into the carton. But it didn't. It just got bigger, thickening and congealing. Jacquot blew on the bone and took a bite. Elaine was right. The rib was spectacular. The meat fall-apart soft but somehow kept together with the sauce, a hot hickory mix of sweet and spicy juice that coated the mouth and stuck to the teeth. But it wasn't pork.

"Goat," said Elaine. "Everyone's expecting pork, and they all look like you that first bite. Like, what am I eating here, 'cos it sure ain't no hog I ever tasted?"

She levered off a wedge of the meat with the same glistening teeth that had drawn off her gloves, and as she pulled it away from the bone, lapping it up with her tongue and her lips and the tip of a finger, Jacquot felt a sudden and unfamiliar urge to lean across and kiss those sticky honeyed lips. It was such a strong feeling, his eyes so fixed on her mouth, that he looked away, sure that she would know what he was thinking if she caught his eye.

But she didn't. Chewing happily, wiping her mouth with her napkin and waving the bare strip of rib like a baton she continued, "Had us some gallery owner and collector down from Savannah one time to look at Harry's work. 'Course he was Jewish or Arab or whatever, and didn't eat pork. So wouldn't touch it. Nothing we could do to make him try it. It's goat, it's goat, we kept on saying. But he wasn't having any. Which made Cook a happy man, I'm telling you. Had a New-York strip sirloin and fries in front of him, quicker than a pint of moonshine down a southern throat."

The ribs were dealt with equally swiftly, one after another, their conversation reduced to murmurs of warm delight as they worked their way through the stack. A blind person, Jacquot mused, might easily imagine these sounds as part of some sexual encounter, and they wouldn't have been too far off the truth, he thought, sucking off the last of the rib meat and watching Elaine do the same. Afterwards, they bunched their napkins again and wiped their mouths, reached for their beers, sat back in their chairs.

"What did I tell you?" she asked, taking a swig. She rinsed the beer round her mouth, swallowed and licked her lips.

"You lied."

"I what?" For a moment she looked startled, caught off guard.

"You lied. They're better than you said."

Elaine laughed. "You mind if I smoke?" she asked, looking around for her clutch.

"You beat me to it." He reached into his pocket, brought out his cigarettes, and offered them.

She took one, leaned forward for the light, cupping Jacquot's hand in hers. The touch was fleeting, but electric. "Tobacco. Just a plain delight," she said, inhaling deeply. "Always suspicious of people who don't smoke. Like people who don't drink. So where were we? Just plain lost my train of thought there, what with those ribs and all."

"You wanted to know where Ballard came from," said Jacquot, lighting his own cigarette.

"That's right. Mr Gap-Teeth."

"Have you heard of a man called Ettore DiCorsa?"

"DiCorsa?" Elaine paused, frowned. "Of course. Who hasn't? Sweet little man. Gay, of course. Lives out on Sailboat Cay. You see him in The Edgewater every now and then."

"He's a member?"

Elaine gave a short little chuckle. "Of course he's a member. Be strange if he wasn't, being the owner and all."

"DiCorsa owns Edgewater?"

"Lock, stock and smoking barrel. And quite a few other businesses around town; out on the islands, too. Way back he tried to make a play for Behrens, buy in and all, and asked me to put in a good word."

"And did you?"

"No point. I may be a shareholder and the sole surviving family member but I got no sway with the board, not when it comes to the kind of thing DiCorsa had in mind. That's what I told him, but he still tried it on. Till they sent him packing, that is. So where does he fit in?"

"You weren't the only person to help Patric out. Ballard was part of the trade-off," Jacquot replied, wondering how The Edgewater's club secretary, Forbes-Temple, got along with DiCorsa.

Elaine tipped back her head, blew out a plume of smoke. "Patric, Patric, Patric… What were you thinking? You should have come to me."

"Maybe he didn't want to worry you. Or was too proud to ask a second time."

"Maybe, but going to DiCorsa was asking for trouble. Tried every trick in the book to get himself a slice of Behrens. When it comes to business that sweet little man is a shark."

Jacquot leaned forward and, in the absence of an ashtray, tipped ash from his cigarette into the rib carton. She didn't know how close to the truth she was.

"So what will you do with your ten per cent, now you know DiCorsa's on the scene?"

"Hold on to it, is what. See what happens. DiCorsa may be a shark but he's a canny businessman. If he's got plans for Baize I reckon I'll wait and see what my ten per cent is worth to him. Ballard's already made me a good offer, but no reason to make him happy. What about you? You being Boni's brother and all. You seen the will?"

He hadn't, but he nodded.

"So what did she have, you don't mind my asking? Twenty, thirty per cent?"

"Something like that."

"And you're the beneficiary?"

"According to her lawyer, Patric's the primary beneficiary. As for me it's just a few shares and some family stuff."

"Well, even a few shares will see you very nicely... accommodated. If you choose to sell them, of course." She stubbed out her cigarette in the rib carton and leaned forward, elbow on table, chin resting in the palm of her hand, eyes sharp and cold, fixing hard on Jacquot. "Maybe sell them to me. I'd give you a good price." She smiled, archly. "Of course, I'd need to know you really are Boni's brother. Which, hey, we both know you're not."

63

Once again Jacquot was caught off guard, just as Ballard had been caught over dinner at Gustave's. Since he'd clearly been rumbled – for whatever reason – he decided that honesty would be the best solution.

"You're right. I'm not Boni's brother. How did you guess?"

"It wasn't a guess, Daniel – if that's your real name?" She cocked an eyebrow.

"It's Daniel, but not Milhaud. Daniel Jacquot."

"So Daniel Jacquot, let me tell you how I know." She reached across for his cigarettes, helped herself to another one, and lit it. "When Patric brought Boni around here the first time – for lunch, at this very table – she was wary of me. Like I said, she thought I was an old flame, wasn't sure what to make of me, or how to handle me. But when she came to understand the nature of our relationship, that Patric and I were friends, and nothing more, well, that initial coolness eased. She warmed up, and we got friendly. Shopping, lunches... the kind of things girls do. But you know what? Not once, in all our time together, did Boni ever, ever, mention a brother, or any kind of family, save her parents were dead. Strange, don't you think? In fact, I recall her saying one time how alike she and I and Patric were – only children, and all alone in the world. No kids, no uncles or aunts, no cousins, nephews, nieces... No family to speak of. Of course, that was Boni's big hang-up. No kids. They tried, but it never happened. Two miscarriages that I know about. Maybe more. And Patric would have made such a great father."

A memory stabbed at Jacquot. The same thing had happened to Boni in Marseilles. A miscarriage. Though he hadn't known it at the time, it had marked the beginning of the end of their relationship.

Elaine let out a stream of smoke. "And like I said, you really do look nothing like her."

"We were lovers, a long time ago. In Marseilles."

Elaine finished her beer, tipped her ash into the empty bottle. Then she tilted her head and narrowed her eyes, as though she had made some connection. "Are you the man who played rugby? The policeman?"

Jacquot smiled, nodded. "That's me."

"Ah, now I know who you are. You were the one before Patric.

The man she left in Marseilles. Boni spoke of you often, but never mentioned your name. She told me she'd had this lover but hadn't treated him well, and felt bad about it."

Jacquot didn't reply. "It was a long time ago," he said at last, dropping his cigarette into his empty bottle.

"But it hurt, when she left you?"

"Yes. It did."

"But you got over it, like we always do. As we must. And you fell in love again, and had kids. "

"I got over it, fell in love, had children. And I couldn't be happier the way it's worked out. But I'll always feel a deep affection for Boni. She was special. It was a wonderful surprise when she came to see me after all this time."

"She came to see you? In Marseilles?"

Jacquot shook his head. "I live here now. A small island off Martinique."

"So why…? After all this time…?"

"She told me she was in trouble. She wanted my help."

"This was about Patric, right?"

"She told me he was missing, that he'd stolen some money, and run off with a girlfriend. And she wanted me to find him."

"And this is money Patric is supposed to have taken from where? Baize, is that right?"

"That's what Ballard told her."

"How much?"

"Around ten million."

"And he hightailed it with that girl?"

"You knew her?"

"Not personally, of course. But after he'd gone I heard the rumours and I was… well, I was shocked. I didn't know Patric played like that. And he had so much going for him. A gorgeous wife, a lovely home. The business. It didn't make any sense then, and it doesn't make any more sense now. I mean, why would Patric want to steal any money and leave Boni?"

"To set himself up with the girlfriend? To start over, somewhere else?"

"No, no, no. He may have had a girlfriend – not many married men around here who don't – but I'm telling you, there's no way he was going to ditch Boni for anyone. They were tight. The tightest."

"Well, Patric and this girl, Sylvie Martin, were definitely together, and they'd made plans to leave the island. Soon as the police heard that, they lost interest. The way it goes, I'm afraid. No crime, just a domestic."

"So Boni asked you to help?"

"That's right."

"And you agreed?"

Jacquot was in the process of lighting another cigarette. He spread his hands, lighter in one, unlit cigarette in the other. "I told her I couldn't do it. I wasn't a cop anymore. I had the kids... It just wasn't possible. I told her to hire a private investigator." He cupped a hand to shield the flame.

"When was this?"

"A few days before she died."

"You were there?"

Jacquot nodded.

"It said in the paper it was suicide." It wasn't a question, but it sounded like one. As though Elaine wasn't convinced.

"It wasn't. She was drugged, had her wrist slit to make it look like suicide. Real cause of death was established a couple of days ago."

The maids returned, removed the rib cartons and empty Kaliks, and replaced them with two fresh bottles, plates of thinly-sliced guava, and a bowl of lime wedges. A moment later, one of the maids returned with a pair of silver ashtrays.

When she'd gone Elaine whistled softly, shook her head. "So if you're not Boni's brother, and you told her you couldn't help, how come you're here now?" she asked, stubbing out her cigarette and squeezing a wedge of lime onto the fruit. "And what are you doing with Ballard of all people?"

"You mean, the man who killed Patric and Boni."

"It was Ballard?" The shock was clear. Eyes wide, a gasp, lips apart.

"Ballard killed Patric. He told me himself. They brought someone in for Boni."

"They?"

"The pair of them. Ballard and DiCorsa."

"You are joking?"

Jacquot shook his head.

"So go to the police. Report them, why don't you?"

"Not so easy. No proof, no evidence."

"But you've got to do something."

"Yes, find the girl, find the money. That's what Ballard wants. DiCorsa, too."

"So you'd do it for them, and not for Boni?" Elaine picked up her fork and sliced through her guava, speared it, slipped it into her mouth.

Jacquot sighed, took a drag on his cigarette. "Let's just say they made it difficult for me to say no."

"Money?"

Jacquot shook his head.

Elaine narrowed her eyes. "They got something on you?"

"My daughters."

Elaine gasped. "You're kidding me? The little shits. They threatened your children? "

"All I have to do is find the missing money. And it'll be fine."

"And you believe that?"

"Right now I don't have much choice."

Elaine put down her fork, shook her head. "I can't believe it. I really can't. So does this Sylvie... Sylvie...?"

"Martin. Sylvie Martin."

"Right, right, so does she have the money?"

"Looks like she might. Or might know where it is. And that's good enough for Ballard and DiCorsa. Find the girl, find the money."

"And that's why you're going to Miami?"

Jacquot nodded.

"Do you know where she is in Miami?"

"She'll have moved on by now."

"Do you know where to?"

"Let's just say there's somewhere I need to check."

She gave him a questioning look.

"It's just a hunch right now. But worth following up."

"And if you don't find her, or the money, what then?"

"Then I'll have to kill Ballard and DiCorsa before they get to my children. I can't see any alternative." He reached forward to stub out his cigarette, then glanced at his watch. "And I really should be going, if I want to make my flight."

Outside, at the front of the house, Patric's Explorer had been parked in the shade. Jacquot opened the driver's door and flung his jacket onto the passenger seat.

"I'm sorry you have to hurry away," she said, standing beside the car.

And so am I, thought Jacquot, surprising himself.

"And if there's anything you need," she continued, "anything I can do to help, just call. My number's in the book."

Jacquot smiled. "I'll be back before you know it."

"Good," she said, and leaning forward she kissed him lightly on the cheek.

Dead Friends

Lourmarin, Provence

France

64

When boarding an aircraft always turn left. That's what Boni used to tell him. It was the only way to fly, she said. And she was right. As Jacquot discovered in the First Class cabin of an Air France flight from Miami International to Paris Charles-de-Gaulle. A little over nine hours of pampered comfort and luxury, thanks to the money Boni had transferred to his account just before her death on Île des Frères, and the smiling, whispered attentions of the First Class cabin crew. Jacquot had accepted a glass of champagne within minutes of taking his seat just two rows back from the Boeing 747's forward bulkhead, and by the time the Jumbo had lumbered down the runway and lifted off into the night sky he was on his second glass, looking down on the line of coastal lights running north from Miami along Florida's eastern coast. A golden grid-like glow one side of the line, the deep dark blackness of the ocean on the other. In terms of luxury and comfort, all he was missing was a cigarette to accompany the champagne.

When the Boeing reached its cruising altitude and the seat belt sign was switched off, Jacquot got up from his seat and looked around the cabin. Only six of the twelve seats were occupied. Two women, three other men, all well dressed, all travelling separately, three of them on one side of the aisle, three on the other, each with a spare seat beside them. Two of the men and one of the women had snapped open briefcases and were rifling through various files and papers, the third man was flicking through the in-flight magazine, while the remaining woman was talking to a stewardess. Jacquot pushed aside the curtain, went through the First Class galley and up a curving flight of stairs into an empty First Class Lounge. A bar, a small buffet, a table stocked with newspapers and magazines, and a spread of leather chairs and sofas. Next, Jacquot wandered down the length of the plane through the Business Class and Tourist Class sections. Down one side, and back the other. And as far as he could see there was no sign of Brock, and no sense of any other passenger showing him anything but the most cursory attention. He had taken the same precaution on the flight from Nassau to Miami, and had kept an eye out for any of its passengers following him through the terminal to the Air France check-in desk. As far as he could tell, he was not being followed. Not a single familiar face. But he knew that he shouldn't underestimate Ballard, or take him at his word. There were probably more than enough unknown Brocks for the man to call on.

Back in First Class, Jacquot ate his dinner, drank his wine, and after tossing back a small cognac he turned off the overhead lights, tipped back his seat, and closed his eyes. He went to sleep thinking of his daughters, and dreamed of them building sandcastles with a woman who was Boni one moment, and Elaine the next.

The following morning, at a little before eleven o'clock local time, the 747 began its descent over the Normandy coast and twenty minutes later, seats in the upright position, tables stowed, and seat belts secured, Jacquot looked through his window onto the low grey sprawl of Paris' western suburbs. Roads, woods, parkland, houses, then tenements and untidy trading estates, and finally, through a slanting, smearing drizzle, the darker grey of a rain-soaked runway and its grass verge. There was a series of short bumps somewhere behind him, a rising whine of engines, and a gentle forward pressure against his seat belt.

Just over two hour's later, after a transfer from Charles-de-Gaulle to Orly, Jacquot took his seat in the First Class section of a smaller domestic airliner, buckled up, and whiled away the time before take-off with a *gran'crème*, and a *balon* of Calvados, thinking about Elaine, surprised with himself that he should have told her so much, but not, for a single moment, regretting it. Her anger at Ballard's and DiCorsa's behaviour, and her kind offer to help in any way she could, had given him an unexpected shot of confidence.

But as the plane lifted off from Orly and banked south for the final leg of his journey to Marseilles' Marignane airport – the same flight he'd taken all those years ago when he first met Boni – Jacquot wondered once more what he would do if he was wrong.

If he couldn't find the girl, couldn't find the money.

It had all made perfect sense in Nassau.

Now he wasn't so sure.

65

Jacquot shivered. The sun had dipped behind the slopes of Le Panier, the sky was a deep dark evening blue, and a chill brittle breeze rippled the waters of Marseilles' Vieux Port. He had forgotten just how cold the old country would be after the winter warmth of the tropics, and he was not prepared. The first thing he did after checking into his quayside hotel was hurry to the shops before they closed and find himself a warm coat.

Suitably insulated in a quilt-lined leather jacket, with a blue check cashmere scarf tucked into the collar, Jacquot dug his hands into his pockets and strolled down the Quai de Rive Neuve. Everything was how he remembered it. The briny scent of the sea, the frantic cawing and swooping of gulls, the evening gridlock of beeping, tooting traffic, and around the old port the strengthening neon glow of bars and restaurants readying themselves for the evening crowds. Marseilles. His city, his home, where he'd been born, grown up and worked, save those few years after his parents' death – first in a Jesuit orphanage and then with his maternal grandfather. It was a wonderful, vibrant city and he loved it with a warmth and affection that still surprised him, even after five years away.

But for all the fond familiarity and affection, Jacquot felt an odd sense of dislocation too, a strange disconnection from the city and from his past. Only five years away, and he could have been visiting Marseilles for the first time. He might know his way round, might know the names of the bars and the restaurants – the Mirador on the other side of the harbour with its unforgettable Bouillabaisse, Gassi's steak-house just a block back from the quay, Café Samaritaine on the corner of rue de la République where his morning *gran'crèmes* and pastries were always accompanied by a warming measure of Calva, and Bar de la Marine where he now took an outside table, sitting directly beneath a gas-fuelled heating lamp to watch the world go by – but this time there was something different about the place, about the way he felt. Everything was as he remembered it – commuters heading home, young lovers clinched on the saddles of passing scooters and motorbikes, the MetroBus with its foggy windows, blue neon interior and swaying strap hangers, and the occasional spark and crackle from its connecting overhead cables – but those five years away, a new life bringing up his two daughters, made him feel no longer quite so much a part of the city. Not even the proximity of his boat, *Constance* – across the road there, snug in her berth, secure under her tarp cover, and kept in trim by his old friend Salette – could quite make him feel at home.

Indeed it was this very familiarity, this closeness with everything around him, that made his sense of dislocation all the more acute. Because the city wasn't his any more. He didn't live here, he didn't work here. He might know Salette, the port's old harbour master, and Madame Foraque, his mothering concierge on Place des Moulins up there on the heights of Le Panier, and all the boys at police headquarters on rue de l'Évêché, working some case up in that squad room on the third floor, but he had no plans to call on them, to renew their acquaintance, to drink with them, or hug them, or find out what had been happening in his absence. Because his real home was half a world away now, on a beach on Île des Frères. And the soul and the heart of that home – and his entire being – were his two daughters, Matti and Béa. The sooner he saw them again, the happier he would be. Maybe next time he'd do the rounds, make the calls. But not now.

There were other memories, too, as he sat there alone, smoking, sipping his pastis, watching the sky darken, the quayside lights brighten. And not such pleasant ones either. Driving along this very road nearly five years earlier. Snow falling. Christmas Eve. Heading out to the clinic at Castellane with a ring in his pocket. A ring for Claudine.

The last time he saw her alive.

Two hours after slipping it onto her finger the woman he loved was dead.

Cold. And gone. For ever.

Maybe it was good he felt this disconnection.

Maybe time, and distance, really had healed the wounds.

66

It was still dark when Jacquot woke the following morning. Back home on Île des Frères he'd be finishing off a last St Clément rum and listening to some soft jazz or the distant crash of surf on the reef. Something warm and peaceful to go to sleep to. But here in Marseilles a new day was about to dawn and, whether it was the time difference or just a restless energy to be done with it all, Jacquot was up and dressed, and ready to greet it. There was no time to waste.

An hour after checking out of his hotel Jacquot was at the wheel of his rental car and on the A55 Littoral heading north-west, with the sky up ahead still a dark bluey grey, but in his rear-view mirror a softening pink over the hilltops of Montredon and the Massif des Baumes. Like the city he was leaving behind, the road was eerily familiar in the dawn's half-light. How many times had he made this same journey, from Marseilles to Cavaillon, and back again? From the cranes and gantries of La Joliette and the swaying masts of the old port, to the dusty melon fields of the Calavon Valley and the wooded slopes of the Lubéron? Enough to know every last twist and turn of the road, every slope and rise, every swoop and plunge, starting with the road tunnel above L'Estaque before spinning down towards Pennes Mirabeau and the Autoroute du Soleil.

Flirting with the speed limit Jacquot sped past the turning for Marignane where he'd landed the afternoon before, and drove on with the sparkling expanse of the Étang de Berre on one side and the creamy bluffs and slopes of Vitrolles on the other. After skirting Rognac and the garrigue hillsides of Velaux he swept down towards Coudoux where the road joined La Provençale, the tarmac humming beneath his tyres, knowing to keep his foot pressed hard on the accelerator to save himself a gear change on the rising slope that led to the Lançon *péage*. A few kilometres further on, he swung left off the autoroute, crossed the Craponne canal and parked in Salon's Cours Gimon as the first shops opened their doors and rattled up their shutters. In a florist shop he chose a small bouquet of tightly budded red roses, in an office supplies store a few doors further down he bought himself some copy paper, and in a second-hand bric-a-brac shop on LaSalle he finally found the portable typewriter he was looking for. Lugging his purchases back to his car, he set off for the Abbé de Launc in the

Roques Hills above Salon.

The last time Jacquot had taken this twisting country road he had sat in the back of a gleaming black limousine with Midou and the twins, following the hearse that carried Claudine to the Abbey's chapel and cemetery, her body laid to rest beside her aunt, Sandrine, in a shawling drizzle that was strong enough to have mourners shuffle together under black umbrellas. Today the sky was blue and the cypress trees that lined the abbey's driveway cast long pencil-thin shadows in the rising sun.

Jacquot started talking when he was still some fifty metres from the small marble headstone that marked her grave.

"Hello, my darling. It's been a long time. It's good to be with you again. And your girls send their love."

When he bent down to place the roses beside the headstone, the first tears welled up in his eyes and he caught his breath in a tightening throat.

"I miss you very much, so very much," he whispered. "And so do the girls. I called them Béa and Matti, but I guess you know that. And you'll know, too, that I tell them about you all the time. What you look like, the sound of your voice, all the little things you do like pushing your hair behind your ear, and tapping a paintbrush against your teeth. Which always makes them laugh. They have a photo of you in their bedroom. Can you guess which one? That's right. You, on the sofa, very pregnant, and me sitting at your feet, wide-eyed and looking shocked but happy."

He stayed with Claudine for another ten minutes, telling her about their life on Île des Frères, how the girls loved to play on the beach, how they were fine swimmers, how Matti was the troublesome one and how Béa was always warm and cuddly. But then, before he left, he told her what he had been thinking about, what he wanted to happen.

"There's someone I've met," he began, feeling oddly disloyal and a little embarrassed. "Her name is Elaine. She's... very nice. Very kind. She's lives in a big beautiful house by the sea. She has maids and a cook, but she still likes to drink beer from the bottle and eat takeaway ribs. And they're good ribs, too. Goat. You'd like them. And I think you'd like her, too. She's got... she's got style, and nerve, and she's the kind of woman who'd keep me on my toes. Like you. And I think she'll love the girls, and be good for them. It's just... It's just

I wanted you to be the first to know... Before anything happens. If it does... I mean, who knows? I've only met her once, but... I just hope you won't mind?"

He didn't expect an answer, and didn't get one. But as he turned out of the Abbey's driveway and set off for Lourmarin, he felt a lightness and a certainty that he hadn't felt for a long time.

Everything was going to be alright.

67

The idea had come to Jacquot on the flight from Miami to Paris. He'd worked it round in his head and it seemed to fit the bill exactly. In the old days, working with the *Judiciaire*, he could have applied for a court order from some obliging *juge d'instruction* like Solange Bonnefoy and let the law do its work. But he wasn't with the police any more, and he knew he needed a cover for the next step or he'd blow everything. The typewriter, copy paper and a well-prepared cover story would be all he needed when he knocked on the door of Château Clos des Roses, Patric's family home a few kilometres outside Lourmarin.

Out of season, the small Provençal town was quiet. No coaches lining the meadow below the looming Château de Lourmarin, and no tourists clogging the narrow cobbled streets. Parking his car on Avenue Dautry he strolled into the centre of town and found what he was looking for. The Tourist Office. The next part of his plan.

"I'm looking for somewhere to stay," he told the girl behind the counter. She was short and dumpy and the buttons on her blue uniform cardigan pulled against the buttonholes that held them. She wasn't pretty but she was bright and friendly and helpful, the walls of her office covered with posters of Lourmarin, always on the list of most beautiful villages in France: its mossy fountains, its ancient château, its ivy-clad buildings, pale blue shutters and blossoming window boxes.

"There are many places in town to choose from," the girl replied, reaching for a rack of brochures.

"Not in town," said Jacquot. "I'm looking for somewhere close by, but quiet, out in the countryside. A *gîte* maybe. I am a writer and I want to stay somewhere for a few weeks to finish my book."

"A writer? Then you have come to the right place, monsieur. Albert Camus lived here, did you know? The man who wrote *L'Étranger* and *La Peste*? He is buried in our cemetery."

Jacquot put on a shocked expression. "Is that how you treat writers hereabouts?"

The girl looked puzzled, not sure how to respond.

"So is there somewhere you could recommend?" he asked, letting a smile ease her frown.

"I am sure we can find you something, monsieur," she said, reaching for a map and spreading it out on the counter, pointing out properties with the point of her biro. "Well, there's the Mas des Couronnes, here? Or perhaps Les Aristides just a few kilometres out of town? Or how about Auberge le Moulin at...?"

"I remember someone mentioning a place called Château de... des something. Des Roses?"

"Château Clos des Roses? *Oh, mais oui, bien sûr*. On the road to Cadenet. It is very pretty. But whether they take guests now, monsieur, I do not know. Some of these places are only open during the season."

"Would it be possible for you to call them, to find out if they have a room? Somewhere where I could work undisturbed." He gave the girl another smile. "It would be a great help, and maybe save me a wasted journey."

"Of course, that is not a problem. It is why we are here, to help our visitors," she replied, and reached for the phone. She checked the château's phone number on her computer screen, dialled it, and held the receiver to her ear.

Ten minutes later Jacquot headed back to his car with directions for Château Clos des Roses where the *gardienne*, a Madame Galinesse, would be happy to show him a choice of rooms. They would be closing soon for the winter but for an important writer looking for peace and quiet to finish his book, well, they would be happy to remain open a little longer. Also, they would provide breakfast, and dinner if he wanted. He only had to say the word

68

Château Clos des Roses wasn't a château in the real sense of the word
– no witch-hat towers, no grand façade, nor lofty battlements. But it
was a substantial property nonetheless, the kind of country home a
prosperous seventeenth-century merchant or landowner might have
built for himself and his family.

Seven or eight minutes after leaving Lourmarin, Jacquot turned
off the main highway and started along a secondary road veined
with cracks and edged with ragged crumbling tarmac. Five minutes
later, after a tight left-hand turn between two steep stone buttresses
covered in steel safety-netting, he straightened out into a long low
valley with leafless vines marching in stark regimental lines up
the hillsides. Across the valley he could see the road begin another
gentle ascent but before then, half-way along on the right, he spotted
a pair of stone pillars and a driveway lined with plane trees. At the
end of this driveway the château fronted a wide gravel turning circle
with a stable block on one side and a barn and manger on the other.
Both these side buildings were covered in the wiry winter remnants
of rambling roses but the house itself, built in traditional Provençal
style with eight blue-shuttered windows on the top floor and six on
the ground floor, had no such embellishment. At its corners a pair of
bookend towers provided a certain softness and gentility but they rose
no higher than the low red-tiled roof, and just four simple stone steps
led up to a sturdy, studded front door, the date, 1699, carved into the
lintel above it. Jacquot put down his case and portable typewriter, but
before he could ring the bell he heard hurried footsteps coming across
the gravel behind him.

"Monsieur Jacquot? Is that you?"

Madame Galinesse was in her fifties, a farmer's wife in a tie-
wrapped housecoat and green Wellington boots. Broad, wide-
shouldered and big-bosomed, with a warm welcoming smile and a
tumbling fall of loose grey curls caught up in a headscarf, she looked
a sturdy, trustworthy type whose easy confidence conveyed the sense
that once she had been a beautiful and alluring woman. Which she
still was, Jacquot decided, as she shook his hand and reached past him
to open the front door. Gesturing that he should go in ahead of her,
she paused to lever off her muddy boots, the first boot toe to heel, the

second against the top step.

The house was warm and smelled of scented candles, the wide hallway light and airy, laid with worn black and white tiles and furnished with suitably château-like antiques – high-backed tapestried chairs, a collection of crossed sabres and muskets, some tusked boar-heads, and an intricately-carved oak buffet set between a pair of foxed, rococo mirrors. A number of panelled doors led off this hallway but Madame Galinesse led Jacquot to the first room on the left, a small music room with delicately patterned floral wallpaper, a line of framed theatre programmes, and a pair of worn leather sofas set either side of a carved stone hearth. There was a box-like harpsichord with a raised and painted lid in one corner, cushioned window seats behind thickly belted silk drapes and, just inside the door, an ancient roll-top desk. With a rattling of slats Madame Galinesse opened it up, took out a key on a long embroidered fob and handed it to him.

"Our last guests checked out a few days ago, and we have an English couple arriving at the weekend, but for now the house is yours. I hope you won't feel too lonely, but at least you will have peace and quiet for your writing. What do you write?" she asked, as she led him back into the hallway and headed for a curving stone staircase hung with tapestries.

"I'm writing a memoire," said Jacquot. "Life in the Marseilles *Judiciaire*."

"*Ooh là là*. You were a policeman?"

"For a long time, I just wanted to write it all down. How it was to work as a *flic* in Marseilles."

"Well, that will make an interesting read, and no mistake."

They reached the landing and Madame Galinesse turned right, leading Jacquot down a long stone-flagged corridor.

"You are the owner, madame?" asked Jacquot, knowing she wasn't.

"Ah, *non*, Monsieur Jacquot," she replied with a laugh. "Just the *gardienne*. I look after the house and my husband works the vines for the owner. We have a small cottage at the side of the house."

"Have you worked here a long time?"

"My husband's family have been here over a hundred years. Me, just the last thirty."

"The owner doesn't live here himself? It is a beautiful home."

She stopped at a door, opened it and showed him in.

"Not here, no. In the Caribbean. But he comes back every couple of years for a week or so."

Jacquot's bedroom was at the front of the house and through the window he could see the line of plane trees along the drive, and the roofs of the stable on his right and the barn on his left. The room was a good size, high and square, with a closely-beamed ceiling, a stone hearth, and a large four-poster bed. The walls were panelled with shields of eau-de-nil damask, and above the hearth was a brightly-coloured canvas, naïf-island style, that Jacquot recognised immediately from the Stuyvesant house on Lyford Cay. A Caribbean market scene, with blurred black faces and piles of red and green fruit under a deep blue sky. It was a striking piece of work – not quite abstract, not quite realist, but full of life and movement. Claudine would have liked it, thought Jacquot – the colours, the bold strokes, the movement. He went up to it, looked more closely. There, in the lower right hand corner, he made out the initials, H.D., and the date, 1997. Harry Drumgoole, it had to be. As Elaine had told him, it was unlikely her late husband's work would ever end up in the auction rooms of Sotheby's but the painting in front of him was still very good. A professional study, in no way uncertain or self-conscious, the chosen subject executed with real energy and skill. For a brief moment Jacquot remembered his own Tuesday market on Île des Frères and felt a wince of homesickness, and distance. And the looming sense of threat and danger, and possible loss, that came with it.

"Monsieur Stuyvesant brought it back with him the last time he visited," explained Madame Galinesse, noting Jacquot's interest. "There's another one downstairs in the dining room. Lovely colours, don't you think? So bright and cheerful." Madame Galinesse paused, looked around. "So, Monsieur Jacquot, I will leave you to unpack. Please feel free to enjoy the house and go wherever you wish. I'm afraid it is a little late for a proper lunch, but if you are hungry I can put together a little something? Some paté, perhaps? Some bread, cheese, wine? I will leave it in on a tray in the library. Second door on your left as you come down the stairs."

"That would be kind, thank you," Jacquot replied, and with a nod and a smile Madame Galinesse left the room and closed the door behind her.

69

After one of those light country lunches that for Jacquot pressed every pleasure button – a thick wedge of rough farmhouse terrine served with crispy green cornichons, a basket of warm crusty bread, dairy-fresh butter, a bullet-hard *crottin* of goat's cheese, and a clay jug of red wine – he took Madame Galinesse at her word and set out to explore his new surroundings.

If the house had appeared plain and austere on the outside, its interior was anything but, the rooms freshly painted and papered, furnished in a homely, comfortable mix of modern and antique, and all the drapes and upholsteries bright and new, not faded or tatty like so many other châteaux that opened up as country hotels and *pensions* to make ends meet. Money had been spent here, and Clos des Roses was clearly loved and well-cared for. He might not have lived here, but Patric had made sure that his family home lacked for nothing. What Jacquot couldn't quite work out was why Patric should have left such a wonderful home in the first place, to build another nest and start another life on the other side of the world? He had no brothers, no sisters, would have inherited the property on his parent's deaths, and could have lived a very comfortable life here as the *propriétaire* of a fine Provençal estate, just as his parents and probably grandparents had done before him. Certainly he had made a great deal of money in the Bahamas, enough to live well there, and cover the upkeep here, but surely there must have been a temptation to return to his roots? Had that been a part of his plan, Jacquot wondered? A family home to retire to? Or a bolt hole to escape to? Somewhere distant and anonymous to set up house with his mistress when he tired of his wife and island life?

After exploring the house, Jacquot pulled on his leather jacket, wound the scarf round his neck and went for a stroll in the grounds. If the house was well-cared for, so were the barn and stables, the former tidily filled with the kind of machinery needed to work the vines, and the stable block equally well-equipped. The tack room, stacked with saddles and hung with bridles and helmets, smelled of leather and polish, and the looseboxes, six a side, were clean and well-kept, the seven horses accommodated in them glossy of coat and clear of eye. Jacquot had never liked horses, failed to understand the power they held over their owners, and as he walked between the stalls he kept resolutely to the centre, the horses watching him as he passed, no doubt sensing his discomfort, snorting and stamping as though sharing a joke.

Leaving the stables through an open set of double doors he entered a flag-stoned saddling yard and from there wandered around the corner of the block, found the drive and started along it. Half way down he turned off onto a path between the vines and made his way around the property until he reached a low ridge and looked back at the château. It was a fine estate; the house, the barn, and stable block a neat square of habitation surrounded by blackened lines of twisted, stunted vines that in summer would cover the hillsides in an emerald green cloak. The only thing he couldn't see was any *pressoir*, and assumed that every harvest the grapes were sent to the nearest co-operative.

An hour later, the breath steaming from his mouth in the chill afternoon air, he returned to the house and realised that the other thing he hadn't seen was the woman he had come to find. Nor any sign of her. Was she hiding, he wondered? Had she moved on? Indeed, had she come here at all?

At the top of the front steps Jacquot pulled off his scarf and was reaching for the door when it suddenly opened from the inside. Madame Galinesse, on her way out, gave a start when she saw him, put a hand to her breast.

"Ah, Monsieur Jacquot. I wasn't expecting you. Out for a walk? Such a lovely afternoon. I was just lighting a fire in the library; it can get chill in the evenings, even with the heating on."

"That's kind of you, thank you."

They paused together on the top step. For a moment Madame Galinesse appeared a little hesitant. "I hope it doesn't sound like an imposition," she began, "what with your work, you know? And just arriving. But I wondered, my husband and I, that is, if you would like to join us for supper? I can easily lay up a table in the dining room if you would prefer to eat alone, but…"

Jacquot smiled. "That would be lovely. Thank you."

"Say eight o'clock? Nothing formal, just a kitchen supper?"

"My favourite kind."

Madame Galinesse looked pleased, and relieved. Easier to invite him to her house, Jacquot supposed, than prepare and set out dinner for one in the château's dining room.

"We're just through there," she said, pointing to an archway between the house and stable block. "I'll leave the light on so you can see the path. You can't miss us. Oh, by the way," said Madame Galinesse, as she started down the steps. "My husband, Bertrand, is sure he knows you."

70

Bertrand Galinesse was a giant of a man, well over six feet tall with a broad, bulging chest, shiny red cheeks, sparkling blue eyes, and hands like meaty spades. He wore a pair of thick brown cords held up by red braces, and a grey woollen shirt that was buttoned up to its turning collar points. His reddish hair was thin, close cut, and still wet from the shower, tidily combed and parted on one side, the comb's tine marks still showing. Jacquot judged him to be about his own age, but a good head taller. When he opened the door to Jacquot's knock, he stood there a moment with his hand still on the door as though barring the way, peering down into Jacquot's face. For a moment he looked unsure, and then he smiled. A big broad smile.

"I *knew* it was you. Recognised the name soon as Dénise told me. And you being with the *Judiciaire*... It just fitted."

They shook hands and Galinesse ushered him into a flagstoned hallway, closing the door behind them with a kick. "I'm right, aren't I? Twickenham. Way back. That try against the English?"

"You're right, monsieur..."

"Bertrand, please."

"But it was a long time ago."

"At our age, everything's a long time ago, my friend. But it doesn't make it any less important or any less memorable. A drink?"

Bertrand showed him into a small salon with a stack of logs blazing away in a blackened ash-filled hearth. He pushed past Jacquot, crossed the room to a corner table, and held up a bottle of whiskey. Jacquot nodded. Two glasses were poured, a generous splash in each.

"Could hardly breathe, you know?" Bertrand continued, handing Jacquot his drink. "Every step you took. No one in front of you, just that English *con* coming up behind."

"But he caught me. Tapped my heel and down I went. If it hadn't been so muddy I wouldn't have made it across the line. *En effet*, I just slid over it."

Jacquot sipped his drink and wondered how many times he had made these same dismissive comments whenever someone recognised him, remembered that try for France so long ago that it sometimes seemed to Jacquot that someone else must have scored it.

"Doesn't matter how you did it," said Bertrand. "Slide, jump, dive, fall – it's all the same. Over the line you went. You scored. And the winning try, too. With just seconds to go. Hell, the café in Lourmarin went wild." He pointed Jacquot to an armchair beside the fire and they both sat, made themselves comfortable. "And now you're a writer, Denise said?"

"I retired. A few years back. Just thought, you know, that I might try my hand at a book. To fill my time. Some of the cases I covered."

"Well, we'll buy a copy, and no mistake. So long as you promise to sign it?"

"You can count on it," Jacquot replied.

"You had a ponytail back then, am I right? But now it's a beard."

"Too old for a ponytail, don't you think? A beard seems more... appropriate. And I always hated shaving."

Bertrand rubbed his chin. "Me too, but the wife, you know...? Ah, here she is."

The two men struggled to their feet as Dénise came in from the kitchen. She carried a plate of small toasts buttered with a generous knife scrape of *foie gras*.

"Monsieur Jacquot," she said, handing the plate to her husband. "Welcome to our home."

"It's Daniel."

"Then you must call me Dénise."

"Something smells very good in the kitchen?"

"Just a *daube*. I hope you're hungry."

As Dénise had said, their supper was taken in the kitchen, at a round table set with four places.

"Our neice, Marie," Dénise explained, when she saw Jacquot glance at the extra place. "She said she'd be home for supper, but..." she looked at the clock on the wall. "The young, always running late, *n'est-ce-pas*?"

"She'll be back soon enough," said Bertrand, taking his chair and inviting Jacquot to join him. "No reason we have to wait for her. Come on, woman, let's get at it."

They were half way through a rich and silky beef stew, Dénise ladling out second helpings to Jacquot and her husband, when they heard the latch on the front door. A moment later a young woman came bustling into the kitchen, struggling out of her coat, hanging it on the back of the door and apologising for her lateness.

"So sorry, so sorry. There was a crash just outside Pertuis. Everything held up," she explained, unwinding a scarf, cheeks glowing from the cold. She was tall and willowy, with a shock of short spiky blonde hair. She wore tight red jeans, green plimsolls, and a sloppy, oversized black jumper whose sleeves she pushed up as she came round the table to kiss Dénise and Bertrand. Then, with an uncertain smile and questioning look, she held out her hand to Jacquot.

He pushed back his chair, got to his feet, and introduced himself.

"Daniel Jacquot, mademoiselle."

"Marie," she replied. "Marie Dufour."

But Jacquot knew that the girl now taking the seat across the table, holding out her bowl to Dénise for a ladleful of stew, wasn't who she said she was. The hair might have been short and blonde, she was taller and prettier than he'd expected, and while her French was good, assured even, she was still not wholly fluent. Just behind the words he could make out a gentle tell-tale calypso lilt.

There was no question about it.

Marie Dufour was Sylvie Martin.

71

It was a late night. After finishing the *daube*, and working their way through some cheese and fruit, the two women – 'aunt' and 'niece' – cleared what was left on the table and shooed the men from the kitchen. Bertrand led Jacquot back into the salon. Another log on the fire, a shower of sparks, more whiskey. And more talk. Rugby, of course. And Jacquot's time with the *Judiciaire*. And then the estate, the wine-making – "Monsieur Patric wants to start up without the co-operative; bring in our own *pressoir*, fermentation tanks. Some real marketing, too. And the wine's good. You've been drinking it tonight and at lunch, so you'll know. It's the way forward, he says. And he's right."

Bertrand spoke with such enthusiasm that Jacquot wondered how he'd take the news that Patric Stuyvesant was dead, that the last of the family line would not be coming home, and that Clos des Roses, sooner or later, would be put up for sale. With Patric and Boni gone, there was no other option. Unless the new owner kept them on, their life here would be over.

The two men had stayed by the fire another hour after Dénise and Marie popped their heads round the salon door to say they were off to bed, and to wish them a *bonne nuit*. When the door had closed, and over another glass of whiskey, Jacquot had asked lightly about their niece.

"Down from Evreux," Bertrand told him, not in the least guarded or suspicious. "Had a job up there but hated it. And there was some man, of course. Some trouble…" He gave Jacquot a look. "Came down a few months ago and we got her working with the horses. Good with the guests, too. Started up some riding tours, which seemed to work, and next year she's planning some cookery courses, painting courses, and the like. A good girl. Hard working, you know? Has her own place out above the stables. Bit of a ruin when she took it over but she's turned it round – a real little *apartement* now."

There was no doubt in Jacquot's mind that this was the story that Patric and the Galinesses had come up with, if anyone bothered to ask, and Bertrand had reeled it off with a practiced ease, even though he knew he was lying through his teeth. As deceptions went, it was convincing enough, as good as his own cover. But Jacquot wondered if Bertrand and Dénise really knew what had happened, what was going on? Who this young woman was? That she was Patric's lover?

Now Jacquot lay back in his bed and watched the flames from the fire in his hearth flicker across the ceiling. When he'd left their cottage, the cold night air stinging his face, Bertrand had told him to light a fire if he felt like it – many guests did, he'd said; he'd find all he needed in the basket by the hearth. And Jacquot had done just that, kneeling on the stone floor, arranging the splintered kindling, setting light to a screw of newspaper, and watching the flames lick up, catch and crackle amongst the wood. There was something primal and ancient about a fire, he decided, as shadows spun and danced across the walls. It wasn't so much the heat it generated, as the company it provided. And the smell of woodsmoke sliding through the room brought back memories of his grandfather's house at Blazy-Landau. But most of all, wrapped in thick linen sheets and soft wool blankets, the overriding feeling was one of relief. For there was not the slightest doubt in Jacquot's mind that the young woman who'd sat across the table from him in the Galinesse kitchen was Patric's lover. The girl who had worked at The Edgewater Club, the girl Patric had taken off with. She might have changed her appearance, but he was certain now that he had found her. He'd been right. Right to come to France. Right to follow his instincts, and come here to Patric's family home. Because this was where Patric had sent her. This was where he knew she'd be safe.

All that remained for Jacquot was to decide what to do next.

He had kept up his cover at supper. A cop turned writer, looking for some peace and quiet to work on his book. And that cover, and the winning try he'd once scored for France, had worked. But as soon as he could, he knew he'd have to confront Marie, and tell her all he knew. About Patric, about Boni, and about the money. The longer he left it, the greater the risk to his daughters.

But what was he actually going to do, after that? Was he going to take her back with him to Nassau? Hand her over to Ballard and DiCorsa? Condemn her to the same fate as Patric and that racetrack runner, Fuentes? A final boat trip to the feeding grounds between New Providence and Abaco? Or just tell them where she was; leave the rest to them?

And what about the money? Where was it? Did she know? Could

she lead him to it? Did she even know that Patric had stolen the money? Maybe, he thought, in return for the money – if he could find it and get the girl to part with it – DiCorsa and Ballard might be persuaded to leave her alone.

A step at a time. A step at a time, he thought to himself. And as the flames flickered liquid gold across the beamed ceiling, the wine and the whiskey finally set to work, his eyes grew heavy, and he fell asleep.

72

The fire had died and a light drizzle speckled the panes of his bedroom window when Jacquot woke up the following morning. The previous day's blue sky had gone, and a gusting breeze rattled the shutters and pushed a low scud of grey cloud over the valley. The greyness matched the dull ache in his head, his movements a little pained and leaden as he levered himself out of bed, showered and dressed.

Downstairs in the dining room, a table for one had been set for breakfast and placed by a warming fire. On a buffet table below another of Drumgoole's paintings – a row of fishing boats hauled up onto a beach, a blue sky, white clouds and turquoise sea all in the same blurred strokes as its companion in his bedroom – Jacquot helped himself from an iced jug of fruit juice, a steaming Thermos of coffee, and a basket of pastries.

"*Bonjour, bonjour*, Monsieur Daniel," said Dénise, bustling through a swing door that must have led to the kitchen. "Something hot for your breakfast? Some eggs, some ham?" She came to the table, reached into her apron pocket and brought out a foil pack of Ibuprofen which she placed beside his plate. "My husband can be a very bad influence," she said, with a smile, "so you might need these too. After mixing his whiskey and wine, he swears by them."

"A bad influence, indeed," said Jacquot. "But it was a fine evening – for which, my thanks – and as much my fault as Bertrand's. And worth the pain, too, which these, I hope, will chase away."

After two milky *gran'crèmes*, some *petits pains* with home-made fig preserve, and a plate of scrambled eggs, Jacquot felt the tightness in his head and shoulders start to ease. Too old for whiskey, he thought. Or rather, too old for too much whiskey. He would know better the next time. And then he chuckled to himself. He said the same thing every time he felt like this, but had still to learn his lesson. Pushing away from the table he got to his feet, feeling just a little bit steadier than when he'd sat down, and left the dining salon. Upstairs he pulled on his jacket, wound the scarf round his neck, and decided the time had come to face the day and its consequences. Whatever they turned out to be.

He started with another walk down the drive, to the gates and back, to properly clear his head, shoulders hunched against the chill, hair and beard lightly sprinkled with the soft rain. It wasn't the easiest walk, but by the time he returned to the château he felt a great deal better. The pills had done their work. He was no longer squinting, his limbs were less stiff, and he knew what he had to do.

He found Marie in the stables, the first place he went to, exactly as he had expected. The door to a loosebox was open and she was brushing down a horse, sweeping a gloved hand along its glistening brown flank, a reaching, rhythmic movement, fluid, controlled. And as she worked Jacquot stood in the doorway and watched her. Ankle boots and gaiters to the knee, a tight, form-fitting pair of grey jodhpurs, a blue open-necked polo shirt, and black quilted *gilet*. And he remembered the photo of her at The Edgewater, in the swimsuit, the long legs and fall of hair, a breeze teasing the hem of her sarong, lifting it. She may have cut and dyed her hair, she may have lost some of her colour, there was no sarong, no swimsuit, but the girl in that photo was the girl in front of him. Except... Except, she was so much more attractive, more alluring, more desirable than any of those photos had suggested. They didn't come close to capturing or conveying the real person. And it wasn't just her youth and prettiness, nor that arched look in the personnel file photo that Ballard had shown him. It was something else, something far more elemental. And for the first time Jacquot really understood what Patric had seen in her. What any man would. She might not have had Boni's poise or beauty or confidence, but there was something utterly beguiling and compelling about her, something quietly and fundamentally irresistible about her. She was simply impossible to ignore, impossible not to look at, and want. And want urgently. The way she moved around the horse, the easy swing of her arm, the stiff pitch of her gaitered legs, the tightening and loosening of her jodhpurs as she bent and straightened. Jacquot had seen the girls in Patric's clubs – the 666 girl, for instance, and the high-rollers' escorts - but not one of them came close to this girl. Nowhere near. Which made Patric's decision to run away with her, his decision to steal a vast amount of money to set themselves up out of harm's way, seem suddenly all the more understandable. Because Sylvie Martin was special, very special indeed.

If the sun had been shining Jacquot's shadow would have stretched into the stable and Marie would certainly have seen him. But with low grey skies behind him he was just dark shape in the doorway, And as he watched her, Jacquot wondered how she would take the news that her lover was dead, that she would never see him again, that this life she had started in his family home would soon be over. There would be no more riding tours, no more cooking or painting courses, just as there would be no *pressoir* for Bertrand. The news he had brought with him from Nassau would bring all their dreams tumbling down.

The horse noticed Jacquot first, gave a snort, stamped a hoof, and swung his head round to fix him with a large chestnut eye. The movement alerted Marie and she stood up, turned in Jacquot's direction.

"Monsieur Jacquot. I didn't see you there. How are you? How's the writing?"

Jacquot came out of the shadows. "I must admit I have felt better," he said. "Your uncle led me astray."

"Then you'll know better next time," she said, with a mischievous chuckle, and pulling off the brush glove, patting the horse on the rump, she walked over to him. And the closer she came, the more Jacquot was aware of her, as a woman not a girl; comfortable in herself, at ease, the kind of woman any man would want to hold, kiss, undress, make love to. And more, that she would want to do the same. For a moment he didn't know what to say.

"Is it okay to smoke?" he managed at last, reaching into a pocket for his cigarettes.

"Only if you have one for me," she replied, and reached for the cigarette he offered. He lit it, she inhaled briskly, and whistled out the smoke as though she hadn't had a cigarette for a long time. "Dénise and Bertrand don't approve, and I'm trying to quit anyway," she said, her warm molasses eyes settling on him, taking him in.

It was a surprisingly direct look, and he felt a certain stir of surprise. Even without a raised eyebrow, it was such a knowing expression.

"So do you like horses, monsieur? Would you like me to saddle up and take you for a ride?" There was suddenly a coquettishness there, too, in the accompanying tilt of her head and, whether it was meant or not, the offer was delivered with an easy suggestive smile and followed by another long appreciative pull on her cigarette. Those photos did her no justice, no justice at all, thought Jacquot.

"Daniel, please," he replied. "And no, I don't like horses. Too big, too strong. Too... wayward."

"And you are right on all counts, Daniel. It is good to understand the opposition. But once you do, then it is only a small step before you become entranced. You are hooked. It is a relationship, rider and horse, like nothing else."

It was the first time they had spoken without Dénise or Bertrand around, the first time they had been alone together, and Jacquot was struck again by her self-assurance... her spirit. There was, too, something challenging in the way she spoke, something increasingly attractive, a low smoky tone to her voice. Without thinking she slipped her hand into the open neck of her shirt to ease the strap of her bra, and worked her shoulder. He knew it hadn't been deliberate, or in any way suggestive, but it was no less intimate for that, a glimpse of white lace, the barely heard snap of elastic on bare skin.

"Have you always ridden? Back home?" he asked, realising he'd had to clear his throat before speaking. Even without make-up, her features were fresh and fine, her skin the lightest shade of honey, her lips full, her dark eyes gleaming with a kind of childish mischief.

"Whenever I could."

"In Evreux, was it?"

She nodded.

"Gorgeous country there."

She nodded again.

"So who looked after the horses before you arrived?"

"There are a couple of girls from Lourmarin who come in to help."

"And Bertrand tells me you live here? Upstairs?"

"Not much room in their cottage, and my uncle takes up a lot of space. This seemed the obvious place."

"Not the château?"

"Rather grand, don't you think? I mean, I just work here."

"And how long will you stay?"

She narrowed her eyes. "Do you always ask such a lot of questions?"

Jacquot gave a short laugh, and smiled. "Being a cop, I suppose. It's what we do, ask questions."

"But you said you'd retired. So you can stop now." She returned his smile. It was warm and friendly still, but the message was clear. She didn't want to answer any more questions.

And Jacquot knew in that instant that this was the moment, this was where he crossed the line and put aside his cover to tell her about Patric and the money, and DiCorsa and Ballard. Whatever the consequences.

He let the silence stretch between them, and then, gently, he said, "I think, mademoiselle, that we should talk."

Behind her, the horse she'd been grooming snorted again, stamped its hoof. She glanced back at it, and then down at her cigarette. She dropped it, put it under the toe of her boot and ground it out. When she looked back at him, she was frowning, uncertain, and he could see a splinter of fear flicker in her eyes.

"Talk about what?" she asked, the words hard and sharp.

"About someone we both know. A young woman called Sylvie Martin," he said. "And her lover, Patric Stuyvesant."

She stiffened, suddenly alert, like a lone creature scenting the closeness of a predator.

Her eyes narrowed and her mouth tightened.

"Who are you?"

73

From somewhere beyond the valley a distant rumble of thunder reached them, filled the silence between them. Outside in the saddling yard the drizzle turned suddenly to rain, pattering loudly now, and a chill slip of breeze slid between the stable doors.

"I'm a friend of Boni's," Jacquot began. "Patric's wife. And you have nothing to fear from me."

She frowned, as though she didn't recognise either name. Or understand why he should imagine she should be afraid of him. But she said nothing. Still playing the game, he thought, the game of safe denial. And Jacquot knew that he would have to make the running. She would give nothing away until she was sure of him.

"Is there somewhere we can talk?" he asked.

Without replying Sylvie Martin turned and walked back to the horse she'd been grooming, untied him from the hitching post, and led him back to his box. Time to consider her options, thought Jacquot, as he watched her coax him in, and bolt the door. When the horse had turned to face her, she reached up, pulled off the head collar, ruffled his nose affectionately, and fed him a cube of sugar from the pocket of her *gilet*.

Jacquot stayed where he was. He would make no move until she initiated it. He would be no threat. He would give her whatever space and time she needed.

Without a word, without a glance in his direction, she hung the collar from a hook, turned from the loosebox and, as though there was no one else there, she walked to a flight of warped wood stairs at the end of the stable and started to climb them.

Jacquot watched her. When all he could see were her ankle boots and gaiters, he flicked his cigarette out into the rain and followed.

Sylvie had taken off her jacket and was spooning coffee into a Bialetti percolator when Jacquot reached the top of the stairs. Her apartment was long and high with whitewashed stone walls, a raftered ceiling, and wide floorboards spread here and there with rugs. The kitchen area, at the top of the stairs, was simply, sparely furnished with a chipped enamel gas stove, a sink, a fridge, a microwave, and a small round table with three rush-seated chairs. Beyond a dividing line of cupboards, topped with a formica work surface, was her sitting room, with a pair of sagging armchairs and a small sofa set around a coffee table and television. There was a bookcase, a CD player, and behind one of the armchairs a wood-panel screen. Around the edge of it Jacquot could see the end of an unmade bed, and an old armoire tilting a few degrees from the wall. Jacquot could imagine Bertrand bringing everything up here bare-handed – the stove, the kitchen table, the bed, the sofas and chairs, the armoire and screen. Furniture from a storeroom, a cellar, or attic. Furniture from the big house, no longer needed. The space was warm and smelled of horses and perfume and candle wax. Rain pattered down on four roof-light windows, two each side, and battered against the window above the sink.

Sylvie waved a hand at the kitchen table, and Jacquot sat down. She lit a match, put it to the gas with a pop, and placed the coffee percolator on a ring of blue flame. When she was done, she leant back against the sink, crossed her arms, and looked at him. She had made sure there was enough space between them for her to make a dash for it if she needed to.

"Do you speak English, Daniel? If that's your real name? All this would be easier for me in English. My French isn't up to it yet."

For someone who supposedly lived in Evreux and was visiting her aunt and uncle, this was enough of an admission for Jacquot to feel a beat of confidence. She was letting down her guard, and they both knew it. A first small step. And now that she was speaking English, the calypso lilt was far more noticeable.

"Of course, if you wish. And Daniel Jacquot really is my name. And once upon a time I really was a cop."

Another low groan of thunder came to them, growling over the hillsides.

"But not a writer?"

He shook his head, spread his hands apologetically. "Not a writer, no."

"You had us all fooled. The retired cop, turned writer. And you really did look the part. The beard, I guess."

"I couldn't really come barging in. It seemed wiser to have a cover. To find out what was going on. Whether you were here or not." And that cover, he decided, had worked. Their supper the previous evening, the four of them gathered around the kitchen table, had provided him with a kind of provenance, an authenticity. Bertrand knew him from the rugby field, Dénise liked him, he'd been a policeman, and he'd been welcomed in their home. If they could accept him, then so could she.

"So what do you want?" she asked, her arms still crossed defensively. "Why are you here?"

"As I said, Patric's wife, Boni, was a friend of mine. Way back. Ten years or more. In Marseilles, where I worked for the *Judiciaire*. Three weeks ago she came to my home on Martinique, told me that Patric had run off with a lover, and asked me to find him."

Again there was silence, save the hiss of gas from the ring, and an occasional squalling spatter of rain on the roof lights and kitchen window. Sylvie turned and took two mugs and a kilner jar of sugar from a shelf by the sink. Clamping the jar in the crook of her arm, she went to the fridge, took out a carton of milk and brought it all to the table.

Jacquot made a point of crossing his legs, settling himself back in the chair. A man lounging in a chair, with legs crossed, was always going to be less of a threat. It would take him longer to get out of his chair and catch her if she did decide to make a run for it. But he felt there was now little chance of that. She would be as keen to know about Patric, as he was to know about her; about what had happened all that time ago in Nassau, and about the money.

On the stove the coffee started to bubble, steam rose from the Bialetti's spout, and the lid began to rattle. She turned off the gas, and brought the coffee pot to the table, filling the two mugs with a steady hand and telling Jacquot to help himself to sugar and milk. She took the percolator back to the stove and reached down to one of the cupboards beside it. When she came back to the table she was carrying a bottle of Calvados and two small tumblers.

"A habit I've picked up," she said, pulling out a chair and sitting down, facing the stairs and still keeping her distance. "But a good way to start the day. Blame Bertrand."

A girl after his own heart, thought Jacquot, as she levered out the cork with a squeak and poured two measures. Jacquot picked up his glass and held it out to her. She looked at it for a moment, then leant forward and tipped her own against it. She nodded, gave a small uncertain smile. Jacquot sensed that she was beginning to relax, to feel easier, but he'd continue to go slowly. As though he had all the time in the world, he sniffed the liquor, took a sip, then tossed it back in one, put down the glass and reached for his coffee. Hair of the dog. Like the Ibuprofen and the walk, he knew it would make him feel better.

For a while there was silence, save the rain and a gusting wind. Just the two of them there. Sitting at the kitchen table. Sylvie sipped her Calva, then reached for her coffee.

"I always think it's better to knock it back in one," he said, lightly, "and then chase it with the coffee."

"That's what Bertrand says. But I prefer to make it last."

Jacquot nodded, gave an easy, each-to-their-own shrug. But stayed silent. After years in the *Judiciaire*, sitting across from a suspect in an interview room, he had learned that silence was often a more effective spur than a direct question. And so it proved to be.

"Do you have another cigarette?" she asked.

He reached for his pocket, handed her the pack and lighter. She took a cigarette and lit it, tipped back her head and blew the smoke to the rafters. "So how did you find me?"

Voilà.

"A stack of letters and postcards in Patric's study. In a desk drawer. From his parents. From here, and from wherever they went on holiday. Sent to different addresses. All the places Patric lived when he first arrived in the Bahamas."

Sylvie frowned, so Jacquot explained how he'd followed the pair of them from the Idlings Motel on Yamacraw Drive – the first place Patric had lived in Nassau – to Mrs Swanson's, and then to Pirate Cay, about Marlon and the flight to Miami.

"It was just a guess I'd find you here," he said.

"A good guess, I'd say. So you really are a policeman?"

"Was a policeman. Like I said, I'm retired now."

"And what about Patric? Have you managed to find him, too?"

Jacquot shook his head. "No, I haven't." He paused for a moment, and then said what he knew had to be said. "And no one ever will. I'm afraid that Patric is dead."

Sylvie said nothing. Just a catch of breath and a low sigh. The slightest slump of her shoulders.

"When did he die?" Her voice was almost a whisper.

"Shortly after you left Pirate Cay for Miami."

"How?"

"He was murdered. Drowned."

She shook her head, closed her eyes. "Talking to the sharks. That's what we say."

Jacquot nodded. "I'm so very sorry."

Sylvie got up from the table, went to the stove, and came back with the coffee pot and an ashtray. She topped up their mugs, uncorked the Calva, and refilled his glass.

Jacquot watched her closely. The hand was still steady, there were no tears, no exclamations of disbelief. Just a kind of resignation, as though she'd been expecting something like this, and the news came as no surprise.

She sat down, laid her cigarette in the ashtray and, putting her elbows on the table, she rested her forehead in the palms of her hands. Maybe now she would cry, thought Jacquot, and he waited for the shoulders to jerk, the sobs to come. But they didn't.

She stayed like that for a moment, her fingers bending open and closed. Then she looked up at him, and a curious, teasing smile played sadly across her mouth.

"You must have been a very good policeman, Daniel," she began, picking up her cigarette. "Following that trail of letters and cards. Finding me. But you have one thing very wrong."

Jacquot frowned. "And what is that?" he asked.

"Patric was not my lover," she said, quietly. "He was my father."

74

A sudden sharp crack of thunder directly overhead made them start in their chairs. It was as if, for a moment, they had forgotten the storm outside. Which wasn't going to happen. Just seconds later a sheet of lightning turned the roof-lights and window panes white, made the day darker.

Sylvie Martin shook her head, took a final pull on her cigarette and stubbed it out. "Is that what everyone thinks? That we were lovers?" She got up from the table, switched on the light above the kitchen table, and came back to her seat.

"Everyone I've spoken to," said Jacquot, trying to gather himself. This was not what he had expected, and he was reeling as much from this unexpected disclosure as the sudden heart-stopping clap of thunder.

Patric Stuyvesant was Sylvie's father? Sylvie was Patric's daughter?

It couldn't be. Or could it?

He tried to think, to clear his head.

Of course it could. She was what? Twenty-four, that's what Ballard had said. Which meant Patric would have been in his late twenties when she was born. Still early days for him in the Bahamas, just starting out. He'd been working on Pirate Cay back then. Had he come to Nassau for a break? Met up with her mother and had some fun after a good run on the tables? A one-night stand for Patric? Just one of many high-rollers for her mother? Or had they been together longer? Had Patric been different? Had they tried for something more? And after their affair had run its course, if that's what had happened, had Patric known about the pregnancy? Or had Sylvie's mother even known who the father was? The questions tumbled over each other in a dizzying succession, one leading to another, an endless, unsatisfying line of speculation. Just how it always was… at the beginning.

Jacquot frowned, trying to get his head around it, yet stay calm and focused at the same time.

Boni hadn't said anything to him about any step-child, or a previous marriage. Had there even been a marriage? And Ballard hadn't said anything, nor Mrs Swanson, nor Cooper, nor Elaine, nor Forbes-Temple … No one. Jacquot smiled to himself; what a secret to keep.

Sylvie turned and gazed through the kitchen window, as though doing no more than wait for the next clap of thunder and flash of lightning which, when they came, just seconds apart, made her smile.

"Lovers," she said, and shook her head.

"They all just assumed…" Jacquot managed.

"I guess that's how it might look," she said. "I suppose you can't blame them."

They looked at each other, Jacquot still lost for words.

Sylvie must have seen the look, and understood it. She smiled again. "You had no idea?"

"None."

"No likeness?"

He peered at her, searching for something familiar; tried to recall the photos he'd seen of Patric. "I never met him," he said at last.

"You didn't know him?"

Jacquot shook his head. "Just Boni, just what she told me about him, and other people who knew him."

She chuckled again. A light, careless chuckle. "So that's you and me both. I didn't know him either. Not at first. Not while I was growing up. Just me and my mother back then. The two of us against the world, you know?" Without asking, she reached across for the pack of cigarettes and helped herself to another, lit it, pushed the pack and lighter back to him. "You want to hear the story? Being a policeman, I'll guess you do."

"Go ahead," he replied, and took a cigarette himself.

"Well, my mother and I lived together in an apartment on Paradise," she began, kissing her lips to blow out the smoke. "She worked the casinos there, waitress, hat-check, general party girl. I mean, she was real pretty. Just gorgeous – the life and soul? And it worked, you know? Just the two of us. When she got back from work, I was getting ready for school. When I came home from school, she was getting ready to go out again. And one weekend a month, we'd go off together. To the beach, to some other island. We were chums. It was okay.

"But when I started college, something changed. She got in with the wrong crowd, started with drugs – using and dealing. One day I came home and she was still in bed… Unconscious. All the gear on the bedside table. When she came to, she promised me she'd stop, promised she'd change, and for a while it was all okay. And then one day I got home and there she was, in her bed again, just like the first time. Only this time she wasn't sleeping. She was dead."

Another silence, followed by more thunder and lightning, Sylvie staring through the smoke from her cigarette, eyes fixed on some distant point.

"Which was when I first became aware of a father. My mother had never said anything about him. He'd just gone. That's the way it is, sometimes."

Jacquot nodded, remembering what Forbes-Temple had told him at The Edgewater Club.

"It was at her funeral service I found out. I'd just left college, like a month before, and was wondering what I was going to do? Where I was going to live? What was going to happen to me? I just felt so alone, you know? And then this man comes up to me after the service and says, can he have a word...?

"My mother being my mother meant there weren't many mourners. Just me and a couple of her pals from the casino, the pastor and the funeral people." Sylvie took a pull of her cigarette, held between long straightened fingers, and the tip glowed like a blown ember. "I only noticed him when the service was over. He was standing by the gate. He came over, like I said, introduced himself, and asked if he could buy me lunch. I told him, no, thank you, I don't even know you..." She shook her head, gave a little laugh. "That's when he told me... Just like that. Out of the blue. The same day I lose a mother, I find myself a father.

"He took me to The Edgewater. And told me everything. About the time he and my mom had spent together, way back. How they had met. How it hadn't worked, and he'd moved on. The way it goes. And then, just before before she died, he said how she'd got in touch with him, told him about me, and asked for help. She was in a bad way, running with a rough crowd, doing and dealing, and she owed some money. He gave her what she needed for the debt, and then kind of took over. Gave her money for me, for the rent, and for treatment – to get her off the drugs. But it didn't work. She just spent it all... On drugs, of course, until she took that one last hit.

"Which, I guess, makes it all just a little bit easier," she said, taking up her glass and finishing the Calva. "I mean, Patric was a great guy, and kind and generous, and I really did like him, the short time we spent together, but... I never really got close to him... didn't really get to know him well enough, to feel... well, what I suppose I should feel. My Dad dying, and all. Sad, of course, but..."

Jacquot gave her a moment. "So what happened?" he asked, at last. "After the funeral?"

Sylvie tipped the ash off her cigarette. "He got me a job at The Edgewater, and I really liked it there. I'd see him a lot; and sometimes we'd go out after work. Just the two of us. To Baize. For dinner some place. Getting to know each other."

"And no one knew?"

"No one knew. And I didn't mind that. It was our little secret. He always promised me that when the time was right he'd tell his wife about me. But she'd just had a miscarriage; things were difficult, he said. And I understood. It was cool."

"Did you know Boni?"

"Just saw her around the club, you know? By herself, having lunch with girlfriends, or with Patric. She was always really nice to me, so polite. All the other staff, too. And really beautiful. But it never happened. He never had the chance to tell her."

Jacquot said nothing. Instead he asked, "So why did he want you off the island?"

"One night we went out together. Patric and I. Back in the summer. Just cruising round in my car, like we did sometimes. He loved stopping off at beach bars, new places he'd found. Places with good food and good music, nothing fancy. But I could tell there was something wrong. He seemed wound up, tight, really anxious. I asked him what was wrong, and he told me he was in trouble; there were some dangerous people after him. But he wouldn't say who, or why. He didn't tell me anything, just that he needed to get me and Boni off the island, fly us all here. For our own safety. Like, right away. So he set it up. First that motel on Yamacraw Drive, then Mrs Swanson's, and then down to Pirate Cay."

"What happened then?" asked Jacquot, wondering if Marlon's account and hers would tally.

"He left me there while he went back to Nassau to sort things out and get Boni. The next thing I know, the pilot, Marlon, comes back to take me to Miami. He's got a flight ticket for me from Patric, and some cash to see me through. The plan is that I go ahead, and they'll meet me here. But when they didn't turn up, and didn't turn up, and didn't… Well, I knew something must have gone wrong. But I kept hoping, you know? That's all I could do. Hope and wait." She ground out her cigarette in the ashtray. "And then you arrived."

Jacquot nodded. "Do Dénise and Bertrand know all this?"

"Patric gave me a letter to give them, explaining everything, and what he needed them to do. They've been wonderful. Just the best. They never had kids, you know? So they've enjoyed having me round."

"Marlon said he gave you a briefcase?"

"That's right. Stuff about Patric's business. Legal things, he said. Things he didn't want to fall in the wrong hands."

Jacquot stubbed out his cigarette, and felt a chill. He reached for his drink, swallowed it back.

"You look inside?"

She shook her head. "Just left it for him, for when he arrived."

"You weren't curious?"

"It wasn't mine."

"And where is it now?"

She gave him a long, level look.

He recognised it for what it was. A judgement call.

Did she trust him, or not?

He could see her making up her mind.

"Bertrand's got it," she said at last.

75

The briefcase was pigskin, with shiny brass locks, the leather a dark brown, puckered and pockmarked. Elegant, expensive. An Air France cabin baggage label was still tied to the handle. Bertrand brought it to the kitchen table, then sat between Sylvie and his wife, the three of them watching Jacquot as he flicked the catches and lifted the lid.

"There can't be much there," said Bertrand, who'd been working in the barn when Sylvie went to find him. "It's not very heavy," he added, with a short little cough to cover the catch in his voice. Sitting beside him, Dénise wiped at her eyes, her face ashen. The news of Patric's death had hit them hard.

"There isn't," replied Jacquot, looking at the single large manila envelope the briefcase contained. The envelope wasn't sealed, but secured with a legal-style button-and-string closure. On its cover were the words: *In the event of my death...*

Jacquot took up the envelope, pushed the briefcase aside and unwound the loop of string. Inside the envelope were two smaller white envelopes. A single word had been written on each one: *Summary*, and *Paternity*. Neither of the white envelopes was sealed.

Jacquot opened the one with *Summary* on it. Four hand-written pages, signed by Patric and dated July 29th 2004, just a week after his poker game with Elaine Drumgoole. A brief but comprehensive record of the events leading up to his disappearance. It was an astonishing story and Jacquot whistled softly, shook his head, and felt his stomach turn and knot as he read it. Things he hadn't known, things he hadn't suspected, things he hadn't even considered. Thoroughly duped, and blindsided. Played for a fool. Just as much as Patric. And DiCorsa, too.

How had it come to this, he wondered?

Five years retired, and living island time, that's what it was.

When he'd finished reading, he pushed the pages across the table to Sylvie, and picked up the second envelope marked *Paternity*. A single sheet of paper. Folded twice. A black letter-head, elegantly embossed and copperplate. A firm of lawyers in Nassau with offices in New York, London, and Zurich. Three crisp paragraphs. Notarised and witnessed. A voluntary acknowledgement of paternity, recording Patric Yves Stuyvesant, of Lyford Cay and Baize Inc., as the legal father and protector of Sylvie Raine Martin.

No wonder Ballard had wanted to find her, thought Jacquot, and get his hands on any documents that Patric might have given her. What a haul it would have been for him. Not just the acknowledgement of paternity, but the damning record of his attempt to incriminate Patric in the theft of company funds. It was all dropping into place.

"You are a very wealthy young lady," said Jacquot, pushing the lawyer's letter across to her. "According to that, you inherit the château here, and nearly eighty percent of all Patric's holdings in Nassau, namely the Baize clubs."

Sylvie read the letter, then sat back, a stunned look on her face.

"But what about Boni? Patric's wife. Surely everything will go to her." And then a worried frown stitched itself across her brow. "Do you suppose she'll let me stay here when she finds out about me? I mean, I miss the island, but I've come to love it here. And there's so much to do…"

Jacquot sighed, shook his head.

Sylvie suddenly looked small, and vulnerable. "What?"

"Boni's dead, too. You're the only one left."

Her eyes widened, and she looked scared. Across the table an astonished Bertrand and Dénise glanced at one another.

"So why are you here?" asked Bertrand. "How are you involved?"

"Because the people who killed Patric and Boni think that I can help them find the money they say he stole."

"What money?" asked Sylvie.

It was a response that Jacquot had been expecting. It didn't surprise him.

"Do the names Ballard or DiCorsa mean anything to you?" he asked.

Sylvie shook her head. And then, "DiCorsa… yes. I do know him. He owns The Edgewater, doesn't he? A funny little man."

"Well, not so funny. His associate, Ballard, told me that over a period of time Patric removed nearly ten million dollars from the Baize clubs. Money that belonged to DiCorsa. Money from DiCorsa's various criminal enterprises that was laundered through Baize accounts." Jacquot looked at the three of them, each with their eyes fixed on him. "And they want it back. The thing is, I believe what Patric says in that summary. Because what Ballard really wants is you. And everything that you now own. The clubs, the house on Lyford Cay, this château, too, if he finds out about it. Either he'll force you to sign everything over to him or, more likely, you will simply disappear. And the money with you. Like Patric and Boni. No loose ends. As though you had never existed. Leaving Ballard free and clear to continue with his deception."

"But why are you working for him, this Ballard? Helping him like this?" asked Dénise, her voice as brittle and choked as her husband's. For all her earlier friendliness, Jacquot knew that she was now the least sure of him. For Bertrand there was the rugby, that try, his time as a cop. For Sylvie, there was Boni and Patric. But for Dénise, he was still the man who'd come into their lives under false pretences. He had taken her in once, and she had fallen for it. Would it happen again?

"I'm working for him because…" Jacquot gave a sigh, spread his hands. "I'm working for him because he and DiCorsa are holding my children to ransom. My two daughters. If I bring them Sylvie, my girls will be released. At least, that's what they've promised."

Dénise gave a little gasp, and Sylvie blinked.

"You're surely not going to tell them where Sylvie is?" said Bertrand, squaring his shoulders and reaching out a hand for hers.

Jacquot smiled. "No, I'm not. I just have to work out what I'm going to do instead. What I'm going to tell them. I need a plan. A good plan."

76

It was Bertrand who came up with the plan, sitting there at the kitchen table. Not so much a plan as a strategy. And in his simple country way, it centred around rugby, the farmer's bright blue eyes shining with conviction as he outlined his idea.

"Confront them on your home ground, my friend. You're an old rugby man. You should know that it will play to your advantage. Better home than away."

Jacquot thought about it for a moment – not mentioning to Bertrand that often a team played with more enthusiasm and determination on away games – weighing up the pros and cons of going against Ballard, and playing the hand his own way.

"*Alors*, you will be with your children, too," Bertrand continued. "You can protect them more easily at home. And you have friends there to help you. So let him come and find you, this *con...*" Dénise gave a start at her husband's profanity, but he paid her no attention. "Put him on the back foot, my friend, and play your advantage."

Which was why, the following day, Jacquot took his return flight, not to Miami and Nassau, but to Martinique's Aimé Césaire airport, thinking about his daughters whom he'd called without success during his lay-over in Paris to tell them of his arrival home, thinking of Claudine on the slopes of Salon, of Elaine on her Nassau estate, and of Patric, Boni's husband and Sylvie's father.

Everything that Jacquot had learned about the man – from Boni, from Sylvie, from Dénise and Bertrand, and from all the people he'd spoken to on Nassau – had convinced him that he would have liked Patric. A man who loved life, and all its glorious pleasures. A gambler, too. A born chancer. But – for Jacquot, the most important thing – an honourable man. And loyal. To Boni, to Sylvie, to people in his past like Mrs Swanson and Sylvie's mother. And to his own parents, keeping all their letters, tidily tucked away in his desk drawer, years after he'd received them. Everyone before himself. And at the hardest of times he had done all he could to make sure that Boni and Sylvie were safe, to keep them out of harm's way. Jacquot wished he had known the man. That they had met. They would have got on well, he was sure of it.

All he could do now was finish the job for Patric. And make his killers pay. As simple as that.

And finish it for himself, and his daughters, too. Who were now just a few short hours away.

After the musty confines of the Jumbo jet – a Business Class seat was all he'd been able to secure – Jacquot stepped out of the plane in Fort-de-France and breathed in the warm tropic heat of a Caribbean afternoon. Another world, he thought, after the chill and drizzle of winter-time Paris and Provence, and less than a day between them. After claiming his baggage from the carousel he had a taxi drive him to the docks at Le Vauclin where the old harbour-master, Merluze, was only too happy to take him across to Îles des Frères. He owed him a fifty after all.

Sitting in the stern of Merluze's fastest speedboat – not his own, of course, but the best of the fleet the old boy looked after for absent owners – Jacquot felt suddenly revived as the sea air filled his lungs and tore through his hair and beard on the last leg of his journey. Watching the twin humps of the island ahead grow larger in the soft evening light, he knew it wouldn't be long now before he was back at Trinité, at his home on the beach, with his daughters running to greet him, flinging themselves into his arms, and asking in a jabber of excited island patois if he'd brought them any presents – which he'd had the forethought to procure at Duty-Free in Paris.

They were only a mile or two from the island when old Merluze beckoned him forward. Cupping his mouth to Jacquot's ear, he said he'd take them straight to Trinité, to the small jetty just a few hundred metres away from the house.

"No point getting a taxi in town when I can drop you right there, near as dammit," said the old boy. "So long as you got a beer and chaser to wash away the salt in my mouth," he added with a grin.

And moments later Jacquot felt the growing, hot thrill of homecoming as Merluze cleared the reef at Pointe du Trinité and brought them into the shore, closing down the revs as they approached the jetty, the speedboat's bow settling into the water, the engine dying, just the lap of the sea sluicing along its sculpted hull. Already he could see the lights of the house winking through the palms, and after helping Merluze tie up the boat he ran ahead, his bag bumping against his leg, his heart pumping with a boundless exhilaration.

And as he came through the palms, their browning fallen fronds rustling and snapping beneath his feet, there was Madame Loubertin, a brush in her hands, sweeping along the porch, the house lights behind her shining bright and golden. When he was fifty metres away, she stopped her sweeping and peered in his direction, a look of astonishment breaking over her face as he pounded up the porch steps and dropped his bag, breathless, expectant, waiting for Matti and Béa to come out, to see who'd arrived.

"Why, Mister Daniel. What you doin' 'ere?"

Jacquot frowned, looked past her into the house. The lights might have been on, but he could see that the place was empty. No sign of the girls. Were they out with Midou? Would they be back soon? He could surprise them. He would hide their presents, make them search the house, following them around going 'hot' or 'cold', the way they did it whenever presents were involved...

But Mama Loubertin's next words shot a numbing shaft of dread through Jacquot's body.

"'Cos there h-ain't no one 'ere. Them done gone to see you up dere in dem Bay-'amas."

77

"Dem gone off coupla day back," Mama Loubertin explained, settling herself at the dining table. "Midou, it was, stopped by an' tell me you done sent for dem, and can I keeps an eye on de 'ouse while dem is away? Her was goin' into town to pick up de girls from school an' h-all. Goin' straight on, dey was."

"Was she with anyone?" Jacquot was pacing back and forth in the salon, Merluze nursing the beer and rum chaser that Mama Loubertin had brought him from the kitchen.

"Just one of dem town cabs was all. Not Solomon, one of dem ferry drivers down from de port. Think it were Thomas from h-over Oubliette way, but can't say fo' sure."

"Did they catch the ferry?"

Mama Loubertin shrugged. "Just said her was going is h-all. Not how. Guess it had to be ferry. H-ain't no other way offen the island I knows." And then she frowned. "So you didn't see 'em? Up dere?"

Not wanting to alarm his housekeeper, Jacquot shook his head. "Crossed wires, I guess. Getting old." He shrugged. "So I better be getting back there before they spend all my money in the casinos." He turned to Merluze. "Looks like it's a trip back to the mainland, if you can handle it?"

"Cost you another round," said Merluze, polishing off his chaser and following with a gulp of beer, cupping a hand over his mouth to cover a low satisfied belch. "Something for to fix my night vision, you understand."

While Merluze set to work on his second beer and chaser, Jacquot went to the phone and dialled Sergeant Balmet's home number. After a couple of rings his mother, Justine, answered and when the usual colourful stream of greetings came to an end Jacquot asked to speak to her son.

"Why, he done gone off on some training exercise *Capitaine* Faubert arranged, up Guadeloupe way," she told him. "Been gone a few days now. Back at the weekend, he is."

When he ended the call, Jacquot didn't bother to replace the handset, just dialled the number for police headquarters in town. One of the deputies on duty took the call, and when Jacquot asked to speak to Jules Faubert he was told that the *Capitaine* was on holiday. He was expected back in ten days.

"When did he leave?" asked Jacquot.

"Yesterday mornin', Monsieur Jacquot. You want I pass on a message iffen he gone call in?"

78

It was late when Jacquot checked in to the Ambassadeur Hotel on Parc Savane in Fort-de-France. The room he was shown to overlooked the park, one floor below Boni's, and two floors below Tarrant or Torrance, the man who killed her.

The first thing he did was phone the concierge to make arrangements for a seat on the earliest flight for Nassau the following day. The quickest flight time was a frustratingly long eight hours, leaving Fort-de-France mid-morning with stop-overs in Puerto Rico and Miami before the final flight into Nassau's Lynden Pindling International Airport. With gritted teeth, he asked the concierge to book a seat, only to be told just the very next minute that the flight was now full and he'd have to be put on the wait list. If he failed to make the flight, the next departure was late in the afternoon.

This was not going well, and knowing he'd never be able to endure such an achingly long delay he asked about private jets. Thanks to Boni there would probably be enough money to book a flight. The concierge told him he'd make enquiries, and call him back. Three cigarettes and thirty minutes later, with a couple of cognacs from the mini-bar to calm himself, the phone rang. He could tell from the jaunty tone that the concierge had good news for him, and his heart lifted. A private jet had come in from Miami that evening and was returning at seven the following morning. An 'empty leg', the concierge told him; the client had only wanted a one-way flight. The pilot would be happy to take Jacquot and land at Nassau en route. Flight time approximately three hours. Would that be acceptable, asked the concierge? It would be, thought Jacquot, and he asked how much the flight would cost. Eight thousand dollars came the reply. Book it, said Jacquot, and gave the man his credit card details. Five minutes later the payment had gone through and that was that. All being well he'd be back on Nassau by lunchtime. Thank you, Boni, thank you, whispered Jacquot, and after putting in a request with the concierge for a four a.m. wake-up call, he put down the phone and got ready for bed.

The wake-up call had not been necessary. Whether it was jet lag or worry, Jacquot spent most of the night tossing and turning in his bed, waking up to the beep of a horn from the road below his room, or a shout from the park, or the loud thumping sound of music in a passing car, dropping into a series of light dozes during which he dreamed fitfully of Matti and Béa and Midou, of his bedroom in Clos des Roses, of the *daube* in the Galinesse kitchen, and of Bertrand, Dénise and Sylvie, the three of them on the steps of the château, waving in his rear-view mirror as he set off for Marignane and his flight home.

Jacquot was already dressed and packed when the wake-up call came through from the concierge. Ten minutes later, he was getting into a taxi at the front steps and, with a salute from the doorman, he was on his way to Aimé Césaire airport just a few miles out of town at Le Lamentin.

The last time Jacquot had left the airport by private jet it had been in the company of John Ballard. This time he was alone, ushered through the charter terminal and out onto the tarmac where a gleaming white Beechjet 400A was waiting for him. A stewardess in a neat blouse and pressed grey trousers greeted him and ushered him aboard, the scent of aviation fuel undercut by the light floral tones of her perfume.

He would have felt like a pampered millionaire businessman, as he took a plush leather seat and was offered a plate of pastries and Buck's Fizz, if it hadn't been for his overriding sense of urgency to get off the ground and into the air as fast as possible. To arrive in Nassau and find Midou and his children. She might only have been his stepdaughter, but he had grown to love Claudine's daughter and he owed it to her mother to make sure that she was as safe as their own children. Strapping himself into his seat Jacquot turned down the Buck's Fizz but accepted the pastries, as fresh and warm as if they'd been bought just minutes earlier from one of Fort-de-France's leading *patissiers*. And maybe they had been, he thought.

Within minutes of boarding, the door was closed and secured, the engines started their rising whine, and the Beechjet began to roll forward, heading for the taxi-way. Up ahead the cockpit door opened and a good-looking young man in crisp white shirt and black trousers came into the cabin, spoke a few words to the stewardess, then made his way down to Jacquot and introduced himself.

"Good morning, Mr Jacquot. Captain Brandon Allen. Pleasure to have you aboard, sir."

"Pleasure to be aboard, Captain. And thank you for making it all possible." Jacquot shook the hand that was offered, and remembered Marlon with his can of beer and dirty shorts, his tattoo and stubble, and the stale, airless stink of his de Havilland Beaver.

"Estimated flight time to New Providence is a little over three hours, sir," said Allen. "Conditions are good, and all being well we should have you in Nassau sometime after ten local time. If there's anything you need, Sharon will be happy to take care of it, and if you want to join us in the cockpit, why, we'd be happy to make room for you. Not regulation, of course, but quite a few of our clients enjoy the experience."

With a nod and a smile, Allen made his way forward and closed the cockpit door behind him. A few minutes later, the Beechjet turned onto the runway, its engines rose to a shuddering roar somewhere behind Jacquot, and they were off, hurtling down the tarmac and lifting abruptly into the air, climbing fast through a low scatter of cloud over the glittering golden waters of Fort-de-France Bay before heading north-west above the island's forested coastline, the sun flashing through the Beechjet's starboard windows, the coastal corniche to Case-Pilote and Bellefontaine that Boni had taken her first day in Martinique just a tiny grey ribbon many thousands of feet below them.

By the time they levelled out at the Beechjet's cruising altitude of forty-five thousand feet, Jacquot was fast asleep.

79

Jacquot could feel a hand on his shoulder, a gentle pushing motion, and the words, "I let you sleep, sir. You looked so tired."

He opened his eyes, glanced around, and wondered for a moment where he was. Sharon, the stewardess, was leaning over him, a bright perfumed smile on her face.

"We'll be landing in thirty minutes. I thought you might like some breakfast."

Jacquot struggled up in his seat, straightened himself, and rubbed his hands over his face. Had he dribbled? Had he snored? Those were his first thoughts. He certainly hoped not. And then, blinking his eyes open, he saw a pot of coffee, fruit juice, and a plate of scrambled eggs on the table in front of him. "Thank you. How lovely. You are kind."

"My pleasure, sir. And there's more if you want it."

The eggs, like the pre-take-off pastries, were delicious, freshly scrambled, he could swear, and just how he liked them, a heaped golden pile on a toasted slice of nutty wholemeal bread. The coffee was just as good, hot and strong, and the orange juice ice cold and squeezed on board. Forget turning left, thought Jacquot, as Sharon cleared away his plates and the Beechjet began its descent. Private jets were the only way to travel.

But there was little time for such pleasant, pampered reflections. Touchdown meant action, and surprisingly refreshed from his three short hours of sleep, Jacquot retrieved Patric's Explorer from the airport car park and drove to the house on Lyford Cay, wondering to himself if he would find Midou and his daughters there, but knowing that if he didn't he'd find them soon enough. Ballard would want him to find them.

Without Beth to care for it, the Stuyvesant house had been left to its own aimless, timeless devices: cool and silent, an airless, echoing space with a late-morning sun slanting across its marbled hallway. And empty rooms; no food in the fridge, no fruit in bowls, no flowers in vases. And no Midou, no children. There had always been a chance that he might find them here, but there was no sign of them.

What he did find, on the kitchen table, was a silver urn and a padded envelope. He knew the contents of both, but opened them anyway. With an easy twist he removed the lid of the urn and tipped its contents to the light. A soft grey ash sprinkled with white flecks. He replaced the lid and then opened the padded envelope, shuffled the contents around, and peered in: an Omega Seamaster, a solitaire ring, a pair of diamond ear studs, and a weighty platinum bracelet. All of it Sylvie's now. Everything as it should be.

Resealing the envelope, he picked up the urn and, after a moment's thought, he left the house and headed for the beach. This was where Boni would want to be, he decided, and passing through the casuarinas and tamarisk he kicked off his loafers and walked down to the shoreline. This was where she had come after all her travelling, living on a beach with a man she loved. And this, Jacquot was certain, was where she would want to stay. There was a gentle stir of breeze and turning his back to it, Jacquot eased off the lid, tilted the urn and watched the ash drift away from him, shawls of grey mist dancing in the air, drifting down to the sand, darkening in colour as the sea touched it. And vanishing. She would be happy now, he thought.

Back at the house Jacquot showered, changed his clothes, and leaving his unpacked suitcase on the bed he drove away from the house, turning out on to Western Avenue, heading for The Edgewater Club. He didn't expect to find Midou and the kids there either, but he could check if any messages had come for him in his absence, and make some phone calls.

Leaving the car with The Edgewater's valet, Jacquot trotted up the steps and into the main hall.

"Good morning, Mr Milhaud," said the receptionist. His name tag said 'Boris'. "How nice to see you again. Are you here for lunch? Can I reserve you a table?"

After being 'Jacquot' for the last few days, it took a moment for the 'Milhaud' to register. Of course, now that he was back in Nassau, he was Boni's brother again.

"No lunch, thank you. But I wonder, has my step-daughter, Midou Eddé, checked in? She'd have arrived with two little girls."

Boris frowned, then shook his head. "No sah, that name is not familiar. But I do believe we have some messages for you." He bent down, opened a drawer in the desk, and leafed through its contents. When he straightened up he had a sheaf of sealed envelopes in his hand with Jacquot's name, or rather Milhaud's name, on the cover. He went through them like a croupier with a pack of cards. "Three, four, and number five, and… six in all, sir." he said, tapping them into a neat square and handing them over.

Jacquot thanked him and slid them into a pocket. "Is Mr Ballard in the club, or booked in for lunch?" he asked.

"Not so far as I know," said Boris. "Shall I let him know you're here if he drops by?"

"No need," said Jacquot. "I'm sure we'll meet up soon enough." And with that he crossed the hall and headed for the Churchill Bar.

"The usual, sah," asked the bar steward, Joe, as Jacquot drew up a stool.

"A thousand members and you remember one order?"

"This is The Edgewater, sah. Don't make no mistakes hereabouts."

Jacquot nodded, and as Joe set to work on his small punch he went through his messages. They were all from Balmet – the first four simply reported that all was fine; the fifth explained that he'd been selected for a course in Guadeloupe, and what should he do? The final message said simply that Faubert would be taking over the surveillance. Jacquot could read the subtext, and knew that Balmet wouldn't have put much store in that arrangement. And he'd been right not to do so. A day or two after Balmet's departure, Faubert had taken himself off on holiday. And someone had come for Midou and the girls.

The rum punch was served and Jacquot slid the messages back in his pocket. So what had happened when Faubert went on holiday, he wondered idly? Whom had he had put in place to keep an eye on Midou and the girls? If anyone. Typical Faubert, he thought. The man wouldn't know a threat if it put a hand up his neatly-creased shorts and squeezed his *couilles*. And if that threat was directed at Jacquot, the man was even less likely to do anything about it.

Jacquot swirled the last of the punch in the glass and picked up the coaster. *"The only thing we have to fear is fear itself."* Jacquot frowned. It sounded suitably Churchillian but it didn't quite ring true. And then he remembered. It was Roosevelt. They must have got the coasters mixed up between bars. With a brief smile at Joe's misplaced trust in The Edgewater's infallibility, he finished his drink, signed the bill, and left the bar.

After making a call in one of the phone booths, Jacquot went down the steps and asked for his car to be brought round.

He knew where he needed to go next.

He didn't expect to find his girls, but there was something he wanted to know, something he needed to confirm.

80

The gates to Elaine Drumgoole's home did not open at his approach as they had on his first visit. Instead he had to climb out of the Explorer and push the button on the entry grille. A minute later the gates parted and he started up the drive. As he closed on the house, he saw Elaine step out of the shadows, cross the verandah and come down the steps to greet him. She was wearing cream slacks and a loose beige jumper that hung elegantly off the shoulder, showing a white bikini top or bra beneath the open weave. She was barefoot, her hair was loose, and as he killed the engine and got out of the car, she brushed back a loose strand and tucked it behind her ear. Just like Claudine.

"So the traveller returns," she said, smiling widely. "It feels like an age."

"Just a few days," he replied, as she reached up and kissed both cheeks.

"Isn't that how you French boys do it?" she said with a grin.

"Three kisses are better," he replied, and showed her how.

"Well, you guys sure know how to make a gal feel special." She glanced at her watch. "You hungry? You thirsty?"

"A drink would be good," he said. "Maybe one of your beers?"

Elaine took his arm and, drawing him to her, matching him step for step, she led him into the house, past the portrait of her great-grandfather, and out to the ocean-side verandah.

"It's the staff day off – there's a family wedding or some such – so I'll get the beers myself. Back in a heartbeat," she said, directing him to a cane-weave sofa and going back inside.

While he waited, Jacquot pulled his cigarettes from a pocket, tapped one out, and lit it. He drew in the smoke, held it a moment, and then blew it out. Everything the same, he thought to himself, yet everything so different. Just a few days away, that's all it was. That's all it had taken to change the game.

Sitting back, he crossed his legs and watched a line of gaily-coloured spinnakers bloom far out at sea. It would be good out there, he was thinking – the wind in your hair, the bow spray on your face, the salty taste of the sea on your lips – when Elaine returned with two opened bottles of Kalik.

"So," she said, taking the seat beside him and tipping her bottle neck to his. "How was the trip? Successful? Tell me all. Did you find her? Did you find the money?"

"I found her."

"Where?"

Jacquot paused, took a swallow of his drink. The Kalik was light, and cold enough to burn a path down his throat.

"Canada," he said. "A few miles outside Ottawa." The lie came easily.

Elaine frowned. "Ottawa?"

"She has an uncle who lives there."

"An uncle? How did you find out about an uncle?"

"From her mother's will. She left him some things, personal items. His address was with her lawyer. Something Ballard should have thought of."

Elaine chuckled. "My, my. You truly are resourceful. A real cop."

Jacquot smiled. Of all the words she could have used. *Resourceful.* The very word Ballard had used back on Île des Frères. How Boni had described him to Tarrant. And he knew, in that instant, with that single word, that Patric had been right. That Elaine Drumgoole was not the woman that either of them had imagined.

"And the money?"

Jacquot shook his head. "All I had to do was find her. That's what Ballard told me. He'd take it from there. And I didn't want to scare her off."

"So what will you do now?"

"Give Ballard what he wants. And get my daughters back."

"Get them back?"

"He took them. While I was away. A little extra insurance."

"You are kidding me?"

Jacquot shook his head. "I went home after Ottawa. Back to Martinique. I was going to call Ballard from there and give him what he wanted, but the girls were gone. I've come back to find them. I've been to the house at Lyford Cay, to The Edgewater, but they're not there. I can only assume they're with DiCorsa on Sailboat Cay."

"Why, that's just terrible," she said, leaning forward, putting a hand on his knee. "What can I do to help? Anything. Just ask."

"There's nothing you can do," he replied. "It's down to me now. Give Ballard the girl's address, and hope he keeps his word. That he'll let me take my daughters and go home. Put it behind us."

"And the girl? Sylvie? What about her?"

Jacquot shrugged. "I don't want to know. It's not my business."

Elaine considered this, then nodded. "I think you're right, Daniel. Let it lie. Just go home and get on with your life, enjoy your daughters."

"You should come and visit some time," said Jacquot.

"Why, that would be just lovely," she said.

But he knew she didn't mean it. Not a word of it.

81

Jacquot parked the Explorer at Arawak Point, and walked over to the timber frame hut that passed as headquarters for Charter Island Airways. He knocked on the door and pushed it open. The single room was empty, hot, airless; just maps on the wall, a Pirelli calendar, a desk, telephone, chair, and green metal filing cabinet. Closing the door behind him, he walked along the jetty to the de Havilland Beaver that had taken him down to the Exumas. He called Marlon's name, peered through the cockpit window in case the ex-Navy SEAL was taking a nap. But there was no sign of him. And then, as he looked around and wondered what to do next, he heard the rising high-pitched whine of a motor-boat. He put up a hand and shaded his eyes. Like the de Havilland, the approaching launch looked a few years and several sea miles past its best, but its engine sounded healthy and it came towards him at a respectable clip. As it drew closer, the sun shifted off the wheelhouse windscreen and he saw Marlon stooping down to throttle back and steer in to the jetty. For a moment it looked as though the boat was going to crash into the pilings, but seconds before impact Marlon threw the engine into reverse and with a roar and a twist of the wheel he brought it in perfectly to kiss the woodwork. Jacquot shook his head; the man drove a boat the way he flew a plane. A natural. A real SEAL.

"You're late," said Marlon, as he hoisted himself up onto the jetty and proceeded to secure the boat.

"If I'm late, then so are you."

"Hey, man, just call it island time an' be settled." The two men shook hands and Marlon gave Jacquot a big beefy smile.

"Did you get what I needed?" asked Jacquot, as they headed back to the office.

"Snug away down in the cabin," Marlon replied. "Nine millimetre, just like you said. A Beretta M9. 15-round magazine. One in the slot. Happened to have a couple back at the house. Old friends from the Service, if you catch my drift."

Marlon pushed open the office door, swung himself down in the chair and reached behind him for the filing cabinet. Second drawer down. Without looking he reached in and came out swinging two cans of Kalik from their plastic grip, all that remained of a four-pack.

"Take a seat," he said, tossing Jacquot a beer. "And tell me what you got in mind?"

When Jacquot had finished, Marlon gave a grunt.

"Gonna cost you, cop."

82

It was mid afternoon when Jacquot and Marlon finally cast off from Arawak Point, and motored west into the channel between Paradise Island and New Providence, passing through a squad of pelicans who moved indignantly out of their way but refused to take wing. On the port side lay the white-sand beaches and gleaming wedding-cake mansions of Nassau's north shore, and up ahead, to starboard, the rusting white hulk of the Crystal Cay lighthouse. The sun was still high enough and strong enough for the shade of the wheelhouse to be welcoming, but when Marlon increased the speed and headed out into open water Jacquot stepped from the shade and made his way to the stern. Looking back at the tilting cranes and gantries of the harbour, dwarfed by a mighty white cruise liner whose balconied flank rose a dozen storeys above its wharves and all but blocked out the pink-walled fastness of the Atlantis Hotel, Jacquot felt oddly calm.

It's nearly over, he thought, turning away from the view and settling himself in the stern seat, watching the water slice past them, feeling the wind in his hair, riffling through his beard. In twenty minutes they would reach Sailboat Cay and he would do whatever he had to do to save his children, to save Midou. Which was why he'd asked Marlon to find him a gun. If he had to use it, he would. Without a second's hesitation.

Of course, there were options. He could simply tell DiCorsa and Ballard what they wanted to know. He could tell them where to find Sylvie, and trust them that they would keep their end of the bargain and let him walk away with Midou and the girls. Just as he'd told Elaine. But he knew that would never happen. And so had she. Men like DiCorsa and Ballard did not leave loose ends. There would be, could be, no witnesses. They would be tidy and methodical and utterly ruthless, and nothing would be left to chance. Whatever he did, he had no doubt that before the day was out they would feed him and his family to the sharks. Like the runner, Fuentes, like Patric, and many more besides. Children or not, DiCorsa and Ballard would consider it a small price to pay to protect and secure their continued and profitable enterprise. And no one the wiser.

Jacquot knew what would happen. On Île des Frères, Mama Loubertin, or Sergeant Balmet would report them missing, would tell

investigators that Monsieur Jacquot had gone to the Bahamas on a
business trip, and that Midou and his children had followed. But that
was all they could say. And Sylvie, Bertrand, and Dénise – if they lived
long enough to discover what had happened – would be of little help
either. Yes, Daniel Jacquot had come to the château, had told them
that his children were being held to ransom, and that he had returned
to the Caribbean to protect them. But that was all. Fingers might be
pointed at DiCorsa and Ballard, but there would be no evidence. No
bodies. The sharks would see to that.

Why don't you go to the police, Elaine had suggested, as he
climbed back into the Explorer? I'll back you up, she'd told him;
I'll say it's true, that your children are being held against their will.
She'd said it to him before, the first time they met, over the cartons of
Earl's barbecued ribs. But Jacquot knew her game now. Knew there
was no chance of that. So he'd told her that was not an option, that
DiCorsa was a respected member of the island's business elite. He
owned companies, he owned The Edgewater, and he undoubtedly had
friends in high places, possibly even the police. If someone had come
to him when he served in the Marseilles *Judiciaire* with such a story,
he would have been hard pressed to obtain a search or arrest warrant
from any *juge d'instruction*, and at the very most would have been
able only to visit the suspect, to get their side of the story – even if
they were prepared to give it. And though Elaine had tried to persuade
him otherwise, he knew she hadn't meant it, could sense her relief
when he turned down the offer.

And now the moment was drawing near. The time had come to see
this through, and put a stop to it. On his own. Once and for all.

Up in the wheelhouse, riding the battering chop with spread legs
and bare feet, Marlon pointed ahead, shouted back over his shoulder.

"Comin' up, boss. You set?"

Jacquot took a breath, and felt the reassuring weight of the gun in
his pocket.

"All set," he replied.

83

Jacquot steered them into the jetty by himself, the first time he had skippered a boat since his days on *Constance* back in Marseilles. As agreed, Marlon had disappeared below deck, squirreling himself away out of sight, leaving Jacquot, to all intents and purposes, on his own. This small deception represented only a slim element of surprise, they had both agreed, but any advantage had to be better than none. Managing rather better than he'd expected, Jacquot brought in the launch with some measure of elegance, and as it settled against the pilings he hoisted himself up onto the jetty to secure it.

His was not the only boat there. Moored on the other side of the jetty were DiCorsa's Mochi and a sleek white speedboat with red upholstery and two mighty outboard motors. He was examining the two craft, both of them empty as far as he could see, when he heard the patter of bare feet and looked up to see the houseboy, Duc, running towards him. He stopped a metre short and, putting both hands together in greeting, gave Jacquot a swift bow, coming up with a broad smile on his pixie-brown face.

"Ah, Mistah Daniel. So please see you. Been expectin' you all day. Come, sah. Come, sah, follow me."

Not sure what else to do, Jacquot did as he was told and followed Duc up to the house. But rather than enter through the front door, the houseboy led him around the side of the building and pointed him through a coral stone archway.

"Mistah DiCorsa busy, sah, with busy ness. He say he join you some time soon," said Duc, bowing. "But chi'dren through there, sah. Such ruvelly, ruvelly girls…"

With a nod to Duc, Jacquot followed his directions and stepped through the archway. What he saw was not what he'd been expecting, and the Beretta in his pocket suddenly felt very heavy indeed. And oddly redundant.

Behind the house, set in a ring of small thatched cabanas, was what appeared to be a long glass swimming pool sunk into the rocky edge of the cay and cantilevered over the ocean. Stretched out on a sunbed beside the pool was a young woman in a blue and white striped bikini that showed off a deep golden tan, a bottle of wine in an ice bucket on a table beside her. As Jacquot watched, the woman sat up and turned in his direction. When she spotted him in the archway, she lowered her sunglasses. It took Jacquot a moment to recognise her. Midou.

"Daniel. It's you," she said, happily. "They said you'd be here today." She swung her legs off the lounger and picking up a sarong, wrapping it around her waist, she hurried towards him, hugging him tight. She smelled of coconut oil and patchouli, her skin warm and smooth, her wide blue eyes sparkling with delight. "You didn't tell me you lived this kind of life. And there I was so worried about you. And the girls have been having just the best time. So spoiled, you won't believe. And they'll be so thrilled to see you." Turning back to one of the cabanas, she called out their names. "Matti! Béa! Come see who's here."

A moment later the two girls came bustling out, brown as berries, hair tied in ponytail and pigtails, wearing nothing but matching ruched bikini bottoms.

Jacquot felt like bursting into tears. Just the sight of them – turning, seeing him there, and then, when they realised who it was, racing towards him, arms flung out. "Papa! Papa! It's you, it's you! Papa, Papa, Papa!"

And then he was down on his knees and they were in his arms, hugging him tight. He could hardly speak, his eyes welling, his jaw clamped tight so the tears didn't come, desperately trying to swallow the huge hot lump in his throat. He had been apart from them for little more than a week but it felt like years.

"Do you know what *gelati* means?" was the first thing Béa said, when the hugs and the kisses had been exhausted, stepping back and looking at him seriously. "It means ice cream in Italian, and I've been eating lots and lots and lots of it," she said proudly. "It's the best ice cream I've ever eaten. All kinds of flavours, and creamy, creamy. Matti says she doesn't like it, so I eat hers as well."

Jacquot turned to Matti. There was a stern, disapproving expression on her face. "I just don't like *this* ice cream," she said, solemnly. And then, wrapping her arms round his neck, she whispered, "When can we go home, Papa? I don't like it here. The man plays funny music. Very loud."

Matti and Béa. Two peas in a pod, but each of them so different.

"Just as soon as you like," whispered Jacquot back.

"Come and see the pool, Papa," cried Béa. "It's just the best pool you've ever seen in the whole wide world." And running towards it she tucked up her legs and jumped in. When she came spluttering to the surface, she cried out, "It's got a glass bottom so it's like you're in the sea with all the fishes. Look, look…"

But there was no time to look.

From the archway behind them came a chillingly familiar voice.

"Ah, my good friend Daniel. You're back. How good to see you again. And looking so well."

Ettore DiCorsa was dressed in pink shorts and a green Hawaiian shirt printed with what looked like lines of dancing pink pineapples. The shorts were big and made his legs look more spindly than they might have been, but his lips were as pink and glistening as Jacquot remembered them. Something wet and hungry about them.

"And your girls," DiCorsa continued. "*Sono così belli, incantando così…*"

Jacquot stiffened, every fibre of his being bristling with a chill, familiar mix of hatred and fear. That his daughters should be anywhere near this man was enough to make him scream out. That they should be here in his home, swimming in his pool, eating his ice cream, was almost too much for Jacquot to bear. He wanted to pull the gun from his pocket then and there, and shoot the man dead, once and for all. And if it had just been DiCorsa, he might have done so. But there was Brock, now stepping into view behind DiCorsa, a black shadow the size of a door, in his signature black t-shirt and trousers. And squeezing past him, Ballard, wearing a white open-necked shirt and shiny blue trousers, with a matching shiny blue jacket swung over his shoulder.

"Welcome back, Daniel," said Ballard, playing his tongue between the gap in his teeth. "I trust your trip was successful?"

"Pah!" said DiCorsa, waving the question aside. "Business! Business! Always business with you! When we have the *bella bambini* to consider… and the gorgeous Midou. So, Matti, Béa, are you ready to go? Have you got all you need?"

Matti glowered and stayed beside Jacquot, reaching for his hand. But Béa had hauled herself out of the pool and was running towards DiCorsa.

"Are we going now?" she said excitedly, grabbing DiCorsa's hand, and twirling around. "Will Duc bring ice cream? *Gelati? Gelati?*"

For all the world, this cold-blooded killer could have been her favourite uncle. And this the same man, Jacquot now remembered, who, on their first meeting, had not wanted to know his daughters' names. Jacquot shivered.

"Of course, of course he is, *mia cara*. He's putting it on board as we speak. So, if we are all, ready, why don't we go? Eh? Eh?" And holding on to Béa's hand, looking at all of them with a wide, expectant smile, DiCorsa turned on his heel and disappeared with her through the archway, with Ballard following behind. Only Brock remained, watching them.

"Do we have to go?" asked Matti. "I'm tired."

"But you love it," said Midou. "It's such fun. And Papa will be able to see how good you are. So let's go and get everything we need," she said, picking up Matti and heading off to the cabana.

For a moment Jacquot didn't know what to do. Follow after Béa, or stay with Matti and Midou? But then he realised that the most important thing to do was tell Midou what was going on. Tell her the kind of man DiCorsa was. Warn her. For she clearly had no idea. So he followed them to the cabana and, standing in the doorway, he watched as they packed a bag. The cabana was luxurious, with a stone-flagged floor, a four-poster bed hung with mosquito netting, and louvred wood panels along one wall to catch the breeze. The furnishings were simple but stylish, and the bathroom looked immaculately equipped. The one thing Jacquot noticed was how tidy the place was. No clothes on the floor, no unmade beds, no tumbled disarray, nothing like the girls' bedroom at the house on Trinité. Duc, he supposed, or some other unseen staff on hand to tidy up after them.

"Midou? Could I have a word?" Jacquot asked, quietly, so as not to distract Matti from her packing, or alert her.

Stepping inside so as to be out of sight of the watchful Brock, he caught Midou's arm and held it tight. She looked up at him, frowned.

"Are you alright, Daniel? You look white as a sheet? Are you ill?"

"He is not what he seems, DiCorsa. All this…" he waved his hand around. "This is not what it seems. He is dangerous. Deadly."

"But he's been lovely," Midou replied, shaking her head in a questioning disbelief. "And you should see him with the girls. So attentive, so generous…"

"Listen, Midou. You have to listen to me. We are in danger. Real danger…"

Instantly her expression changed. "You're serious…"

"Very, very serious. Whatever you do, whatever happens, look after yourself and the girls. Before anything else. And do as I say. Without question. Do you understand?"

"Of course, if you really think…"

But suddenly there was Brock, walking towards the cabana.

"The boss says to hurry up," he called out. "It is time to go. They're all waiting."

84

When Jacquot, Midou, and Matti arrived at the jetty, DiCorsa, Ballard, and the skipper, Stephen, were already on board the Mochi, its engine chortling happily.

"Why don't I take my boat, too?" suggested Jacquot. "Give everyone a bit more room."

"No need," said DiCorsa, who was helping Béa with her life jacket. When he had it properly cinched he settled himself in a corner of the stern seat, opened up an ice box and presented her with a gaudily-wrapped ice cream. "We have plenty of room here, don't we, *bella*. Enough for everyone. *Tutta la famiglia*."

"Come on, Papa," said Béa, ripping off the ice-cream's wrapping. "It's so much fun. You'll love it. And you won't believe how good at it we are."

With a glance at his boat, hoping that Marlon would be able to follow at a safe distance, Jacquot helped Midou and Matti into the Mochi, then jumped in after them. Up on the jetty, Brock untied the lines and joined them.

After fitting Matti with a life jacket the three of them settled in their seats and, with the same fluid turn that Jacquot remembered from his first outing on the Mochi, Stephen pulled away from the jetty, pushed down on the throttles, and they were soon speeding past the jagged rocky edge of Sailboat Cay, accelerating into open water and heading north – the same direction they had taken the last time.

Jacquot, every sense alert, suddenly comforted by the weight of the Beretta in his pocket, looked around the cockpit and sized up the opposition. Ballard and Brock in the wheelhouse with Stephen, and DiCorsa eating an ice cream with Béa. Though he could see no weapons there was little doubt that Brock and Ballard and Stephen would know where to find some if they were needed, and wondered what was planned for him, and for the girls. It was clear that DiCorsa and Ballard wanted him to imagine another Fuentes re-run, with Midou and his children in the race-track runner's place, something to encourage his co-operation. But that was never going to happen. He would never allow it.

For now, though, he sat tight, his arm wrapped around Matti, working out what he would need to do when the moment came to settle this terrible affair. Somehow he must contrive to get the girls below decks, safely secured in the main cabin or locked away in DiCorsa's for'ard stateroom. Or maybe he should leave them here, and lure DiCorsa, Brock and Ballard below deck. Whatever happened he had to make sure that the girls were out of the line of fire, and that they did not witness what their father was going to do.

As for targets, Brock was the more immediate threat and would have to be brought down first. Ballard would be next, and DiCorsa last. But he would not shoot to kill. He would shoot to wound, to incapacitate, to neutralise. With Midou's help he would then bind and secure them, above or below decks, before putting a gun to the skipper's head with a request that he call up the coastguard and police and return to Sailboat Cay. And with any luck he might even have Marlon to help him out. As casually as he could manage, Jacquot looked behind him, over the churning trail of wake, but could see no sign of his friend and ally. Surely he should have left the jetty by now? If he was to be of any help, he couldn't afford to leave it much longer.

They were no more than a couple of miles from Sailboat Cay when DiCorsa called out to Stephen to kill their speed. The skipper did as he was told, the Mochi's engine dropped to a low hum, the bows sank down, and the launch came to a gradual halt, the water lapping against its hull as it turned with the current. As if everything had been planned in advance, Brock climbed round the wheelhouse and came back with a coil of rope, and a large bundle of blue plastic. Kneeling on the stern seat between DiCorsa and Jacquot he clipped one end of the rope to a steel stanchion that he levered up from its housing in the transom, and attached the other end to a ring in the blue plastic. Opening the deck hatch from which he had pulled Fuentes all that time ago, Brock reached down and brought out a length of hose, plugged it into a nozzle in the blue plastic and flicked a switch. With a sudden stir the blue bag unfolded with a whoosh of compressed air. An airbed. A large, triple-sized airbed with three holding handles lifting up from its leading edge like three blue horseshoes. Disconnecting the hose, Brock hoisted the airbed and dropped it over the stern, keeping the rope tight so the inflatable stayed close.

"So, my little treasures," said DiCorsa, getting to his feet and taking Béa's hand. "Are you ready to show your Papa how good you are, and what fun you've been having?"

With a squeal of delight, Béa tossed what was left of her ice cream over the side of the Mochi and held out her arms to Brock, who, with an effortless sweep, deposited her onto the bobbing airbed where she squirmed into position, and reached for a handle.

Leaning across Matti's head Jacquot whispered to Midou, "Stay with the girls. Whatever you do, stay with the girls." And then, to Matti. "Go on, my darling, show Papa what you can do. And Midou's coming, too."

Rather than let Brock take Matti, Jacquot did the lifting himself. He could tell she didn't want to do it, for whatever reason, and he prayed she wouldn't make a fuss. But when Midou took off her sarong, pulled on a life jacket, and clambered over the stern to join her, she seemed to calm a little.

"It smells funny," Jacquot heard Matti say, and he saw her wrinkle her nose as Midou took her place on the airbed.

"It's just the hot plastic," Midou replied, and smiled up at Jacquot; a reassuring smile – everything would be fine.

"Come, too, Papa! Come, too. You'll love it," cried Béa excitedly.

"Next time, my beauty," said DiCorsa, heading for the wheelhouse and the cabin below. "Your Papa and I have some business to attend to. And then he can join you."

Now, thought Jacquot, as Brock unreeled the line and Stephen engaged the throttle to take the Mochi forward. Now is the moment to act. The girls are out of the way. It's just me and them. He watched the line play out and tighten, saw the airbed swing forward and start to follow, picking up speed, bouncing over the water, Midou raising an arm to wave, the two girls screaming – Béa with delight and excitement, Matti because she didn't want to be there.

Now, now, now.

With a final wave to the girls Jacquot reached into his pocket for the Beretta, wrapped his hand round the butt, and was about to pull it clear and spin round when a hand gripped his wrist.

"Daniel, Daniel, Daniel," came Ballard's voice, whispering warm and close in his ear. "Is that the way to behave with old friends?"

85

Jacquot tried to pull free, but Ballard's grip was firm. He twisted Jacquot's arm up between his shoulder blades, slipped the gun from his fingers, and slid it into his pocket. Pushing him forward, they followed DiCorsa to the wheelhouse and down the companionway into the main cabin.

"Make yourself comfortable, my friend," said DiCorsa, settling himself at a length of polished mahogany table. The cabin was luxurious with a black leather banquette around the table, burr walnut panelling, and a thickly-carpeted deck. But the ceiling was low and neither Jacquot nor Ballard were able to stand upright. "Sit, sit, or you'll end up hunchbacks."

They did as they were told and slid along the banquette, Jacquot first, followed by Ballard.

"So, tell me, how was your little *avventura*?" asked DiCorsa. His voice was soft, smooth, gently enquiring. "Have you brought us good news? The money? The girl? Did you find her?"

"Yes, I found her," Jacquot replied.

"Ah… I had no doubt if it. My colleague, here, was right. You are, indeed, a resourceful individual. And the money? You found that, too?"

"There was no money. At least, the girl didn't have it."

"She told you that, did she? And you believed her?"

"I believed her. She was telling the truth."

DiCorsa nodded, as though this made perfect sense. "Of course, she was. Of course, she was," he said. "So it appears, my friend, that while you may indeed be resourceful, you are also… *un po' troppo ingenuo*. How do you say? Just a little bit gullible. Easy to persuade. Too big a heart for this kind of work. A pretty girl, soft words…" He waved a hand as though to conjure up the scene.

Then, suddenly, with a lurch, the launch reduced speed and swung round in a long turning circle.

"Ah, someone has fallen off. Your step-daughter, maybe, or one of the *bambini*," said DiCorsa, with a slow smile.

Jacquot made to leave the table, but Ballard caught his wrist, held him back. "Stay where you are. Brock and Stephen will handle it."

The launch came to a drifting halt, and from beyond the wheelhouse came the sounds of excited chatter and laughter.

"There, you see. All is fine," said DiCorsa, taking a lip balm from his pocket, unscrewing the lid and delicately applying a fingertip's worth of the lotion. "And in just a minute we will be off again," he continued, working his lips and returning the balm to his pocket. "So, you were saying…"

"What I'm saying," said Jacquot, pulling his wrist free from Ballard's grip, "is that I will tell you nothing until Midou and the children are safely back in Nassau."

DiCorsa chuckled. "No, no, no. You do not understand. You are going to tell me everything now, and then you can take your children, and go back to your home and your life. Only then, *amico mio*, only then."

Up in the wheelhouse, Stephen increased the power and the Mochi started forward. Before the engine drowned out any sound, Jacquot heard Béa shriek with delight as the line tightened and the airbed surged ahead once more.

"What guarantee do I have that you will keep your word?"

DiCorsa shrugged. "At this moment, none. But if your information is sound, then be assured you will all be put ashore on New Providence in the time it takes us to get you there, and supplied with all you need to return home. With a little… consideration for all your work on our behalf. And some gifts for the *bambini*, of course. Something for them to remember me by. And that, I assure you, would be the outcome I would prefer. You see, the alternative will not be to your liking."

"And what alternative is that?"

"Why, the children, of course. As we speak, a tiny, tiny little hole in the airbed – no more than a pinprick – is leaking…" He turned to Ballard. "What is that word again? What is it leaking? The fish thing?"

"Chum," replied Ballard, turning a thin little smile on Jacquot.

"Chum, chum, that's the word. Of course. Such a… friendly little word, no?" DiCorsa played the tip of his tongue across his lips. "Anyway, that is what is leaking into the water as we speak. Just small, tiny amounts. But enough for your clever little daughter to smell it when she climbed aboard, and certainly enough to attract the attention of my friends in the deep. And the longer that airbed stays in the water, and the faster Stephen goes, well, slowly but surely that hole will grow bigger, and the chum will flow faster. Ingenious, wouldn't you say?"

Jacquot went cold.

"We did this once before, didn't we?" asked DiCorsa, turning to Ballard.

Ballard nodded. "Twenty minutes. That's how long it took. Like game fishing, but with live bait on the end of the line."

Jacquot felt a rash of icy goosebumps race up his legs and back. There was no time to waste, no point wondering what might happen if he did, or didn't tell them what they wanted to hear. The children had been on that airbed long enough. Right now, the most important thing was to bring Midou and Matti and Béa back on board just as swiftly as he could manage it.

"Well," he began, "you're not going to like what I have to tell you, either of you."

DiCorsa spread his hands. "Please allow us to decide what we like and don't like."

"Well, to begin with, the girl, Sylvie, is not Patric's lover," Jacquot began. "She's his daughter." He nodded at Ballard. "As your colleague here knows only too well."

DiCorsa frowned. "His daughter? Is this true?"

"It's the first I've heard of it," replied Ballard, coolly.

"Oh, I don't think so," said Jacquot, taking Patric's four-page summary from his jacket and laying it on the table. "At least, that's not what Patric says." He pushed the folded pages across to DiCorsa. "You should read it. I think you'll find it interesting."

DiCorsa patted his pockets. "I don't seem to have my reading glasses with me. Why don't you give us the bones of it, my friend? Tell us what Patric had to say for himself."

"Well, let's start with the fact that he wasn't the one who stole your money. It was your associate here, John Ballard. Working with Elaine Drumgoole."

Ballard sat back, and laughed. "What? That's preposterous."

DiCorsa put a silencing hand on Ballard's arm. "Shush, shush now. I'm sure it is," he said. "I'm sure it is, but do let our friend continue. Such an entertaining story. I long to hear how it will end. Like a wonderful fairy tale. The plot of a grand opera. Do, please, continue."

"You see, Elaine Drumgoole wasn't just Patric's friend, she's the executor of his will. And as sole executor it is she who'll decide how

Patric's assets – shares in Baize, property, and such like – will be distributed in the event of his death. Which is why she and Ballard, here, hatched a plan to steal the money they would need to buy those assets when Patric, and his sole beneficiary, Boni, were dead. In other words, they planned to buy Baize with your money."

Ballard looked shocked. "That is quite ridiculous. I mean, if what you say is true then Mrs Drumgoole is easily wealthy enough to buy those assets all by herself, without any need for me to take money from Mr DiCorsa."

"Actually, she is not," said Jacquot. "According to Patric, her wealth is held in a family trust administered by four board members of Behrens Bank. Under the terms of this trust she is provided with a generous annual allowance to cover all necessary domestic and personal expenses, but that allowance does not extend to the purchase of a business like Baize, no matter how profitable it might be. Which is why the two of them came up with this particular plan. Skim the money they needed, place it in an anonymous shell company account with Behrens Bank, and wait until Elaine was called upon to perform her duties as Patric's executor. An eventuality that Ballard was already preparing for. And this being the Bahamas…" Jacquot spread his hands.

"And why, pray, would the charming Mrs Drumgoole do all this?" asked DiCorsa. "As I understand it, she and Patric were the very best of friends."

"Patric didn't say, but I can hazard a guess. Because that's all they were – the very best of friends. And I believe that Elaine wanted more. Much more. And what Elaine Drumgoole wants, she gets. Just a spoiled woman who doesn't like losing. And talking of losing, Mrs Drumgoole had never beaten Patric at the table, in any of the games they played. But now she has the upper hand, now she's going to win at last. Or so she thinks."

"Really," said Ballard, impatiently. "This is just…" he paused, spread his hands, as though he couldn't find the right words.

But he had paled. And DiCorsa had seen it.

"And?" said DiCorsa. "Is that it?"

"Not quite," Jacquot replied. "Everything was going according to plan until Patric discovered that he had a daughter from an old liaison and asked his good friend, Elaine, what he should do about it. Boni had recently had a miscarriage and he wanted to know how best to break the news to her. Elaine, of course, advised caution, saying he should keep it to himself until Boni had fully recovered, or better still, fallen pregnant again. That would be the time to tell her, she said. And only then. In the meantime, Elaine wasted no time passing on the bad news to our friend here. Now it wasn't just Patric and Boni they'd have to get rid of, but the daughter, too. The problem was, they didn't know who she was, or where she was. So Ballard decided to flush her out by telling Patric that a large amount of money had gone missing from Baize – the ten million dollars that he and Elaine Drumgoole had taken – and that you, Mr DiCorsa, had found out about it. Which was true, because by now Ballard had told you, pointing the finger at Patric."

"Go on," said DiCorsa, in a quiet voice.

"Well, Patric knew he was innocent, but he knew, too, that he was in trouble, and didn't have time to hang around and argue his case. The first thing he had to do was get his daughter and his wife off the island. Which was what Ballard was waiting for. But Patric had smelled a rat. If he hadn't stolen the money, which he hadn't, then who had? It could only be Ballard. So he and Sylvie disappeared, just dropped out of sight, keeping themselves hidden until he could get her off the island and out of harm's way. Which he did, very successfully. Which was when he found out about Elaine, that she and your man, here, were lovers–"

"Lovers? What rubbish, total rubbish. A daydream," said Ballard, with a disbelieving chuckle, and a carelessly dismissive wave of his hand. "Really…"

But Jacquot paid no attention, simply carried on with his story. "You see, getting Sylvie off the island was always going to be easier than doing the same thing with Boni. Patric couldn't risk just turning up at the house at Lyford Cay, and the chances were that the phone was tapped. So he decided to call on his old friend, Elaine, and have her invite Boni over for supper. Once she was there, he was going to put her aboard a boat and head for the mainland. So he drove over to Elaine's house in his daughter's old Honda and was about to turn up the side-road leading to her gates when a car up ahead did the same thing. A car he recognised." He turned to Ballard. "Yours. That's when he discovered that you and Elaine were lovers. He parked further down the road and came back to the house along the beach. The two of you were on the verandah, a little *diner à deux*. He got as close as he could, close enough to hear what you were talking about, and when the two of you went upstairs together, he knew he'd have to come up with another plan, a plan that didn't involve Elaine. And that's where his story ends. Those pages there," said Jacquot, pointing to the summary on the table. "He wrote it all down, put it in a briefcase with the paternity papers he'd drawn up, acknowledging Sylvie as his daughter, and sent it to her. And either that day, or the day after, as he tried to work out how to get Boni off the island without Elaine's help, Ballard, here, had him picked up, desperate to find out about the girl – who she was, where she was... But Patric wouldn't play, wouldn't tell him anything, until finally he was taken out on this boat and fed to the sharks."

Jacquot paused, looked at the two men. DiCorsa appeared relaxed, mildly interested, eyes half-lidded. Ballard was frowning, had started work on a thumbnail.

"Tell me, Mr DiCorsa, were you there for Patric's final moments?" asked Jacquot. "Or did your friend here act on his own initiative?"

DiCorsa gave it some thought. "I was in the States. Some friends. Some meetings. But John kept me informed. I knew what was going on."

"I'm sure you did," said Jacquot. "So you'll know that after Patric had been disposed of, Ballard started watching Boni. Maybe she knew about the girl; maybe Patric had told her where she was. Which was when Boni decided to call on me..."

"Yes, yes, I know all that."

"But what you won't know," said Jacquot, "is what Ballard and Elaine talked about at their cosy little supper. What Patric heard them discussing."

Beside him, Jacquot felt Ballard stiffen.

DiCorsa frowned. "And what might that have been?"

"Why their plans for you, Mr DiCorsa. As well as taking over Patric's assets, your trusted associate had also decided that your client list would be better served under new management. His. In short, Mr DiCorsa, your days behind the wheel–"

But there was no time to finish.

In a sudden blur of movement, Ballard pulled the Beretta from his pocket and swung it towards DiCorsa, firing off a single shot that left a tiny hole in the Italian's cheek and a splash of blood, hair and bone splinter on the panelling behind him.

Then he turned the gun on Jacquot.

86

As the ringing, blasting sound of the single gunshot hammered away into a numbing silence, a black backlit figure appeared in the Mochi's hatchway, a lowering golden sun casting a long shadow into the cabin. It was Brock, gun in hand.

"You okay down there?"

"He shot the boss," said Ballard, shuffling along the banquette. "He fucking shot DiCorsa. We need to get out of here. And fast."

For a moment Brock didn't move, taking in the scene. The slumped lifeless figure of DiCorsa, head flung back, mouth agape, pink lips stretched tight; Jacquot beside him, frozen, deafened; and Ballard, finally getting clear of the table, his gun levelled at Jacquot.

"You hear me?" he said, over his shoulder. "Let's get moving."

"Back to Sailboat?"

"Out, out. Usual place."

Brock stepped away from the hatch, and honeyed sunlight spilled back into the cabin.

"And cut the line, cut the kids loose," Ballard called up to the wheelhouse, turning just a fraction to make sure Brock had heard, taking his eyes off Jacquot.

It was all Jacquot needed. Rather than move along the banquette he ducked beneath the table, put his feet against the edge of the seat, and pushed himself out, reaching for Ballard's legs in a desperate attempt to topple the man, wrestle the gun off him – shoot him, shoot everyone; save his children, save Midou. Because whatever happened in the next few seconds, Jacquot knew that Ballard wouldn't shoot him. Wouldn't dare shoot him. Couldn't afford to shoot him. If he did, he'd never find Sylvie.

But he knew too, as his fingers snatched at the hem of Ballard's shiny blue trousers, that his timing was out, his grip not sure enough, the attack misjudged. Years before he might have managed it, but not now, not here.

And he'd pay the price. There'd be a beating, for sure. Ballard would lay into him. The butt or barrel of the Beretta slammed into his face, a kick or two maybe, and Jacquot prepared himself for the pain.

But he was wrong.

Instead, Ballard swung the gun down and fired, a brief burst of flame from the muzzle, another deafening blast in the panelled, upholstered confines of the cabin. But he was sufficiently off balance, trying to step away from Jacquot's snatching hands, and just a little blinded from the sun streaming through the hatch, that the shot went wide, the bullet thudding into the carpet and splintering the deck just a few inches from Jacquot's head.

His second shot went wide as well, as the Mochi suddenly surged forward and swept into a tight turn.

But the third shot found its mark, as Jacquot's arms finally wrapped around Ballard's legs, pulling at his knees and bringing him down.

But he was too late.

Jacquot felt a violent jolt, a molten burning pain... and then, darkness.

87

The girls didn't see the first shark.

Its slim, curved dorsal fin broke the surface fifty metres behind their drifting airbed. It passed to and fro, from left to right. Idling, curious. Following the curling stream of scent in the water. Sometimes the fin dropped below the surface, leaving just a swirl of bubbles, but never for long, rising up again to pass this way and that, the long sinuous body beneath it gliding effortlessly through the water.

Clinging to their airbed, the girls didn't see the second or the third shark either, joining the first to follow the thin, deadly trail of blood and guts in the water. Fins crossing left and right, right and left. Slow, easy passes.

The sun was low now, a shimmering golden globe that touched the horizon, turning the water into a sheet of shifting iron blue. Long shadows dancing over the swell towards the drifting airbed. Water lapping around them in the silence of the sea.

Midou and Matti were quiet, but Béa whimpered.

"Where are they going, Midou?" she asked. Such a tiny, frightened voice. "Why have they left us? Where's Papa?"

"The line must have snapped," said Midou. "They'll be coming back any minute to pick us up. Just you wait and see."

But she wondered if they would, if they'd even be able to find them on this darkening ocean? Or if they'd cut the line deliberately, had no intention of coming back for them?

We are in danger. Real danger... Jacquot had told her. And she could hear his voice, remembered the look in his eyes.

And deep inside Midou suddenly, fearfully, understood, and knew he'd been right.

They were in danger, real danger, and she tried hard to stop the tightening, knotting sense of dread stealing icily through her. She must be strong, she must be brave, she must protect the children and keep them safe. She must believe they'd be coming back. Any minute now. Any minute.

But as she watched the Mochi's lights flickering above the water, she realised they were getting smaller, the sound of the engine diminishing, that the boat was drawing away from them. This really couldn't be happening. Could it? Or were they looking in the wrong place? Should she shout? Should she scream? Would they hear her? Would they care?

"I'm cold," said Béa, in a shivery voice. "My legs are cold."

"Mine, too," said Matti.

"Here, come closer," said Midou, taking her right hand off the handle to draw Béa to her. Then the left hand, to bring Matti nearer.

And as they squirmed against her, their little arms around her, it seemed to Midou that the airbed was somehow softer, its skin not as taut, the plastic wrinkling, sinking slightly, a wash of cool water swilling between the airbed and her belly, her jacket chafing against her skin. There had to be a tear, she thought. Somewhere the air pumped into it, the air that had made it tight and swollen, was leaking away.

A slow, bubbling whisper, unseen, not heard, somewhere below them.

How long until the airbed was just a sheet of plastic, she wondered?

How long would it be before it finally crumpled, a dead drifting shroud in the ocean? And would it sink? How long would they be able to cling to it?

With a final golden blink the uppermost edge of the sun sank below the sea, just a few strands of pink and blue remaining at the edge of the world.

"I'm frightened, Midou," whispered Béa. "And I can't see them any more."

Nor could Midou. No lights from the Mochi. Just a distant faraway glow between sea and sky. A coastline somewhere. An island. Sometimes lost in the rise and fall of the ocean. Switching on, switching off.

Ahead now, where the sun had been, the thin strands of pink and blue were fading fast, and a few pinprick stars began to wink. Midou turned her head and looked behind them. A black endless void, stealing over them, sparkling with stars, thousands of them, big and bright and sharp.

And then, in that liquid starlight... Something else. Something closer.

A shifting scar of phosphorescence. There, and there.

To the right of them. To the left.

Creamy green lines shimmering on the black lapping surface of the sea. Fading, then reappearing. Long lines, short lines…

Something following them. Closing on their airbed.

She knew what was out there. She knew what was following them.

"Pull up your legs," said Midou. "Cuddle into me. There, that's good, that's right."

But there was no room on the airbed for her own legs. So she bent her knees and tried to lift her trailing feet from the water. But the edge of the airbed, now just a thick plastic skin, sank beneath the surface, under their shifting weight, and water surged up between her thighs.

And with a shiver of icy fear, she wondered how long…?

How long until…?

She looked ahead and saw the first fins, black slanting triangles slicing through the water, balancing on bubbling phosphorescent scars.

And heard, in the inky stillness, the first whisper as the fins drew closer…

And felt the weighty press of something pass beneath them.

"There's something under us," whispered Matti. "Did you feel it?"

"What is it, Midou? What is it? I felt it, too," said Béa.

"It's nothing, nothing," said Midou, whispering back, clenching her jaw, her teeth starting to chatter. "Just the current, a swell, just the sea…"

But as she said it the first shark came up from the depths and hit their airbed from below, tenting the thin sheet of plastic, sending the three of them spiralling into the air, tumbling down into the water, coming up for air and screaming, legs and arms thrashing …

And in the splashing, bumping, crowded, snapping blackness of the sea…

Screams and shouts…

"Midou, Midou…?" called Béa.

"Midou, where are you?" called Matti.

"Matti, Béa… I'm here… I'm…"

88

From a deep, dark, distant place Jacquot began to surface, his senses starting to operate once more, his body sending in signals – of cold, of fear, of helplessness.

And pain. Two hot pulsing points of it in his left side, front and back. Where the bullet from the Beretta had hit him…

In and out. Right through. The round that had put him down…

And echoing through the lightening darkness in his head came the sound of his children's screams…

Just a dream, he decided. A nightmare. It had to be.

Or was it?

Where were they? Were they safe?

Would someone find them? Was Marlon out there…?

"He's coming round, boss."

Brock's voice, and Brock's big meaty hands under his armpits, hauling him like a sack of rice across the deck, the pain in his side screaming, dropping him beside another body. DiCorsa.

"Get some tape round his legs. Just in case." Ballard's voice. And then, "Are we there yet, Stephen?"

"Getting close, boss. Not far now…"

Jacquot opened his eyes, blinked, and saw a shifting blackness above him and bright tiny lights, felt the sway of the sea, the hardness of the deck, heard the soft throbbing of an engine somewhere below him, and smelled its rich oily scent. Somewhere close by he heard the tearing sound of tape being ripped from a roll, and hands clasping his ankles together, winding the tape around them.

And all the time wincing at the pain in his side, wanting to weep at the hurt shooting through him, feeling a warm pulse of blood trickling into his groin; and thinking of the girls, little Béa and Matti, and Midou, out there somewhere…

Out in the darkness.

The three of them. All alone.

Pushing away the pain, he closed his eyes and prayed for them…

Dear God, stay with them, protect them, until I can… until I can… Do what?

But there was no time for prayers. Jacquot felt something hard press into his throat. The muzzle of a gun. The bristles of his beard prickling against his skin at the pressure. The muzzle still warm.

"Where is she?" It was Ballard's voice. Close, cold, and calculating.

Close enough for Jacquot to feel the man's breath on his face. He turned his head, opened his eyes, but all he could see was a shadow blocking out the stars...

"Tell me where she is, or you go to the sharks. Tell me, and I'll make it quick." He pulled back the slide on the Beretta, clicked the hammer into place. "And don't give me fucking Ottawa..."

Through the pain, through the fear, for himself and his children, Jacquot knew now for certain that Patric had been right. Elaine had called Ballard. Had told him about Ottawa, the mother's lawyer, the uncle... The story he had spun for her. The story she had fallen for, and passed on. The story Ballard would never now believe.

"Not Ottawa," he whispered.

"Now that's more like it. So where? Where is she?"

"Close..."

"Close? Where? The island, the mainland?" The muzzle jammed deeper into his throat.

"Miami..." whispered Jacquot, as his left leg began to cramp, thigh and calf muscles suddenly tightening like a vice, forcing the knee to bend, raising the leg to accommodate the pain, the shortening of sinews. Oh, hell, it hurt, it hurt so much... And getting worse, so much worse, tears springing into his eyes.

"Tell me, and I'll go back for the girls. I'll put them ashore, free to go. Just tell me."

"Miami," he whispered again. "Ten miles north... Her grandmother..."

The same lie he'd told Elaine, but different...

Anything to keep himself alive, to play for time.

And then, beside him, he felt DiCorsa's body move, an arm pressing against his. Was it the boat, the swell of the ocean? It had to be. And then Jacquot heard a soft hiss of breath, a gargling groan.

Ballard and Brock heard it, too.

"Jesus. The boss. He's alive," said Brock.

"He can't be," said Ballard.

Jacquot felt Ballard shift away from him, lean over the body beside him.

"Shit, he is."

For a moment there was silence, just the low hum of the Mochi's engine, and the lapping of the ocean against its drifting hull. Ballard thinking, working out the next move. Jacquot knew what he would say. And he was right.

"Okay, that's it. We've got to move. Get a hold of him, let's get him over."

Jacquot felt a foot push him aside, Ballard's or Brock's, he couldn't say. Felt hands reach for DiCorsa, haul him away, up off the deck.

"Hey, Stephen," Ballard called out, his voice suddenly lighter, more confident now. Back in control. "Get the lights on, put on some music. Let's give the old bastard a send-off."

A moment later, the sound of a chorus filled the night. Ten, twenty singers, and the voices of a man and a woman, duelling voices, deep and strong, high and piercing.

Jacquot tried to raise his head, focus his eyes. He saw the lights of the wheelhouse, Stephen at the wheel, looking back over his shoulder, watching Ballard and Brock lift DiCorsa's body away from him, blood dripping onto the deck from the ragged opening in the man's lolling head, the dancing pineapples on his shirt drenched a dark scarlet.

No need now for Brock's cut-throat razor, thought Jacquot.

But how had the man survived that shot, he wondered? The hole in his cheek, the splash of blood and bone on the panelling. How could he still be alive?

But Jacquot knew there was nothing DiCorsa could do to defend himself. A kind of consciousness, perhaps, but no strength to do anything, no ability to stop what was about to happen. Just like him.

With a grunt from Ballard, the two men hoisted the body onto the transom and, with a final push, they rolled it over.

There was a splash, and the Mochi rocked gently.

And Jacquot knew that he would be next. Unless he could do something, unless he could stop them from dragging him to the edge of the boat and pushing him over, too.

But when he tried to move the pain in his side exploded again, and a fresh gout of hot blood pumped out over his skin, another cramping spasm wrenching through his leg and hip, twisting his body...

How could he do anything when he couldn't even get himself into a sitting position...?

How could he ever...?

And then, "You see it?" he heard Ballard say, the words accompanied by a soaring trembling note from the speakers, a great clash of orchestration.

"Where?"

"Coming into the light... There... On the left."

"Jesus, he's big. And coming in fast..."

There was the slashing sound of water, a grunt, and a crunch.

"Whoa! That was a bite," said Ballard, his voice pitched now with excitement, Jacquot momentarily forgotten...

Beyond the Mochi, Jacquot could hear more thrashing and grunting, and a series of rippling waves slapped against the hull. Sounds that took him back to Fuentes.

Those black shapes homing in... That wild, snapping frenzy...

He didn't need to see what was happening. He knew...

But there was no sound from DiCorsa. Not like Fuentes. No cries, no screams. No begging for mercy. Just that foaming, frothing eruption of water.

And then, at last, there was silence...

No sound from the sharks. Just the music.

It was over. For now.

Ballard gave a low whistle. "Well, that's what I call a show," he said. "Doesn't matter how many times you see it, just... unbelievable."

"Just gone," said Brock, chuckling. "He's gone... like he was never here."

"They tear you apart, and they leave no trace," said Ballard. "Couldn't be tidier. And now for their second course. You ready?"

The next moment, Jacquot felt hands grip his bound ankles, drag him to the side of the boat. He tried to kick out, but the pain was too great to do any kind of damage, or stop what was happening. And from the speakers, as another pair of hands slid under his shoulders and gripped tightly at his armpits, the duelling voices faded and Jacquot heard the first haunting notes of another familiar sound...

Dum... di-dum-dum...

Dum... di-dum-dum...

The same tune that DiCorsa had played for Fuentes...

Carmen, and Callas...

And as that sweet, soaring voice broke through the music Jacquot felt his body lifted from the deck and hoisted over the seats to the transom.

And there was nothing, save feebly flailing arms and weakening mermaid kicks, that he could do to stop them...

Nothing he could do to fight off his killers or, when the moment came, the sharks...

Waiting for him, down there, in the shifting green circle of spotlit, bloodied sea that now came into view...

"You got a choice, Jacquot." Ballard's voice, soft, cajoling, close to his ear. "One last chance. A bullet, or the sharks. Give me an address, and it's over. You won't feel a thing. And maybe, just maybe, I might go back for the kids. All alone, out there somewhere. Wondering where their Papa is... Give me what I want, and I'll go find them, I promise, and let them go..."

Jacquot shook his head. "No, you won't. And no, I won't."

Ballard chuckled. "You think you're so clever, don't you? So brave. But you're not. You're dead meat. And your kids, too. Even if they're still out there. Probably gone already, eaten up. But you know what? It doesn't matter. Because I will find Sylvie. With or without your help. And she'll die, too. Just the same as you. Just as painfully, just as badly." Ballard leant back, took a deep breath and blew it out. "So, there we are. The end of the line, my dead, dead friend."

And Jacquot felt Ballard place a hand on his hip and a hand on his shoulder, felt the hands push against him, the pressure building then easing... building and easing... and felt his body start to rock backwards and forwards on the narrow ledge of the transom... picking up speed, gaining momentum.

"So, *adieu* Monsieur Jacquot, Monsieur *Flic*, and happy days," whispered Ballard, and then he raised his head to the shifting spotlit ocean and called out in a clear, ringing voice, "*Et bon appétit, mes amis...*"

89

Somewhere close by a muffled blast.

The whizzing, sparkling climb of a firework soaring into the night sky. And seconds later a bright burst of magnesium light. Bright as a white sun. Wavering. Like a searchlight swinging above them. Slowly descending from the heavens, bathing the Mochi and the sea in a blazing play of shimmering daylight.

Teetering on the edge of the transom, Jacquot saw Ballard and Brock look up, their faces shining in the light, and heard a gun shot. Close and loud. And a fleshy thud as a bullet smacked into Ballard's shoulder and jolted him backwards, sent him sprawling onto the deck. And Brock, suddenly spotlit as another beam of light cut through the whiteness of the flare, looking back at Ballard, and down at Jacquot, and with a snarl of hatred stepping away and raising his hands.

"Heave to, *Aria*," came a deep, booming voice. "Heave, to, *Aria*. This is the Coast Guard. Lay down your weapons and heave to, prepare to be boarded…"

And as Jacquot lay there on the transom, too weak to move, he saw in the beam of light from the Coast Guard's searchlight and in the flickering glow of the flare, the bows of a launch drawing close. A familiar craft. And a familiar figure, Marlon, at the wheel…

And Midou clambering up past the wheelhouse…

And the two girls in the cockpit calling out his name…

"Papa! Papa! We're here. We're here…"

Tear sprang into his eyes, and with a groan of pain, Jacquot tipped himself backwards, down onto the Mochi's seats.

Stared up at the light swinging in the sky.

Heard his children's cries…

And knew, at last, that it was over.

After all this time, it was finally over…

They were safe. At last…

90

Jacquot opened his eyes. Mouth dry. Body numb.

Shapes. Figures. Around a bed. His bed.

Four faces. Two at the foot of the bed. One on each side.

He turned his head, left and right. Two little children. Matti and Béa, sitting on chairs drawn close to the bed, each of them holding one of his hands. He could feel their fingers gripping his fingers.

He tried to smile.

Someone said, "Is he awake?"

Later. Night-time.

Now when Jacquot opened his eyes, the focus was clearer. He could see a room, cream walls, one of them a panel of glass. Outside, in a dimmed corridor, nurses passed to and fro.

A monitor, a drip.

Hospital.

But that was all.

The first thing he saw when he opened his eyes was a clock on a wall. The hands danced a little but then settled. Eight-twenty seven. It was light outside, so morning.

But which morning? How long had he been here?

And then, for the first time, he remembered what had brought him here. DiCorsa, Ballard, Brock. Stephen and the Mochi. The girls on the airbed. Sharks. Gunshots. Pain.

But he was alive. The children were alive. Midou was alive.

The door opened, and a nurse bustled in, smiled.

She looked like…? Beth. The same motherly smile. Just as broad and bulky, but taller.

"So you come wake at last? Been a while, handsome. Lazin' there, and no mistake. Makin' us do all the work."

"I'm in hospital." His mouth was still dry. His voice croaked.

She came to the side of his bed, looked down. "And got your wits about you, too. An' 'ospital is right. Princess Margaret."

"How long?"

"Like I say, been a while. A week, mebbe?"

A week? How could it have been a week?

"You in bad shape, Mister Daniel. But we done sort you out, and that's fo' sure. So there's people waitin'… You wants to see 'em?"

He was sure he'd said 'yes', but he hadn't been able to keep his eyes open.

Now, when he came awake, the clock showed a few minutes past twelve. Still light outside, so midday. But which day?

He tried to sit up, but couldn't manage it. No pain, just a wooden stiffness. As he eased back down he saw the door open and there was Midou. She came to the bed, leaned down, kissed him. She smelled of flowers and coconuts. She smiled Claudine's smile, but there were tears in her eyes.

"Welcome back. We thought we'd lost you. It was close."

"Close, yes," he said.

"And I've got two young ladies outside who are desperate to say hello to their Papa."

Jacquot nodded. His throat was thick. He knew he couldn't speak.

They came in quietly, holding hands, eyes wide. Not sure how to behave. As though they were in church.

Jacquot raised his fingers, patted the sides of the bed, and they clambered up, carefully. They kissed him, tugged his beard, clasped his hands in theirs.

"You got lemonade in a bag there," said Béa, pointing under the bed. "I want one of those."

"It's Papa's pee-pee, stupid," said Matti.

"You were sick, Papa," said Béa. "We were worried."

"Sick from a bullet," said Matti, with a stern expression. She knew about pee-pee and bullets.

"Bullets are bad," said Béa. "You shouldn't play with guns."

Marlon came next. Later that day.

Clean t-shirt and clean shorts. Jacquot couldn't see his feet, but knew he'd be wearing crumpled socks and laceless boots.

"Brought some Kaliks, but they took 'em off me."

"There's water."

"Yeah? That's good." He said it as if he didn't know what water was. He pulled up a chair, sat down, crossed one leg over the other. Jacquot was right. Crumpled socks and laceless boots.

For the next twenty minutes, Marlon brought Jacquot up to speed. Following them out from Sailboat Cay. Picking up the girls from the airbed. Calling in the Coast Guard, but keeping his distance from the Mochi until he heard the gunfire.

"You French guys sure know how to party."

"You were in a bad way," said Midou, that evening. "They brought in a helicopter. Airlifted you out. It was touch and go."

"The doctor told me."

"You know about the kidney?"

"Works as well with one as two, that's what he said."

Midou nodded. "You'll have to watch the rum."

"He told me that, too."

And then Jacquot asked the questions he'd been thinking about.

"Who came for you? Why did you leave Trinité?"

"Your friend, Elaine Drumgoole. She flew down, came out to the island, and said you'd asked for us. *Capitaine* Faubert vouched for her, offered to come with us, so… we went. A private jet, no less. And she was so nice, brought presents for the girls…"

Jacquot filed that one away. Now he knew how Ballard had known about the girls in their Sunday school dresses.

"And Ballard?"

"…is in custody," Midou told him. "Murder, conspiracy to murder, money laundering… And that's just for starters. The list of charges is impressive. Brock and DiCorsa's skipper share the same ticket, bar the money laundering. And all their assets seized."

"The clubs? Baize?"

"Patric's daughter, Sylvie Martin, is on her way over from France."

"And Elaine…?"

"In custody. Conspiracy to murder, accessory to murder, fraud… Another long list."

Jacquot sighed. The lady wouldn't be eating any goat ribs from Earl's Smoke Shack any time soon.

"Do you know when they're letting me out?"

"Another week, they say. If you do what you're told."

"Will you be okay?"

Midou laughed. "We'll manage. The Stuyvesant house on Lyford Cay isn't exactly what I'd call a hardship posting."

"And the girls?"

"Loving it."

Jacquot smiled fondly, remembered the beach, remembered Boni.

And then, "When you were adrift, on the airbed," he asked, "were there sharks?"

Midou frowned. "Didn't see any. Why?"

Epilogue
Six weeks later…

The *gendarmerie* on Île des Frères was one block back from the main promenade, on the corner of rue des Pêcheurs and rue St-Agathe. It was a single-storey coral stone building painted a bold peppermint green, with blue shutters, a steep red-tile roof, and a knee-high picket fence set around its corner plot of patchy brown grass. A line of white painted stones edged the path that led from the gate to the front steps. When he reached the top of these steps, a week after his return to the island, Jacquot pushed through the green swing doors and entered the reception hall. Two gendarmes lounged behind the worn lino-topped counter, and behind them Sergeant Balmet sat at his desk filling out an incident form on an old Adler typewriter.

"Just called by for a word with *Capitaine* Faubert, if he's in," said Jacquot, as Balmet rose from his desk. But Jacquot didn't wait to be announced. With a nod and a wink, he passed the sergeant and pushed open the frosted glass door to Faubert's office. He had a final score to settle, and he wanted to make it personal.

Faubert was perched on the edge of his desk, sipping a *demi-tasse* of coffee and going through the racing pages of the daily paper. As usual, he was dressed in finely-pressed shorts and blue uniform shirt. A white bandolier, fed through a shoulder epaulette, stretched across his chest and a white belt was set neatly around the top of his shorts. His long black socks were folded back below the knee, and his lace-up shoes were brightly shined. When Jacquot marched into his office, Faubert turned, put down the newspaper and cup, and got to his feet.

"Monsieur Jacquot, to what do I owe this–?"

He got no further. Jacquot's fist hit fair, square, and forcefully in the middle of Faubert's face. His nose exploded in a shower of blood and mucus, and he spun backwards across his desk, knocking over his cup and saucer, desk lamp, and chair, and landing in a heap on the floor.

"That's from Midou," said Jacquot, and without breaking stride he came round the side of the desk, leaned down, caught hold of the bandolier, and hauled a dazed Faubert to his feet.

"And this one's from Béa and Matti." Holding him upright, Jacquot's second punch landed between his blood-splattered lips, taking out his two front teeth with a single sharp bony snap.

Faubert's head jerked back from the blow, slammed against the wall, and then swung round on his shoulders as though his neck had lost the ability to hold it straight. The breath came from his broken nose and ruined mouth in a gasping, hissing spray of blood, and his eyes seemed to spin round in their sockets.

"Now, I'm not going to hit you again," said Jacquot, pushing Faubert up against a map of the island, "because I want you to hear what I'm going to tell you."

Faubert mumbled something and tried to take a swing at Jacquot. But Jacquot brushed the fist aside and pushed him harder against the wall, his forearm pressing into the man's throat.

"So this is what you're going to do, *mon Capitaine*. You're going to come back from hospital in a couple of days and you're going to sit at this desk and you are going to write a letter of resignation, with immediate effect. In that letter you will recommend in the strongest terms possible that Sergeant Balmet be promoted to *Capitaine* and installed as your replacement, also with immediate effect. And when you've written that letter you're going to pack your bags and leave the island. And Martinique. In fact, the whole goddamned Caribbean. For good." He pressed his arm tighter against the man's throat. "Because if you don't, if there is a single second's hesitation on your part to do what I'm telling you, I'm going to present to the *Judiciaire* in Fort-de-France a sworn statement from John Ballard outlining your involvement in his criminal activities, along with another sworn deposition from my step-daughter detailing how you aided and abetted in the kidnap and unlawful transportation of my children. Since you might have trouble speaking at the moment, just nod your head if you've understood clearly what I've said to you."

With a feeble grunt, and a loose, swivelling nod, Faubert acknowledged that he had, indeed, understood what Jacquot had said to him.

"Good," said Jacquot. "I'm pleased to hear it. But you know what?" he continued. "I lied… I am going to hit you again, quite a few times, so you don't get to waste any of Doctor Cornel's valuable time."

There followed a single crunching punch to the solar plexus that doubled Faubert over, a sweeping uppercut to the point of his chin which made his remaining teeth snap shut on his tongue, and then two mighty left and right haymakers to the sides of his head.

As Faubert slid down the wall and crumpled to the floor, Jacquot stepped back and delivered a final swinging kick between the man's legs that hoisted him a good few centimetres back up the wall.

"And that one's from me, you *petit tas de merde.*"

Rubbing his knuckles, Jacquot walked to the office door where Balmet and the two constables, eyes wide, with unbelieving smiles on their faces, stepped aside to let him through.

As he passed between them, he turned to Balmet and said, "I think you had better call an ambulance, don't you? That was a very nasty fall your *Capitaine* just suffered, and there's no telling what kind of damage might have been done."

Afterword
From Daniel Jacquot…

My dear friends,

Some time ago, when Boni Stuyvesant came here to ask for my help, I told her that I had retired. As you will all know by now, on that occasion I had no choice but to do what she asked. But now that it is over, I really am retired. I am done. There will be no more cases for me to investigate.

I am aware, however, that in the last few years my various adventures with the Marseilles Judiciaire *and with the Regional Crime Squad in the Lubéron have found favour with you, and that you have enjoyed reading the books written by my good friend, Martin O'Brien.*

The last time Martin was here on the island, I gave him a number of files, old cases from Marseilles and Cavaillon, and the names of various useful contacts who could help with his research. I have no doubt that he will find something of interest, something intriguing, as he has done before, and that there will be more new stories for you to enjoy.

For now, though, it is time for me to sign off, and to wish you all well. It is Christmas Day, there is a birthday party on the beach for Matti and Béa, and I know they will be cross with me if I delay any longer. So….

Adieu,
Daniel

About The Author

After graduating from Hertford College, Oxford, Martin O'Brien joined Condé Nast and was travel editor at British Vogue for a number of years. As well as writing for Vogue he has contributed to a wide range of international publications, and his books have been translated into Russian, Turkish, French, Dutch, Spanish, Portuguese, German, and Hebrew. He lives in the Cotswolds with his wife and two daughters.

19181258R00198

Printed in Poland
by Amazon Fulfillment
Poland Sp. z o.o., Wrocław